THEY PROMISED ME
THE GUN WASN'T LOADED

THEY PROMISED ME THE GUN WASN'T LOADED

JAMES ALAN GARDNER

TOR

A TOM DOHERTY ASSOCIATES BOOK

New York

This is a work of fiction. All of the characters, organizations, and events portrayed
in this novel are either products of the author's imagination
or are used fictitiously.

THEY PROMISED ME THE GUN WASN'T LOADED

Copyright © 2018 by James Alan Gardner

A Tor Book
Published by Tom Doherty Associates
175 Fifth Avenue
New York, NY 10010

www.tor-forge.com

Tor® is a registered trademark of Macmillan Publishing Group, LLC.

The Library of Congress Cataloging-in-Publication Data is available upon request.

ISBN 978-0-7653-9878-9 (trade paperback)
ISBN 978-0-7653-9877-2 (ebook)

Our books may be purchased in bulk for promotional, educational, or business use.
Please contact your local bookseller or the Macmillan Corporate and Premium
Sales Department at 1-800-221-7945, extension 5442, or by email at
MacmillanSpecialMarkets@macmillan.com.

First Edition: November 2018

Printed in the United States of America

0 9 8 7 6 5 4 3 2 1

To Anne Bishop
Long-time booster and friend

THEY PROMISED ME
THE GUN WASN'T LOADED

1

Deimatic Behavior

I'M THE SMARTEST ACTUAL human on the planet.

Also the strongest. And the fastest.

But despite my best efforts, I'm not the drunkest. This stupid airplane hasn't stocked enough booze to do the job.

It doesn't help that I'm competing for alcohol with three Darklings up in first class. My hearing is (of course) the best a human's can be, and I can hear quite clearly that they're having a drinking contest.

I saw the Darklings when I got on the plane: a vampire, a werewolf, and a demon one-off whose hide is a patchwork of human skin, mammal fur, bird feathers, and insect chitin. That's only what I could see on her face and hands; under her Armani, she likely has an entire zoo's worth of integument. Fish scales. Tortoise shell. Jelly from *Cnidaria*. Maybe tree bark and vegetable rinds, too. Even stuff from extraterrestrials.

I should ask if she'd let me examine her—I need a project for Biology 399. But she'd likely tell me to go to hell. I've never met a Darkling who wasn't a mean drunk.

All three Darklings sound like drunken assholes. They're loud enough that even the normal people around me can hear them. At this moment, the Darklings are hassling the cute guy who's playing air host for first class.

On major flights like New York to London, the airlines *know* that first-class attendants will have to deal with obnoxious Darklings, so every attendant gets an amulet or psi-shield to defend against magical mind-stomps. But gadgets like that are ungodly expensive; on pissy little runs like this one from Edmonton to

Waterloo, the staff are expected to resist through sheer force of will.

Yeah, right. Even back here in sub-sub-economy, I can feel the Darklings flaring their Shadows. Every passenger on the plane is staggered by the effect—faces pale, hands trembling. A couple folks are puking into their barf bags.

The first-class air host is probably hyperventilating into an oxygen mask. But I can't tell for sure—the curtain is drawn between the first-class cabin and ours. Still, it pisses me off.

Oh, look, I'm up on my feet.

I'm not immune to the force of Darkling Shadows, but being a superpowered Spark, I have a dollop of mental resistance. On a scale from zero to shitting myself, walking toward the Darklings matches what I felt when my academic adviser told me I was close to flunking out. Or maybe more like before a hockey game, when our team is up against strong opposition. I just tell myself that fear won't improve my game, so I go on offense.

Like I'm doing now.

I force myself forward rather than running back to the bathrooms—partly because a crowd is already stampeding to bathroom-land, but mostly cuz I'm a heroine, fighting fuckery wherever I find it.

Also I'm half-drunk and making bad choices. So there's that.

I push through the curtains and enter first class. It's empty except for attendant-dude and the three Darklings. Two other seats have a lived-in look, with their TVs displaying a business channel and with hastily discarded copies of the *Financial Post* covering damp spots on the upholstery. The occupants of those seats are nowhere in sight—probably locked in the up-front washrooms.

Good. It means I don't need to worry about bystanders. I just have to figure out what I'm going to do.

Aw, fuck this, I'm drunk. I'll wing it.

"Yo!" I say. "What's holding up my drinks?"

The Darklings turn their eyes toward me: vampire red, werewolf green, and the demon's one-brown–one-composite. The werewolf is already furry. Thank you, baby Jesus. Actually seeing a werewolf change is enough to make your bladder crawl out of your panties. If that part is done, the worst is over.

I'm assuming, of course, that the Darklings won't actually fight me. That's a reasonable assumption: the Dark are as rich as fuck, so they don't like getting their hair mussed. Usually, they pay other people to do their rough tough dirty work. Besides, these Darklings probably own stock in this airline, so they won't want to cause costly damage. On the other hand, they may be drunker than me, if only because first-class passengers get all their hooch for free.

After a moment of silently staring at me and wondering, "Who the fuck is this bitch?" all three Darklings amp their Shadows in an attempt to turn my brain into pudding. In Bio 370, we called this deimatic behavior: attempting to intimidate other creatures by physical displays, like cobras flaring their hoods or poison frogs inflating their butt cheeks. Most normal humans would collapse under the psychological onslaught. However, it's common knowledge that alcohol makes some people immune to Darkling Shadows. I won't endanger my secret identity if I pretend not to feel their mental mugging.

More interestingly, the hottie air attendant doesn't seem too crushed either. His skin is a perfect black—I mean really black, and also perfect, making me want to rub my face all over his body—so the guy will never go pale, no matter how frightened he gets. But despite being here at ground zero of the Darkling auras, Mr. Dude only looks a bit shaky. He hasn't even retreated behind his coffee cart.

Maybe the airline *did* give the guy a defensive talisman. Or maybe he's the one-in-a-million human with natural resistance to magic. Or maybe, like me, he's just numbed himself with C_2H_6O, which makes perfect sense if you know you're going to spend a three-hour flight rubbing elbows with the Dark.

"Miss," the attendant says, "please return to your seat."

I say, "I will, but not empty-handed." I'm surprised the words come out anywhere near intelligible—the Darklings are still trying to make my brain cells shrivel.

With every passing moment, retreat gets more attractive. I came up here because I thought the Darklings were making waves without adult supervision. Now that I see Mr. Hottie isn't jabbering in panic, I'm okay with letting him deal with the situation. It's his job, after all; and while I happen to be the most tactful, diplomatic human on the planet, and therefore a better smoother-overer of Darkling jackassery than Mr. Air Host Cutie Dude, I'm also hella respectful and would never undermine his authority by trying to do his work for him. I'm also not so completely in the bag as to ignore the chance that me and the Darklings are gonna brawl if diplomacy fails. Since a three-on-one Darkling-slash-superhero fight is a bad idea at thirty thousand feet, I'm prepared to retire graciously without further ado.

As soon as I get another shot of Captain Morgan.

Or Smirnoff.

Or Johnny Walker whatever-color-is-cheapest.

"I'll have what they're having," I say to Cutie Boots. I point to the row of single-shot bottles in front of the Darklings. "They have way, way more than they'll ever need. Consider this redistribution: down with *r*, up with *g*, one for you and three for me. Or else I'll just drink these three job creators under the table and prove that a real human's tolerance for alcohol poisoning beats candy-ass magic every time."

The three drunks stare at me for a long, long moment. Then the demon with the patchwork skin gives me the Morpheus *Matrix* hand gesture. *Come on, little girl; show us what you got.*

"You want to join the contest?" the demon asks. She sets an unopened bottle on the seat tray in front of her. "We'll deal you in."

"About fucking time," I say. I plop myself in the big comfy chair at the end of their row. "Hi," I tell them, "I'm Jools."

AN HOUR LATER, WE begin our descent into the Region of Waterloo International Airport. The airport is only "international" by the skin of its teeth—once a day, there's a round-trip to Chicago, and most weekends, you can catch a flight to Cancun if you're sick of imported tequila. Otherwise, the airport's traffic stays exclusively in Canada, mostly between Waterloo and Ottawa or Alberta.

I'm okay with that. My family lives in Edmonton, and I went to see them for Christmas. Ten days of R&R with my father and four snoopy sisters. Fortunately, their questions were all "Do you have an actual boyfriend yet?" rather than "Have you accidentally acquired superpowers?"

So I didn't spend my vacation telling lies. Still, I'm glad it's finally January, and I'm coming home to Waterloo.

Weird to say it straight out like that. But yes, Waterloo feels like home. And when you're as drunk as I am, everything you feel is the absolute truth.

How drunk am I? Well, I won the drinking game with the Darklings. Okay, technically I only beat the demon and the werewolf. I tied with Karthik the vampire, but that's still a moral victory. Vamp hearts don't beat and their fluids don't circulate, so when they drink, the liquor just sits in their stomach, immobile and chemically unreactive. Basically, vampires are undead wineskins: alcohol doesn't affect them, but it fills them up volumetrically. The cutoff point is when the booze rises all the way up their throats and reaches their epiglottis. Any more after that and it drains into their lungs, which burns like a son of a bitch even if vamps don't have to breathe. Turns out Karthik and I had identical fluid capacities, so the match was a wash.

That means I won. Toss-ups always go to the human, right?

As for Marie the werewolf and Iza the demon, they gave up the moment they tasted bile.

Tsk. Wusses.

Mark, the air-host dude, makes me go back to my seat when the pilot says, "Prepare for landing." Mark ought to have sent me packing an hour earlier, but he realized my sparkling presence had pacified the Darklings and kept them from scaring other passengers.

BTW, Mark asked for my Snapchat ID. *Ka-ching!* Of course I gave it to him. It'll be a novel experience to sleep with someone who has a job.

I'M JUST GETTING BACK to my seat when a voice speaks inside my head. «*Hey, girl, you there?*»

It's Grandfather. Not my personal grandfather, but the primal granddaddy of the human race: the first male *Homo sapiens*, born more than a hundred thousand years ago. At least that's what he claims. He might be a deluded old coot driven batshit by whatever glowing meteor gave him superpowers. Or he might be a *wily* old coot who uses the Grandfather persona to grease his way into your confidence. He makes you feel he's your favoritest relative; you can trust him with your wallet and your secrets.

I'm able to hear Grandfather's voice thanks to a communication ring I'm wearing. It's a telepathic doodad I got from a Spark known as Invie. "Invie" is short for "The Inventor"; what he invents are gadgets above and beyond physics. They're what we call "Cape Tech" because "Mad Genius crap that defies the laws of God" sounds judgy. Anyhoo, Invie divvies out comm rings to anybody he thinks suitably heroic, giving us a super chatroom where we can share info, call for help, and generally shoot the shit.

«*What's up?*» I ask. I wonder how I'm coming across. If I spoke to Grandfather with my actual mouth, my words would be a slur of drunken mumbles. But speaking straight from my brain has to come out more clearly, right?

Yeah, Jools, clear as fucking crystal.

Hope I didn't think that out loud.

«*You got trouble,*» Grandfather tells me. «*Are you on a plane?*»

«*Yup.*»

«*Then you're going to be arrested the moment you land.*»

«*Arrested? Why?*»

«*Don't know,*» Grandfather says. «*But Invie listens in on official comm chatter. The folks at Waterloo airport just went into a tizzy because a couple Mounties put the place on security alert.*»

«*Mounties? Weird.*» The Royal Canadian Mounted Police operate differently in different parts of the country. Back in Alberta, they're the official provincial police—you see them all over. But Waterloo is in Ontario, and the province has its own separate police force. Mounties don't have much presence here, except to handle big-ticket stuff like drug trafficking and terrorism.

«*I'll tell you what's weird,*» Grandfather says. «*We haven't heard anything about this on normal Mountie channels. Either they're using some new comm network that's off Invie's radar, or this isn't the real RCMP.*»

«*But what does this have to do with me?*» I ask.

«*These Mounties, or whoever, gave airport personnel the following description: twenty-one-year-old female, short brown hair, brown eyes, five-eleven, athletic, probably drunk . . .* »

«*Did they actually say that, or are you editorializing?*»

«*I'm saying it sounds familiar,*» Grandfather tells me. «*And they gave the name Julietta Walsh.*»

Well, shit. Apparently, Grandfather knows my real name. But I should have guessed he'd find out eventually—he saw me using powers before I got a proper costume, mask, and code name. There's a wonky pseudoscience effect that prevents people from connecting your Spark identity with your normal human ID, but it doesn't protect you if you do superstuff in your civvies. It might have been inevitable that Grandfather would figure out who I was, but I'm pissed off it happened so fast.

He says, «*If it's any consolation, they aim to arrest your everyday self. Nothing in the message about you being super. So this may just be a follow-up on the lab explosion thing.*»

That doesn't make me feel better. My three roommates and I got superpowers a few days before Christmas, thanks to a fiasco at the University of Waterloo. Lucky for us, the mess was mostly caused by a bunch of Darklings, so the Dark establishment hushed up the whole thing. In exchange for not being prosecuted, my friends and I signed nondisclosure agreements promising we'd never spill a word about what happened.

That was supposed to be it: everything finished, case closed, buh-bye. But now I'm about to be arrested? What the living fuck?

«*That's all I got,*» Grandfather says. «*Invie asked me to warn you so you don't do something stupid if you're caught by surprise.*»

«*Do something stupid? Moi?*» But yeah, drunken me might react on impulse if I suddenly got armlocked by police. That would be bad.

Except now that I think about my being a reckless drunk, I'm not nearly so swiggered as I was. I still have a three-beer buzz on, but considering how much I drank with Karthik, Marie, and Iza, I should be a puddle of drool. I have the gift of super-healing, but it isn't supposed to handle alcohol; booze is the one toxic substance I can't shrug off. But apparently my gift of regeneration isn't all-or-nothing: it'll let me get moderately plastered while saving me from complete and utter collapse.

Good to know.

«*Well, thanks for the heads-up,*» I tell Grandfather. «*I'll be on my best behavior when the gendarmes put me in irons.*»

«*Don't be too meek and mild,*» Grandfather says. «*If you literally let them put you in irons, we might never see you again. I've heard of magical restraints that nullify superpowers. There's even some that blank out your brain and turn you into a zombie.*»

«*Noted,*» I say. «*If things get too fugly, I'll call on my besties for help.*»

«*You do that,*» Grandfather says. «*I'd hate to lose a granddaughter.*»

I think, «*I'd hate to be lost.*» But he's already hung up.

THE PLANE LANDS SMOOTHLY. I've been on flights where the passengers applauded a safe landing, but our group is too chill for that. Instead, there's just a flurry of thumbs on phones despite the flight staff's warnings that the plane will go up in a fireball if anyone turns on an electronic device before we've come to a complete stop outside the terminal.

Me, I don't start texting. Or Facebooking. Or whatever it is that my fellow passengers have to do so fucking urgently. The only people I might want to contact are my roommates, and if necessary, I can telepath them through my comm ring.

But despite what I said to Grandfather, I refuse to tell my roomies I'm in trouble. They'd come running to save my ass, and that would really piss me off.

The others think I'm helpless, the weak link on the team. No, wait, it's more than that. They think I'm stupid.

My powers make me smarter than the three of them put together. But they still think of me as the clueless fuckup who failed every course last semester.

That was so ten days ago. Now I'm the Chuck Norris of human intelligence. The Richard Feynman. The Beyoncé. Maybe I'm not as hyperastronomically clever as one of those Sparks whose IQ is a superpower, but I'm equal to the smartest humans in history: Newton, Einstein, Mozart, and . . .

Nah, I can't be bothered to make a culturally diverse gender-balanced list. But I could. Cuz I'm Just. That. Clever.

Me and Socrates are BFFs. Me and Confucius get together to discuss analects and shit.

Yet my friends still think I'll end up working at Mickey D's. Well, screw 'em; I won't call for help. Not yet, anyway.

And yes, I know this is a loser-girl move, purely because I've talked myself into a sulk. But I'm drunk and that's my excuse. Just like always.

WE TAXI TO THE terminal. Then we begin the chaotic hassle of debarking, with everyone dragging thirty-kilo suitcases from the overhead compartments. Since it's January 2, most passengers are university students coming back after Christmas break. Their luggage is crammed with enough clothes and parentally supplied dental floss to last the whole winter term. Without thinking, I find myself helping everyone around me wrestle down their bags. I'm a Spark and I'll come to your rescue whether you want me to or not.

I'm not literally super-strong, but I'm maxed out on everything a normal human can do. When it comes to lifting weights, I'm a perfect match for some four-hundred-pound dude named Boris who set the world record at the last Olympics. Unless you're a Spark or a Darkling, I'm stronger than you. So I sling luggage around with abandon, until I notice the dirty looks I'm getting. In these cramped quarters, people can smell the alcohol on my breath, and for some unfathomable reason, they're pissed that a drunk is smearing her fingers all over their dainties.

But even when I see them getting mad, I have trouble stopping. I just keep thinking I can patch things up if I try really hard. It's the logic of someone who's well and truly in the tank. Mark, the air-host guy, finally taps me on the shoulder and suggests I leave well enough alone.

He doesn't look so charmed by me anymore. Oh well, he was probably a creep anyway. Shame on him for chatting up a girl who's blitzed.

Now he's giving me the stink eye. Maybe he's received word that I'm wanted by the Mounties. The cute Mr. Mark has started wondering if I'm a drug mule or the hench-wench of some super-villain. Or else he just sees me as a stupid drunk slut who deserves to be locked away from decent people.

Great. Now I'm depressed.

I slump along with the crowd toward the plane's exit. My Darkling drinking pals are long gone from the first-class cabin. They were ushered out ahead of us sweat-stained plebeians. I picture them being driven in gold-plated golf carts to some superfast baggage claim. Meanwhile, the rest of us clog up the exit of the plane like gunk in a Drano commercial.

At least it gives me a chance to see what awaits me outside. We don't go straight into a terminal like in upscale airports; it's down a ramp to the tarmac, then across a stretch of pavement before actually entering a building.

And look! Two persons of lawful authority stand at the foot of the ramp: a man and a woman, both in dark blue suits and their forties, imbued with officious dude-i-tudes. People keep a nervous distance, as if the pair of them are bristling with poisonous spikes. I'd bet dollars to dachshunds these two have spent years drinking blood from some Darkling master. It's made them into Renfields: strong, fast, and wrong in the head. Even if they look superficially human, they give off monstrous vibes that creep the hell out of normal people.

Renfields are almost as intimidating as Darklings. However, I can tell that these dudes are only minions, not full-on members of the Dark. Why? Because their suits came off the rack from Moore's—specifically the Kenneth Cole Awearness line. (Yeah, I know shit like that. One of my not-quite-superpowers is that my brain automatically downloads useful trivia when I need it. I call it WikiJools: instant mental access to all public knowledge.)

The point is, true Darklings wouldn't be caught undead in mass-produced clothing. These two Renfields may be serious heat, but they're not the biggest flames in the furnace. On the other hand, they're probably stronger than I am: not just human, but superhuman. I have to assume they're faster, too, and maybe tough enough to take bullet or two without getting mopey about it.

I ask myself if I should reassess my decision not to call for help. I'm looking at Mulder and Scully's evil twins; I may be in over my head. But hey, I'm a Spark. Even if these heavies are stronger and faster than me, they won't be nearly as smart.

Cuz I'm brilliant now, right? And Renfields have the IQ of Styrofoam. When you drink Darkling blood, what you gain in muscle, you lose in intellect and independence.

I can outwit these dudes. My inebriated brain says it'll be fun.

So down the ramp I go. And yes, they're definitely Renfields: the stink of blood surrounds them like the haze around Pepé Le Pew.

It proves they aren't honest-to-artery vampires. You never smell blood on vamps—that's part of their magic. As inexplicable as the ability to suck a person dry through two piddly holes in the neck.

Fucking magic is so *semantic*. I mean, if *I* were going to suppress the smell of blood, I'd have to think about scent molecules and blocking olfactory receptors. Reams of biochem and anatomical analysis. But with magic, it's just, "Blood, smell, block," and it's done. That's offensive, is what it is, especially to those of us who pissed kidney stones to squeak out a 52 percent in organic chemistry.

The Dark has no respect for mundane reality. Neither do the Renfields waiting for me; I can tell that just by looking. They're plasma-scented tools of the powers that be: not just ordinary po-po, but members of some vague yet menacing government agency that does dirty deeds for the Darklings who run our country.

RCMP? It is to laugh.

The male minion blocks my path as soon as I hit the tarmac. "Julietta Walsh?" He plumps up his aura of intimidation to add more butterflies to my fluttering stomach.

FYI, I hate people who call me Julietta. It's like dealing with one of those ATMs that read the name on your card and then repeat it umpteen times during the transaction. "Welcome, Julietta! You're broke, Julietta! Stop crying, Julietta! If we actually let you have cash, you'd only waste it, Julietta! Have a wonnnderful day and come back soon, you bankrupt trash bag . . . oops, we mean our precious respected customer, Julietta!"

So I don't acknowledge the name and I don't acknowledge the man. That just means I get buttonholed by his partner. She flashes a card. "RCMP. Would you come with us, please, Ms. Walsh."

"Whoa," I say. "Show me that card again."

The woman looks taken aback. I'm supposed to be cowed by the megajoules of magic pounding my brain with "Respect my authoritah!" But passengers from the plane are waddling all around us, and dozens are within easy earshot. Whatever this run-in eventually becomes, these two Slytherins want to appear legit, at least for the time being.

So the woman lets me look at her ID again. She allows me plenty of time to admire the ornate seal of the Royal Canadian

Mounted Police embossed on plastic-coated card stock. There's a photo of the woman labeled STAFF SERGEANT BARBARA L. STEVENS. It looks very official . . . except inside my head, WikiJools does a download to brief me on Mountie minutiae.

Staff Sergeant Barbara L. Stevens, you're busted.

The card the woman showed me is a perfect reproduction of what Mountie IDs used to look like. Just one problem: the format changed eight months ago. The new cards have embedded RFID tags, similar to the EMV microchips on bank cards.

Staff Sergeant Barbara L. Stevens is chipless. With her out-dated card, she couldn't even get into a Mountie parking lot.

She's Fakey McFakeface. I give her a smile. Set kid gloves to Off.

Of course, I don't do anything rash. I'm supposed to be a normal university student, not someone in the know about Mountie IDs, and definitely not the type to cause a fuss with the police. Besides, I don't want to endanger the innocent people around me. If I get rambunctious, who knows what will happen?

Anyway, I want to see where this game is heading. What are these fakes up to? And why with me?

So I don't resist when they parenthesize me, one on either side. They take my arms, but their grip is light; they don't try to cuff me or use those plastic restraint strips that make you feel like a freezer bag. The word "arrest" never burbles into the air. I'm simply going along with the nice pseudo-Mounties for purposes we're all too polite to mention.

It occurs to me that a normal girl would ask, "What's this all about?" So I do.

"We can't talk here," the man says. "It's a confidential matter."

Uh-huh. It's so confidential that this dude hasn't even showed me his ID. I believe I will christen him Staff Sergeant Bobby L. Stephens. That way they can be Stevens with a "v" and Stephens with a "ph"—like Thomson & Thompson in *Tintin*, but without the comb-overs.

To be fair, Stevens & Stephens don't look alike, despite their similar suits. Stephens (male) is the same height as me, but built like a bulldog. Or a fireplug. Or whatever your favorite simile is for someone denser than seawater. Stevens (female) is a few inches shorter, but just as blocky as her partner. She has bottle-blond hair and a reddish complexion that is either windburn from skiing or . . . oh, fuck, my brain just downloaded a medical encyclopedia full of skin diseases.

Barf. It's not the first time this has happened. I hope it's the last.

I look away from Stevens-female and back to Stephens-male. His skin color is Mediterranean. Dark brown hair. Bloodshot eyes. He's wearing green-iris contact lenses, and he's had them in too long.

But why does he need contacts? Renfields usually have super-acute vision. I'll bet this dude has been drinking Darkling blood for so long, his eyes have mutated to look nonhuman. He needs contacts to hide the degeneration. Maybe Lady Stevens's reddened skin has a similar cause.

As I thought from the first, Stevens & Stephens are longtime Darkling suck-ups. That makes them more powerful than run-of-the-mill Renfields, but also more mentally unstable. Like the original Renfield from *Dracula*, they may eat bugs in private or have even less savory hobbies.

Ooo. Yummerific.

STEVENS & STEPHENS GRAB a porter and order him to take my carry-on to the main Arrivals area. They march me off in a different direction, into the terminal building and through nondescript corridors until we reach a door labeled AUTHORIZED PERSONNEL ONLY. We go another short distance, then reach a door that clashes with the glass-and-chrome ambiance we've seen so far in the airport. The door is solid mahogany, oiled and polished, busy with intricate carvings of devils.

When Stevens & Stephens open the door, the first thing I see is utter blackness: like a curtain hung just inside the entrance, but so blackity-black-black, it eats photons for breakfast and never bothers to shit them out. I've seen its like before—it's a blinder wall. A magical privacy barrier that Darklings use to block prying eyes. High-quality blinders can't even be pierced by sorcerous scrying or superpowers; they cloak clairvoyance and X-ray vision, to make sure that shenanigans go unseen.

Stevens & Stephens escort me forward. There's a moment of total sensory dep as we pass through the blinder, then suddenly we're in a brandy-scented gentlemen's club straight out of 1890s London. We're talking actual gaslight. Oak paneling. A genuine fucking hearth with a genuine fucking fire, and over the mantelpiece, a huge painting that to my alarmingly expert eye looks like an authentic Watteau. (Two rosy-cheeked women are reading in a forest. "Ooo, *chère* Hélène! Let's put on impractical gowns and walk in the woods, so we can read dirty bits from the *Decameron* while deer look over our shoulders!")

Screw Watteau. I turn my eyes toward the bar: specifically toward the bottles of booze, each of which would cost a year's tuition just to sniff the cap. Whiskies and brandies and gins, oh my! And no bartender in sight. As if you can just walk up and fill a glass from whichever bottle you fancy. I'd say it's like I've died and gone to heaven, except that with a free, open, and expensively stocked bar, I might simply die without heaven being involved.

The only features that clash with the room's decor are the people who currently occupy it. Two paper-pale women sit with mugs of blood on the table in front of them. A dude with the head of a jackal eats a plate of I-seriously-don't-want-to-know. And a human-shaped mass of flies is reading *The Wall Street Journal*. As one does.

For lo, this must be the luxury lounge where the .01 percent wait for their Learjets to get refueled. Every person here is a multimillionaire, rich enough to afford the Dark Conversion. Every person is also a festering bleed of mystic corruption . . . which is why the ceiling is cobwebbed, the paneling is cracked, and tribes of deathwatch beetles peek out from the upholstery.

It's the same wherever Darklings gather. Airport staff must try to keep this place free of decay, but unless they scrub continuously 24/7, the rot sets in. No doubt some first-rate wizard has cast a preservation spell on the Watteau, but otherwise the lounge is allowed to molder. Darklings don't mind—they find decrepitude homey. But every few months, the airport must have to trash all the bug-infested wood and rusted metal, then start again from scratch.

Well, heck, why not? Darklings can afford it. They openly *enjoy* conspicuous waste. What they don't enjoy is intruders. A moment after we enter, one of the vampire women rises from her padded leather chair and addresses my escorts. "Were you looking for someone?"

She *has* to know that Stevens & Stephens are Renfields. If they smell bloody to *me*, a vampire must be able to sniff them from thirty miles away. And if the woman knows they're Renfields, she can deduce they have a master: some Darkling who supplies them with blood and calls the shots. To the vampire woman, Stevens & Stephens are someone's personal pit bulls. So why are they here, off the leash?

Meanwhile, the woman doesn't give *me* the tiniest glance. I'm not even as important as a Renfield; I'm beneath her interest.

But I'm interested in *her*. For one thing, she looks old. If she were human, I'd put her in her fifties. That's unusual, especially for vampires. Lots of vamps are trust-fund kiddies who Convert on their eighteenth birthdays. That leaves them stuck forever looking like high schoolers. And vamps who convert when they're older get younger as they feed—not all the way back to eighteen-year-olds, but usually to their early thirties.

So every vamp I've ever seen looks to be in the age range from eighteen to thirty-five. What does it mean when a vampire looks fifty? Either she's incredibly ancient—so old that the power of blood can only get her down to middle age—or else she's *made* herself look older with a magical glamour.

Another thing I notice: her British accent. I've only heard her speak a single sentence, but I can already tell she's rocking Received

Pronunciation. Or so WikiJools informs me. For a long, long time, RP was considered the apex predator of accents—the difference between the hoi and polloi in Oxford and the BBC. Attitudes have mellowed in recent years . . . but RP is still the accent of choice for people whose first language isn't English but want to hide that fact.

It takes work to replace your native accent with something more posh. The people who go to that effort do it because RP sends a message: I. Have. Class.

One way or another, this woman is not your run-of-the-mill vampire. Maybe she isn't a vamp at all, despite her Kleenex-white skin. She could be a different type of Darkling: one of the many called demons for lack of a better name.

Maybe she's something exotic from non-Western folklore. Apart from her pallor, she looks Southeast Asian: dark Pacific Rim eyes and straight black hair that's unfashionably long for someone her age. Her lips are ebony, and I don't think the color comes from lipstick. In fact, she's not wearing much makeup at all. That's atypical for Darklings—most are obsessed with the way they look, and I don't just mean the women. Whether or not a Darkling aspires to be conventionally attractive, every single one of them wants to look *striking*.

I can't help noticing this woman wears a loose full-length dress. Black silk with gold embroidery. From the waist up, she looks like a normal woman—trim and well built for someone her age. But from the waist down, under that dress, she could look like anything. My drunken brain imagines her slurping around on octopus tentacles like Ursula in *The Little Mermaid*.

"Well?" the woman says to Stevens & Stephens. "For whom are you looking?"

"Sorry, ma'am," Stephens says, "I can't answer that question." Both he and his partner have tensed up like cats who've run into a Doberman. The Dark Pact says Darklings can't hurt humans except in self-defense; but Stevens & Stephens are Renfields, and to a Darkling, they aren't people, they're just property. If the woman in black decides to get pissy, she can smash them however she chooses. The only penalty she'll pay is reimbursing their owner, like when you accidentally break a neighbor's window.

But the pale-skinned woman doesn't resort to violence. Instead, she only cocks an eyebrow. "Your patron must be formidable if you're willing to annoy so many of us. Your patron is also a boor to deem this a suitable place for meeting with your kind and this mortal. However, I won't punish you for obeying orders. I will hold my disapproval until your master arrives."

The woman gives one last glare at all of us, then returns to her seat. The other Darklings in the room give us scowls of their own. (Well, at least the ones who have faces.) Then they all turn away pointedly, and pretend we deplorables don't exist.

I'm left with nothing to do except stare at the bar with saliva-filled longing. I wonder what Stevens & Stephens would do if I went over and got a drink. Maybe something from the Highlands and older than my father. Would the bar have something like that? Not bloody likely. This may be a luxury lounge, but Waterloo is a backwater. I'd expect to see quality hooch, but nothing world class.

The bottles are calling my name. *Jools! Jools! Wrap your lips around us and suck!* But if I take one step toward the bar, Stevens & Stephens will . . . no, forget what they might do, the woman in black will turn me into a newt. Or a vole. Or some other animal whose name is fun to say.

I can feel her watching me now. She's pretending to read: a fat red morocco book whose cover has faded with age. I think it might be a codex, written by hand instead of printed. The woman moves her finger along the page—not left to right but downward, as if the writing is Chinese. But she's not really reading. She's eyeing me with an unblinking stare, hiding her gaze under her eyelashes.

For all I know, she could be casting a spell. Maybe she's hexed me and I can't even tell. Legally, Darklings aren't supposed to use their mojo on mortals without consent . . . but legally, people aren't supposed to shoplift nail polish and that happens all the time. Specifically, every Sunday afternoon around three thirty at the Shoppers Drug Mart in Waterloo Town Square.

Maybe I'll ask the woman right to her face why she's checking me out. But before I can muster the nerve, there's a kerfuffle in the hearth. The flames go agitato, and a dude balloons out of the fire.

It looks like he's inflating. He starts as a dot among the embers that fills with hot air and puffs up into a full-sized man. A full-sized man holding a big fucking scythe. He wears robes from head to toe, with the fabric a shade of dirty gray that might have been chosen so that fireplace ash doesn't show too noticeably.

The robes have a cowl, and all I can see of the dude is his face. Surprise, surprise, it's a skull.

The hands on the scythe are skeletal, too. Don't ask me how the finger bones don't fall apart into separate carpals, cuz as far as I can tell, Scythe Dude has no ligaments holding his pinkies together. But that's magic for you. It doesn't have to make sense physically, as long as it works as a story. Concept: living skeleton. Done and done.

I glare at Scythe Dude as he strides from the hearth, tracking soot over the genuine Persian carpet. I say, "Really? Really? Doesn't J. K. Rowling have a patent on that?"

"Belief is a lubricant," Scythe Dude says. His voice is predictably sepulchral, like James Earl Jones wearing a Darth Vader helmet while standing at the bottom of a well. "When the public believes in a particular type of magic spell," drones on Scythe Dude, "casting the spell becomes easier. Thanks to Harry Potter, travel from fireplace to fireplace takes far less effort than other forms of teleportation."

"So it's also easier to fly on broomsticks now?"

"Yes," says Scythe Dude.

"But it makes you look like a *memek*," mutters the woman in black.

Memek. WikiJools tells me that's an Indonesian vulgarity. Or should I say "vulvarity."

Well, that's informative.

Scythe Dude ignores the woman and turns to me. "Are you Julietta Walsh?"

"Call me Jools," I say, striding forward and extending my hand. Behind me, Stevens & Stephens lose their shit as they realize I just slipped from their grip like soap in the shower. Scythe Dude seems equally taken aback as I grab his bony fingers and give a hearty shake.

I know I'm supposed to be retching into my Reeboks in his presence. I feel his Shadow trying to stroke its bony fingers up my sides and make me shiver. But between my buzz and my resistance from being a Spark, this Death dude doesn't scare me. And as per always, I'd rather make a splash by leaping forward than hanging back with the girls who behave.

"Pleasure to meet you," I tell Mr. Scythe. "Gonna tell me your name?"

"You may call me Reaper," Scythe Dude says.

Me and the woman in black both snigger. I mean, really. Before this dude bought the Dark Conversion, he had a name like Bernard Skank-Huffington the Third. Now, he's christened himself Reaper? That and the scythe and the robes and James Earl Jones are enough to make Freud say, "I told you so."

Look, if Scythe Dude wasn't compensating for feeling like the bottom man on the broomstick, he'd wear regular clothes, use his real name, and avoid entering rooms through the fireplace. He def-o-lutely wouldn't try to impress me by having his flunkies bring me to the luxury lounge, and he'd carry a regular briefcase instead of a farm implement.

The only message this bullshit sends me is that Reaper is a Darkling loser: the unpromising son of wealthy parents who paid for the boy's Conversion in the hope he'd become a badass Death Lord. Instead, all they got was the bass guitarist for a Black Sabbath tribute band.

"So what's this all about, Reap?" I ask, maxing out my volume and bonhomie.

I can almost see wheels turning inside Reaper's head. (Whoa, now that I think of it, if the dude really did have wheels inside his head, I could see them through his eye sockets. That would be awesome! But all I see are empty air and shadows. Sad!) Reaper turns this way and that, scoping out the other Darklings in the room. I guess he's debating whether they have enough security clearance for hearing whatever top-secret horse crap he has to say. Finally, he makes a decision. "Ms. Walsh, would you follow me, please?"

"Why the heck not?" After all, he said *please*. I know he's taking me somewhere where shit can transpire without witnesses, but I just can't work up much concern. Reaper, Stevens, and Stephens are too Yakko, Wakko, and Dot to make me sweat.

But as the four of us troop from the room, I look back at the Darklings lounging in the lounge. They're ignoring our group with an air of "I'm pretending you were never here, *fa-la-la*." All except the woman in black, who stares at me without blinking.

Her eyes meet mine for a moment of meaningful I-don't-know-what. Connection? Interest?

That's not good. Attracting a Darkling's attention is playing with fire. Considering how powerful the woman likely is, maybe it's like playing with plutonium. Still, I'm tempted to stick out my tongue at her, but there's not enough booze in the world to push me over that line.

Aww, fuck it. I give her a wink. She doesn't wink back.

Interspecies Competition

REAPER LEADS THE WAY through more of the airport's AUTHO-RIZED PERSONNEL ONLY. Stevens & Stephens have grabbed my arms again, and this time they're applying strength. It must have rattled them, how slickly I slid out of their grasp, so now they're giving me the jailhouse clinch. I can still break free if I need to, but aikido will be involved.

Joint locks and pain. Maybe fractured wrists.

Picturing what I'd have to do to them turns my stomach. I've thrown my share of punches playing hockey, but it seldom adds up to much. Everyone on the ice wears decent protection, including a helmet. Besides, hockey gloves are so thick, the padding reduces their impact. A scuffle lets off steam and sends a message without anyone getting more than a black eye.

But I've also seen real injuries. Broken bones. Severe cuts. And once . . . shit, I don't want to think about it.

Hockey violence is 90 percent show: deimatic behavior. But true violence gets ugly real fast. When I think about hurting Stevens & Stephens—I mean *sincerely* hurting them . . .

Ick. I just won't do it. Unless they give me no choice.

Shit. All this thinking has sobered me up. I mean literally: I can feel it. The booze just got purged from my bloodstream like draining a cake of tofu.

I *hate* being a Spark. I hate how all of a sudden I have to get serious. Dammit, I'm a student in university; this is the time of my life that's supposed to be *fun*.

I feel my eyes getting damp. Oh no. Before I embarrass my-self, I scramble for a distraction.

And support.

I finally call for backup.

«*Yo, dudettes!*» I transmit mentally. «*Could be I might need a hand.*»

«*What's wrong?*» a voice answers immediately. It's my roommate-slash-teammate Miranda. She replies so quickly, it makes me wonder: Is there a telepathic equivalent of holding the phone and waiting with your finger over the Accept button? But more likely, it's just her superfast reflexes. Miranda isn't one of those Sparks who can race across the continent in the time it takes to say, "I want sushi," but her reaction speed beats any mere human's.

I say, «*It's possible I've been busted by two fake Mounties and a demon who calls himself Reaper.*»

«*What did you do?*» Miranda demands.

«*Nothing,*» I answer, «*and thanks for thinking the worst of me.*» (By the way, all this time, Stevens & Stephens have been walking me in firmly held lockstep between them. I approve—it means I don't have to watch where I'm going while I Skype telepathically.)

I say, «*Two Renfields heavy-handed me when I got off the plane. It's snaky as fuck. Did I mention they were fake RCMP? As in counterfeit IDs?*»

«*How do you know they're counterfeit?*» Miranda asks.

«*I know things, remember? So can you please stop thinking I shit the bed, and start giving me some teamly support?*»

«*Sorry,*» Miranda says. Since she almost never apologizes, this counts as a major concession. «*You're at the airport? I can be there in five. You want to be rescued?*»

«*Don't need it at the moment. Besides, it'll look suspicious if a big glowing Spark shows up out of nowhere to save unimportant little me. But I'd love you to be within striking distance if striking becomes necessary.*»

«*Understood,*» Miranda says. «*And I'll bring Zircon with me. Can't trust Zirc alone with the cookies.*»

«*Hey, I heard that!*» says Zircon. Zirc is my roommate Kim. Or maybe Kim is Zircon. All Sparks are identity-fluid, but Kim is more fluid than most.

«*I'd love both of you to be ready in the wings,*» I say. «*Is Dakini around too?*»

«*Visiting relatives in Toronto,*» Miranda says. So Dakini, the fourth member of our team, is off the roster for the moment. Toronto is an hour away from Waterloo by car. Miranda flies faster than any car ever, but Toronto and back will still take too long to be practical.

Too bad. Dakini reads minds, so she could tell us what Reaper is up to. But we'll just have to wing it in ignorance: the story of my life.

«*See you soon,*» I tell my friends. «*Let's hope I don't need you.*»

Miranda and Kim both snort in disbelief. They have this idea I'm a walking disaster, like an alcoholic stick of dynamite. An alcoholic stick of dynamite who plays with matches. An alcoholic stick of dynamite who plays with matches, and isn't very bright, and maybe hates herself a little.

Such judgmental meanies! I almost regret asking for their help. But not really. To be honest, I'm relieved they're on the way.

MEANWHILE, MY ESCORTS HAVE walked me into a baggage-handling area. This isn't like the ones you see in movies, with conveyor belts rolling, and a maze of catwalks, scaffolds, etc. Waterloo is just too small for such mech. Glancing around, I'm led to conclude that the airport can handle all its baggage needs with two luggage carts pulled by lawn-mower tractors, and a shopping trolley with ZEHRS FOOD MART printed on the handle.

The most eye-catching feature of the area is a whacking big vault: made of solid steel, three meters high, and the same distance wide. It's locked up tight and deeply embedded in the room's concrete floor. I can't tell for sure, but I'd be super disappointed if the walls weren't strong enough to shrug off missile fire. Just to ice the cake, sorcerous runes have been etched in the metal, then painted Day-Glo pink.

I stare at the runes and hope that WikiJools will tell me more about them. Nope. I get stabbed with a hideous headache and have to look away real fast. I don't know if the pain is backlash from the runes themselves, or if it's what happens when I try to access data on forbidden topics. One way or another, WikiJools gets a flatulent 404 on the infodump request.

Looks like I need a Plan B. I point to the vault and ask Reaper, "What's that? Apart from a scary-ass safety-deposit box."

Reaper hesitates, then says, "Planes occasionally transport dangerous cargo. All airports are required to have storage facilities where such cargo can be held securely awaiting shipment or pickup."

"So this is where FedEx stores Necronomicons when people buy them off eBay?"

"Essentially."

Reaper does some hocus-pocus on the vault. It involves hand gestures, guttural chants, and other mystic fapping. I pay close attention. Not that I'll be able to reproduce the spell—since I'm not a Darkling, I can't do magic no matter how loudly I shout, *"Fhtagn!"* But I'm a science student even if my marks are in the toilet, and the habit of gathering info has been lovingly beaten into me.

So I memorize what Reaper says and does. Or at least I try. But my brain refuses to remember a single word or twitch of the fingers.

I think it's because I'm a Spark. Nature may abhor a vacuum, but it absolutely *loathes* attempts to combine the Light with the Dark. Magic and weird science don't mix. Period. This doesn't stop idiots from trying to merge the two, but it's like stashing matter and antimatter in the same suppository. Hilarity ensues.

But Reaper has no problems getting his wizard on. After ten seconds of making shadow puppets and James Earl Jones incantations, Reaper smacks the vault with the tip of his scythe. Click goes the door . . . then it creaks open melodramatically, wider and wider, until finally I can see inside.

The upper part of the vault has movable shelves. They're currently hiked to their highest position, leaving the lower half of the space for something large and gleaming: a gun the size of my leg, apparently made of diamond.

Picture a tapered diamond cylinder with dozens of weird protrusions: helical antennae and octahedral knobs, cruciform outgrowths and randomly arranged handles. It looks deliberately baroque, as if someone had a Barbie's Diamond Decoration Set and decided to glue everything from the kit onto a giant diamond Nerf gun.

That's one way of looking at it. The other is to say it's a leg-sized bazooka with a shit-ton of diamond bling. I could totally see myself hoisting this bad boy onto my shoulder and blasting a panzer tank into My Little Pony glitter.

"Sweet," I say. "Where can I get one?"

Reaper asks, "Have you ever seen anything like this before?"

"Uhh . . . bar mitzvah present for Kim Jong-un?"

Reaper glowers. "Ms. Walsh," he says, "approximately two weeks ago, on the night of the winter solstice, you entered a lab filled with unusual equipment. Is that not correct?"

I nod. Warily. Lots of shit went down that night, some of which involved my civilian self and some my superhero identity. I'd better keep straight which parts were which so I don't give away any secrets.

The events in the lab all happened when I was Jools; and like an upstanding citizen, I gave a full report to the cops. Eventually, I signed that NDA to keep my mouth shut, but since these dudes are supposedly Mounties, hiding the truth would be suspicious. "I saw plenty of weird stuff in that lab," I admit. "Why does it matter?"

Reaper asks, "Do you know who made that 'stuff'?"

As it happens, I *do* know. But I say, "Nope."

"It was made by a Spark terrorist," Reaper says. "A so-called Mad Genius named Diamond. Have you heard of him?"

I pretend to wrack my brain. WikiJools has obligingly filled my brain with gigabytes of info about Diamond—all the crazy schemes he's dreamed up, from robot dinosaurs to zombie plagues—but I say, "Is he the Mad Genius who put his butt on Mount Rushmore?"

"No," Reaper says, "that was Zettajoule." Despite having only a skull for a face, Reaper looks smug that he knows more than me. *Or so he thinks!* "Diamond," says Reaper, "is best known for having a battle suit that appears to be made of diamond. He also has a fondness for diamondlike devices."

I nod toward the bazooka in the vault. "Exhibit one?"

"That's what we're trying to determine." Reaper peers at me. Inside his eye sockets, beady red lights glow like LEDs in a cheap Halloween decoration. "Are you sure you haven't seen this object before? Or anything similar?"

"There was diamondy stuff in the lab," I say. "One machine was like a refrigerator made of diamond. Except inside, it had crazy stuff: a metal hand . . . a ray gun . . . a brain inside a jar . . ."

"Yes, that's what you told the police," Reaper agrees. "You may not realize, Ms. Walsh, but you're one of the only people who's ever inspected Diamond's technology. Or rather, you're one of the few who survived. Diamond's equipment is built to self-destruct if examined by strangers."

"Yeah, so I noticed." The diamond fridge blew up real good. My friends and I were lucky it didn't kill us.

"You're also trained in science," Reaper continues. "That makes you even more valuable as a witness."

I say, "I'm in biology, not, uhh . . . woo-woo-istics or whatever you call the study of Mad Genius tech."

"Even so," Reaper says, "you can help us."

"Help you do what?"

"Identify this item," Reaper says, gesturing toward the diamond bazooka. "It was recently discovered in a storage cache here in Waterloo. As you can see, it's made of a diamondlike material, and we know that Diamond spent several months in this area."

I say, "So you think it was made by Diamond?"

"That *is* a tempting conclusion. However . . ."

Reaper reaches toward the bazooka. He almost touches it; but at the last second, he pulls back his hand without making contact. "As I said, every device irrefutably linked to Diamond has obliterated itself. This gun is the first to be found intact. If it's genuine . . . well, you can understand why we'd be interested. But also why we find it hard to believe."

I stare at the bazooka. I worry it'll blow up this very second. From my brief encounter with Diamond several days ago, I can totally picture him leaving a prezzie for Darklings to find, then detonating it in their faces. If the bazooka hasn't exploded yet, it may just be waiting for a prime opportunity to murder a whole bunch of people. Exploding now will only kill me, the Renfields, and Reaper. If the weapon waits till it's surrounded by Darklings and scientists . . .

I say, "Look, have you even pulled the trigger on this gun? That would tell you a lot, right? If it shoots out something Mad Geniusy, you've hit the jackpot. But if nothing happens, maybe it's a high-school kid's art project." I give the gun a look. "Maybe middle school."

Reaper stares at me for a long moment. "Would *you* be willing to pull the trigger, Ms. Walsh? When you know Diamond's weapons invariably explode if they fall into the wrong hands?"

"No way in hell," I answer. "But an engineer should be able to rig a little lever that pulls the trigger while everyone stands well back." (My head immediately fills with schematic diagrams for making such a lever. Then for making a fully robotic triggering mechanism. Then a semiautonomous robot ten meters tall that can fire four bazookas simultaneously. Come on, brain, don't be that guy.)

"We've already tried what you suggest," Reaper tells me. "An expert built a device to pull the trigger. No result. We weren't surprised—even conventional technology can make guns that only shoot when held by an authorized user. Fingerprint recognition, that sort of thing. It would be no challenge for Diamond to build a gun that only he could use. Or . . ."

Reaper pauses. The bastard wants me to ask him to finish his sentence. I'd love to leave him hanging, but I'm too curious to hear what he wants to say. "Or what?" I ask.

Reaper's skull somehow grins. "One of our scientists believes the weapon is powered by the Light. I don't mean ordinary light; I mean the energy that makes superpowers possible. If that's correct, the gun can only be fired by a Spark. Imagine how useful that would be, for identification."

A chill goes through me: I can imagine it all too well. Darklings have always been frustrated by Spark anonymity. It's hard as hell to tell if someone is superpowered when they're in civilian identity. Because, sure, you could shoot them point-blank and see if the bullet bounces off; but courts really frown on that sort of thing, so good luck on getting a warrant. Besides, plenty of Sparks aren't bulletproof. But if you could just hand someone a bazooka and see if they can fire it . . .

That must be what Reaper is hoping for. And if it works, he could test me right now to see if I'm super.

Not good.

But to brazen it out, I say, "What does this have to do with me?"

"According to the statement you gave police," Reaper says, "you actually touched the equipment in Diamond's lab. Is that correct?"

I decide it's way too late to lie. "Uh, yeah. I touched the diamond refrigerator."

"Good," Reaper says. "We know for certain that that device was built by Diamond. When you touched it, you established a sympathetic connection with him."

"No way," I say. "No sympathy for Diamond at all. He's total dog dirt."

"*Magical* sympathy," Reaper says. "You touched something he touched; that forms a link. It's extremely weak, but sufficient for us to use. If this weapon"—he indicates the gun—"was truly built by Diamond, we'll detect a resonance between it and you."

I give him a dubious look; but a second later, WikiJools tells me that Reaper isn't totally off his meds. Darklings are paranoid about letting outsiders know exactly what magic can do, but it's common knowledge that mages can tell if someone has touched a particular object. If two people have touched the same object, maybe a top-notch wizard could sense the connection.

I say, "What do you want me to do?"

"One moment, please." Reaper leans his scythe against the side of the vault, then reaches under his robes (ew) and pulls out a strip of sparkly black fabric. It's the same length and width as a scarf, but it's constructed more like an afghan: crocheted with an interrupted V stitch, so it's mostly a lacework of holes. (And for once, WikiJools isn't planting outside info. I learned to crochet when I was seven, thanks to bonding experiences with my sisters. Ignorant assholes call me a tomboy, but I'm actually quite good at girly-girl things. And if I refused to learn how to knit, it's because wool is scratchy and ugly and gross, not because I kept dropping stitches.)

Reaper hands me the cloth. It's freezing. I don't mean it's merely as cold as the ambient winter air. The moment I touch the strip, my bare hands ache as if I've plunged them into an ice bucket. Is Reaper that cold under his robes? Or is the fabric rigged with cold-based magic?

I look more closely at the strip of cloth. It sparkles because thin metal wire has been threaded in with the crocheted yarn. I see gold, silver, copper, and something perfectly clear, like thin optical fiber. In other words, the cloth has "genuine magick artifact" written all over it.

"What *is* this?" I ask Reaper, as I pass the cloth back and forth between my bitterly cold hands.

"A connection tester," Reaper says. "Made by a master wizard." He gestures toward the bazooka. "Tie yourself to the gun."

"What?"

"Use the tester strip to tie yourself to the gun. No need for fancy knots. Just a loop around your wrist and another around the barrel. There's plenty of cloth."

"Do you know how freezing cold this sucker is?" I ask. "It's giving me frostbite."

"Then stop arguing and get it over with."

"Why should I?" I toss the cloth to the male Stephens. He automatically catches it. His face tightens in pain; he may be a big strong Renfield, but the frigid cold still hurts him. I wonder if the strip is icy enough to damage flesh. With my powers, I can tolerate cold temperatures as stoically as any human alive—let's say like some veteran Inuit hunter whose people have spent umpteen generations straddling the Arctic circle. But if I were a normal candy-assed white girl, my fingers would be bloodless, numb, and ready to snap off like icicles.

"This is bogus," I say. "You haven't formally arrested me. You haven't shown me a court order. You haven't read me my rights or asked if I want a lawyer. Do you know how much it hurts to touch that stupid thing? I'll bet it counts as torture. Making me tie it to my wrist violates the Geneva convention."

I stop ranting, mainly because it's hard to think straight when WikiJools is downloading an entire law library of judicial precedent. My goal here is to sound like a run-of-the-millennial biology student, not a justice of the Supreme Court.

Reaper lays his skeletal hand on his scythe. He doesn't raise the weapon; he leaves it propped against the side of the vault. But he strokes the wooden handle, and he amps up his Shadow to squeeze me like a fist. "This could all be over in a minute," he says. "Then we go our separate ways and you forget it ever happened. Alternatively, I could charge you and your roommates with multiple felonies for your adventure in Diamond's lab. The charges wouldn't even have to make sense—they'd be heard behind closed doors by a Darkling judge who specializes in terrorists too dangerous for public trial. That's the nice thing about a world with supervillains in it: those pissers are a pain in the butt, but their existence justifies draconian legal procedures that the public would never accept otherwise." Reaper takes the magic cloth away from Stephens and thrusts it back into my hands. "Now get this done or you'll never see daylight again."

Well, at least he's not going to test to see if I'm a Spark. And if worse comes to worst, I can punch my way to freedom. The odds are three against one, but the element of surprise should let me grab Reaper's scythe. That would be a wonderful equalizer:

enough to hold off these douchebags until my teammates arrive to bail me out.

But fighting would end my civilian life. Even now, I'm on thin ice. Magical auras of fear are flooding my way, both from Reaper's Shadow and from whatever juju oozes off Stevens & Stephens. An ordinary person should be puddling her panties, not debating constitutional law. Soon these dudes will start wondering why I don't melt through the floor.

So fuck it. I have to knuckle under.

I glare at Reaper and knot the cloth around my left wrist. Just an overhand knot—simple enough to tie with my free hand. The frigid cloth chills every drop of blood passing through my forearm. I tie the other end of the strip around the barrel of the bazooka. As I do, I take care not to touch the gun with my fingers. Given the conversation about Diamond's stuff exploding, I think I'll avoid direct flesh-to-gun contact.

"Done," I say to Reaper. "Is that it?"

"Don't be impatient. I have to cast an activation spell."

"Well, get your ass in gear," I tell him. "I've lost sensation in my arm."

Reaper reaches under his robe again, moving with what seems like deliberate slowness. I wonder what will happen if my hand turns to ice and falls off. I mean literally. Because a few minutes after that, my hand will start to grow back thanks to my gift of regeneration. I don't have a ton of respect for either Reaper or Stevens & Stephens, but they might just be observant enough to notice a fucking hand sprouting back from nowhere. "Come on, come on, come on," I mutter to Reaper.

He doesn't move any faster, but he finds what he's after: a scroll scribbled with sigils. The scroll is parchment, an animal skin scraped clean and bleached to beige. At least, I hope it's animal skin. The haystack of legal information still needling my brain includes the worrisome fact that our government recently passed a law that allows the use of human remains for . . . well, anything.

Reaper's scroll could have been flayed off some dead dude's

corpse. And now that I think about it, that isn't the worst-case scenario.

Reaper begins to read. As with the spell that opened the vault, the words from the scroll are gibberish. I hear the sounds but they don't stick to my brain. Since becoming a Spark, my memory has been perfect—it records every photon and phonon I perceive, without ever losing a qubit. But Reaper's mystic recitation slips away like white noise.

My head starts to throb and go dizzy. My eyes cross; I can't straighten them out. It's hard to breathe, like my lungs have lost the knack. If I don't consciously force myself to inhale and exhale, I'm afraid I'll pass out.

No idea how long the wooziness lasts. I'm not conscious of anything but the need to keep breathing. Then heat flashes like a cheese grater scraping the length of my arm, and the cloth connecting me to the bazooka bursts into flame. The fabric burns to ash with the speed of blazing plastic. Just as fast, my hand goes dead, all the nerves completely cooked. They'll regenerate soon, but if I were human, I wonder if I'd be living the rest of my life with a shortage of one in the hand department.

"We're finished, Ms. Walsh," Reaper says. "Your government thanks you for your cooperation."

"And what's the verdict?" I ask, as I massage my dead hand with the other. "Is this Diamond's gun or not?"

"You don't have clearance for that answer," Reaper says. He gestures to Stevens & Stephens. "Take Ms. Walsh back to Arrivals. Her luggage should be waiting at the—"

Boom! The wall of the baggage area explodes in on us.

FLYING FRAGMENTS OF CINDER blocks gash my skin with their sharp little edges. To add insult to injury, the cement barrage is immediately followed by a cloud of pink: shreds of the insulation that used to be inside the wall. The shreds grind into my new nicks and cuts, setting me asquirm with itching.

Oh, and while I'm being peppered with concrete pellets and

panther-pink, I'm also flying backward from the impact of the *kaboom*. I land in a kneeling pose because I'm just that good. A moment later I'm up again, diving for cover behind a baggage cart. The cart has flipped on its side from the force of the blast; the luggage that used to be stacked on the cart has tumbled onto the floor. Still, the cart itself is solid wood held by a reinforced steel frame, so it should be a passable shield against whatever just broke in.

I peek around the edge of the cart. A huge woman stands where the wall used to be. Her skin is rusty black iron, and that's no metaphor—she looks like something produced by a blacksmith's forge back in pioneer days, which then sat collecting rust for a century and a half. Her body approximates a sphere, what with her short legs, small head, and a bulging belly she stole from Santa Claus . . . that is, if Santa was made in a metalworks, and if he came smashing through your living-room wall instead of sliding down the chimney. I think Ms. Iron-and-Oxide is wearing a Sparkish "tights and tank top" costume, but since it's the same rusty black as her body, it's hard to be sure.

What I *can* be sure of is the name that pops into my mind. WikiJools says the woman calls herself Wrecking Ball.

Of course she does.

A moment after telling me who the woman is, WikiJools tosses in her group affiliation: she's one of Robin Hood's Merry "Men."

Oooo-kay. Things just got interesting.

Robin Hood is the kind of super-dude who's culturally inevitable. Think about it—actual monsters now control the world's money and power. How long before some Spark takes the name Robin Hood and thrusts his Sherwood Forest up the Dark establishment's ass?

Naturally, our modern-day Robin steals from the rich and gives to the poor. Or so he claims. And maybe he does. It's just impossible to tell one way or the other.

After all, suppose Robin openly gives everything he steals to the Red Cross or UNICEF—some altruistic group that truly fights the good fight. Charities can't take stolen money; they'd have to give it back to the original owners. Maybe even pay fines and interest. Also, every government in the world would go over the organization's books with a fine-tooth comb to make sure they haven't taken any other illicit donations. End result: more harm than good.

So whatever Robin Hood does with his ill-gotten gains, he has to keep it hush-hush: buried so deeply that even the best forensic accountants can't tell where the money goes. For all I know, Robin Hood may honestly be feeding the hungry and healing the sick. On the other hand, he might spend his loot on blood diamonds, drugs, and underage girls. No one knows.

Whatever Robin does with his cash, he has plenty to throw around. He and his outlaws take credit for six of the ten most lucrative heists in human history. That's quite an accomplishment, considering the gang is competing with Mad Geniuses and other assorted super-criminals.

If Rockin' Robin has come to Waterloo—or even if he's just sent Wrecking Ball, who's one of his top lieutenants—then tonight just escalated from "Jools in a little hot water" to "Guess what'll dominate the next forty-eight hours on CNN."

I hear a yell. Enter Reaper, brandishing his scythe. But the scythe has upped its game from "kitschy farm implement" to "enchanted instrument of death." It glows bright black, and yes, that defies common sense, but I stand by my statement. Under the lights of the baggage area, the scythe is surrounded by a jet-black nimbus, as if it's destroying any photons that venture too close to the blade. The photons don't die easily; the scythe itself is utterly silent, but the nearby air makes a curdled crumpling noise, as if the fabric of reality is having an allergic reaction.

My nose is bleeding. What the living fuck. That scythe is *bad*.

Perhaps I've underestimated our grimly reaping pal. He might lack the little gray cells, but he's way more lethal than I thought.

Wrecking Ball comes to the same realization. She backs away fast from the scythe and grabs a chunk of concrete that broke off from the wall. She hurls it at Reaper's bony head with all the super-strength at her disposal. But Reaper spins his scythe in front of his face, weaving a complicated pattern that would give Bruce Lee nightmares. The blade intercepts the concrete and shatters the chunk to dust.

Note to self: Don't fuck with the scythe.

Oh, yay, and now we've got gunfire. Stevens & Stephens have finally pulled their thumbs out of their badges and are giving their boss SIG Sauer support. This is not a positive development. Any idiot knows that bullets bounce off ladies made of iron . . . and when the lady in question is spheroidal, the ricochets zing in unpredictable directions. Bullets ping at random around the room, including a few that embed themselves in the luggage cart I'm hiding behind.

«*What a surprise,*» says a voice in my brain, «*you've gotten into a firefight.*»

It's my roommate Miranda, except now she's Aria—a snarky Spark songstress with supersonic powers. She continues, «*And here I was wondering how I'd find you in a big place like the airport. I should have known you'd make it easy.*»

«*Are you okay?*» asks Kim, who is also Zircon. At least one of my so-called friends cares about my health.

«*No sucking chest wounds yet,*» I tell my "rescuers." «*Where are you?*»

«*Observing from on high,*» Aria answers. «*Zircon says I shouldn't blast anyone until you give the word.*»

«*Zircon is right,*» I say. «*Right now, we've got Wrecking Ball from Robin Hood's crew tussling with a Darkling named Reaper. I see no reason to help either one out. Let 'em hack and slash on their own.*»

Aria says nothing, but I'm sure she wants to lend a hand to Wrecking Ball. Aria is a "Fight the Power" girl. She considers a week wasted if she doesn't attend at least one protest against Darkling overreach. But siding with Robin Hood's gang is more serious than waving signs at a sit-in. Every government on the planet has declared Robin a terrorist, maybe even with good reason. If half the stories about him are true . . .

Well, who knows? I have no doubt at all that Darklings have fabricated lies about Robin. But when a superpowered dude picks fights with the Dark, it's damn hard not to cause epic collateral damage. Even if you manage to avoid vivisecting bystanders, what about all the Darkling minions you smack around? Many of those minions are ordinary joes: not Renfields, but cops and security guards.

And some of Robin's crew are freakin' psychopaths. Ninja Jane, for example—the popular perception is she's putting on an act, like some bad-guy wrestler who snarls at the camera and cusses out the crowd. But WikiJools tells a different story. Witnesses have seen her chop and drop anyone who gets in her way. The only reason her butchery isn't public knowledge is that someone in Robin's merry band can clean up murder scenes and expunge every microspeck of evidence. Now *there's* a superpower.

All things considered, helping out Wrecking Ball would align us with extremely problematic allies. Not something to do on the spur of the moment. But throwing in with Reaper isn't any better. Not only would it make Robin Hood our enemy, it'd piss off the millions of people who idolize Robin as a hero.

Our group is new at being Sparks. Best not to risk our reputations by backing the wrong horse, especially when we haven't a clue what the fuck is going on. Why is Wrecking Ball even here? Apart from the fun of kicking through walls and fighting a demonic scythe.

I watch as Wrecking Ball continues to back away while hurling debris at Reaper's head. She's retreated completely out of the building; now she's on the pavement that surrounds the terminal. I can see the undercarriage of a plane through the hole in the building's wall. The winter night is dark, but the outside area is lit by the overhead lights that illuminate much of the airport. The shine gives a sodium-yellow tint to Wrecking Ball's rusty black body, and to the steam that billows from her mouth as she breathes.

Reaper advances with his nosebleedy scythe knocking Wrecking Ball's attacks aside. Reaper goes slow, not trying to close in. He must be hoping to drive Wrecking Ball away without a full-on fight. I don't blame him—once the gloves come off, you can't predict how combat will go. One fluke of luck, good or bad, may turn the tide.

Besides, even if Reaper's scythe is megaintimidating, who knows if it'll pierce Wrecking Ball's skin? Maybe the blade will bounce off. Maybe it'll slice her like a hard-boiled egg. When Dark powers crash into Light, the results are a crapshoot until you test them for real. Neither Reaper nor Wrecking Ball wants to risk finding out who's impervious to whom.

«*Why are they fighting?*» Zircon asks inside my head.

That's an excellent question. But since Robin Hood's MO is stealing big-ticket items, I can put two and two together. I say, «*There's a honkin' huge bazooka sitting right in front of me, ostensibly built by our BFF Diamond. Wrecking Ball likely wants to steal it. Reaper demurs.*»

«*Demurs?*» Aria repeats. «*Did you just say, 'demurs'? And 'ostensibly'?*»

«*You betcha,*» I say. «*I got the OED on the tip of my tongue, and Merriam-Webster up my ass.*»

Zircon says, «*Do we want either of these kumquats getting their hands on a Diamond weapon? Robin Hood is no saint, and this Reaper guy . . . he's running with your fake Mounties, right?*»

«*They aren't Mounties,*» I say, «*but they're probably government issue. Your point still stands—I wouldn't want these wanks to get their hands on Diamond's tech.*»

«*Then let's take away their chew toy.*»

A figure in white appears inside the vault. It wears a white top hat and tails, with a blindfold covering the eyes—like a cross between Fred Astaire and blind Lady Justice. That's actually pretty appropriate: Zircon aims to straddle the line between male and female. Then again, Zirc contends that no such line exists, and to hell with your confabulated gender binaries.

Seeing Zirc, I couldn't argue even if I wanted to. I'm too over-whelmed by Zircon's Halo. All Sparks emit an aura, akin to a Darkling's Shadow; but Darkling auras are scary, whereas Sparks have a wider emotional range. Zirc in particular smacks my brain like an ancient force of nature, something more primal than a god and more punch-in-the-face awesome.

It's a good thing Zircon spends most of the time shrunk to the size of an insect or even smaller. At human height, Zirc takes my breath away. I'm not affected when I'm in costume, too—well, okay, I'm affected a bit—but at times like this, when I'm ordinary Jools, seeing Zircon reminds me how small and trivial I am compared to the vastness of the universe.

Think of staring at the Grand Canyon. Or a volcano. That's Zircon. Shaped like a human, but projecting the feel of primordial stone. It's daunting as hell. And actually Zirc *is* made of stone: from a distance, Zircon's skin looks like standard-issue flesh, but up close you can see that it's finely faceted rock, carved and colored to resemble a person. I don't know what kind of rock it is, but it's tough enough to take a serious pounding without getting damaged.

Zircon would be awe-inspiring even without the Halo.

Zirc stands inside the vault, out of sight from everybody but me. She picks up the bazooka, clearly struggling with its weight. Like all of us, Zirc has acquired lean, mean muscles since becoming a Spark, but the bazooka was built by a dude who wears super-powered armor. Diamond can sling five hundred kilos as easy as juggling eggs. Zirc, on the other hand, may be able to bench-press a year's worth of textbooks, but hoisting the bazooka is a whole 'nother thing. Zirc can barely stay upright while holding the weight . . . but after a moment, she and the bazooka both disappear, shrinking too small to be seen.

«*Omnimorphic field for the win!*» Zircon says.

«*You just say that to make me crazy,*» Aria mutters.

Aria has a point. She's a physics major, and anally obsessive when it comes to the (finger-quote) "laws of nature." She hates that Zircon can shrink at all, but Zirc makes it worse by claiming to have an "omnimorphic field"—a pseudo-science surrounding that will shrink down anything Zirc is holding. It makes no rational sense, but it's hella convenient at times like this.

My attitude is let's not look a gift field in the mouth. Aria, on the other hand, gets all hung up about "logical consistency." As if anything in the world has ever been logical. Magic and superpowers are the universe's way of saying, "Chill."

«So, Zircon,» I say, «whatcha gonna do with the big-ass gun?»

«Would you let me take it home and hang it on my bedroom wall? I feel like redecorating.»

«Yeah, no,» I answer. «Swag made by Diamond has a habit of blowing up. Of course, if you let me examine it, I could probably shut off its defenses.»

«No way,» Aria says. «You do NOT get to analyze Mad Genius inventions.»

«Come on, Mom, I'll be careful.»

«No. It might give you ideas. BAD ideas. You're already too—»

Kablammo.

I WISH I HAD Zircon's fancy vision powers. Zirc can see at a distance, without even looking in the appropriate direction. Me, I've only got the eyes in my head, and they have an unobstructed view of the flames that have suddenly started spewing through the hole in the wall. A wave of fire sweeps across the room so gorram fast I don't have time to duck.

In the nanosecond before I'm hit, I can't help thinking of those Hollywood explosions that people can outrun on foot. Yeah, right. I sprint the hundred-meter as fast as Usain Bolt, but the flame tsunami doesn't care as it bursts my eardrums and ignites my face.

My eyes burn out of their sockets. The experience sucks.

I mean it really, really sucks. Like for serious.

As I'm finally going unconscious, I think, *Why couldn't I shut down sooner?* I've taken a shitload of crap since becoming a Spark, but getting set on fire is grade-A the worst.

I guess that's the price of being human max in everything. Someone somewhere holds the record for suffering the most. I get to match that record. Joy.

But I regenerate. So there's that.

I WAKE UP WITH the worst hangover of my life. That's saying a lot—on many mornings after nights before, I've had brain-splitting headaches, sometimes with the added fun of groin aches, ass aches, and whisker burn. But after having my face *literally* burned off, I apologize to whiskers everywhere. I also apologize to alcohol for all the unkind words I've muttered. In the days to come, I promise nothing but respectful adulation. I sure as fuck could use some booze for the purpose of self-medication.

Let's take stock, shall we?

Vision: a blur. But my eyes must have mostly grown back or I wouldn't be seeing a thing.

Inhalation: each breath feels like knives cutting ragged chunks from my nostrils, but breathing through my mouth is worse. I'm not sure I have actual lips at the moment . . . just pan-seared tatters of flesh draped across my teeth. I don't want to picture what that looks like, but I'm thinking Reaper's ugly stepsister.

General skin tone: flaky. Crispy Flakes of Jools, your favorite new breakfast! I wonder whether I'm sunburned red or charred all the way to black. But I'm like some annelid worm who only has eyespots rather than actual eyes. I can tell light from dark, but beyond that, all bets are off.

Anyway, I couldn't see my baked flesh even if my eyes were functional. I was crouching behind that baggage cart when the fireball tore through the room. Only my head and shoulders were exposed to the flames. I don't feel too bad from my boobs on down—no doubt I got scorched, but the sheer screaming agony of everything above my collarbones drowns out any *oww*s from below.

I wait. After plenty more ungodly pain, my sight deblurs, my eardrums reskin, and my lips reconstitute from ash.

I feel like it takes forever. However, WikiJools checks with some ultra-accurate timekeeping website and tells me that, start to finish, it's only been six minutes since I got flambéed.

I sure hope no one has been watching. It's hard to pretend you don't have superpowers when your eyes regrow from nothing in the time it takes Miranda to brush her hair.

I stay on my back even after I'm healed, just to gather my wits and strength. Fire alarms blare loudly off in the distance, but the world is more hushed nearby. I'll take that to mean I'm not in immediate danger of catching fire again. Awesome.

Finally, I sit up. My shirt and ski jacket immediately fall to my waist. Well, shit: the tops of my clothes got incinerated, too, and my wardrobe doesn't do super-healing. Too bad I wasn't wearing my Spark costume—it magically repairs itself, thanks to a deal Zircon arranged with a goblin. But no, I was only wearing my day-to-day. The fabric wasn't all that flammable, but still, neither the jacket nor the shirt has shoulders anymore. I'll have to use my hands to hold up what's left if I don't want to go flashing the airport.

No, let's rephrase: what's *left* of the airport. Cuz I'm sure I'm not the only thing that caught fire.

I force my aching eyes open. I'm not in the baggage area. I'm in a corridor, sprawled beside a thick metal door with a sign saying FIRE DOOR, DO NOT PROP OPEN. Obediently, the door is closed.

I wonder if I staggered here after getting blasted by the fire. My body may have a previously undiscovered superpower that makes it stumble away from danger if my brain goes unconscious. More likely, Zircon or Aria carried me here so I'd have a safe place to regenerate. Then they went off to help other people. I'm still not sure what happened, but the fireball I swallowed was likely part of a whole big thing that set the airport ablaze. In which case, hundreds of people may need to be evacuated.

I could check in by mentally calling Zirc and Aria. But I refuse. I don't want to hear them fuss over me. *Poor nonsuper Jools, always getting smacked down!* Well, I'm fine now, aren't I? Apart from the ongoing sting of having my eyes and cheeks set on fire. I'll just rest a tad longer, till I feel fit enough to start rescuing people myself.

Footsteps coming down the hall. Oh, look, it's the witchy woman I saw in the lounge. The one as pale as a vampire, but who used an Indonesian swear.

She stops in front of me. "You're alive."

"Apparently so." Since my hands are busy holding up my clothes, I plant my feet on the floor and use leverage to shove myself upward. My partly bare back slides up the wall. "What the frak happened?"

"An airplane exploded," the woman says. "I don't know why."

"There was a fight," I say. "Between those people who dragged me into your lounge, and a woman made out of metal." Should I admit I know who the woman was? Why not? Robin Hood and his gang are pretty famous, so it wouldn't be odd if I recognized one of them. "I think the woman was Wrecking Ball. A friend of Robin Hood's. She and Reaper and those gun-happy Renfields decided to go aggro right next to a plane. I didn't see exactly what happened, but I can connect the dots."

"And you survived," the woman says. "How remarkable."

"Actually," I improvise, "I was saved by a local Spark. Called herself Ninety-Nine. She picked me up and carried me to safety. Heroic as fuck."

The Darkling woman looks at me keenly, like she's examining a slime mold under a microscope. "You aren't afraid of me, are you?"

I hesitate. Given the strength of this woman's Shadow, a normal person should have drenched her delicates. But it's too late to pretend I'm shaking in my boots. "You're scary," I say, "but I had a lot to drink on the plane."

"So I've heard. After you left the lounge, your friends Karthik, Maria, and Iza dropped by. They told me you hung out with them for at least an hour." She continues to stare at me hard. "You have a surprising tolerance for the presence of Darklings."

"Matches my tolerance for alcohol."

Tolerance for Darklings or not, I'm beginning to get nervous. The woman and I are alone in a corridor that apparently doesn't get much traffic. She's eyeing me like a chef picking out meat for dinner.

But then the woman says the magic words: "Would you like a drink?"

I say, "Uhh . . ."

"I don't mean that swill they serve on airplanes," the woman says. "Something good. Something *sippable*." She gestures down the hall. "Our lounge isn't far." When I hesitate still, she adds, "It will actually be safer in there than out here. The lounge is protected by numerous charms. The rest of the airport could burn to the ground, but in the lounge, we wouldn't even feel the heat."

She gestures again. For a moment, the superhero in me wants to say, "No can do, I must hie myself hence to rescue innocents!" But playing the hero card in front of a Darkling would jeopardize my secret identity, and my "surprising tolerance for Darklings" is already mucho suspicious. Besides, Aria and Zircon have surely been pulling people from the flames since the fire started. Can't be many folks left to save.

And this woman has promised me booze. *Sippable* booze. "Sounds good to me," I tell her. "I'll enter freely and of my own will."

THE WOMAN WASN'T LYING—the lounge is just around the corner. My Darkling host opens the door and ushers me inside, placing her hand lightly against my back as she does. She actually touches my bare skin (exposed where my clothes burned away). The woman's hand is warm. Without thinking, I say, "You aren't a vampire. You may be pale, but you aren't cold."

The woman smiles. Her teeth are as white as a dentistry ad, but there's no extra length to her canines. "In the pigeonholes of this modern world, I'm classified as a demon." She rolls her eyes.

"A useless label. I'm Calon Arang. But I doubt that you've ever heard of me."

It's true I've never heard the name before, but WikiJools fills in the gap. Calon Arang: a legendary witch-devil from the island of Bali. Tradition says she was evil, and the Balinese hold festivals to celebrate her defeat by the hero Empu Baradah. But some scholars think her story is classic patriarchy bullshit. Once upon a time, there might have been a *real* Calon Arang who was probably a strong tribal leader. Empu was a warrior from some other clan who butchered Calon and her people, then made up stories for why she deserved it. *Wicked bitch got what was coming.*

But the details don't matter. The big question is whether this is the *real* Calon Arang or just a Darkling who's stolen the name. The real Calon (if such a woman actually existed) would be at least eight centuries old: in other words, an Elder of the Dark. Undoubtedly crazy strong.

I'm hoping she's only a pretender—someone who bought the Dark Conversion at some point in the last thirty-five years. That would put her in the same class as Reaper: a glorified cosplayer, trading on an unearned reputation.

But the woman I'm with doesn't feel like she's bluffing. Even if she's not the original witch-devil, she still seems like a powerhouse of the Dark. Either that, or her Shadow is spoofing my brain to hell, and she's just a silly wannabe like Reaper but with a better Charisma roll.

One way or another, does it make a difference? Monstrous is as monstrous does. So I hold out my hand and say, "I'm Jools." Calon hesitates, then takes my hand and gives it a shake. Once again, I can't help noticing how *warm* she is: several degrees above my own body heat, and definitely not vampirically chill.

"Pleased to meet you, Jools," says Calon Arang. It sounds like she means it—weird, considering how hostile she was the first time I entered the lounge. She treated Stevens & Stephens like ick on her shoes, and me like sick on the ick.

So I ask straight out, "Why are you being so nice to me?"

Calon chuckles. "You interest me, Jools. Your mental resilience. And . . ." She waves her hand at my burned clothes. "Your physical resilience, too. You clearly had a close brush with the fire, yet you seem uninjured."

"I got saved by Ninety-Nine," I say. I'm proud I remembered my cover story. "Maybe she healed me, too. But I don't know what all her powers are. She showed up in Waterloo just before Christmas and nobody knows much about her."

"Interesting." Calon's dark eyes grow distant for a moment, then refocus. "Well, I promised you a drink, didn't I? Let's not keep you waiting."

Calon heads toward the bar. She moves so gracefully, it's almost as if she's gliding. Vampires are the same: no quirks in their movements. Living humans are subject to tiny glitches in their muscles and nerves—biology just isn't perfect. But vampires slide along with unnatural smoothness down the middle of the uncanny valley.

Apparently, Calon Arang has a similar deal. And hey, she's wearing that dress that hides everything from the waist down. For all I know, she could be gliding cuz she's got wheels.

"Scotch?" she asks from behind the bar. "Or brandy?" As if those are the only conceivable options, even though I recognize many old friends winking at me from the racks—the highest-end labels from Tanqueray, Stolichnaya, Angostura. And when I say old friends, I mean like Ryan Gosling and Chris Pine: friends I've never met but whom I'm sure would be my devoted pals if we ever bumped into each other.

"Scotch," I say, because I'm not stupid. Now that I think of it, I am (of course) an Olympic-class expert on artisanal beverages from the Glens. I'm your girl for rhyming off deadpan, "Peaty with overtones of pepper, pears, and privilege, leading to a finish of oak and bagpipe spit."

So bring on the sixty-four-year-old Macallan Lalique. I will drink the *shit* out of that brew.

All Calon can find is a 1938 Glenfiddich. *Tsk.* But I'll rough it.

Calon pours two snifters and hands me one. I prove my classiness by not tossing it back in a single gulp. In fact, I do the swirly sniffy crap that proves I'm queen of the cognoscenti. Then I sip (without slurping) and say with superlative suavity, "So why the fuck are you buttering me up?"

Calon smiles. "Why do you think?"

"It can't just be cuz you want to drink my blood. I'd let you have that for a shot of ouzo."

"Please," Calon says. "Polluting my hands with low-rent liquor would be more trouble than you're worth."

"So why I am worth any trouble at all?"

Calon looks at me in silence. I meet her eyes for several seconds before I remember that's a bad idea. If you make eye contact with certain kinds of Darkling, you might wake up ten days later as a toad. But since I'm already deep in the shit, and since Glenfiddich is pleasingly scratchy in my throat, I decide, *Oh, fuck it,* and hold her gaze.

She smiles. "That's why." She sips her Scotch. "What are you doing tomorrow night?"

"Uhh . . ." After a moment, I pull my jaw off the ground and say, "No plans at the moment. What did you have in mind?"

"There's an event," Calon says. "I assume you've heard about the Darklings who recently died at the Goblin Market?"

I say, "Sure, it was on the news." I do *not* say, *I was there myself and nearly got blown to pieces.*

"Well," says Calon, "the Darkling community has arranged a memorial service. Not somber—more like a wake than a funeral. I've been invited. And I can bring a guest."

"Uh-*hunh*." I stare into her eyes again. "Just as a clarification, I'm straight. Totally into penises, and vice versa. But if you're looking for a date, I have a roommate who's obsessed with Darklings and . . . no, actually, I don't know what Kim's preferences are, but I'll bet they're more fluid than mine. I could see if she'd like to set up a meeting—"

Calon interrupts me with a laugh: a genuine laugh. I can't

remember hearing a Darkling laugh before. They're more into smirks and gloating *bwa*-ha-has. "Oh, honey," Calon says, "if I truly wanted your *memek*, your taste for penises wouldn't stop me. But that's not what this is about."

"So tell me," I say.

She's still smiling broadly. "Superficially, it's about position. If everyone else brings a guest and I don't, ill-bred oafs would sneer that I couldn't find a companion. I would then be forced to put those oafs in their place, and unpleasantness would ensue. It's better that I attend with a presentable plus-one, thereby avoiding the need to defend my position with aggression."

"You need an entourage," I summarize, "or people will talk. And you really think I'll impress people as arm candy?"

"You're young, you're attractive, and you're one in more than a million when it comes to withstanding Darkling Shadows. That makes you a rare treasure. Most other mortals who attend the event will have to wear protective talismans." Calon rolled her eyes. "Admittedly, some members of the Dark enjoy making their companions wear talismans—the more ostentatious, the better. Fetishes made from decapitated chicken heads. Medicine bags filled with reeking herbs. Slave collars." She makes a disgusted sound. "But those of us who've outgrown such displays place a high value on aesthetics. When people see I'm accompanied by a human wearing no talisman at all . . . well, I won't deny it, Jools, you're a status symbol. People will envy me."

I say, "So, what, you're showing me off like a girl you can fuck without a condom?"

For a moment, Calon looks shocked. Then she gives a belly laugh. "Yes, Jools, essentially. Fucking will not be involved, but you don't need an amulet to tolerate my company. You'll make many Darklings quite wistful."

"Huh," I say. I drum my fingers on the bar. "Now why do *really* need me?"

Calon's laugh dries up. She gives me an appraising look. "You *are* one in more than a million, Jools."

"So tell me the truth."

"Not until you say yes."

I take a sip of Scotch . . . where *sip* is closer to *gulp* than etiquette dictates. Mmm: peaty with overtones of pepper, pears, and privilege.

I'm tempted to go for it. I really am. Because no one else I know would do something so rash. I almost laugh at the thought of my roommates' faces when I tell them. Anything for a reaction, right? When it comes to manic pixie dream girls, I ain't no pixie, but I got manic down cold.

But then Calon says, "I'll get you a suitable gown. Something fine that will fit you to perfection. Jewelry, too. It's a Darkling event, so you'll have to look the part."

Just like that, the mood is broken. I know I have nothing good enough for a Darkling gala. Even that nice green dress I wore to Science Ball will look like cheap trash. But I won't let Calon buy me clothes and jewels. That's just too tawdry for words.

"No, thanks," I say, "I don't think so. It's not my kind of thing."

Calon shrugs. She twitches her fingers and a white business card appears in her hand. "If you change your mind, give me a call. And if not tomorrow night, there'll be other events. If you get bored." She lifts her glass of Scotch. "Or thirsty for finer things."

She dangles the card in front of me. Well, what can it hurt if I take it?

So I do. I hold it in my hand and read CALON ARANG in plain block letters. Nothing else on the front or back except a phone number.

When I look up from the card, I'm not in the lounge anymore. I'm standing in the Arrivals baggage pickup area.

The whole place is full of smoke.

THE AREA HAS BEEN evacuated—no surprise considering the smoke in the air and the racket of alarms going off. The ceiling has a sprinkler system, and there's a slick of water on the floor. But nothing is sprinkling now. Either the danger has passed, or something has destroyed the pipes that are supposed to bring in water.

My luggage sits alone in the middle of the room. Everybody else on my flight had plenty of time to pick up their bags and leave. The porter assigned to watch my stuff must have run when everything went to hell. I can't blame him, but I'm docking him marks for not taking my luggage with him.

Or maybe the porter left my bags cuz he was helping actual people get to safety. Which I should have been doing, too.

Except now that I think about it, I should have been helping people *after* they'd been rescued. I'm a world-class paramedic. Doctor. Surgeon. All those things. I could have been saving lives.

Should have thought of that sooner. Instead, I dawdled away, drinking Scotch with Calon Arang.

I'm just so accustomed to being useless and stupid. Shit. Another straw on my haystack of shame.

No one's around, so I scream. The sound is barely audible above the fire alarms. Before I lose control and break down crying, I give my face a hefty smack and use my comm ring.

«*Hey,*» I transmit, «*I'm finally awake. Where should I be?*»

«*Home in bed,*» replies Aria. «*Do you know how burned you looked?*»

«*I'm fine now,*» I say. «*I could model for* Elle. *Or at least* Horse and Rider. *Now how can I make myself useful?*»

«*We've cleared all the buildings near the fire,*» says Zircon. «*I search, Aria rescues, it's all good.*»

«*Do we know what caused the explosion?*» I ask. «*And please don't tell me it was one of you.*»

«*It's never our fault!*» Zircon snaps. «*I think it was Wrecking Ball. She yelled something that sounded like Latin, then started to glow.*»

WikiJools does a fetch-and-serve. «*She was likely calling Friar Tuck,*» I say. «*He's another of Robin Hood's outlaws. He has weird powers based on summoning super-animals. Number one in Tuck's menagerie is a horse that can teleport. Robin's gang always uses it for escapes.*»

«*Then Reaper must have known about the horse,*» Zircon says. «*When he heard Wrecking Ball yell, Reaper tried to take her down before she got away. He charged straight at her, waving his scythe. They were right beside that airplane. Next thing I knew,* whack-a-boom.»

«*Let this be a lesson, kids,*» I say. «*No roughhousing near jet fuel.*»

«*You say that now,*» Aria grumbles, «*but how soon before we catch you fighting on top of an oil tanker?*»

«*It's on my bucket list,*» I say. But truth to tell, I hate getting cremated. My face hurts like hell, even though it's fully healed. My throat is raw from screaming in a smoke-filled room. My shoulders are bare and my top still wants to fall down. Good thing I don't actually need to rescue anyone or I'd end up on YouPorn.

I say, «*So are we done?*»

«*Wrecking Ball has disappeared,*» Zircon reports. «*Ditto for Reaper and his flunkies. Fire trucks have arrived and my skill set sucks for putting out flames.*»

«*Let's get out of here,*» Aria says. «*Tell me where you are and I'll pick you up.*»

IT TAKES ARIA ALL of ten seconds to reach me. The smoke whips into a frenzy as she flies in, a beautiful blond prima donna in a Venetian bird mask and a lacy gold dress.

When I say "beautiful," I mean it. Just as Zircon's Halo says "force of nature," Aria's says "elegant beauty." Or maybe it just says "queen." Her aura grabs my brain and squeezes out words like "gracious" and "glorious." Also "dignified" and "reserved": there's a distance between Aria and the rest of the world, just as there's a distance between a queen and scruffy old commoners like me. I love Aria, and I love Miranda, and the two of us joke around . . . but Aria-slash-Miranda guards herself with walls of steel.

At this moment, she's also guarding herself with a force field, a luminous golden sphere that protects her from the elements as well as the super-crap that Sparks face on the regular. As soon as she lands, she extends her force field around me too. It's as warm as a hug, and somehow full of clean air devoid of smoke.

"Ready to go?" she asks.

I wrap my arms around her neck. Her body goes stiff for a heartbeat, then she scoops me up in her arms. I'm not a lightweight—last time I checked, I weigh in at a hundred and fifty pounds. But Aria lifts me as easily as a kitten, and holds me as she takes off into the air.

The lace of her dress is scratchy. And as soon as we get outside, the warmth inside the force field drops considerably. The field still blocks the brunt of the wind, but my bare shoulders pucker in the cold.

It gets worse as Aria heads higher. She doesn't like flying too close to the ground for fear that drivers will gawk and get into accidents. She also likes the quiet, peaceful feel of soaring high in a sealed glowing bubble. I get that: off on your own, away from the world, too far up to see any people. But it's bloody fucking freezing at three thousand meters. Brass monkeys are bereft, and I don't even want to think about witches' tits.

Seriously. *No witches' tits!* Get out of my head, Calon Arang!

«*What was that?*» Aria asks. «*Did you think something at me?*»

«*Not hardly,*» I say. «*I'm utterly devoid of thought.*»

Surprisingly, she doesn't give me snark. Then again, when you're jetting along at the speed of sound, maybe you need to concentrate on flying.

But she holds me a tiny bit tighter. She can probably tell I'm cold.

3

Mutualism

HOME IS OUR TOWN house, toasty and warm. I damn well hope.

Aria does a low-altitude flyby and neither of us sees anyone who'll notice us sneaking into the house. Then again, why *should* there be anyone watching the skies above our town house complex? It's eight thirty on a Friday night and classes don't start until Monday. Half the students who live here have gone out to pubs, and the rest aren't back yet from holidays.

Still, we have to be careful. Aria lands behind the gas station that's a short way down the street. As stealthy as the best ninja in the world, I slip over the fence and make my way to our unit's back patio. Once I get the door open, Aria zooms inside so fast she's a blur. She doesn't quite break the sound barrier, but she sure rattles its teeth.

Moving that fast ought to stir up a hurricane; it doesn't. I've stopped scratching my head for a logical explanation. Sometimes the best you can say is, *If superpowers had natural side effects, they'd be a lot less useful. So they don't.*

It's enough of a pain in the ass that we all have to sneak around. But so far, we've had it easy. We got our powers on December 21 when most students had already left the city for Christmas. All our neighbors will be back by Monday when the University of Waterloo starts its winter term. After that, people will be awake at all hours. If somebody pulling an all-nighter glances out the window, we really don't want to be seen creeping in our back door while dressed in super costumes.

How do other Sparks do it? Do they dig tunnels between their basements and abandoned lots? Or maybe Old Navy has a secret super section, selling Cape Tech clothes that make you invisible.

No, forget Old Navy. If I'm such a super smarty-pants, why can't I make my own damned invisible clothes?

Not a cloak of invisibility—that's too passé. *Toe socks* of invisibility!

No, I can't see a way to do it. But it *might* be possible to generate an invisibility field with two anklets, two bracelets, and some ear cuffs.

No, stop! Bad Jools! Constructing super fashion accessories is the first step down a slippery slope toward Mad Genius.

And Mad Genius is bad. Super-intelligence tends to make people go, "Surrender, mortals, and bow down before me!" A handful of super-smart inventor types have managed to stay sane, but dozens of others spend their time prancing about in jackboots and building armies of giant zombie dinosaurs. Whenever I tell myself I'm strong enough to resist that temptation, a voice in my head says, "You can't resist Cheezies. You think you're gonna resist going evil?"

So, whoops, I have voices in my head. Not a sign of mental stability.

I'm pretty sure it's safe to invent stuff that uses genuine science. No harm in being brilliant, as long as I color inside the lines. But the moment I mess with upsilon waves and transdimensional quasi neutrinos, it's a fast downhill slalom to calling myself Queen Sadista and skanking around in clothes that require Boob Glue.

Ooh, I've just thought of how to make an awesome new Boob Glue! I could cook some up with barnacle cement glands and hyperaxions.

No, no, no! Gotta anesthetize my brain before it gets me in trouble. I wonder if there's anything in the house that could do that. Perhaps something in the form of a tasty beverage.

I announce, "I'm going to my room." Hastily I add, "I need to change. Out of these burned clothes." I silence my babbling lips before they can add, *I'm definitely not going to drink my entire stock of vodka.*

"Are you getting into costume?" Aria asks.

"Why? Do we expect trouble?"

Aria shrugs. "We should maybe look around. If Wrecking Ball is in the area, the rest of Robin Hood's gang might be, too."

"Sounds like you want an excuse to break someone's face."

Aria shrugs again. "There's nothing to do here at home. Not till classes start. And I really like flying. It's exhilarating."

I look at her in surprise. Aria-slash-Miranda isn't usually "exhilarated" by physical experiences. She gets off on opera and physics, but she isn't a *bodily* person. Her most vigorous activity is yoga . . . and while she goes to classes several times a week, she treats it as maintenance, not pleasure. Like brushing her teeth, only in downward dog.

"We can go out if you want," I say. "Just let me get changed. And where's Zircon?"

"Don't know. Zircon has the gun, so ze is probably putting it someplace safe."

"Huh," I say. "Zirc wants to be called 'ze' now?"

"Yeah, 'ze' and 'zir,'" Aria replies. "Maybe partly because the pronouns match with *Zircon*—you know, they all start with zed. And out of costume, ze doesn't want to be Kim anymore. Just K."

I nod. WikiJools helpfully informs me that gaining superpowers often precipitates personal changes. It kind of shakes things loose. And I'm not referring to Sparks who go through complete mental transformations, the ones who become raging monsters or homicidal stalkers. But if you're blocked up and spinning your wheels in life, acquiring new abilities is a smack upside the head. It breaks you out of your rut. Gives you confidence to take the next step.

So I shouldn't be surprised that Kim is upping her game. Oops, sorry: *K* is upping *zir* game. K's been leaning in that direction for quite some time. I guess now ze's taking the leap.

"Okay," I say to Aria. "I know I'll fuck this up at first, but I'll try to get the pronouns right."

"You and me both," Aria says.

* * *

I HEAD UP TO my room. I'm glad K isn't in the house, since ze (I'll have to get used to that) can see through walls and might check up on me. K isn't the type to spy—all four of us roommates are good at respecting boundaries, which is why we haven't murdered one another after a year and half together. But K has started worrying I get drunk too often . . . and the number-one psychological change in people who gain superpowers is a heightened tendency to intervene in problematic situations.

Translation: even polite roommates end up saying, "What the fuck, Jools? Put down the bottle and get some help."

Or maybe I'm putting my own words in someone else's mouth. Good thing I know how to shut myself up.

I do so. Using vodka.

It's vodka-tasting vodka, not that berry-flavored shit. Then I play my own striptease drinking game: take a shot . . . take off some clothes . . . take another shot . . . dal segno.

But I run out of booze before I'm all the way naked. Good thing I wasn't with a guy or I'd be embarrassed.

And I really had intended to keep clothes and booze in sync. *You're such a screwup, Jools!* Plenty smart enough to calculate how big each drink should be to make the timing work. But here I am, still in my undies and nothing to drink.

Pouting, I go in reverse: alternating between putting on parts of my superhero costume and eating raw mouthfuls of toothpaste to cover the smell of alcohol.

I end up fully dressed but with toothpaste left over. Is that a loss or a win? I'm too drunk to decide.

But at least I'm geared up and ready to go. For the first time since I retreated into my room, I'm willing to look in the mirror. No longer Jools: I'm Ninety-Nine. And I look damned good if I say so myself.

My outfit is black on black: a hockey uniform with all the pads and armor. The armor is only fiberglass, which will never stop a bullet. However, if I keep on getting into superpowered fights, fiberglass is better than nothing. The helmet protects my head, and I've coated my face with black greasepaint. You wouldn't believe it could hide who I am, but being a Spark is special: as long as you wear a costume and mask, and you go by a code name, you absolutely can't be recognized. Weird super-science redraws your fingerprints, changes your voice, and even scrambles the DNA on the hair and skin cells you shed. Your own family won't recognize you. The only way your true ID can be exposed is if you mess it up on purpose . . . like telling someone who you are, or dropping big hints, or doing super-stuff in your civvies.

I might do that someday, cuz I'm stupid and reckless. But as far as I know, I'm still good. I haven't endangered my friends.

I clump down the stairs, holding the banister for support. I'm wearing Reeboks, not skates, so I'm not as wobbly as I could be. Even so, ever since I boarded the plane in Alberta, I've been drunk enough to kill an elephant . . . and I mean an adult African bull, not one of those little Indian pishers. *Loxodonta africana ebria*— that's me. The rare African bush lush. But if you can say "bush lush" three times quickly, you're sober enough to fight crime.

Bush lush, bush lush, bush lush.

"What?" asks Aria. But I ought to call her Miranda, since she's taken off her mask.

"Nothing," I say with perfect diction. "Have you heard from Zircon yet?"

Zircon appears out of nowhere. No wait, it's only K. Ze still wears the top hat and tails, but ze has taken off zir blindfold, so ze's officially in civilian identity. And may I have a hallelujah for nailing the pronouns, even when pissed to the operculum?

Hallelujah, Sister Jools. Amen, and also with you.

"I'm back," K says.

"Where's the bazooka?" I ask—proud that I say *bazooka* without flubbing it. (I'm the best in the world at not appearing drunk. With great power comes great responsibility.)

K says, "I shrank the bazooka and left it in a corner of Diamond's old lab."

"The lab that blew up?" Miranda asks.

"That's the one," K says. "It's all sealed up. Got a new steel door with a serious lock, so I doubt anyone will go in there anytime soon. As a bonus, if the gun starts giving off wonky radiation, people will think it's just residue from Diamond's tech."

"What if the gun self-destructs?" Miranda asks.

"At the moment, it's the size of a fruit fly," K says. "Can't make a very big bang. Anyway, it's behind that steel door, so the blast will be contained."

Miranda still looks worried. "You couldn't have taken it farther away? Like out in the country?"

"I don't fly fast," K replies. "*You* might be quick enough to dump the gun in the middle of nowhere, but me, I need ten minutes to fly a block. Besides, you never know if we'll need the gun on a second's notice."

"Why?" asks Miranda.

"Because being a Spark is insane. For all we know, Godzilla might start stomping downtown Waterloo, in which case we'll be glad to have the bazooka within close reach."

"Also," I say, "I'd love to dissect how that sweetheart works."

Oops. That just slipped out. Weird how toothpaste makes you impulsive.

K and Miranda give me the wary eyeball. "You sincerely want to analyze Mad Genius tech?" Miranda asks.

I say, "I'm a teensy bit curious. Know your enemy, right?"

"Only a few days ago," says Miranda, "you got seriously upset about possibly being a Mad Genius. Remember?"

Of course I do. The night we got our powers, I had a mini-major breakdown when designs for Mad Genius inventions started popping uncontrollably into my head. Miranda stayed with me and talked me down, till the flood of bad ideas subsided. I told her I was swearing off that shit: I appointed Miranda my sanity sponsor, authorized to rein me in if I got out of hand.

But I suck at following the advice of trainers. Just ask the people who've coached me in hockey. There's a reason I got thrown off the varsity team, and it wasn't because of my grades . . . even if that's the story I told my friends.

"Look," I say—and even as I do, I wonder why the hell I'm doubling down—"I won't go cray-cray just from looking at the gun. It's a bazooka, not Cthulhu. And we should learn as much about it as we can."

"Why?" asks Miranda.

"Because first, that guy Reaper claimed it might only work when held by a Spark. See the implications? If Diamond has technology that operates like that, he can tell who's a Spark and who isn't. And so can whoever has the gun."

"Ouch," says K. "That would be a disaster."

"I know, right? Because if anybody got something like that, how hard would it be to . . ." Shit. A flood of ideas geyser into my brain. Any one of them might work as a foolproof Spark detector. I so, *so* wish I had a bottle in my hand to wash those ideas away. All I can do is take a deep breath and say, "It'd be trivial to make a remote detector, something to scan a crowd and pick out anyone who's a Spark."

"Okay," Miranda says, "I'm officially scared."

"And another thing," I say. "We're gonna face Diamond again. You know that, right? We stopped his stupid scheme and hurt him bad. Once he heals, he'll come back for revenge. He's a mass-murdering supervillain. He won't let bygones be bygones."

Miranda looks at K. K grimaces. "Jools has a point," K says. "I read up on Diamond over the holidays. He's got an ego the size of Betelgeuse, and he never lets things slide. He'll want serious payback, and sooner rather than later."

"See?" I say. "If only for self-preservation, we should learn what we can about his tech. If he really has some gadget that can tell Sparks from ordinary schlubs on the street, I need to find out how it works and how to jam it."

Miranda looks very unhappy. "Jools . . ." she says. Then she brightens. "No way you can analyze something like that. You don't have the proper equipment. The only analysis thingie in the house is that piddly little hand lens K uses to look at rocks."

"It's not piddly," K says. "It's a precise optical instrument. My mom ordered it from Zeiss."

"It's a 10X lens the size of a thimble," Miranda says. "You really think it can analyze a superweapon? And for all we know, the bazooka is a Trojan horse. Diamond could have left it behind because he *wanted* it to be found. Maybe it contains a hidden camera that Diamond can watch from. When he spots a suitable victim, he'll push a button and *auf wiedersehn.*"

Miranda has a point—that's Diamond's brand of jam. But if so, why hasn't the gun gone *boom* already? Reaper implied it was found by government agents. Diamond would *love* blowing up government agents. If not that, there'd been a golden opportunity for mayhem in the baggage area. An explosion would have caught me, Stevens & Stephens, Reaper, and Wrecking Ball. Or what about when Zircon picked up the gun and cradled it like a baby? Diamond *loathes* Zircon. If he could make the gun blow up, he would have done it then.

Absolutely. Positively.

I lay out my reasoning . . . and while I'm talking, WikiJools pulls another useful fact from the cloud. "You know what?" I say. "We can analyze the gun without using K's lens thingie. The university has facilities for examining Cape Tech."

"It does?" Miranda says.

"Yes. A brand-new lab. Funded by anonymous backers."

"Who must be Darklings," K says. "Nobody else could afford it." K pauses. "No, wait—Darklings always put their name on the door. They want bragging rights, not anonymity."

"It's probably funded by the government," Miranda says. "They have this approach-avoidance thing about Spark technology. They'd love to ban it, but they'd also love to know how to reproduce it."

I say, "It doesn't matter who put up the money. All I care about is that we've got a nice shiny lab full of everything we need."

Miranda scowls. She *always* scowls. She's the Boy Who Cried Wolf of scowlers. She says, "We have a horrible track record with labs at the university."

"Then it's time we turned over a new leaf," I say. "Benevolent basic research for a worthy cause."

"What if somebody's *in* the lab?" Miranda asks.

"On a Friday night? On the second of January?" I scoff an Olympic-level scoff.

Miranda says, "There must be security alarms."

I say, "We have someone who can shrink under doors, not to mention yours truly, who happens to have mad burglary skilz. No, wait, not 'mad.' Poor choice of words. Nothing mad about me."

"Shut up," Miranda says, trying not to smile. "If you really want to do this, we'll *all* go, to keep you out of trouble. Then we'll come back and watch *Frozen*. I got the 3D-V for Christmas." She glares at me. "You will sit through the movie, you will not make rude comments, and you will let me sing along."

"Yes, Elsa," I say.

She scowls me a scowl. We head out.

ARIA TAKES ZIRCON AHEAD to fetch the bazooka from where it's stashed. I'm happy for the chance to clear my head: five minutes of fresh air as I jog from our town house to the University of Waterloo.

The city is snow-a-rama between our house and campus. The roads are clear and the sidewalks are shoveled, but the shortcuts I usually take are buried under thigh-deep drifts.

The snow isn't natural—it was deposited by a blizzard that Diamond created in order to bog down cops on the night of his hijinks. And I can't help wondering how Diamond produced so much snow. The night had started clear and cloudless, not much humidity in the air. So where did Diamond get enough H_2O to make a blizzard? Did he teleport it from elsewhere? I don't know how teleportation works, but I assume it takes humongous energy, especially when you port several millions of tons of vapor.

How did Diamond *do* it?

How would I?

A Mad Genius needs resources—matter and energy, plus shitloads of cash. Where does it all come from?

Set Diamond aside for a moment. Let's think about a more recent Mad Genius fiasco. On New Year's Eve, Doctora Desafío attacked Buenos Aires with an army of giant robots. To build them, she needed truly colossal quantities of steel, electronics, mechanical parts, and God knows what else.

It must have cost billions of dollars. Where did she get the money? And how did she buy the raw materials without being detected by antiterrorist agencies? Especially when said agencies have their cyberhooks embedded in every financial database on the planet, plus honest-to-Gygax magic spells filling in the cracks. Super-smart freaks like Doctora may be able to hack the computers that are watching for trouble, but no Mad Genius can finagle sorcery. Sparks can't cast spells: period, full stop.

I suppose if Desafío had billions of dollars, she could bribe Darkling wizards to cover her tracks. Darklings are obsessively money-centric. Expert magicians will sell out for the right price. But the Elders of the Dark try to prevent that from happening— they've created the Dark Guard, a secret police force, to stomp any Darklings who go rogue.

The Guard are the best of the best: powerful Darklings trained to sniff out anyone who breaks the Dark Pact. The details of the Pact are a deep Darkling secret, but the gist is well known. Any Darkling who helped Desafío before, during, or after the fact would be the Dark Guard's public enemy number one.

But as *The Great Gatsby* tells us, wealth breeds careless people. Darklings crash through life without considering the results. How could there ever be problems that money can't solve?

And even when the Dark Guardians catch and execute some sleazebag, it gets hushed up. Publicizing the punishment wouldn't act as a deterrent, cuz careless people can't conceive that the rules apply to them.

Besides, Darklings hate airing their dirty laundry in public.

So, with enough cash, Doctora Desafío could hire a Darkling with the smarts to hack magical surveillance as easily as Desafío hacked other types of tracking. After that, she was free to assemble her robot army in peace.

In her massive underground lair.

That she somehow constructed without being noticed by anyone in the neighborhood.

An underground lair where she received deliveries of high-tech components day and night for months on end, while she built a million robots all by herself.

Or maybe she built a thousand machines that could each build a thousand robots.

Or she built a single machine that built a thousand machines that could each build a thousand robots.

Fuck, she'd have to be a genius just to plan the logistics, never mind the actual inventing. And she'd have to be insane to go to such trouble. Why spend billions on a stupid scheme that you *know* will be foiled by do-gooder heroes, when you could fill your day with booze and hot willing men for a fraction of the cost?

I don't understand it. And whoopee for me. Maybe it means I won't turn into Waterloo's own Mad Genius.

Instead, I'll just be a high-IQ underachiever.

That's my niche. Fits me like a glove.

I GET SO DISTRACTED by these thoughts, I almost run past the building I was heading for. It's one of the newest on campus, tucked in an out-of-the-way corner behind the big smokestack that says WE ❤ FOSSIL FUELS.

Welcome to the T. V. Tagore Energy Research Centre.

WikiJools helpfully supplies me with the résumé of T. V. Tagore, but please: she's just another Darkling donor who wanted her name on something cool. If it wasn't a research center, it'd be a football stadium or proctology clinic.

I circle the building to make sure no lights are shining inside. Nothing but EXIT signs. By the time I get back to the main entrance, my friends have arrived.

"Any problems?" I ask as Aria holds the door open for me.

She shakes her head. "We have the bazooka. Zircon has gone ahead to check out the security."

Clear sailing. When we reach the lab we want, Zircon transmits from inside, «*I can open the door anytime you like, but there's an alarm pad—the kind that gives you thirty seconds to key in a number code, or else sirens go off.*»

«*No problem,*» I say.

"You know the code?" Aria asks.

"No, but I know the lullaby."

She gives me a quizzical look, then shrugs. «*Okay, Zirc, let us in.*»

The door opens. I move inside, playing it cool AF as I look at the number pad. It's a Singatec Model 3C, child's play for an Olympic-level expert in B and E. I pry off the faceplate, yank loose a wire, then knuckle-punch the control wafer. The wafer cracks down the middle and I pull out both pieces.

"We're good," I say.

Aria says, "Where by *good*, you mean we've successfully committed breaking and entering, trespassing, destruction of public property . . ."

I say, "In Alberta, that's what *good* means."

Zircon snickers. Zirc's from Alberta, too.

I hit the light switch beside the security pad, then turn to scope out the room. It's less than a year old, so it's uncannily fresh: clean white paint and unstained floor tiles. No dents in the drywall or any of the other wear and tear one expects in a lab used by university students.

As an Olympic-level architect, I can tell the far wall was originally supposed to have a bank of windows, but at some point the plans were changed. You can still see the window frames, but instead of glass they hold titanium steel plates. Gawkers can't see in, and shrapnel can't shoot out. It wouldn't surprise me if the window plates included a layer of lead—all the better to block X-ray vision and radiation leaks.

As for the lab's equipment, each piece seems blankly anonymous. These days, analyzer machines are basically just boxes. There's a slit for inserting your samples, but you can't see anything else from the outside. Any melting, pulverizing, and/or Kirlian scintillation is done in tightly sealed internal containers.

Before I became super, I would have seen nothing here of interest—just a bunch of off-white metal boxes of various sizes, each with a computer attached. Now I recognize everything; even as I take stock of what I've got to work with, I'm figuring out how to proceed.

What are my goals? Number one: to avoid setting off any self-destruct surprises in the gun. Number two: to determine if this is really Mad Genius tech—with so much showy bling, the bazooka may just be a prop for someone's homemade movie about supervillains. Number three: if it *is* Mad Genius tech, try to understand how it works . . .

Or not. Comprehension is risky. Can I get my head around a Mad Genius's work without twisting my brain in the process?

Guess we'll see.

"Where's the bazooka?" I ask.

Zircon shrinks out of sight, then grows back holding the gun. Aria takes it quickly, before Zirc falls over from the weight. Aria is about to hand the weapon to me when she thinks better of it. "Where do you want me to put it?"

I point to a nearby worktable. It's basically a kitchen island, with a hard plastic work surface on top and casters so you can wheel it around the room. Attached to one edge is a magnifying glass the size of a dinner plate. It's on a long metal arm with hinges and ball joints so you can turn the lens any direction you want. "Set the gun there," I tell Aria. "We'll give it a once-over."

"Anything special you're looking for?" Zircon asks. "My Spark-o-Vision can scan better than any lens."

"I don't know what to expect," I say. "But feel free to take a look-see. Tell me if you find anything scary."

Aria says, "It's too bad Dakini isn't here. She could link you to Zircon telepathically, so you could see through Zirc's eyes."

Zircon's mouth tightens. "Dakini should keep her telepathy to herself. Now shush, let me scan."

Zirc shrinks to the size of a Barbie and/or Ken and walks the length of the gun like a shopper checking out the frozen-food aisle. I can barely restrain myself from leaping forward to make my own inspection. But deep down I know Zirc's Spark-o-Vision is the most sophisticated analytic equipment in this room; I'd be stupid not to use it.

So I wait. At last, Zirc finishes zir painfully slow stroll-by. "Well, it's definitely . . ." Zirc stops. When Zirc is that tiny, zir voice is an ultrafalsetto. It sounds like a Pokémon chickadee: enormously cute and enormously undignified. Zirc grows back to normal height (which is still pretty short) and starts again. "The gun is definitely more than mundane. My Spark-o-Vision sees magic and superpowers as weird-colored glows . . . and there's something right *here* with serious shine." Zirc points to a section of the gun barrel right above the trigger.

I say, "I don't see anything."

"You wouldn't," Zirc says. "The glow is the size of a pinprick and deep inside the weapon. Still, it's like a bright pink LED."

"Maybe a power source?" Aria suggests. "A Cape Tech battery?"

"Don't know," Zirc replies. "I zoomed in for a microscopic close-up, but I don't see anything special. The light doesn't come from any specific component. It's just a fleck of I-don't-know glued to the inside wall of the gun barrel."

I ask, "Have you ever seen anything similar?"

Zirc shakes zir head. "No. And that's odd too. Up till now, my Spark-o-Vision has been consistent. When Aria uses a power, the glow is always gold. Ninety-Nine, you're green, and Dakini is violet. It's the same with Darklings—no matter what powers or magic they use, each Darkling radiates their own personal color. Like for instance, that vampire, Lilith: every supernatural thing she did lit up with the same shade of red."

I say, "So?"

"So I've always seen Diamond's powers as bright white. Even

when he pretended to be someone else, his powers didn't change color. The tech he made shone the same color, too."

"But the glow in the bazooka is pink," Aria says.

"Exactly," Zircon says. "And the rest of the gun doesn't glow at all."

I think for a moment. "If this gun was made by Diamond, it's defective, right? Otherwise, it would have self-destructed by now. Maybe it glows the wrong color because it's broken."

"Or maybe it wasn't built by Diamond," Aria says.

"You think two different supervillains stashed weapons around Waterloo?"

Aria shrugs. "Or else Reaper lied to you. Or somebody lied to him."

"Lots of 'or's," Zircon says. "That's the problem with magic and superpowers. Whenever you play detective, you're dealing with umpteen weird possibilities that you can't rule out."

"Then let's gather hard data," I say, pulling down the magnifying glass and angling it into position.

"Ooh, look at you!" says Aria. "Acting all like a scientist."

I say, "I fart in your general direction." I *am* a scientist, dammit, and I can figure out what's going on.

So I look. I examine. I test.

E.g.: I pry off glittery niblets from the barrel of the gun, have Aria crush them to powder with a sound blast, and run them through the mass spectrometer.

E.g.: I fire up UV lamps and go inch by inch along the exterior to see what fluoresces.

E.g.: I scrape off flakes of bazooka using Zircon's pocketknife and look at them under a microscope. (This is Zircon's *ordinary* pocketknife I'm talking about—the one ze carries in case a rock's hardness needs testing. I don't mean Zirc's *magical* knives; as far as I'm concerned, those horrors should be locked in a rowan-wood coffin and sunk into Challenger Deep. I think Zircon agrees with me: ze's hyperextremely reluctant to pull the knives out of their sheaths. Let's hope that lasts forever.)

I soon zone out, getting blurry drunk on science. I'm still teching and it feels productive . . . but the Jools part of me is off the clock.

It's restful. I wouldn't call it pleasant, just as I wouldn't say being drunk is giggly bouncy fun time, but my battered brain gets to go AWOL.

No worrying. No beating myself up.

It lasts maybe an hour. When my mind finally returns from the Nothingness Spa, I expect to be staring at results. Instead? Fuck all. I have a cartload of superficialities—printed numbers, scribbled notes, graphs on computer screens—but none of it sparks any comprehension.

Maybe I'm just too stupid. After all, my powers only make me human-best in everything. Maybe to understand Mad Genius tech, you have to be *more* than human: beyond the house-trained end of the scale where knowledge politely uses the litter box, and into the part where there's shit all over the house.

This should make me happy. *Hey, Jools, you won't go crazy: you're too dumb!* But I'm sick of feeling like a moron. It's the story of my life since I got to uni, and I hate it.

I WANT TO BE SMART, DAMMIT! I DON'T WANT TO FEEL LIKE EVERYONE ELSE UNDERSTANDS THINGS I DON'T.

I want to believe I can *force* my brain to catch on if only I focus. Like when I'm training for hockey, and don't have the strength for another chin-up, but I try anyway. There's a moment when you aren't using muscles anymore, but just pure determination. It feels like you're going to rupture a vein, but you steal one more chin-up from thin air.

I've always been able to do that with physical stuff. I've wished and wished I could do it mentally, too.

Am I getting a glimmer about the gun? Through absolute stubbornness, am I pulling back an edge of the curtain? Or am I lying to myself, same as always?

Can't tell, cuz I get derailed. Zircon suddenly hollers inside my head, *«Aria! Get me out of here!»*

"What?" says Aria. "Why?"

«*Just do it!*» Zircon snaps. «*Please!*»

Ze collapses to the size of a Barbie. Aria looks worried as fuck, but she has superhuman reflexes. She snatches up Zirc in one hand and bolts out the door so quickly it slams behind her. I'm left standing in the lab, *Hommina hommina*, and wondering whether to expect a zombie invasion or a hail of frogs.

MAYBE ZIRCON JUST HAD to pee. That's serious when your costume is white. But since Zirc can shrink to the size of *E. coli*, ze could strip down naked without being seen and take care of business.

So what the hell is up? Did Zircon's Spark-o-Vision detect a flock of hungry velociraptors? But then why not just say that? Why would Zirc demand to bug out but not worry about leaving me behind? Especially when Zirc can hide from damned near anything just by shrinking out of sight.

The lights just flickered. Crap, now they've all gone out. The only light comes from computer screens . . . and there is *nothing* scarier than the muted glow of monitors in the dark.

Flashbacks to playing *Alien: Isolation* till three in the morning. Creeping around dark labs filled with ambush predators.

Crap. Crap. Crap.

Smoke starts to seep under the door. No, not smoke. Oh, fuck.

I snatch up the diamond bazooka. I have no idea what will happen if I pull the trigger, but the gun looks imposing as hell. Whatever is leaking into the lab from the hallway should be nervous about finding itself in the crosshairs.

"Dude," I say to the Definitely Not Smoke. "Not to be confrontational, but you're hovering where I'm about to shoot."

Creepy laughter of the sort that usually needs a reverb microphone. The smoke congeals into a transparent human form: a man, thirtyish, with stringy hair, hollow eyes, and an emaciated body draped in a long leather duster. The duster reaches to the floor, but the man's body doesn't; he dims at the waist, trailing off into nothingness.

"Oh," I say, "Wraith. Short time no see."

"Ninety-Nine," he says, tipping his head in a little bow. "You're not who I expected to find."

Who *did* he expect? Zircon? My friends and I met Wraith on the night we became super, but I picked up definite vibes that Zircon and Wraith already knew each other. Zirc never explained how ze might know a Darkling ghost. But hey, we all have secrets. Zirc would tell us if it's important.

Still, it's clear that Zirc saw Wraith a'coming and ran off spooked. It could be time for a team meeting.

Now that I think about it, I'm the only one in our group with experience being on teams. Miranda, K, and Shar all occupy the lone-wolf end of the spectrum.

Then again, if I'm such a great team player, why am I here on my own?

"What are you after, Wraith?" I ask.

"Your toy." He nods toward the bazooka that I'm aiming at his chest.

"Why do you want it?" I ask.

Wraith purses his desiccated lips. "I can't tell you."

"Because?"

"I signed an NDA. That means a nondisclosure—"

"I know what an NDA is!" And since Wraith is a Darkling, it's no doubt an NDA with *teeth*. Darkling contracts aren't *necessarily* signed in blood—Wraith doesn't look like he *has* blood—but whatever the technical niceties, Darkling contracts can fuck you up good.

If you sign a Darkling NDA, either you'll find yourself physically incapable of saying certain things—your mouth simply won't form the words—or else you can say them, but you then suffer serious blowback. You could literally get struck by lightning . . . and that's tame compared to other punishments I've heard of.

If Wraith truly signed an NDA, I'd be wasting my time trying to wheedle him into talking. I say, "Fine, your lips are sealed. But that means you're working for someone. Hopefully not the same bozos as Reaper. He was supposed to keep the bazooka safe; he screwed up royally."

Wraith says nothing. I continue. "Yes, I know about Reaper. I happened to save that nice Jools Walsh when the airport caught fire. She told me everything she knew. So if you were working with Reaper, you'd probably flash official-looking ID and say you were claiming the gun on behalf of national security. You haven't tried that. Nor have you tried to beat me up, or to play ghostly mind games and make me drop the weapon."

"I can do that if necessary," Wraith says. "But I'd rather you be reasonable."

I laugh. "Is it reasonable to give a superweapon to someone I barely know?"

He hesitates, then says, "Ask Zircon about me. She'll tell you I'm trustworthy."

Interesting. I say, "Zircon is a 'ze' now, not a 'she.' Just FYI. And ze isn't here at the moment." I stare at him, thinking, *I don't think ze trusts you as much as you believe.* "Speaking of Zircon," I say, "Zirc's the one who commandeered this gun in the first place. Jools saw Zircon sneak in while Reaper was fighting Wrecking Ball. Zirc decided neither could be trusted, so ze took the weapon into protective custody."

Wraith says, "We figured that was what happened. Sparks are as territorial as wolves. Your team has claimed Waterloo as your turf, so naturally you'd turn up when the airport went to hell. You'd also believe you had the right to confiscate anything you thought would disturb the peace."

"You said 'we,'" I tell him. "You and who else?"

"Me," says a voice from the doorway.

Big surprise. I *knew* someone else would be waiting to make an entrance.

It's a vampire woman with skin the same white as our kitchen Corelle. But unlike Calon Arang, this newly arrived vamp is a classic second-gen Darkling. She must have taken the Dark Conversion the moment she turned eighteen, so she'll look that age for all eternity . . . or at least until someone cuts off her head and stuffs it with garlic. The woman wears dark-rimmed serious glasses, a short serious haircut, and sharp-pressed serious Armani, all to project an air of gravitas; but she looks like a Goldman Sachs Barbie, or one of those stock photos where a teenage model wears a business suit and points at fake sales charts.

And I've seen this vampire before. It was back on the night of the solstice, when she and I tried to pound the crap out of each other in the middle of our local landfill. The chick was dressed differently then—I remember sneak-in-the-dark clothing and razor-sharp claws. But I actually enjoyed the battle. Of all the Darklings I've had to duff up, this vamp was the only one with combat training. Pity she won't remember our fight; my teammate Dakini erased several hours of the woman's memory.

Knowing Dakini, she likely snarfled up information from the vampire's brain while wiping away the memories. But Dakini didn't share. Neither did Zircon, even though this vamp had some kind of hold on Zirc's mind. But I never got the details. I just know that I whacked this woman unconscious without learning who she was or what the heck she was doing in the dump.

At least WikiJools gives me a name. "Hi," I say. "Elaine Vandermeer, right?"

The woman's face freezes, the vampire equivalent of gaping in shock. (When a vamp is taken aback, she doesn't tense up in surprise. Her body does absolutely nothing, like a robot with its power off. Nothing happens till the vamp's brain recovers and can give her muscles new orders.)

Elaine finally puts on a curious expression. "It's odd that you'd recognize me."

I smile. "I know things." Thanks to WikiJools, I know that Elaine belongs to a wealthy Calgary family who made their money during the oil boom sixty years ago. Every member of the Vandermeer clan is now a vampire, except the youngest son, Nicholas. He became a ghost.

Hi, Wraith. Now I know who I'm dealing with.

Elaine says, "You really should give us the gun."

"Why?" I ask.

She shakes her head. "I can't tell you. I signed the NDA, too."

"Of course you did."

I consider the situation. Being alone with a vamp and a ghost, I'd be crazy to put up a fight. Besides, why bother? I'm clearly too stupid to figure out how the damned bazooka works. And it may still self-destruct explosively. Possibly the first time anyone pulls the trigger.

If I were truly a hero, maybe I'd do that: blow up myself, the lab, and the Vandermeers in order to eliminate the gun. But after an hour of getting nowhere, the damned bazooka just pisses me off. I sure as hell don't want to die for it. I want it out of my sight.

But should I give it to the Vandermeers? No good reason why. But what's the alternative? Handing it over to the cops? The gun might blow up the police station; and if not, the cops would likely pass on the gun to Reaper and Stevens & Stephens.

I like Elaine better than those morons. She and I share a bond: we tried to kill each other.

Still, I refuse to give the gun away for free. I say, "What are you offering in exchange?"

Wraith gives a laugh—creepy and sepulchral, of course, but it sounds genuine. "Now you're talking our language."

"What do you want?" Elaine asks. "Money?"

I roll my eyes. "I'm a Spark, not a Darkling. Don't care about money."

Elaine shrugs. "Robin Hood and his outlaws are Sparks. They care about money. A lot."

"Do they?" I ask. "The way they talk in their YouTube videos, they just steal from Darklings to make you look like idiots. The money is icing on the cake."

"Interesting," says Elaine. "You watch Robin Hood's YouTube videos?"

"No, I just know things." At this second, I know how much

these two apparently care about Robin Hood and Company. A datum to file away.

"If you don't want money," says Elaine, "what are you asking for?"

I ponder. When an answer pops into my head, it's so surprising I let it slip directly out of my mouth. "Invitations," I say.

"To what?"

"The memorial tomorrow night." I watch as Elaine does another vampire freeze. Wraith goes temporarily misty. I grin. "The memorial takes place here in town, correct? To honor the people who died at the Goblin Market."

"You *do* know things," says Elaine.

"Our Spark team should be there," I tell her. "Just in case."

"In case of what?"

"Anything. Like, what if Diamond shows up? If *I* know about the event, he does, too. And plenty of the partygoers will be Darklings who survived the fiasco. Diamond may want another crack at them."

Elaine says, "There'll be security measures to deal with Diamond."

I say, "Security measures so reliable you can't use four Sparks as backup?"

"You won't be backup," Elaine says. "You'll be provocations."

"Without us," I say, "the body count at the market would have been much worse. Don't we *deserve* invitations?"

Wraith turns to Elaine. "They'll come whether we invite them or not. Sparks can't let anything happen on their home turf without getting involved."

"I suppose you're right," Elaine says. She turns to me and says, "Fine, I'll get you put on the guest list. What names?"

"Ninety-Nine, Aria, Zircon, and Dakini," I say. "Plus four unnamed guests."

Elaine raises her eyebrows. "You're worried that Diamond will attack, but you want to bring dates?"

Actually, I just want to cover our asses in case we decide to show up in civilian ID. In a party with geysers of flowing booze, I'd rather wear a dress than a bulky hockey uniform. Besides, I'll be able to thumb my nose at Calon Arang and say, *Ha! I got here without you.*

I say, "I'm just thinking ahead. We may want backup of our own. Maybe Sparks from Toronto."

"Whatever," says Elaine, waving her hand in dismissal. "I'll leave eight entry cards at the reception desk. Anything else?"

I try to think of other perks to scrounge. I'd love to squeeze these two for whatever they'll give, but I'm operating in the dark. Should I ask for stock tips? A fruit basket? No. I've seen what happens to fruit around Darklings: it rots. "That's enough," I say. I slide the bazooka off my shoulder. "Which of you wants this?"

The gun floats out of my hands of its own volition. Clearly, Wraith could have taken it anytime he wanted. Brownie points to us all for acting so civilly.

Still, I want one more shot at figuring out what's going on. I say, "So you really won't tell me why you want the bazooka? *The Globe and Mail*'s 'Report on Business' says your family specializes in mining and oil, not weapons."

Elaine says, "No comment."

She goes to the door and opens it. Aria stands outside, surrounded by a fiercely burning force bubble. I'm sure she's been lurking in the hall for several minutes, just waiting in case I needed backup.

Elaine shows no surprise at seeing her. She nods and says, "Aria."

Aria nods back. "Elaine." She pauses for a long deliberate moment, then steps back out of the doorway.

Elaine and Wraith leave quietly. I yell after them, "The shindig tomorrow has a free bar, right?"

They don't answer. Now that they're out in the hall I can't see them, but I'll bet Wraith summons a ghostly fog so they can vanish into the mist.

4

*Fixed Action Patterns**

ARIA STAYS IN THE corridor as she watches the Vandermeers depart. I shut down the equipment and start erasing all signs of our presence.

I can't fix the broken security pad, but we caught a break on that—Wraith stood in the same place long enough that the floor tile started yellowing with age. Add to that the cobwebs and ants that have appeared out of nowhere, and our campus cops will leap to an obvious conclusion: some Darkling broke in for reasons unknown. They'll probably decide that it's not worth investigating. Bothering Darklings just earns you a call from some VIP saying, "Stop it right now!" . . . whereas letting Darklings get away with indiscretions often leads to generous cash donations.

Just to be safe, I fire up my flawless memory so I can clean up every spot where I left a fingerprint. They won't be Jools's fingerprints—when I become Ninety-Nine, my fingerprints change (and yes, they really do). It's part of the whole Spark anonymization thing, making it impossible to connect your Spark identity with your civilian one. Still, I don't want Ninety-Nine's fingerprints being found in the lab, either. Don't want either of my identities branded as a thief.

So note to self: always carry surgical gloves. Also a good multitool, so the next time I need to disable a security system, I can do it with finesse.

---

*A sequence of behaviors that an animal performs "robotically" from start to finish, without being able to stop.

Maybe I'll make a fanny pack with useful odds and ends. Or a utility belt! I could build a utility belt! Cuz nothing says "super" like someone whose belt weighs ninety-five pounds and sags down to show her butt crack.

Aria enters and closes the door behind her. "That worked out well," she says. "I don't like them having the gun, but I'm glad it's gone."

"You aren't mad I gave it away?"

Aria shakes her head. "Better for you to avoid Mad Genius things. You remember how you worried about—"

"Yeah," I interrupt. "But that was then, this is now. I've had time to get my act together."

Aria stares at me for a couple of heartbeats, eye contact and everything. Finally she says, "What's this about a memorial service?"

"Tomorrow night. For those who died in the market."

"I got that. How did you find out about it?"

"I know things," I say. And I do—WikiJools is feeding me details even as we speak. "The party is at the Transylvania Club," I tell her. "Starts at eight. They're expecting most of Canada's Darkling community, plus bigwigs from around the world. Plenty of people had friends and family die."

Aria looks sour. "I respect the idea of grieving for the dead. It's actually more human than I expected from the Dark. But the event will be a target for Diamond and every other nutjob with a mad-on for Darklings."

"The event has been kept pretty secret," I say. "If they can hush it up for another day, it might not turn into a circus. At least no protesters or reporters."

"There's nothing wrong with protesters," Aria snaps. "Although in this case . . ." She grimaces. "If the shit hits the fan, protesters will become collateral damage. I'll check the online places where protests usually get organized. If I see something starting, I'll try to head it off. Shouldn't be hard—I'll point out that protesting at a funeral looks bad. Even if you have no sympathy for Darklings, plenty of humans died in the market, too. They deserve to be mourned, and a protest will hurt the movement's reputation."

I nod. Aria (or rather Miranda) has clout in anti-Darkling circles. She may well be able to prevent sit-ins and speeches on blowhorns. But our best bet is still for the event to stay secret from the public. The fewer complications, the better.

Speaking of complications . . . "What was that with Zircon?" I ask. "Did ze say what was up?"

Aria shakes her head. "I decided we didn't have time to talk. I just flew zir to the far side of the city, then hightailed it back in case you needed help. But when we get home, we need to have a conversation."

I nod. With Zircon in the hot seat, it would only muddy the waters if I mentioned my chat with Calon Arang. Besides, I refused Calon's proposition. No harm, no foul. And now we have legit invitations to attend the memorial, so the point is moot.

Moot. I like that word. Moot. I'm tempted to say it out loud, but Aria would look at me funny.

WHEN WE'RE DONE CLEANING the lab, Aria and I leave the same way we arrived: me jogging and her flying. She goes to pick up Zircon, while I race through the cool night air.

Running is good. And when I go back to brooding that I'm too stupid to understand Diamond's bazooka, I can run even faster. So fast I get home too soon, so I circle the block, sprinting flat out until I'm wheezing. Then I jog home cross-country, scurrying through backyards and parkouring over fences until I reach our patio door.

No one's watching . . . I think. Fuck, but we should come to a better arrangement than looking over our shoulders and hoping.

The patio door is unlocked. I don't think that's my fault. No, I can hear Miranda and K upstairs in their rooms. They must have left the door open for me. I lock it and head upstairs myself, feeling sad that the vodka is gone. Guess that just leaves tequila. Olé!

Minutes later, I'm in yoga pants and a T-shirt that doesn't smell too bad. I should have done laundry before I left for Christmas, but if I had, Miranda would have thrown me against the wall and demanded to know what I'd done with the *real* Jools.

I'll put "laundry" on my to-do list. Right underneath "buy toothpaste." No need to remind myself about picking up other essentials. Besides, I don't want to put "purchase lethal amounts of alcohol" down in cold hard ink. I'd rather be in denial.

It occurs to me that I must be an Olympic-class denier. The denying-est denier of the *Homo sapiens* species. I'm number one on the planet . . . unless there's a Spark with superhuman levels of denial, and I don't even know what that means.

Probably they babble nonsense about denial to distract themselves from facing it.

WHEN I GET DOWNSTAIRS, K and Miranda are busy not communing with each other. K is in the kitchen making unhealthy quantities of popcorn, while Miranda sits in the living room, reading tweets on her damned Linux phone. ("It's more secure, Jools! It's end-to-end encrypted." Add to my to-do list: *Hack Ubuntu*.)

I consider pulling out my own phone and firing up Facebook, but why bother? As soon as I form the thought, my brain magically fills up with my Facebook feed, downloaded straight from the mother ship.

It's garbage. Consider it ignored. And it's easy for me to do that—I'm not addicted to social media, cuz alcohol beats the competition.

I'm only enslaved by one vice at a time.

"So what's up?" I say as I arrive in the living room, thereby proving I'm an Olympic-level conversationalist. I can sense my roommates gritting their teeth; one reason we manage to live together without bloodshed is that we have similar boundaries and senses of privacy. We agree on where to draw the line between sharing and oversharing.

But the time has come for K to share, even if it makes us squirm.

With a sigh, K emerges from the kitchen carrying three jero-boam bowls of popcorn. Ze can barely get zir arms around the load. The bowls are duly passed out, and we space ourselves around the living room, automatically maximizing the distance between us: K with zir legs tucked up in the rocker, Miranda with perfect posture in the armchair, and me on the couch. The atmo-sphere is strained enough that I don't even sprawl.

No lights on in the room—just spillover from the kitchen, and that's only from the overhead light of the stove.

K says, "You want to know why I freaked."

"Only if you want to tell us," Miranda says.

"I don't," K replies, "but I have to." Sigh. "So Elaine Vander-meer—she's a vampire, right? And back in high school . . ." K blushes; not something I've seen very often. "For a while," K says, "I had a thing with Elaine's brother. Nicholas. That's Wraith, by the way: when Nicholas took the Dark Conversion, he turned into a ghost. Anyway, I hung with the Vandermeers quite a bit, and one time . . . the details aren't important, but I let Elaine drink my blood."

"Willingly?" Miranda asks sharply. "Full consent?"

K hesitates, then nods. "Nothing you could call coercion. I was an emotional wreck at the time, but Elaine didn't use magic to make me agree. And I wasn't drunk or anything. I was dumb and desperate, but said yes of my own free will."

"How old were you?" I ask.

"Eighteen. By-the-book legal."

"Forget about the law," I say. "At least, not *human* laws. What matters are the laws of magic, and they aren't always—"

"Jools, stop," K interrupts. "Arguing won't fix this. I willingly let Elaine drink my blood. Now I'm hooked with a blood bond."

K's face has gone pale in the darkness. Maybe ze turned into Zircon to feel less fragile. Stone, not flesh.

Softly, Miranda says, "Are you sure?"

"Of course I'm sure!" K snaps. "How do you think I knew Elaine was getting near the lab? I *felt* her. It was all I could do not to fall on my knees. *How may I serve you, mistress?* The only reason I can resist at all is because I'm a Spark. Normal people bound to a vampire wouldn't *dream* of fighting the compulsion. I had just enough willpower to ask you to take me away. If I'd stuck around, Elaine would have played me like a fiddle."

"But you did have some resistance," says Miranda. "Maybe you can build it up. Maybe eventually, you can fend her off completely."

K says, "Or maybe she'll break down my weak little blocks and I'll be totally under her power."

Miranda turns to me. "You're the one who knows things. Is that how it works?"

I wait, but WikiJools gives me nada. I say, "I only know things you can Google: reasonably public knowledge." I shrug. "If anyone knows how blood bonds work on Sparks, they're keeping it very secret. Neither Sparks nor vampires want the truth splashed around."

Miranda scowls, then turns back to K. "This is so stupid! If Elaine tries to influence you, why can't you just say no?"

"Because it doesn't work!" K sounds close to tears. "A blood bond isn't *persuasion*, Miranda, it's a disease. When you've got cancer, you've got cancer. Stubborn thoughts don't help."

"That's the blood bond talking," Miranda mutters.

K glares at her. Me, I wrack my brain to see if there's a Cape Tech way around this. I may not be smart enough to understand Diamond's gun, but surely I can invent some gizmo to save K from Elaine. A super tinfoil hat? Or maybe just a total blood transfusion to purge the contamination.

But I doubt such tricks will work. Using tech against magic is like using calculus against cannibalism. Totally different wavelengths.

"We need our own private sorcerer," I say. "Someone who can break a blood bond."

"Don't get your hopes up," K says. "Elaine is one of the strongest wizards in the country. Average Darklings don't have the power to break her hold. We'd need an exceptional Darkling even to give it a try, and anyone like that would be reluctant to mess with another Darkling's property."

"We're Sparks," Miranda says. "We can do impossible things. We can try to find a wizard who'll trade a favor for a favor."

K gives an eye roll. "Trading with Darklings? Every legend since forever says that'll blow up in our faces."

"What about the Goblin?" I suggest. "He's a whiz when it comes to sorcery. And he seemed to like you."

"Maybe," K says, "but I don't want to trust him. He's so innocent and innocuous, it's like he's using magic to make himself likable. And in stories, dealing with goblins never ends well."

K has a point. The Goblin helped us once—he enchanted our costumes so they clean and repair themselves, no matter how much they get wrecked during battles. But he did us that favor because we helped save his market. Asking for something else may be going too far.

Miranda says, "We're bound to see the Goblin tomorrow night, right? The memorial is for the people who died in his market; he'll have to be there. We'll talk to him. Find out the possibilities. Nothing wrong with that, is there?"

Instead of answering, K crams popcorn into zir mouth. We all do, out of sheer discomfort. Miranda, who hates Darklings, has just proposed we get into bed with one. If not the Goblin, then someone else. There must be plenty of Darklings who'd love Sparks owing them a favor. But it won't end well. We all know it.

After several loud seconds of popcorn crunching, K mutters, "One other thing."

I wouldn't have thought I could get any more tense, but voilà. And by the sound of it, Miranda is in the same boat. She says, "What?"

"Nicholas and Elaine," K says. "I think they're with the Dark Guard."

I wince. "Why do you say that?"

"When Nicholas was doing all that stuff on solstice night, he claimed he was just doing business work for his father. But you saw him—he was snooping around like a cop investigating Diamond's background. And Elaine . . . supposedly she was having a fling with Diamond, but she flat out told me she was faking. She only got close to him to gather info. That's Dark Guard stuff. Sleeping with the enemy in order to take him down."

"Elaine slept with Diamond?" Miranda says. "Ew. When Shar gets back, I need her to erase that image from my mind."

K shrugs. "I thought you should know. If Elaine were on her own, she'd use our blood bond for fun. Like a cat playing with a mouse. Humiliation. But if Elaine is with the Dark Guard, she might use me *strategically*. That's bad for you, me, and everyone."

"Enough!" Miranda says. "We can't fix this tonight. Maybe by tomorrow, we'll have a brainstorm. Or maybe Dakini can do some mental repair . . . no, don't glare at me, K, I know how you feel about brain stuff, but if we can deal with this in-house, you'll be free. So don't moan."

With a determined look, Miranda uses the remote to turn on the TV.

Frozen. Which I have to admit is good, even though it's Darkling propaganda. Poor Elsa, treated so bad by mean old humans simply because she can do magic.

But the whole idea of magic makes me think of Calon Arang. Possibly an Elder of the Dark. I'll bet she can slice through a blood bond like snipping off thread.

I find Calon's business card in my hand. I don't even know how it got there—I put it in my pocket when she gave it to me, but I'm not wearing the clothes I had on at the airport.

Yet here it is.

I palm the card like a magician. I'm such an Olympic-level prestidigitator, I doubt even K's Spark-o-Vision noticed my move. Then I roll off the couch and head for the stairs.

"Oh no," says Miranda, "you are *not* running out on the movie."

"Gotta pee," I say. "But I'll be back before fractals start spiraling."

Miranda looks grumpy but holds her tongue. K's too distracted to care—likely brooding about Elaine, mental dominance, and other awfulness.

Don't worry, dude, I'm gonna fix that.

IN OUR UPSTAIRS BATHROOM, I lean against the sink, Calon's business card in one hand, my phone in the other.

K might be watching me; I'm pretty sure Spark-o-Vision can see through closed doors. And if I call the number on Calon's card, Miranda may hear every word—her super-sensitive ears pick up firefly farts at twenty paces. If I try a stupid trick like turning on the tap to cover my voice, it'll just draw attention. I'm tempted to start tickling the tulip, cuz that'll get both of 'em to block their eyes and ears . . .

But in the end, I just decide to have faith. Miranda and K are my BFFs. Superpowers or not, they won't pry. Not even when I'm about to do something with "bad idea" written all over it.

I punch in the number from Calon Arang's card. She answers immediately . . . which is totally not how cell phones work, considering all the connection protocols that have to take place before a call goes through. WikiJools starts to download a bunch of IEEE standards pertaining to wireless telephony, but I ignore the infodump and say, "Hello?"

"Jools," says Calon Arang. "Lovely to hear from you."

"You knew it was me?"

"Of course. Just a moment."

I figure she's just adjusting her grip on her phone. But two seconds later, there's a flash of Day-Glo pink light and I'm back in the airport lounge. Calon sits in front of me on one of the big leather armchairs. She's like a queen on a throne, except she's wearing a terry-cloth bathrobe. An upscale one—black with gold embroidery. The robe is long enough to cover her legs and feet completely. Once again, I have the feeling she might not have legs at all—possibly a fish tail, or maybe something more awful. After umpteen zoology courses, I've seen tons of icky body designs, but Calon might be worse than anything occurring in nature.

As for me, I'm just in my T-shirt and yoga pants, feeling like a slob in such a swishy environment. Then again, I doubt that I'm really here. The place seems too precisely like before, even the exact same arrangement of logs in the fireplace. (Yes, my memory is that perfect.)

"Illusion?" I say to Calon.

"Of course," she replies. "This is just inside our heads. It's convenient to use a setting we both know."

"If I take a drink from the bar, will I actually taste it?"

Calon laughs. "Feel free to investigate."

I walk over to check out the liquor. Calon stays in her seat. "I assume you've changed your mind about my offer?"

"I'm prepared to discuss it." I make a show of scanning the bottles, which lets me avoid making eye contact with her. I pull down a bottle of Yamazaki Single Malt and pour a glass. After a sip, I ask, all smooth and casual, "How are you with blood bonds?"

"I've established a few in my time," she says. "Is that your price? You want a blood bond over someone?"

"Fuck, no!" Isn't it just like a Darkling to think I'd want such a thing? Does Calon imagine there's a guy I want as a slave? "Can you *break* blood bonds?" I ask.

"Possibly," she says. "But I don't see bonds on *you*."

"It's on my roommate," I say. "My friend. Got bonded to a vampire named Elaine Vandermeer. Know her?"

Was that a twitch in Calon's eye? Very tiny, but I'm world class at reading micro-expressions. Calon says, "I've met Elaine. I've met most of the Darklings in Canada. How did your friend become bonded to her?"

I hate to give away K's secrets. But if Calon's going to help, she likely needs the facts. "My friend used to date Elaine's brother. My friend wanted to get on Elaine's good side, so . . ."

Calon finishes my sentence: "Your friend let Elaine drink some blood."

"Yeah."

"Complete consent?" Calon asks. "And an actual bite, not just licking a cut or some such?"

"The full monty," I say.

"Your friend's a fool," Calon tells me.

I shrug. "I've personally done worse. I'm making a deal with you, aren't I?"

Calon smiles. "So you are." She stands up from her chair. She seems taller than before—the same height as me. She begins walking toward me. "So to be clear: if I remove the blood bond from your friend . . . or if I persuade Elaine to sever the connection . . . you'll join me at the memorial?"

"Yeah, sure," I say. "Do I have to make a fuss over you? Like make a big entrance hanging on your arm, and let you feel me up or whatever?"

"I told you, Jools, this isn't sexual. Nor is it crass. Certain members of the *nouveau* Dark might want you clinging to them worshipfully, but I'm too old to require servility. I'll leave an invitation for you at the reception desk; be at the party by nine and look me up when you get there. We'll chat for a bit, then walk around and meet people. Oh, and sometime during the night, I'll require you to perform a small service."

"So now we get to what this is *really* about," I say. "What kind of service?"

"Less than ten seconds of your time. A single easy action. Then we're quits. Transaction completed, over and done with."

I say, "You aren't going to tell me what you want, are you?"

"No."

"Then how will I know what to do?"

"If we shake hands on this," Calon says, "you'll do your part automatically when the time comes."

I say, "You don't want me to kill someone, do you? Assassinate the prime minister? Nothing like that?"

"Jools," Calon says, pretending to be wounded, "Darklings fully comply with human laws. Surely you know that. I promise you won't do anything illegal."

"Can I have that in writing?"

"This won't be a written contract," Calon says. "Young Dark-lings obsess about documents, but I prefer traditional ways."

She holds out her hand. I stare at it for a moment, as I digest that she's admitted to being an Elder of the Dark. Or at least older than the Darklings who've been made since the 1980s. She's prob-ably the real Calon Arang, and who knows what else beside—any creature that lives for centuries has probably used many names.

Making a deal with such a thing is totally fucking insane.

I say, "My friend's name is K. Or Kim. You'll really break the bond?"

Calon closes her eyes and takes a deep breath. I have the weird impression she's seeing into the future. She opens her eyes and says, "The bond will be permanently broken within twenty-four hours of you fulfilling our agreement. You have my word."

She holds out her hand again.

Making a deal with the devil is nuts, but this is for a good cause, right? This is for K.

I take Calon's hand.

I half expect her to yank me in and bite my throat. But she simply gives a straightforward handshake. A bright pink glow blooms around our grip. I feel nothing except her slightly rough flesh. It's several degrees hotter than mine.

After a heartbeat, Calon lets me go. "I'll send you something to wear," she says.

"Look," I say, "do you really have to go all sugar daddy? It makes me feel nasty, and not in a good way."

"Jools," Calon says, "I can't have my entourage looking shabby."

"Don't judge me on what I wear around the house," I say, try-ing to suppress the urge to cover my clothes with my hands. "I have some very nice outfits."

"I don't want *nice*, I want *spectacular*. You reflect on me, Jools. I won't settle for what you let yourself get away with."

She says that as if she *knows* me. Knows all about me. It's enough to make me grab my glass of whisky and take a gulp.

Suddenly, I'm back in the washroom of our town house. The whisky glass is still in my hand.

Now I really do have to pee.

FOR AN HOUR AND forty-two minutes, Miranda sings along with *Frozen*. She sometimes tries to sing pop-style, but always slips back to being an opera soprano: full volume, articulation, and vibrato. It clashes with the soundtrack, but I don't mind; I like to see her happy.

Every time we do this, Miranda encourages the rest of us to sing along, too. We never do; K is too self-conscious and I refuse to sing unless I'm drunk. Tonight it occurs to me that I can now sing as well as Miranda. Actually, I must be better—I'm as good as any professional diva on the planet, whereas Miranda is only a well-trained amateur. Then again, Miranda = Aria, and Aria's voice is literally superhuman. For all I know, she can sound like a hundred-voice choir.

Note to self: don't try to outsing the super prima donna.

My mind starts to wander. First it goes back to the stupid fucking bazooka and my stupid fucking brain. Then, because contemplating my inadequacy makes me want to drown myself, I shove my thoughts in other directions.

I bemoan all the hassles of being a Spark: not just getting my face burned off, but jumping through hoops to maintain two separate identities. Much of the hassle would go away if I could quick-change from costume to civvies and vice versa. And this isn't just a selfish concern. I want to be able to help other people if anything bad ever happens while I'm out in public. But it takes forever to change into Ninety-Nine, and that's even assuming I'm carrying around my full uniform. Then, after a stint of heroic supering, I need a safe and foolproof way to flip back to myself so I can walk into the house without giving away my Sparkosity.

I need something that yanks off whatever I'm wearing and shoves on a different outfit, even if that outfit includes hockey pads and fiberglass protection. I can't just wear my costume under my street clothes—tomorrow night, for example, I'll be rocking a swanky dress, courtesy of Calon Arang. If it's the sort of gown I'm imagining, I won't even be able to wear undies, let alone a full hockey outfit under the dress. But this memorial is exactly when I may need to become Ninety-Nine at a moment's notice. How the hell am I going to do that?

I cogitate. My mind turns to quick-change artists in nature. I'm still a biologist at heart, even if I'm now a pro at everything.

Lots of animals change appearance quickly. Chameleons and octopuses are obvious examples. Cats raise their hackles . . . pufferfish puff up . . . jellyfish open wide or clench down small to avoid trouble . . .

Jellyfish. Jellies. Phylum *Cnidaria*. Distinguished by poisoned stingers that they can shoot out at high speed.

The stingers are called nematocysts. They spike into targets, inject a load of toxin, then reel in their prey.

Hmm.

Suddenly the movie is over, the TV is off, and we're sitting in darkness. K and Miranda poke the nuggets of unpopped popcorn at the bottom of their bowls, probably asking themselves, *How bad would it be if I ate those, too?*

They're feeling the late-night blues. But me, I'm stoked. I've got a plan. If it's not exactly Mad Genius, it tilts in that direction. A Slightly Loopy Savant. An Erratic Engineer.

"I'm going for a run," I announce.

"You're kidding," Miranda says. "It's midnight."

"That's only ten, Edmonton time. I'm reverse jet-lagged and I need fresh air."

Miranda and K look at me, then exchange glances. I can almost hear mental gears grinding as they debate offering, "Why don't I come with you?" They suspect I'm up to something. On the other hand, they know I've gone running several nights a week ever since we started living together. It would almost be suspicious if I *didn't* go for a run.

Inside my head, K says, *«Call if anything happens.»*

"Sure," I say aloud. I whip up to my room and put on a running jacket. I also put on leather gloves . . . but considering that it's January, K and Miranda will just think I'm keeping my hands warm. A nip of tequila, then I'm out the door.

First stop: a lab in the Heather C. Williams biology building. WikiJools gives me the exact location of a freezer containing hundreds of tissue samples, including several species of *Cnidaria*. The lab with the freezer doesn't even have an alarm—just a lock on the door. It's a pretty good lock, so it takes a full minute to pick open. Still, it's 12:05 A.M. on Saturday, January 3, and ain't nobody here to say boo. I finesse my way into the lab, I find the freezer . . .

. . . and my Joolsness goes offline.

It's not that I black out. I'm awake and alert and at ease. But it's like when I analyzed the bazooka: my Joolsy self goes bye-bye. Parts of my brain reallocate. Instead of the messy business of performing *Jools*, millions of neurons switch to different chores.

A prissy voice in my head says, "That's not how neurons work!" The brain may be adaptable, but it can't just decide to repurpose cells at the drop of a hat. You can't say, "I don't need to talk right now, so you cells that usually handle verbal processing, you're reassigned to differential equations. Now shut up and calculate."

It's ridiculous. But it's also ridiculous that Zircon shrinks and Aria sings golden force fields. Sparks do grotesquely impossible things; changing the specs on my brain is actually on the sedate end of the spectrum.

So instead of being Jools, I crunch numbers. I invent. Any pinprick of selfhood that survives just serves as a bookmark: like a go-to label in old computer code that my brain will jump to when the grunt work is done.

Till then . . . zzzz.

COME MORNING, I WAKE up sitting at my desk back home. My computer is on, with the screen showing words in eighteen-point

Comic Sans type. Awesome. Mad Genius Jools has left Dumbass Jools a cryptic message:

> Bra and panties in each jar
> One for one, one for the other
> Four in all
> Cued to thinking the phrase
> "Ninety-Nine Power, Make Up!"
> "Zircon Power, Make Up!"
> Etc.
> Return with "Jools Power, Chill Down!"
> Etc.
> Lied to K about needing blood
> Said it was trying to break the blood bond
> Better smooth over

Okay, what?

The?

Living?

Fuck?

I stand up and look around the room. There are four big aquariums on the windowsill, all with standard-issue air pumps bubbling to oxygenate the water. I cannot have acquired these legally—not in the middle of the night. Besides, the aquariums look like ones we used in Bio 310, when we were working with *Planaria* and other aquatic beasties. I hope these aquariums are unused extras, and that I didn't dump a bunch of unhappy critters down the drain when I stole their water tanks.

Wait, there's a worse possibility: that I *used* those critters as raw materials to make what's now in the tanks.

Cautiously I approach the closest aquarium. It contains salt water; I can smell the briny goodness, thanks to the pump throwing salt-scented bubbles into the air. The tank looks mostly empty—no sand on the bottom, no plants, nor any of the usual nonsense people buy for tropical fish. Despite my best-in-the-human-world eyesight, it takes me time to spot what the tank *does* contain: two delicate glassy objects like transparent jellyfish, except that they're shaped like a filmy bikini top and an equally filmy bikini bottom.

You have *got* to be shitting me.

No, *I* have got to be shitting me. I'm the one who made a two-piece swimsuit from marine invertebrates.

No, not a swimsuit. This is underwear: a bra and panties. Which I made from sea life I scrounged on campus.

That's . . .

That's so cool!

I reach into the aquarium and pull out the panties. They feel like half-set Jell-O. I remember a lecture where some researcher talked about extracting protein fibers from hagfish slime to make extremely strong fabric—tougher than Kevlar, more natural than nylon. This looks like the stuff. It has the appearance of cling wrap but the texture of snot.

It's drying out fast. In seconds, it changes from goo into something smooth and silky. Another few heartbeats and it feels more slinky than the undies I usually wear. It's like a high-thread-count fabric that breathes. (Heh.)

I reach into the tank and pull out the other piece: bra-shaped slime. It has long dangly tie strings like a bikini top. Just like its sister, it dries out in seconds until it's transparent, silky, and sheer.

It's too flimsy to provide support. Just pulling on the tie strings stretches it out to a flat strip of gauze. But when I stop pulling, it relaxes back into sort-of kind-of cups. Memory fabric. It's too see-through to wear on a beach, but it could fit under a regular bikini just fine. And nearly invisible on my skin.

What the hell, let's try these jelly babies on.

Doff clothes. Don *Cnidaria*. They don't feel gooey at all. And not like plastic wrap, either—they're thinner and permeable to air. I barely feel them once they're on; they shape to my skin without crinkles. I can move any old which way without them binding or chafing.

All underwear should feel this good. I could make good money selling this stuff.

Admittedly, "Slap on some slime!" won't compete with whatever slogan Victoria's Secret uses. And I'll have trouble getting Miranda to so much as touch these things with the tip of her pinkie, let alone apply them anyplace intimate. But if these do what I think they do . . .

I stand in front of my full-length mirror. I'm wearing nothing but my tattoos, the jelly strips, and my comm ring. (The ring is important, I think. It turns thoughts into radio transmissions, and that seems like part of the setup.)

I take a deep breath, then say inside my head, «*Ninety-Nine Power, Make Up!*»

The bra and panties explode. Kind of. Specifically, they shoot out masses of thin strands that must be nematocysts. The strands envelop me—even around my eyes. For a moment I can't see anything. I imagine myself surrounded by little fibers, making me look like I'm swaddled in cotton. Then silently, the fibers slurp back from whence they came and I look exactly the way I started.

Well, maybe a little more erect.

But I get it. I think. It boggles my mind, but I get it.

I put on my Ninety-Nine costume: the pads, the guards, black jersey and all. I even smear on the black greasepaint that serves as my "mask." When I'm ready to throw body checks for justice, I think, «*Jools Power, Chill Down!*»

As silently as a Portuguese man-of-war, the nematocysts shoot out. This time, they have something to grab hold of. They stab the clothes I'm wearing, they inject whatever is stored in their poison-payload reservoirs, then they reel back in whatever they've managed to spear.

The whole process takes a second and a half . . . and now I'm naked again, except for transparent *Cnidaria* undies. Even my face paint is gone, dragged off by greedy tentacles.

Ho. Lee. Shit.

Where did the costume go? The slime silk on my boobs is marginally darker than before—a teensy bit smoky instead of transparent. I sure as hell hope my superhero clothes haven't been digested.

«*Ninety-Nine Power, Make Up!*»

Whoosh! The nematocysts envelope me in their cloud. Whump! They retract and I'm dressed again. Even the greasepaint is back.

Shit. Lee. Ho.

The clothes went away and came back, like zits on my chin.

Only one explanation . . . especially considering that note on the computer about taking blood from K. K can shrink. I must have extracted something from zir blood and distilled a shrinking potion. Then I used it to fill the fluid reservoir in each jellyfish stinger. When the stingers stab clothing, they inject the potion and shrink the fabric to microscopic levels. My costume literally shrank into the bra, like a thin film of microbes. Then I said the magic words and the process reversed: the stingers sucked away the shrinking potion, and the costume returned to normal size.

That's brilliant! Also ludicrous, impossible, and just plain stupid. But hey, that's the superhero biz.

«*Jools Power, Chill Down!*»

Costume goes away. Nothing but me and my ink in the mirror.

Quickly, I dress in street clothes: leggings, a tank top, and for funsies, my ski jacket. Before I say the magic words, I swipe some eyeshadow on one eyelid—proof of concept.

«*Ninety-Nine Power, Make Up!*»

Bye-bye, street clothes; hello, hockey. If the hockey stuff was stored microscopically inside the bra, then the street clothes must get stashed inside the panties. That way they're kept separate, and I don't end up with half-and-half leggings and hockey shorts. End result: a perfect clothes swap in less than two seconds. I can't see what I look like while the swap is happening, but it must be like a cloud of cotton batting bursting out of me and then getting sucked back in.

«*Jools Power, Chill Down!*»

Back to street clothes. Including the eyeshadow.

Fuck me, I'm a genius. A Mad Genius wearing undies made of jellyfish stingers and hagfish slime, but still.

Science rools!

I look at the clock: 8:43 A.M. It's Saturday morning, but K will be up. Maybe Miranda, too. I go downstairs.

Miranda says, "Why do you have eyeshadow on only one eye?"

K SITS AT THE kitchen table, poking stray Cheerios as they turn soggy in zir bowl. K doesn't turn to look when I come in, but says, "So how did it go?"

"Total success," I say. "Watch this."

K doesn't turn for several seconds. I don't think it's lack of interest—zir body language gives the impression of paying attention. But these days, K's eyes are purely ornamental: not used for seeing at all. Instead, Spark-o-Vision gives a clairvoyant 360-degree view of zir entire surroundings.

If K's not careful, ze's going to forget how normal humans engage. But eventually, K realizes that politeness requires actual eye orientation. Ze shifts in zir chair and turns to face me.

Behind me, Miranda says, "What's this about?"

"My first cool invention. Watch." I think, «*Ninety-Nine Power, Make Up!*» The nematocysts do their stuff. In the time it takes for my friends to gasp, I'm completely costumed up.

"Holy shit," Miranda whispers.

"I know, right?" I say.

K doesn't even speak.

"How did you *do* that?" Miranda asks.

I'm half a second away from explaining how everything works. But for Miranda's sake, I'd better not lead with stingers and slime. "I whipped something up," I say. "Isn't it awesome?"

I think, «*Jools Power, Chill Down,*» and I'm back in my civvies.

"O-kayyyy," Miranda says, "that's definitely Mad Genius." She doesn't say it in a *Jools, you rock!* kind of way. More like, *How could you be so reckless?*

"It's not *Mad* Genius, it's *Nice* Genius," I say. "We had a problem; you know we did. We'd never have enough time to gear up in an emergency. It was even a hassle going in and out of the house. But with this, we can pop behind a tree and change easy-peasy. No more risking a high-speed sneak through the back door."

"But Jools," Miranda says, "weren't you afraid . . . *aren't* you afraid . . ." She shakes her head. "You *told* me you were terrified of becoming like Diamond. You were the one who kept saying 'slippery slope.' And of course it's convenient if we can change clothes quickly. But what's next? What will it be convenient to make tomorrow?"

I ask, "Are you afraid I'll make some weapon of mass destruction? Not a problem. I'm stupid with weapons; you saw that last night."

"Is that what this is about?" Miranda asks. "You hated not understanding Diamond's bazooka, so you made this as a means of compensation?"

"I made this as a means to change clothes!" I say. "I solved a *problem*. This is where you say thank you."

Miranda just tightens her jaw. After a moment, K says quietly, "Thank you, Jools. How did you do it?"

"You probably don't want me to describe the exact mechanism." I glance at Miranda. "It involves biology."

K says, still softly, "I probably wouldn't understand the exact mechanism. But how did you go about it? I heard you come and go several times in the night. And of course, you woke me up that once. Do you remember?"

"Uh, sure," I lie.

"So where did you go?" K continues. "Where did you get the raw materials? What facilities did you use? Did you break into a lab on campus? Multiple labs? Are you sure you covered your tracks? Are the cops going to show up and say, 'Hey, you folks broke into a lab before Christmas, and now we've had more break-ins. Where were you last night and can you prove it?'"

Oh. I hadn't thought of that. And I have no clue how well I covered my tracks. In my zoned-out state, maybe I cleaned up perfectly. Or maybe I didn't make the slightest effort.

K's not psychic, but I think Spark-o-Vision makes it easy to read my face. K says, "Do you remember anything at all?"

I say, "Um."

Without another word, I go to my room and shut myself in.

5

Punctuated Equilibrium

I SPEND THE REST of the morning wishing I had homework. But classes haven't started yet, and there's no point even reading textbooks—if I glance in a book's direction, I immediately know its contents. No, rephrase that: I've *mastered* its contents. I understand the material as well as the author or better. So reading the actual text would just be masturbation.

Which is another obvious way to pass the time. But I'm not horny at all, so I spend the morning making a shitload of money.

It's Saturday, and stock markets are closed. Still, I can make online bets on sports and horse races—mostly in Europe, since it's too early in the Americas, and too late in Asia and Australia. I'm not perfect, but I'm an Olympic-class gambler. I know the odds perfectly and I know all the relevant facts. Also, I'm not a gambling addict like many people who frequent online betting joints; I don't feel compelled to bet when there's no good choice.

By noon, I've amassed more than four thousand dollars. I've also established a string of false online identities. As soon as the paperwork goes through, I'll have an anonymous bank account in the Virgin Islands.

I hear a rustle behind me. A dress has appeared on my bed: a flame-red evening gown finer than anything I've worn in my life.

A gift from my sugar daddy. Sugar mommy. Sugar witch-demon-unhealthy-relationship. I stare at the dress a moment, then turn away.

Minutes later, a knock comes at my door. I say nothing, but the door opens anyway. So that tells me who it is: my third roommate, Shar, is finally back from holidays.

Astonishingly, she has bright purple highlights dyed into her black wavy hair. They look great: a good contrast with her dark Sri Lankan skin.

"Wow," I say. "I love the new look."

"So do I." Shar cocks her head and smiles at me. Conceivably, she's reading my mind. Shar has all the mental powers you've ever heard of: telepathy, mind control, telekinesis, and more. Some of the powers give off fluorescent violet glows. Others she can do invisibly. "You're in the doghouse," Shar says, waggling her finger at me. "You hurt K's feelings. You've upset Miranda, too—she's afraid you'll become a Mad Genius. She wants to save you from yourself but doesn't know how."

"So they sent you up to deal with me?"

Shar chuckles. "No. They're too busy sublimating their feelings by listening to *Hamilton*. Besides, they're annoyed with me, too."

"Why?"

"For making household decisions without consulting them."

"What kind of decisions?"

Shar smiles. "I thought you'd never ask." A disk of violet light floats around from where it's been hiding behind her back. Curled on top of the disk is a sleeping black kitten, all fragile and beautiful. I'm torn between grabbing it for an immediate cuddle, or leaving the little darling to sleep in peace.

"You got a cat?" I whisper so as not to wake it up.

"I got *us* a cat," Shar corrects me. "We needed a pet—that's what turns a house into a home. And my cousins in Toronto have a cat who had kittens. The kittens are just old enough now to be adopted, so I took it as a sign."

I stroke the kitten's head with my finger. The fur is impossibly soft. I say, "I'll bet Miranda is allergic to cats. She's the type."

"She's a superhero now," Shar says dismissively. "If she can be punched in the face without flinching, she can handle a harmless little kitten."

I don't bother explaining that allergies have nothing to do with toughness. Shar is a chemistry major and supposedly steeped in scientific thinking. However, she won't believe in anything she finds inconvenient.

"Is the cat a him or a her?" I ask.

Shar grins. "With K in the house, haven't we gotten past the need for gender pigeonholes?"

I roll my eyes. "All right. What's *zir* name?"

"I thought we should decide that together," Shar replies.

"Because we've done so well choosing a name for our team?" After ten days and dozens of suggestions, the four of us still can't agree on a team name. Miranda doesn't even *want* a team name. ("Why can't we just be individuals?") But Shar thinks a team name is vitally important. It looks like she's decided she'll thin-edge-of-the-wedge us by forcing us to name the kitten.

Naming will also force us to buy into having a pet. Because it *is* pretty high-handed of Shar to get a kitten without asking the rest of us. At the very least, we'll all have to cat-proof our rooms. Then there's the cost of food, and vet fees, and toys, and who'll clean out the kitty litter? But if the four of us spend time deciding whether to call the kitten Felis or Jub-Jub or Tigresse . . .

"I've got a basket and a litter tray," Shar says, "and some packets of the kitten food that . . . oh, what a lovely frock!" She's caught sight of the dress on the bed—hard to miss, considering its color. "Did you get that for Christmas?" she asks.

"My sisters all chipped in," I lie. "Did K and Miranda tell you about the memorial tonight?"

"What memorial?"

I explain. Shar gives me a quick hug, then hurries off to assemble a suitable outfit. She takes the kitten away with her, still floating on its bed of violet.

Now that I think about it, what *are* "suitable clothes" for a memorial? It's basically a funeral, right? I get the feeling it's not somber, but it's still intended to pay respect. Why did Calon send me something so drop-dead crimson? To dress for a Darkling wake, does etiquette demand you look like arterial spray?

I have this mental image of everybody else dressed in black, and me a blaze of color in the midst of the crowd. Like marking the chosen victim. On the stroke of midnight, everyone rips me to shreds.

Maybe I should skip the bright-red gown. I own a passable LBD that would blend in much better at a serious event. But when I say "passable," I mean "passable for anything I've ever gone to," not "passable for a gathering of the richest people in the country." I don't want to hobnob with the prime minister while I'm wearing something I got for thirty bucks on Amazon.

Besides, Calon will be mad if I don't wear what she sent me. Reluctantly, I pick up the dress. Underneath it on the bed are matching underwear, shoes, a purse, and . . . holy shit, are those real diamond earrings? And a diamond necklace?

Of course, the diamonds are real. I have an eye for jewels as good as the best appraiser in Amsterdam. I'd better keep these rocks away from K or I'll never get them back.

And the dress! It's softer than the kitten. Almost literally lighter than a cloud. I'm sure it'll feel amazing.

But I'll have to keep Miranda from fingering it. She'll instantly figure out that my cover story is a lie. Miranda knows clothes—fancy clothes like this dress—and she'll realize that even if my sisters chipped in their total annual incomes for a Christmas present, they'd still come up short. This dress is a crimson flag saying, "Jools has a deep Dark secret."

Maybe I should tell them all the truth.

Nah.

If they call me on the dress, I'll just say I'm fucking a banker.

I TRY ON THE dress, and holy shit, I *could* fuck a banker. Not that the outfit is sleazy—I won't be flashing my cleave to the country's elite. But you can be totally covered up and still look *hot*.

Smokin'.

I already had a good ass from skating and running. Becoming a Spark then sweetened the whole Jools package. On Boxing Day,

K commed me to ask if I'd developed belly muscles . . . and while I already had killer abs thanks to actual exercise, I can't deny that my six-pack is sixier and more packed. As for up top, my old bras still fit, but way better. I don't know if my girls have actually changed in weight or geometry, but they've blossomed to a more uplifted outlook.

That leaves my face. Which is a perfectly passable face, even if I'll never get called pretty—not unless there's a craze for chicks with long noses and an overbite. Just label me a respectable five.

My hair occupies the same numeric ballpark. I cut it short because I don't think mermaid hair works with a hockey helmet (even if some girls disagree). But I've often wished my hair were less flyaway.

And I think it's improved. Becoming a Spark has given my hair more body. And maybe my nose has shortened a little. Not dramatically, but. My recent changes are like the opposite of a passport photo. Passport pictures take your real face and make it look like crap. Becoming a Spark does the reverse, like having a really good makeover.

Since I turned super, every photo of me looks great. Seriously, I can take a selfie in the bathroom mirror two seconds after I wake up—while I still have sleep in my eyes and total bedhead—but the result looks like a shot from a Hollywood movie. I'll never be a glamour girl, but I look like someone *interesting*.

The only truly blatant changes to my body are my feet. They used to be like everyone else's: grungy, squashed, and hard-used. Now they're soft and *cute*. I could model sandals for *Vogue*. When I was home at Christmas, I never went barefoot for fear that my sisters would squeal and demand my secret.

It's *good* that I have cute feet, cuz Calon sent me high-heeled sandals: glittery black with silver braids that weave up and down my calves. I'd be totally screwed if WikiJools didn't explain exactly how to strap the darn things up. WikiJools also gives me a list of what to scrub, shave, and paint in order to wear this outfit properly. Luckily, I have all the supplies I need . . .

. . . except maybe the ideal shade of nail polish.

You'd think with all the polish I've stolen, some color would suit the dress. But no. Maybe God is teaching me a lesson. If I actually *paid* for a bottle, it'd match perfectly.

I sigh and face the inevitable: I have to talk with Miranda. Her polish collection is bigger than mine, nicely organized in a spice rack. I step out my door and take two steps down the hall . . . whereupon Miranda's door opens before I'm halfway there.

Her hearing is so damned acute, she could probably hear me moving around in my room, even though I was barefoot on carpet. How long has she been waiting to bump into me "accidentally"?

She wears a fluffy white bathrobe that would make a polar bear shout, "Cousin!" I can tell she's getting ready for the memorial, too, even though it's barely one o'clock.

Miranda loves dressing up. It's her favorite art form after opera. And Miranda doesn't dress to impress other people; certainly not to attract *guys*, or girls, or whatever floats her boat. (I've never known how Miranda swings. As far as I know, she's never gone out with anyone—I mean, not in a romantic or sexual way. She just enjoys looking fabulous, the same as she enjoys singing in the shower.)

She dresses for her own satisfaction. And if I looked like her, I might get off on making myself an art form, too. Spectacular as I'll look in Calon Arang's gown, Miranda will put me to shame.

"Hi," says she.

"Hi," says me.

She hesitates, then says, "Want to give me a hand?" She looks away quickly. "I could do my own hair and nails, but it's easier with help. And I guess now you're good at makeup stuff."

"Best in the world," I say.

She pauses, then says, "I hate fighting with you, Jools. It makes me all hurt and I can't think about anything else."

I hug her. She hugs back. She whispers, "I don't want you crazy or evil."

I don't know what to say, so I hug her more. After a few seconds, she detaches herself and nudges me toward her doorway. "Come on," she says. "Let's make each other look amazing."

SOME TIME LATER, WE get a mental call from Grandfather. *«Hey, Waterloonies, you know about this idiocy tonight?»*

«You mean the memorial service?» Miranda asks. She's sitting in front of the mirror, warily watching as I fuss with her hair. I don't think she's worried that I'll make her a mess. The problem is I'm holding a bunch of hairpins in my mouth. I didn't think about how it would affect her until I put the pins between my lips . . . but now I can see she's afraid that sooner or later I'm going to get my mouth germs all over her hair. If I say or do anything to acknowledge her nervousness, it'll fluster her into a meltdown.

She hates that this freaks her out, and so do I. But neither of us can think of a way to back off gracefully. So we're grateful when Grandfather provides the distraction. I immediately take the pins out of my mouth, as if I need to be ready to speak. I put them in the pockets of my robe, and I'll do my best to leave them there.

«It's not just the memorial,» Grandfather says. *«It's worse than that.»*

From elsewhere in the house, K says, *«Worse than gathering a hundred Darklings in one place, so anyone can take a potshot at them?»*

«Yeah,» Grandfather says. *«I've heard there'll be backroom business. Wheeling and dealing. Private negotiations.»*

«Well, duh,» Miranda says. *«Get Darklings together in one place, and they immediately start scheming.»*

I say, *«People of the same trade seldom meet together, even for merriment and diversion, but the conversation ends in a conspiracy against the public, or in some contrivance to raise prices.»*

Silence.

«That's Adam Smith,» I say. *«The Wealth of Nations?»*

"Thank you, Wikiquote," Miranda says aloud.

It's nice to hear her snarky again. For a while there, she had me worried.

«*This won't just be the same-old, same-old price-fixing,*» Grandfather says. «*Rumor has it someone got their hands on a superweapon made by Diamond himself. Since dozens of dignitaries will be in attendance, they're gonna get together and decide what to do with the weapon: whether to let the government keep it, or sell it to the highest bidder.*»

«*I knew I should have asked for money,*» I say. «*Somebody is going to get rich instead of us!*»

«*You had the weapon?*» Grandfather asks.

«*Briefly,*» Miranda says. «*A big fucking gun. But we got rid of it.*» She glances at me in the mirror. «*Giving it away really was our best move. Things might have gotten unpleasant.*»

I mouth "Thank you" to her.

«*I know all about 'damned if you do, damned if you don't,'*» Grandfather says. «*But the Darklings intend to show off the gun at their memorial. Perfect time to hold an auction if that's what they choose. Lot of high rollers in attendance.*»

Shar says, «*They'll actually have the weapon there? Surely they aren't so foolish.*»

«*Can't hold an auction if the bidders can't examine the goods,*» Grandfather replies. «*Well, okay, you can, but you won't make nearly as much money. People won't bid through the roof if they can't see what they're buying.*»

«*But having the gun there is asking for trouble,*» Shar says. «*There's already a risk that Diamond will attack . . .*»

«*And,*» I add, «*Robin Hood might take another stab at stealing it.*»

«*That's what I'm talking about,*» Grandfather says. «*Darklings can be oblivious to how humans think, but this smells like deliberate provocation. And I heard these rumors from multiple sources. Their security leaks like a sieve. As if someone wants villains to know.*»

«*Wonderful,*» Miranda groans. «*But why?*»

«*It's a trap,*» K says. «*For Diamond. Or Robin Hood. Or both.*»

I think about Reaper and Stevens & Stephens. Those fuckwits are just the sort to think they can make themselves look good by catching Diamond red-handed.

The big bad D is one of the world's most powerful supervillains. Whoever takes him down will become a law-enforcement *star*. But until Diamond came to Waterloo, he'd never been known to venture outside Australia. I wouldn't be surprised if Reaper and his bosses are high-fiving each other that Diamond has come within their reach. Now they've hatched a harebrained scheme to take down a guy the Australians couldn't capture.

I say, «*This is going to be bad.*»

«*A fucking disaster,*» says Miranda. «*Every villain and their dog will show up: Diamond, Robin Hood, and who knows what other crazies.*»

«*Heroes, too,*» K points out. «*The Australian All-Stars have fought Diamond at least a dozen times. If they hear about this, they'll show up, too. Diamond is their nemesis. They won't pass up a chance to nail him.*»

«*The All-Stars are already here,*» Grandfather says. «*It makes sense: if you were arranging a trap for Diamond, you'd call the All-Stars right away. They might never have caught him, but they've defeated his schemes over and over. They can tell you what to watch for.*»

"Arrgh!" Miranda says. «*So who are we expecting? Diamond . . . Robin Hood and his merry assholes . . . the Oz All-Stars . . . random gate crashers . . . and a whack of Darkling VIPs. Is it too late to run off to Tahiti?*»

«*You can't run,*» Grandfather says. «*You're the only Sparks in Waterloo. You're like the city's official babysitters. But if you want help, just ask. Invie can arrange party invites for us. Provided we won't just be two extra headaches for you to handle.*»

I exchange looks with Miranda. She grimaces; I shrug. Miranda says, «*You'd better come. We'll need all the help we can get.*»

Murmurs of agreement from K and Shar. «*Okay, then,*» says Grandfather. «*When you decide how you want to use us, drop us a comm. Or just meet us at the bar.*»

«*At the bar,*» I say, maybe a bit too eagerly. «*And thanks for the warning.*»

«*De nada,*» Grandfather says.

There's no sound of him hanging up, but after a few seconds, it's obvious he's gone. «*Team meeting downstairs?*» Shar suggests.

«*Five minutes,*» I reply. First, I have to pin up Miranda's hair.

WE GATHER IN THE kitchen. Shar sits at the table as if she expects us to join her in a boardroom-style conference. Ain't gonna happen. I sprawl against a counter, K sits on top of the stove, and Miranda paces.

Each of us is halfway through getting prommed up. Miranda still wears her polar-bear bathrobe; Shar wears a skimpy dressing gown made of bright green silk; K and I are both in shorts and sloppy sweatshirts. I don't know what underwear the others have on, but I have nothing except invertebrates.

I wonder how one cares for jellyfish lingerie. Does it have to be fed? Can I wear it in the shower? Should I keep it in salt water overnight?

Yes to salt water—that's probably why I stole the aquariums. Probably no to the shower. Water pressure might damage the tissue, and besides, I think it's a great idea to take off the slime on a regular basis and scrub hard wherever it's touched my body. As for feeding the fish, I suspect jelly undies will happily chow down on sloughed-off flakes of human skin. I also suspect I shouldn't mention this to my roommates. Nonbiology students are squeamish.

"I notice," says K, "that we're all getting primped. But is this really a good idea? I keep wondering if I should just wear my Zircon costume."

"Wear what you like," I say. "But I got a killer dress for Christmas, and this is my chance to wear it."

Oh, look, doubling down on my lie. Typical Jools.

"It's wise to go undercover," Miranda says. "If we're there as Sparks, we'll be easy to track. Also to target. If Diamond or anyone else wants a shot at us, wearing our costumes puts us right in the crosshairs. But if we look like normal humans, we'll blend in and be ignored."

K snorts. "You won't be ignored, Miranda. You accumulate men." K looks at me. "The same for you, Jools, except you do it by grabbing any guy who gets within reach."

"You haven't seen my dress yet," I reply. "Tonight, I'll be crotch-deep in guys without a single headlock."

Shar tells K, "It really does seem best to go incognito. We'll have the element of surprise if someone attacks. But with Grand-father and the Inventor in attendance, there'll be an obvious Spark presence to discourage bad behavior."

"The All-Stars, too," I say. "They're an imposing lot. They're also good at what they do."

Shar tilts her head and looks at K. "Are you leaning toward your costume because you don't have anything else to wear? I'm sure we could assemble a suitable outfit."

"I have something to wear," K says. "I, uhh . . ."

K is blushing! If ze were an anime character, there'd be big beads of sweat and a nosebleed! Sheepishly, K mumbles, "I've deci-ded maybe it's time I stop being a wallflower. So over Christmas, my mother and grandmothers . . . they've finally accepted I'm never going to wear pink chiffon, so when I asked, they took me out shopping for something we could all agree looked nice."

"That's wonderful!" Shar says. I'll bet she's mentally making a list of people she can pair up with K. But one debacle at a time.

"So, clothes, not the problem," K says, with reddened cheeks and lowered eyes. "What we need is an excuse for being there. Because . . ." K takes a breath. "Nicholas and Elaine Vandermeer—they're sure to be at the memorial. And when we run into them, it'll be hard for me, okay? If I'm there as Zircon, they won't give me grief. But if I'm me . . ."

"If they say one nasty word," I promise, "I'll punch the two of them out."

"Unnecessary," Miranda says. "I can handle them. I have expe-rience with their kind." She grimaces. "You all know a lot of my cousins are Darklings. And as it happens, my cousin Todd got hurt at the Goblin Market. Nothing serious—well, okay, he nearly got burned alive, but you, Shar, pulled him out of the flames. Since he's a werewolf, he healed within a day. NBD. But Todd owes me a favor. I went to a wedding as his date last summer and I let him pretend we weren't related. I'll inform him he's inviting me to the memorial, and the three of you, too." She smiles triumphantly. "So there, problem solved. A perfectly valid excuse for us to be there."

I silently ask myself, *How many invitations do I have now? A group of four from Calon, two groups from the Vandermeers, and now one from Cousin Todd.* All I say is, "Works for me."

K hesitates, then nods. "If Nicholas and Elaine had any sensitivity, they'd wonder why I'd want to go *near* this damned memorial, considering all the bad experiences I've had with Darklings. But the thought won't cross their minds. They'll both assume I'm hungry to spend time with the Dark."

Shar says, "K, dear, you *do* have a thing for Darklings."

K glares. "Not anymore. Me. New leaf. Turning over. Gonna find someone whose heart actually beats, and have a normal relationship." Pause. "For a flexible version of normal."

"Okay, then," I say. "Anything else? Or are we good?"

Miranda scowls, then grudgingly lets it go. "That thing you made—the one for costume changes."

I say, "The one that's definitely not a Mad Genius invention?"

Miranda grits her teeth. "We'll need it, won't we?"

"What's this about costume changes?" Shar asks.

I think to myself, «*Ninety-Nine Power, Make Up!*» Instantly, I transform to Ninety-Nine.

"Oh my," Shar says.

I change back. "Ta-da."

"Yes, we'll need that," Shar says. "Most definitely."

K grumbles, "I guess." Inside my head, K says, «*We need to talk about that when we're finished here.*»

Uh-oh. K's «*We need to talk*» sounds like «*We. Need. To. Talk.*» But I only answer, «*Okay.*» Aloud I say, "I'll set you all up with a costume-changer and teach you how to work it. But, uhh . . . look, you're my friends, and if you ask, I'll explain the exact mechanisms involved. But trust me: knowing won't make you happy."

Miranda looks aghast. "It's not, like, ground-up babies or something?"

"Of course not! I'm *not* a Mad Genius. But I *am* a biologist, right? And the process involves . . . biology."

Miranda looks sick. "We have to do something biological?"

"You have to *wear* something biological," I say. "But you're used to that. Cotton is biological. Silk is biological."

K says, "Something tells me we aren't talking about cotton or silk."

"I'm going to my room!" Miranda announces. "And I'm going to play *Tosca* very loudly so I can't hear what you say next." She literally flies out of the kitchen and up the stairs, so fast that the hem of her bathrobe flaps in the wind.

Shar laughs and gives me a smile. "I don't care how it works. Biology is only chemistry that thinks it's special." She gives K and me a finger-wave, then heads with queenly dignity back to her room.

Silence in the kitchen. I finally say, "Well."

K is still sitting on the stove. Ze's across the kitchen from me and not looking in my direction . . . except that with Spark-o-Vision, K is always looking in *every* direction.

Ze asks, "Do you remember last night at all?"

My reflex is to lie, but that won't make things better. I say nothing.

"You came into my room at two in the morning," K says. "You wanted a sample of my blood. When I asked why, you seemed surprised—as if you never imagined you might have to justify yourself. Then you told me you had an idea for how to break my blood bond with Elaine, but you needed a sample to test." K sighs. "You said a lot of things, Jools. And when you want to be, you're the best persuader in the world, aren't you? Besides, I was half-asleep. So I said yes." K finally raises zir head and looks me in the eye. "Do you remember any of that?"

I take a deep breath, then let it out. "Not really."

"Well, good," K says. "Because you manipulated the fuck out of me. If you were in your right mind, I'd hate you. I mean, shit, Jools, you wanted my blood! And I'd already *told* you what Elaine did to me. When she drank my blood, the fear and humiliation nearly destroyed me. And it left me with a blood bond that scares me to death. *Not a good time to ask if you could take some of my blood!* Yet that's what you did, Jools, as casually as if you wanted to borrow a paper clip. And you weren't truly working on the blood bond. You used my blood for your costume-changer, right?"

I want to run away. And I want a giant drink. Why the fuck am I not drunk?

K waits for an answer. I say, "The costume-changer shrinks clothes for easy storage. I must have used your blood to make that happen. Somehow."

"But you don't remember?"

"No."

"Does that scare you?"

. . .

"Yeah."

But the truth is I don't feel scared. I'm too hot with shame to feel anything else.

K slides off the stove. "I don't know whether to hug you or slap you."

"Your choice," I say.

I wait, not looking in K's direction. After a long pause, ze wraps zir arms around me. Lightly. A duty hug. I hug back just as carefully, but it takes all my willpower not to squeeze and cling like I'm drowning. K is so short, zir head is against my chest. Ze says into my sweatshirt, "I'm worried for you, Jools."

I don't say anything.

Ze lifts zir head and sniffs. "I don't smell any alcohol on your breath."

I think for a moment. "I haven't had anything to drink all day."

"Jools," K says, "I'm not a fan of your drinking, but what does it mean when a night of inventing replaces your desire for alcohol?"

Oh, dude, I'm desiring it now! But K's right. It's only in the last few minutes that I've seriously wanted a drink. I spent most of the day without it even crossing my mind.

Okay. Now I'm scared.

6

Social Grooming

I FLEE TO MY room and have a shot of tequila. I drink a second glass more slowly as I brood over the aquariums on my windowsill.

I'd love to never think about the costume-changers again. It's scary enough that I blanked out while making them, and that I ran around breaking into labs and stealing whatever I wanted. But I also exploited K. I used my powers and trampled zir feelings without hesitation. Afterward, I'd been so sated and relaxed, I forgot all about my old friend alcohol.

This is bad. Like, split-personality serial killer bad. Not that I've killed anyone, but what if blacked-out me decided it was necessary? How far would I have gone?

I glare at the aquariums with loathing. I consider pouring their contents down the toilet. But we *need* the costume-changers. And if I throw out the jellyfish underwear, it means I treated K like shit and don't even have anything to show for it.

But at least I've made the deal with Calon Arang. K will soon be freed from Elaine's blood bond. That'll make up for what I did, right?

Right?

I have to believe that.

Eventually, I put on my big-girl panties and set out to introduce my roommates to nematocyst bikinis.

I start with Shar. She won't give me drama. For all I know, she's already romped through my brain and read my memories. She may know what a shit I've been.

Yet she smiles as she opens the door to me. She lets me pet the kitten, and she makes small talk till I calm down.

Even better, she's cool with slime. She doesn't gag when I pull see-through goo from an aquarium. She immediately sees how to use the undies, and is eager to test them out.

Shar starts undressing even before I get out the door. I don't know if it's a Sri Lankan thing or personal to Shar herself, but she has no qualms about her body. The only reason she doesn't walk around the house nude is that Miranda might explode.

Next stop, K . . . and thank you, baby Jesus, K is satisfied with verbal instructions. Ze doesn't ask me to strip down and model the jelly bikini. Then again, K probably uses Spark-o-Vision to look underneath what I'm wearing and see exactly how the slime-wear goes on. I consider apologizing that the outfit includes a bra; is that insensitive with someone who wants to be as gender-unspecific as possible? But I don't think either of us could handle another raw emotional moment. So it's "Thanks," and "You're welcome," then I scuttle from the room before anything traumatic gets said.

That only leaves Miranda. I know she'll want complete operating guidelines, plus a demo and a lengthy Q-and-A. I fortify myself with tequila before going to her room. As promised, the opera *Tosca* is playing loudly, but I don't even have to knock before the music stops and Miranda opens the door.

I say, "You heard my footsteps over the music?"

She shrugs. "I hear a lot."

"Doesn't it deafen you? Or get confusing?"

She shakes her head. "My hearing is sensitive, not delicate. I can hear sounds other people find inaudible, but nothing hurts, no matter how loud. All those explosions before Christmas did nothing to my eardrums. As for confusing . . . you know the cocktail-party effect?"

I nod. "Even in a loud cocktail party, people are amazingly good at following specific conversations."

"Same for me," Miranda says. "If I concentrate, I can pick out the things I want, despite other noise."

I don't ask why she was trying to hear my footsteps, or what else she's been listening to in the past few minutes. I just start my spiel about the costume-changers.

Miranda immediately interrupts. "I've been reading about Mad Geniuses."

She points to the computer on her desk. It's showing a badly formatted web page with cyan text on a black background. "Most of what's out there is bullshit," Miranda says. "Propaganda sites sponsored by Darklings. They claim that Mad Geniuses shouldn't be viewed as aberrations. They say that *all* Sparks are dangerous narcissists who set themselves above the law and society. Mad Geniuses are just more open about it." Miranda rolls her eyes. "But if you go deeper, you can find real facts."

I look at the screen again. The page has the hallmarks of a wacko conspiracy site: the amateur layout, the terrible color scheme, the masses of nine-point text. Miranda reads such websites devotedly. For someone who swears by hard science, she's weirdly enamored of screeds against the Dark.

She says, "It turns out that many so-called Mad Geniuses are sane. Relatively, anyway. Like our friend the Inventor guy. He's pretty balanced, right?"

"Miranda," I say, "he's currently a basset hound. Sane people don't spend their time as dogs."

Miranda waves her hand dismissively. "That happened by accident. A miscalculation. And for a Spark, it's run-of-the-mill. Superheroes mutate, get possessed, lose their powers, even die, then come back stronger. It's nothing important. It's just churn."

"So you're saying we'll all turn into dogs eventually?" I hold out my hand. "Pinkie-swear that when it happens I get to be a husky. I like huskies. But what kind of dog would *you* be? I want to say a golden retriever, but you hate me obsessing that you're blond."

"Jools, focus," Miranda says. "The point is that Sparks can be Geniuses without being mad. Like Maid Marian—she's one of Robin Hood's group."

"She calls herself Maid Marian, but you think she's sane?"

Miranda glares. "The point is she's a Genius and she's been

around for years, but she's never made a doomsday device. She just builds useful stuff for Robin: vehicles, gadgets, defenses. She's the main reason Robin's group have never gotten caught. Like, they must have a headquarters somewhere, right? But it's shielded so well, no one can find it."

I say, "Has anyone checked Sherwood Forest?"

"They've checked *everywhere*, Jools. The Dark Guard use clairvoyants, scrying rituals, and heaven knows what else. They really want to bust Robin Hood's ass. But thanks to Marian, Robin's headquarters are undetectable."

My brain idly toys with two threads of ideas, one envisioning ways to hide a base from all efforts to find it, and another devising ways to find something that's so well concealed. I have no particular urge to rat out Robin and his outlaws, but I'm intrigued by the challenge of beating defenses that no one has ever pierced.

No, Jools, stop, before Miranda notices. "So are you saying you're okay if I invent stuff?"

"Provisionally. Yes." She takes a deep breath, then launches into what is obviously a prepared speech. "Because if you're drawn to that lifestyle now, and it's not guaranteed to drive you mad, then we should make a safe space for you, right? We should say, *If that's who you've become, we'll be supportive.* Which I will be, Jools, I really will." I can see her trying not to make a face. "Even if you want me to wear something made of biology."

I have to hug her—she's trying so earnestly to meet me halfway. She hugs me back gingerly. Miranda is not a natural hugger, but she's working on it. She's made it a goal.

When I let her go, I say, "You'll love this. Seriously."

I show her how the jelly undies work. It's only a tiny bit awkward. When she digs down deep, Miranda can throw a mental toggle switch to change from prima donna to physicist. She drops her high-maintenance instincts and starts to *investigate*.

A perfect example: Miranda is squicked out by blood, but if a friend is bleeding, she switches over to clinical mode and has no hesitation washing a wound, applying antiseptics, and bandaging you up to perfection. Afterward, she seems unfazed; maybe she falls to pieces when she's finally in private, but she doesn't show any revulsion while she's with you. At worst, Nurse Miranda chews you out for trying to chop veggies while drunk, but she only turns into a scold when the worst is over.

So demonstrating the slime isn't a nightmare. I do have to take off my clothes and let Miranda examine the jellyfish at point-blank range. But she doesn't make it weird; it's more like a trip to physio, where the people who have to fix your dislocated shoulder are polite but treat your body like a car without a passenger in it. Miranda asks questions, but all of them are practical: "How do I," "What if," and "When." She stringently avoids inquiring what the bikini parts are made of, or how I procured the raw materials. When she's in this frame of mind, Miranda excels at compartmentalization—she keeps her brain on a very short leash and makes sure it doesn't stray.

Of course, she also stays wrapped in her bathrobe with the belt cinched tight and double knotted. She's not going to put on the slimewear with me in the room. Even in clinical mode, Miranda has rock-solid boundaries.

So when Miranda runs out of questions, she sends me packing so she can try on the undies alone. I'm not the only person who needs a safe space to be who she's become.

SO WE HAIR. WE nails. We face. We garb.

Not necessarily in that order. I don't know how the others finalize their on-fleek-dom, because we prep the last hour in private till it's time for The Reveal. And because being a Spark means a life adrip with coincidence, we emerge from our rooms simultaneously like the end of a montage in a movie.

Me in the red dress from Calon Arang. Diamonds in my ears and around my neck. Hair extensions inserted so I'm ready to mermaid with Ariel. I look like a fucking Bond girl walking into the Monte Carlo casino.

But there are two types of Bond girl: the A-list stars who get their names in the opening credits, and the C-list also-rans killed by the end of act one. Alas, I'm the act-one girl—hot enough for the promotional photo spread in *Maxim*, but not hot enough to sit with Bond at the grown-up table. The A-list honor belongs to Miranda, who's red-carpet ready in strapless white. WikiJools tries to inform me which big-name designer made the dress, but I tell it to fuck off. We all know Miranda is rich; let's not rub it in. I'm jealous enough that she looks like a Disney princess . . . and one of the *modern* ones with arm muscles.

K is Disneyesque, too, but the movie is *Mulan*. K's outfit is a full-length silk robe with a Mandarin jacket. Both robe and jacket are black, embroidered with golden dragons. It's the first time I've seen K wear anything that reflects zir Chinese heritage. I think it's brilliant, simultaneously dressy and unisex. The finishing touch is a black Mandarin hat, possibly to hide K's shockingly short white hair. Then again, K has never shown any reticence about flaunting zir punk hairstyle, so let's just chalk up the hat as a fashion statement.

Speaking of fashion statements, Shar has gone *loud*. Never mind that Buddhists traditionally wear white to funerals. Shar looks like a bowl of Froot Loops: she wears a green sari cloak over a red petticoat skirt and an orange choli blouse. Blue slippers. Purple head scarf. Gold bangles.

It's typical Shar. Day to day she wears blue jeans or leggings, but when she gets the chance, she goes Sri Lankan to the max. I don't know if she's reveling in her heritage, or just being fabulous. But she says that dressing ultra-Asian has the great advantage of pissing off her mother, who is super-mega-Westernized—I've never seen Shar's mom in anything but a pantsuit. (Momma Chandra is a wiz at computerized finance simulations. She's rich enough to go Darkling, but the prospect doesn't interest her. All she cares about is economic models . . . and fighting with Shar.)

So here we are: three hot babes and one hot abstention. Miranda is the only one who'd get on the cover of *Cosmo*—I'm too horsey, Shar too 3-D, and K too hip for the room. But all four of us are rocking our peak potential. I lick my finger, touch each of the others, and make sizzling sounds. Shar laughs. "We'll achieve quite the entrance, yes?"

"Oh yeah," Miranda says. We grin at each other.

"And costumes?" I ask. "We're set for that, too?"

Simultaneously, we activate our slimewear. Two seconds later, we've changed into badass Sparks.

More grins. We switch back to glam.

K says, "So let's go mourn the dead."

We head for the car.

WE TAKE MIRANDA'S CAR: a gold-colored Solfeggietto from I-Light Industries. The car was designed by our basset-hound friend, the Inventor, and I think it was intended as a big middle finger extended toward other car companies. It's solar-powered, with an ordinary 110-volt power cord to top up the battery if the sun stays too long behind clouds. The car seats four people comfortably. It has such good safety features, they're practically superpowers. And it sells for less than any car on the market, partly because there are no dealers to take a cut as middlemen. If you want a Solfeggietto, you sign on to I-Light.com; you specify a color, payment method, and delivery address; and five days later, a car teleports into your driveway.

So *of course* Miranda owns a Solfeggietto. (It doesn't hurt that the name comes from a famous piece of music by C. P. E. Bach.) And *of course* we're going to drive it to a gathering of Darklings, where it will stand out in the parking lot like a dove among crows. More precisely, it will stand out like a bright gold sun-mobile among the black gas-guzzling limos that each take up multiple parking spaces at the Transylvania Club.

But during our drive to the club, we talk things over and decide to avoid parking in the actual lot. We expect trouble, and that starts with T, and that rhymes with D, and that stands for Diamond. Miranda doesn't want her beloved Sol-fa getting damaged by superweapons, gunfire, magic, or any of the other destructive forces that might run amok during the evening. So we park on a side street several blocks from the venue, and walk in all our glory to our appointment with Fate.

We walk at a fast clip. Waterloo never reaches the blistering cold that Edmonton does, but I have to admit the night is pretty darn frigid. WikiJools tells me it's minus ten degrees Celsius, with a windchill dropping down to minus fourteen. I can resist icy temperatures as well as any human on Earth, but I'm still bloody freezing. Shar cheats by surrounding herself with a wafer-thin force field to shut out the breeze. I'm surprised K doesn't cheat, too—it would be simple for zir to shrink and hitchhike a ride in somebody's hair.

But K doesn't take the easy way out. In fact, by the look on zir face, K is obviously suffering from more than the temperature. After a minute of walking, K grimaces and says, "Shar. Do you know about me and Elaine Vandermeer?"

"Yes," Shar says. "Miranda told me."

Miranda looks guilty. "Sorry, K, but I had to. Keeping that kind of thing secret is asking for trouble."

"I know." K draws in a breath "So, Shar, can you protect me? Wrap my head in a mental shield or something?"

It's obviously hard for K to ask. The night we got our powers, Shar used her mental mojo on K without permission and K has been mad at Shar ever since. It shows how much K fears Elaine that ze will ask Shar for help.

"I'll do what I can," Shar says. "But this is my first time encountering a blood bond. I'm not sure how to oppose it. I'll also be in civilian clothes, so I can't use my full strength; otherwise, I'll glow and give us all away. But I'll do my best. If worse comes to worst, I can . . . well . . . even if I can't block the bond, I'll stop you doing anything you'd regret."

"You mean knocking me out?"

"If needed. I'm sure I'll notice if Elaine attacks you mentally. If I can't deflect the assault, I'll twist it and cause an overload."

"That sounds dangerous," Miranda says.

Shar nods. "But it's not like I have a wealth of experience countering Darkling magic. This is unexplored territory."

"Well," K mumbles, "do your best."

Ze suddenly shrinks out of sight. In our heads, K's voice says, «*I'll fly ahead and pick up the invitations.*»

K's not good with interpersonal tension. And someone *does* have to pick up the invites.

The pickup process is trickier than it sounds. While shrunken invisibly small, K changes costume into Zircon. Then K flies to the club and claims the invitations set aside by the Vandermeers. With invites in hand, Zirc shrinks out of sight again and comes back to meet us in the shadow of a tree. Zircon reverts to a full-sized K and hands us each an invitation.

So much jumping through hoops . . . and for something as simple as getting into a party for which we have legit invitations! Does every Spark have to deal with this shit?

But never mind. We're good to go. We're *great* to go. Flashing our invitations, we enter the heart of Darkness.

7

Natural Habitat

THE TRANSYLVANIA CLUB HAS a lobby with a coat check and a security station. We show our invitations again and get waved through a magical body-scanner. It's similar to a conventional walk-through metal detector, except it's covered with sorcerous runes that make my eyes cross when I look at them. Briefly, I wonder if our slimewear will set off alarms. But the four of us sail through as if we aren't wearing anything super.

Inwardly, I cheer. Then I realize that if the scanner can't recognize our slimewear, it might have a blind spot for Cape Tech in general. Diamond, Robin Hood, and other dangerous Sparks could waltz in with their pockets full of death rays, and no one would be the wiser.

But maybe there's a glimmer of hope. Beyond the scanner, a wrestler-sized dude stands on guard at the doorway that leads into the main part of the club. He's heavily invested in the Men-in-Black look: dark suit, white shirt, and sunglasses. His feet are comfortably spread and his gloved hands are folded in front of his waist, bodyguard-style. He could easily be mistaken for run-of-the-mill security, except that he has no wrists.

Seriously. There's a five-millimeter gap between the ends of his jacket sleeves and the beginnings of his gloves. The gap ain't got nothing but empty.

Cool.

When I look more closely at Wrestler Dude's face, I can tell that it's totally makeup. I'm not seeing skin, I'm seeing a paint job on cheeks, lips, and forehead. Under the Estée Lauder, the dude's invisible.

Hey, WikiJools, who dat? As fast as a speeding Bing, the answer hits me. I'm looking at Mister No One of the Aussie All-Stars. His file says he's a tough guy who happens to be invisible. One of his favorite things is disguising himself to blend in with crowds.

«*Yo, dudes,*» I say with my comm ring, «*that beefy guy is an Aussie All-Star.*»

«*How did they get that name?*» Shar asks. «*It feels so ill-advised. And 'Aussie' is problematic. It sounds like an ethnic slur.*»

A WikiJools lookup later, I report, «*The All-Stars didn't choose the name themselves. It came from some rando's internet post. But it stuck.*»

«*See?*» Shar says. «*If we don't pick a name for our team, someone else will. And it's bound to be dreadful.*»

She has a point. K says, «*Let's not get distracted in enemy territory. The important point is that the All-Stars must be here in an official capacity. That man is stationed at the door, and making himself obvious. The other All-Stars are probably doing the same in other parts of the building.*»

«*They sure aren't being subtle,*» I say. «*They planted Mister No One where everyone could see. That's a message to Diamond: we're here, so back off.*»

«*Oh noes!*» says a new voice over our comm rings. «*The All-Stars are gonna get me! I'm weeing in my wellies.*»

Male voice. Australian accent. Eek.

«*Hey, Diamond,*» K says calmly. «*Still tapping our phones?*»

The guy gives a creepy laugh. Oh, just awesome. We're conference-calling with Hannibal Lecter.

«*Go fuck yourself,*» Miranda tells him. Meanwhile, I'm looking around the lobby, but I don't see anyone with a supervillain vibe. Some people nearby are obviously Darklings, but most others could pass as human. Since nobody knows what Diamond looks like, anyone here could be him. He could even pass as a woman or were-beast: I'm sure a Mad Genius could whip up a device to disguise his real appearance.

And why should I think he's in sight? The comm rings have unlimited range. Diamond might be on another floor of the building. Hell, he could be lying on a beach in Bora Bora and yanking our chains just to troll us.

«*What's your plan?*» K asks him. «*The usual senseless slaughter?*»

«*My slaughter is never senseless,*» Diamond replies. «*But these rumors about finding one of my weapons . . . they're an obvious ruse to draw me out.*»

«*You're saying the bazooka isn't yours?*» I ask.

«*The weapons I cached nearby all destroyed themselves,*» Diamond replies. «*That's what they were designed to do, and that's what they did. Anyone claiming I left a loose end is trying to piss me off.*»

«*Because of course,*» Miranda says, «*it's impossible you'd ever screw up.*»

«*Don't taunt me, girl,*» Diamond says. «*I may be a sociopathic narcissist, but I'm not that easy to bait. I intend to— Shit!*»

His voice cuts out. "Damn," Miranda says out loud, "that bastard sure is annoying."

«*Apologies,*» says a new voice inside our heads. This one is nasal and familiar: our friend the Inventor. Invie says, «*I attempted to backtrack Diamond's signal in order to locate his position. However, I triggered some kind of detection protocol. Diamond disconnected before I could pinpoint him.*»

I say, «*Do you have a rough idea where he is?*»

«*Somewhere in Waterloo Region,*» Invie says. «*We should discuss this. Please meet Grandfather and me at the main floor bar.*»

«*Now you're talking,*» I say. I tell my friends, "Bar. Now. Fast."

THE TRANSYLVANIA CLUB HAS three stories and a beer cellar, each divided into sections that can be booked for weddings and such. I've been in the club before—I came last year for Oktoberfest. Back then, however, the place was only filled with humans, all of them drunk and eating sauerkraut while trying to dance the polka. Now I'm surrounded by Darklings. My lizard brain screams, "Run, run, run!"

Now that I think about it, this is only the second time I've been in a big crowd of Darklings. The first was when we went to the Goblin Market. That time, however, I had the benefit of being in Spark ID, so I was surrounded by a Halo that partly warded off the Darkling auras. Now, I'm less protected. I still have more resistance than most humans do, but without my costume and my Halo, I'm only half armored up.

So I get pummeled by Darkling Shadows. They induce fear, disgust, self-loathing, and a bouquet of other shrivel-up-and-die emotions. I want to escape; I want my daddy; I want to hide under the covers while hugging Bear-Bear and sucking my thumb.

But Miranda takes my hand, and K takes the other. We draw strength from one another . . . and we glare in envy at Shar, whose smile never wavers. She must be using her mental powers to insulate herself from the onslaught. That's so unfair! Or maybe my resentment comes from some nearby Darkling's Shadow that stirs up animosity among friends.

I squeeze the hands that grip mine, then let them go. Suck it up, Jools. Don't dampen your dress.

The club's usual ambience has been Darkified. The electric lights are turned off. Instead, the illumination comes from hundreds of candles. Spiders lurk in the cobwebbed corners; a rat eats crumbs off the floor; everything smells of decay and defeat.

But I can deal with the Shadows and damp-rot. What drives me to the edge is the ghosts.

Normal memorial gatherings commemorate the dead with photographs. That's what I expected here: pictures of people who died at the market, plus a book for writing condolences, and the usual shitload of lilies.

But the Darklings have summoned the actual ghosts of the lamented. Transparent forms float limply through the furniture; and unlike Nicholas "Wraith" Vandermeer, the *real* ghosts seem pathetically bewildered by their state. They remind me of my gran in the horrible months between her stroke and her death, lost in confusion and misery.

So awful. I can't stand remembering what happened to her. But even if I could block my memories of Gran, I can't shut out the sight of ghosts around me.

They're *suffering*. Some mutter, some flutter, some repeat the same movements incessantly. This *can't* be how Darklings want to remember their dead. And surely, magic must be able to lay these ghosts to rest. Can't the Darklings hold a mass exorcism? Just say, "Go rest in peace, it's over."

But every Darkling I can see just tunes out the ghosts, as if they're nothing but smoke from furtive cigarettes. I even wonder if I'm merely imagining the dead. But no, my friends see them, too. Miranda freezes up as if she fears a ghost will touch her. K has gone pale, and Shar seems furious as she glares at the see-through phantoms. Shar almost never gets really truly angry, but her eyes have narrowed, and she's glowing a faint violet.

"You, you, you, and you!" she says pointing at four nearby Darklings. "Hand over your invitations. We're going to trade."

Miranda whispers, "What are you doing?"

"Your invitations," Shar repeats to the Darklings. "Trade with us. Now."

Confused, the Darklings give us their invitation cards and we give them ours. The Darklings make the exchange quite docilely— Shar is likely controlling their minds. But as soon as we've swapped invitations, the Darklings' eyes go wide . . . while in our own eyes, the ghosts disappear.

"Thank you," Shar says to the Darklings. "Now go. Forget us."

The Darklings wander away, almost as dazed and unhappy as the ghosts appeared to be a minute ago. But for me and my friends, the ghosts have nearly vanished. If I concentrate hard, I can still see wisps and can feel a faint phantom melancholy. But the feeling just blends with the fear and other emotions imposed on us by dozens of Darkling Shadows.

It's bearable. We can breathe.

"Those fuckers," says K. Ze's clenching zir fists.

"I don't understand," Miranda says. She's very upset. K and I take her hands, and she doesn't shake us off.

"The invitation cards," Shar says. "The ones for Darklings have spells that prevent you from seeing the ghosts. But the ones set aside for us had no such protection."

"How did you know?" I ask.

"I read some minds," Shar says, "then put two and two together."

"Those fuckers," K says again.

I say, "You mean Elaine and Nicholas Vandermeer?"

K's expression stays fierce for a moment, then relaxes. "I shouldn't jump to conclusions. It's possible Elaine and/or Nicholas deliberately left invitations they knew were unprotected. But maybe they just didn't know what was up." K shrugs. "It might even be an accident. Somehow a few invitations didn't get enchanted. Darkling wizards aren't always meticulous."

"But the ghosts are still here?" asks Miranda, looking around. "They felt so lost . . ."

I squeeze her hand. "Dude, ghosts aren't dead souls. Trust me, I know things." I tap the side of my head. "Ghosts are leftover energy: they're echoes of people, not the real thing. They feel empty because they *are* empty."

"That doesn't make sense," says Miranda. But she doesn't ask any more questions—which is good, cuz I'm totally lying. Or rather, I'm picking the most comforting hypothesis from the many ideas about ghosts, the afterlife, and What It All Means.

No one actually knows this shit. Which is weird. People have literally died and come back from the dead—that crap happens to Sparks and Darklings all the time. But their tales of the afterlife don't agree. Some folks see fancy light shows and get sucked down bright tunnels. Others have gone through trials and sentencing. Some experience endless black nothingness. A few experience nothing at all: just the fading moments of life, then boom, they're back . . . even though days or weeks might have passed while they were out of the picture.

I choose to conclude that we're free to believe whatever helps us through the night. I was raised a half-assed Catholic, but my percentage of Catholic assness has dropped to single digits. Now my religion is mostly "Don't be a dick," mixed with nostalgia and aspiration.

Miranda squeezes my hand, then lets go. "I think we were heading for the bar?"

"Fuck yes." I take the lead, pushing quickly through the crowd.

ON OUR WAY TO the bar, we pass all manner of Darklings: vampires, were-beasts, and Other. Very Other.

Among those who still look human, many took the Dark Conversion the moment they turned eighteen. They look too young to drink. So basically, it's like Oktoberfest with tuxedos instead of lederhosen. And with dragon men, snake women, and an oozy mass of mouths and hands . . . oh, wait, I met a guy like that at Oktoberfest, too.

Hey, there are my drinking buddies from the plane: Karthik, Maria, and Iza. I wave. They wave back, but in that totally fake way that everyone uses when they're thinking, "Who the hell is that?" With my hair looking chic, and wearing more than minimal makeup, not to mention a kickass dress instead of a T-shirt and jeans, I bear no resemblance to the lush from yesterday's flight. I'm tempted to go over and launch into effusive conversation just to make the three of them sweat; but my urge to shit-disturb isn't as strong as my urge to fill my mouth with cold white wine or throat-scraping Scotch, so I move on without renewing old acquaintances.

Our progress forward is snail-like. None of us wants to get caught on the barbs of some nettle-bush demon. But slowly we close the gap between us and the booze. Then, just when the bar is in sight, we're waylaid by the Vandermeers.

Nicholas is doing his free-floating full-torso vapor routine. In honor of the occasion, he wears a suit instead of his usual ghostly robes. But his hair is still long and scraggly—he's basically Riff Raff from *Rocky Horror*, but without the legs.

Sister Elaine is more chic: full-length black Chanel, with glittering speckles all over the dress. Compared to last night, she's pulling out all the stops to maturify her dewy teenage looks: horn-rim glasses and a serious chignon with gray strands dyed into the brown. Her skin is even paler than the white Corelle shade we saw in the lab—like kids who starve themselves before prom, Elaine looks like she skipped her daily O-negative so that she'd be the whitest chick at the party.

K, on the other hand, is red-faced. I think it's part rage, part sex-flush: the usual conflicted feelings toward a blood-bond mistress. K looks at Shar, who nods. If I had Spark-o-Vision, I'd probably see K's head protected by a shell of violet light.

"Well, hello," Elaine says to K. "Look, Nicholas, it's little Kimmi. How she's changed!"

"*Ze*," Miranda says immediately. "It's K, not Kimmi, and 'ze,' not 'she.'"

"Well, isn't that a surprise!" Elaine stares at Miranda, then the rest of us. She's pumping up her Shadow, hoping we'll flinch. If I weren't a Spark, I'd be curling into a fetal ball. "So, *K*," Elaine says, with smarmy emphasis, "why don't you introduce your friends?"

"These are my roommates," K says in a mumble. I can't help but notice that K's defiance has sagged through the floor. Shar's face is starting to dampen with sweat, so I assume she's straining hard to shield K's brain from Elaine's influence. But Elaine is winning.

I'd love just to punch this bitch in the tits, or stomp a stiletto through her undead foot. But before I can get into position, a Darkling emerges from the crowd. "Elaine. Stop. Behave."

The new arrival is a woman. Maybe. At least it has womanly hair: waist length, silver, tied into multiple braids. The Darkling's face could be male or female, and it's wearing a brown batik kaftan that's shapeless enough to hide distinguishing characteristics. The voice is gender-neutral: it's much like K's, with a pitch that splits the difference between alto and tenor. At first glance, you might think that this was an ordinary human, following the same nonbinary path as K. But this is very much a Darkling, as evidenced by the pupilless white eyes and the tiny turquoise beads that sprout directly from its skin.

The beads are part of the Darkling itself: not stones embedded in the flesh but growing from the inside out. They're like chin stubble, but they swirl all over the Darkling's face, tracing out pebbled lines. It's an awesome look; and the Darkling's hands have the same turquoise swirls, so the designs probably extend all over the creature's body.

Pretty. But this *is* a Darkling, and it has a Shadow that radiates terrifying vibes—like a poison frog that's so deadly it can afford to advertise its lethality with eye-catching colors. Even Elaine and Nicholas look disconcerted by this newcomer. Then Elaine says, "Mother. I didn't know you were back in the country."

Mother? Oh, snap! But I'm not half as floored as K, who was gaping goggle-eyed at Mama Vandermeer even before Elaine spoke.

So much for K giving up zir thing for Darklings. New leaf, my ass.

Nicholas clears his throat. "Uhh, Mother, this is Kimmi. I've told you about her."

K leaps to shake Mama's hand. "I call myself K now. And I prefer 'zir' to 'her.' I mean the pronouns. 'Zir.' 'Her.'"

"I understand," Mama says with a smile. "I've considered changing pronouns myself, but the children would never adjust." She shrugs and smiles again. "I'm Lee, by the way."

She smiles a third time.

Yikes.

K smiles back. "Lee, these are my roommates." Introductions ensue, and handshakes all around. Lee's hand feels ordinary, body heat and all. Her Shadow makes the handshake intimidating—like touching something venomous—but physically, the sensation is perfectly normal. There's also the pleasure of seeing Elaine and Nicholas squirm in embarrassment and horror.

How can I resist making them writhe a little more? "So, Lee," I say, "I'm surprised this is the first time you've met K. I thought ze had met the whole Vandermeer family."

"The Vandermeers and I parted ways ten years ago," Lee says. "I see my children as often as I can, but I live in Berlin now. It suits me."

"Why are you back, Mother?" Elaine asks. Despite the tricks Elaine uses to make herself look older, she now sounds like an exasperated teenager.

"I thought I'd catch up with old friends," Elaine's mother answers. "And it's lovely to see you two, of course. Is your father here?"

"He had business," Nicholas says.

"Of course he did," Lee says. "So you see? It all works out." She turns back to K. "And what brings *you* here? Do you have friends in our little community?"

Miranda, with her super-quick reflexes, says, "I'm the one to blame. A cousin of mine was hurt in the Goblin Market fire. He invited me to this event, and I asked my roommates to come for moral support."

"I see," Lee says. "Yes, a gathering like this can be intimidating."

"I'm not intimidated," K says.

Lee laughs. Nicholas goes so white, he's semitransparent. Elaine looks like she's swallowed hydrochloric acid; if she had any blood in her veins, she'd be red in the face. She glares at K with a sudden intensity. K stiffens. So does Shar. Blood-bond fuckery is clearly afoot.

"Elaine!" her mother says sharply. "Don't be a beast." She steps between Elaine and K. "Stop. This. Now."

Elaine's fierce glare fades into a sulk. K's stiffness fades, too. Shar relaxes.

"We'd better go," I say. "We have to meet someone at the bar."

"My cousin," Miranda says. "The one who invited us. Todd."

Lee turns toward me and my friends, still keeping herself between K and Elaine. "It was lovely to meet you all. I'm sure we'll talk again."

Lee smiles at K. K smiles back.

Miranda grabs K's arm and we leave posthaste.

"OH. MY. GOD!" MIRANDA says to K. "Were you hitting on your ex's mother?"

K says, "More important, was she hitting on me?"

"Yes and yes," Shar replies.

K looks at Shar with a hopeful look on zir face. "Do you *know* that? Like . . ." K taps the side of zir head. "Did you read it in her mind?"

Shar chuckles. "A, I thought you didn't like me reading minds without permission. B, it's difficult to read a Darkling's mind, especially a powerful one . . . and trust me, Lee is *extremely* powerful. Also, C, I didn't need to be a mind reader."

Miranda is still looking flabbergasted. "But K, she's like . . . I don't know, sixty years old? Sixty, K. Seriously. Sixty."

"Don't be an ageist," says K.

"But she's also a Darkling," Miranda insists. "I thought you were turning over a new leaf."

"Hey," K says, "I'm in geology. What do I know about leaves?"

"Unless they're fossils," I say.

K glares at me. "Don't you start, too."

Shar says, "I wouldn't call Lee a fossil, but I suspect she's *much* older than sixty. Perhaps a hundred and sixty. A *thousand* and sixty. Considering how resistant she was to my telepathy, I wouldn't be surprised if she's an Elder."

Miranda gapes at K. "You hit on an *Elder*? You're lucky she didn't eat your eyeballs."

"The night is still young," I say. "Let's get to the fucking bar before Satan shows up and asks for a dance."

I hustle the others through the crowd. Even near the bar, it's not a *crowd* crowd—nothing like the loud sweaty crush during Oktoberfest. Tonight, the density of people reminds me of an average day at the mall: plenty of folks, but with adequate room for passing.

And for every Darkling, there are at least four normal humans, including waiters, security mooks, arm candy, and other clinging scraps of entourage. I can't help but notice they're all wearing talismans of the type Calon talked about: protective amulets and bracelets and headbands, all ostentatiously inscribed with sigils or decorated with pieces of dead animals.

You'd think it would be possible to defend against Darkling Shadows with something less obtrusive—enchanted undies or a Hand of Glory hidden in your purse. But apparently not. Stashing something in your purse must not be direct enough for protection . . . and as for undies, I can't see anyone wearing them. The building is full of commandos, and panty lines are the enemy.

Finally, *finally*, we make it to the bar. AND IT'S FREE. COMPLETELY OPEN.

I ask for Glenfiddich and the dude pours me Glenfiddich. He doesn't even have a tip jar. Best of all, he doesn't look at me like I'm trash. The guy gives me an honest-to-God smile, not the professional-courtesy kind. He's cute, and I think he likes me. He's an Asian guy as tall as me, and he seems quite pleasantly fit.

So bugger, fuck, and damn, this complicates things. If the barkeep were a sour-faced dude, I wouldn't mind hitting him up for three drinks in quick succession—I wouldn't care what he thought of me. But under the gaze of Cute Friendly Guy, I need to drink like a lady.

Have to nurse my glass. But that's for the best—Grandfather is seated at the bar, and he'll get judgy if I drink too much. He wears the same clothes as the last time we saw him: like a dark-skinned Abraham Lincoln, with a stovepipe hat, an old-fashioned black suit, and a black bow tie. His face is painted with colored dots, daubed on with his fingertip. They spiral all over his cheeks and forehead, but are concentrated around his eyes to make a greasepaint mask. He looks like an African medicine man, a cheerful one who beams with delight, as if he's having so much fun he might burst out laughing.

On a seat beside Grandfather perches the Inventor. Invie is still a basset hound, so he makes quite a picture with his rump on a barstool and his paws on the bar itself. But he's far from the only animal in sight; we've got wolves and tigers, eagles and snakes, and even a few giant insects. They're Darklings, of course: were-beasts. Some wear clothes, and some don't. Invie only wears a collar . . . but I shouldn't say "only" since I happen to know the collar is full of Cape Tech gadgetry.

"Evenin', ladies," Grandfather says.

Loud throat-clearing from K.

"Evenin', my fellow *sapiens*," Grandfather amends. "How's every little thing?"

"Can't complain," I say.

"Yet," Miranda mutters.

"I hear you," Grandfather says. "This event is redefining powder keg." He smiles as if the prospect tickles his funny bone. "You noticed Mister No One at the door? The other All-Stars are hanging around, too, some circulating, some watching the exits. They asked me to pass on apologies for venturing onto your turf without a courtesy call. They just didn't know how to get hold of you."

Shar narrows her eyes at the rest of us. "As soon as we decide on a group name, we'll set up a secure website. Right? Right?"

Miranda ignores her. "Speaking of security," Miranda says to Grandfather and Invie, "what are you going to do about Diamond hacking our comm rings?"

Grandfather says, "We've known about it for a while—Zircon sent word to us before Christmas. So Invie has had time to make improvements. Voilà! Rings 2.0."

Grandfather digs into a jacket pocket and pulls out four simple gold bands. They look like wedding rings—as if Grandfather is proposing to all four of us. "Not going to jinx things by claiming these are unhackable," Grandfather says. "But even Diamond will have trouble beating these fellas. They've got a whole new type of encryption that even a super-duper genius won't figure out soon." He lays the rings on the bar. "Trade your old ones for these."

"Could we keep the old ones?" K asks. "We could use them to broadcast disinformation. Maybe fool Diamond into a trap."

Grandfather shakes his head. "He knows we're onto him. He'll be watching for tricks." The old man eyes us shrewdly. "And maybe he can ID you by tracing the old rings' signals. Do you really want to wear them when you aren't in costume? Invie and me already know what you look like in real life, but you don't want Diamond to know, too." He taps one of the rings. "These are safer. Invie says they got antitracking gizmos."

"Which Diamond will eventually defeat," Miranda says.

"Sure," Grandfather agrees, "but not tonight. This is the first time these have been used for anything. And by the time Diamond figures 'em out, Invie will make Rings 3.0. If we're ridiculously lucky, maybe we or the All-Stars will capture Diamond in the meantime."

He nudges the rings toward us. I'm the first to pull off the ring I'm wearing and swap it for a new one. I slip the new ring on my right ring finger. For a moment after it's on, the ring is way too big; then it reshapes itself into . . .

Um.

It's slimewear.

A strand of transparent bio gunk wraps around my finger. At least it's not ugly; it's barely visible. It resembles a strip of clear plastic like the smallest size of Band-Aid. But my previous ring was wonderful, a whacking great reproduction of the 1988 Stanley Cup ring, gold and diamonds and all. This new one is nothing. Like I'm not worth any precious metal.

My friends have put theirs on. For them, the new rings look much like the old. Shar's is barely different at all—a simple gold band that blends with all the other rings she wears. Miranda put the new ring on her right ring finger, just like I did . . . and the ring has turned into a ladylike signet bearing the crest of the University of Waterloo. K's new ring is plain gold with a clear colorless crystal: it's either diamond or cubic zirconia, but I'd need a good lens to tell which.

And I get slimewear? This sucks.

Except I know that these rings read our minds. When they reconfigure themselves, they base their new shapes on thoughts plucked straight from our heads. I don't want to know what this says about my brain; so I think really hard, *Change, you bastard!*

After a moment, it does. It becomes a set of golden links. Not loose like a necklace, but stiff and squeezing my finger. Inside my head I growl, *I said "Change," not "Chain"!* But the ring maintains its shape and unpleasant tightness. The phrase "golden fetter" leaps unwelcome into my mind. I grab the ring and pull; it holds on fiercely, like how my father's wedding ring is so embedded in his flesh, it'll never ever come off in his lifetime.

I scowl at the ring. It stays the way it is. Well, at least it *looks* like a ring. And it doesn't clash with my outfit. So I let it be, despite its distracting grip on my finger. If I don't get used to it soon, I'll do some Mad Genius tinkering to loosen it up.

«*Now we can talk in private,*» Grandfather says inside my head. "If we need to," he says aloud. "But since we're face-to-face, no sense in telepathy. You folks have a plan?"

I say, "Nothing comes to mind except spreading out to watch for trouble."

Grandfather shrugs. "Not much of a strategy. But the All-Stars are doing the same, and they have experience dealing with Diamond."

«*They're scanning the area on multiple wavelengths,*» says Invie inside our brains. «*Their technical expert, Sensorium, is flying above the building. I've dealt with him before, and he's admirably competent. He promises to alert me if he notices anything suspicious.*»

Okay: Sensorium. WikiJools tells me he's a super-smart engineer just like Invie. He's built himself a flying battle suit equipped with gazillions of sensors. Usually serves as the All-Stars' eye in the sky.

"Can he actually see the whole building?" K asks. "The last time we dealt with Darklings, they put up blinder walls that blocked remote sensing."

Invie pauses, then says, «*Sensorium reports a blinder wall around the third floor. But the blinder spell is weak, and Sensorium is the best at what he does. He can see through the wall.»*

"What about ignorance spells?" K asks. "Magic that makes you ignore things in plain sight."

Invie pauses again. *«Sensorium has experience with ignorance spells,»* Invie informs us. *«It's the nature of such spells that you do not notice their effect on you. But Sensorium is aware of the possibility, and is trying not to be misdirected.»*

"This is weird," K mutters. "No ignorance spells, and blinders so flimsy you can see through them? What are the Darklings up to?"

"It's a trap," Miranda says. "For Diamond. Maybe for Robin Hood, too. The Dark have advertised the bazooka is here, and they want the place to seem wide open."

"They don't mind endangering their own people?" Shar asks. She gestures at the Darklings around us. "Diamond killed dozens of Darklings at the Goblin Market. The Dark are basically tempting him to do it again."

"Now that I think of it," Grandfather says, "I haven't seen any heavy hitters here. Not the prime minister. Not even cabinet members. Nor any important CEOs. Just second-in-command folks and such."

"Ouch," I say. "And remember what the Vandermeers told us? Their father couldn't come because, air quotes, he had business."

Miranda looks scandalized. "He sent his children to a potential bloodbath but stayed away himself?"

K says, "Mr. Vandermeer is not what you'd call a loving father." The look on K's face suggests ugly stories, but ze doesn't give us specifics. Instead ze says, "Anyway, Nicholas and Elaine can take care of themselves. In terms of magical strength, they're both more powerful than their father."

"That makes sense if their mother's an Elder," Shar says. "They'd stand to inherit her level of power."

"You really think Lee is an Elder?" K asks.

"Stop calling her Lee," Miranda says. "Memorize this phrase: 'my ex-boyfriend's bloodcurdling Precambrian mom.'"

"Not gonna touch that one," Grandfather says. "But if there's an Elder on the scene, she may be here to help fight Diamond. Or Robin Hood. Or both. Those two guys are pains in the Dark's collective ass. Could be that the Elders have finally decided to sweep them off the board."

"That's just great," I say. I think of Calon Arang, probably an Elder herself, who must be lurking someplace in the fest hall. We're standing in the dumpster where the Dark wants to light a fire.

I grin and put my arms around K and Miranda. "This is going to be a disaster. I can't hardly wait."

8

Adaptive Coloration

TIME TO CIRCULATE AND mingle. We spread around the fest hall, me and my roommates, plus Invie and Grandfather, covering all three floors and the basement.

The Transylvania Club didn't used to be so huge, but it's expanded a lot in recent years, thanks to Darkling funds. Once upon a time, this building was just a social club for people of Transylvanian extraction, but because of the name, the TC has become a go-to venue for the local Dark community. The resulting revenue has paid to upgrade the place considerably, especially on the third floor.

When I came to the club for Oktoberfest, the third floor was off-limits, guarded by heavy steel doors, a burly man, and a huge stone gargoyle. The gargoyle showed no signs of coming to life—it might have been an ordinary statue, just used to intimidate drunks like me. But in my inebriated state, I could easily believe the gargoyle would wake if needed and bite me in half with its strong stone beak.

Tonight, the gargoyle is right where I remember, and no more animate than before. The steel doors, however, have been thrown open wide, and the burly security dude has been replaced by an equally burly woman scowling at everyone who comes up the stairs. I recognize the woman as Gator Glaive, one of the Aussie All-Stars. As her name suggests, her skin is reptilian, as tough as an alligator's. On top of that, she wears armor like the kind that riot police wear, except made from alligator hide.

Gross. When you're basically a gator, should you wear the

flayed skins of your cousins? But as always, Spark ethics dance to a different didgeridoo.

As for the other part of GG's name, WikiJools tells me that a glaive is a honking great sword blade on the end of a two-meter pole. Gator Glaive has no such weapon at the moment, but she can pull one out of thin air whenever she wants. *Ka-ching*, you're facing an angry alligator armed with a sword on a stick.

I want to bump fists with her cuz I do something similar: I can summon a glowing green hockey stick made of pure sizzling energy. But Gator gal gives me a cold-blooded stare that doesn't say, "Hey, let's chat." She likely thinks I'm here as some rich dude's penthouse pet, or else I've come on the hunt for Darkling dick. Anyway, it's no wonder she's in a bad mood. Who could be happy, standing half a world away from home and waiting for your most notorious enemy to start a massacre?

I feel for you, babe.

Past the Gator and the gargoyle stands a sheet of unwavering blackness. A blinder wall. Unless you're Sensorium, blinder walls prevent you from seeing what's on the other side. Not even Zircon's Spark-o-Vision can penetrate a blinder . . .

. . . but now that I think of it, Invie's rings transmit just fine through such walls. That doesn't make sense: if a blinder wall doesn't stop radio waves, then it's not impervious, is it? Then again, the comm rings probably don't use plain old radio. And I shouldn't expect consistency from either magic or Cape Tech. Both have a huge because-I-say-so factor; they work by "it makes a good story" more than rigorous principles.

I pass through the blinder and enter the club's Darkling sanctum. Or should I say "swank-tum"? I'm looking at a ballroom out of *Pride and Prejudice*: candles and crystal and even a zombie or two. Plus spiders and, for some reason, a skeleton laid across a pentagram drawn on the floor. Then again, the skeleton might just be a Darkling who's passed out from carousing . . . and drawing a pentagram around him might be the demonic version of tucking him under a cozy blanket and letting him sleep it off.

But the centerpiece of the room is a glass case containing Diamond's bazooka. The case looks like it was originally designed for showing off the British crown jewels: it has a solid mahogany base with inlaid marquetry, and under the glass, a bed of red velvet on which the gun reclines.

I take it for granted the case is enchanted with vicious spells to fend off thieves. But I could be wrong. A were-boar is shoving his huge wet nose against the glass for a better look at the gun, and he's not getting electrocuted. He hasn't even set off any alarms.

Perhaps the case is a decoy, and the gun inside is a mirage. The real bazooka may have been shipped to a secret vault in Inuvik. But if the gun is fake, the powers that be have gone all in to back up the ruse—Reaper and Stevens & Stephens stand close by the case, looking like hair-trigger attack poodles ready to nip anyone who swipes their bone.

I wave at the three of them. They pretend I don't exist. How rude. Then again, they're busy keeping an eye on Mr. Were-Boar. The cost of cleaning pig snot off the glass likely comes out of their pay.

While I'm watching the three *estúpido*s, Calon Arang swishes up to greet me. She's wearing white, and I think it's couture—a simple gown that's not daring, but obscenely well made. It's like something a famous opera diva would wear for her eightieth birthday. And for once, WikiJools fails to tell me the gown's designer. That means the couturier is so ultrachic, his or her stuff isn't a matter of public record.

Then again, someone like Calon may be able to *extrude* elegant clothing by magic. Anything to avoid buying retail.

"Jools," she says, "so glad you've arrived." She looks me over with approval . . . but her gaze lingers on my gold-chain ring, as if picking out the single flaw in my appearance. She makes no comment, however. I guess I'm allowed that minimal gleam of personalization.

Calon looks at the whisky in my hands and sniffs disdainfully.

She takes the glass away from me and sets it on a nearby table. "That's from the *downstairs* bar," she says. "You can do better."

"It was Glenfiddich," I say.

"*Ordinary* Glenfiddich," she says. "A mere twelve years old. Never ask a child to do a fifty-year-old's job. Besides, this is a special occasion."

She takes my arm and leads me to the bar. I notice she swerves me around a wispy strand in the air. It's some ghost who's almost invisible, one of the baffled dead who's no longer easy to see, thanks to the "good" invitation cards. I say to Calon, "Those ghosts . . . the people who died . . . you know about them?"

"I see them clearly," she answers. "But I'm surprised you know they're here. I arranged for your invitation to have extra-strong concealer spells."

"The invitations got mixed up," I say. "The problem was eventually sorted out; but why are the ghosts *here*? I mean *here* here. If they died in the Goblin Market, shouldn't they be there? Or some other place they feel connected to: their home, their favorite squash club, or whatever."

Calon squeezes my arm. "I *knew* you were special—you understand ghosts. And you're right: spirits are usually tethered to their place of death, or to some other spot they find meaningful. It took a great deal of magic to fetter them here instead. You can see how disoriented they are. Well, no, you *can't* see that, can you? But they are. Like fish out of water."

"Because someone brought them here?" I ask.

"A committee of sorcerers," Calon says. "It wouldn't be much of a memorial without the guests of honor, would it? At midnight, we'll hold a cleansing ritual to sever the dead from this world: to propel them on to the next stage of existence. Darklings believe in *practical* funerals. We like to get the job done."

This might be kindly intentioned—freeing the dead from whatever holds them back. But Calon makes it sound like scraping off barnacles. I guess if you're an Elder, you've seen a lot of ghosts stumbling miserably through the world. Maybe you consider them flies to swat if they're a nuisance; otherwise, you simply let them bumble around till they vanish on their own. Flies don't live very long, do they?

We've almost reached the bar when Calon stiffens. She snaps her head around and stares at the doorway. I turn to look. A moment later, K enters the room with Lee. Or should I say, K enters with zir ex-boyfriend's bloodcurdling Precambrian mom.

K and Lee are arm in arm. Considering that I'm arm in arm with Calon, I shouldn't judge . . .

. . . but whoa.

I wonder if K sought out Lee, or vice versa. Or if Fate simply brought them together with neither making an effort.

"You know Lee?" I ask Calon.

"Which one's Lee?" Calon replies.

"The Darkling. The other is K, my roommate."

"Lee." Calon laughs. "She's calling herself Lee? How economical."

"What's her real name?" I ask.

"Speaking it aloud could provoke the apocalypse."

I look at Calon. I decide she's joking. Yes. That's definitely the most reassuring way to take it.

I say, "How bad is it that Lee is interested in my roommate? Is she going to devour K's soul or something?"

"I have no idea," Calon says. "She's an unpredictable entity."

"Ouch," I say. "Anything called an *entity* isn't a good dating prospect."

I take a step toward K and Lee, but Calon yanks me back. "Do *not* get between them," Calon whispers harshly.

I try to shake her off. Calon tightens her grip. "Leave this alone," she says. "I need you in one piece."

"So comforting," I say. "I am now thoroughly convinced my friend is safe. By the way, that's the same friend who has the blood bond with Elaine. The bond you promised to break? Remember that?"

"I remember," Calon says. "And I will keep my promise."

She pulls me toward the bar again. We have to pass the bazooka where the were-boar still has his nose pressed against the case. Dude is black-and-white with shovel-sized ears that shift back and forth as he gapes. He smells like he's recently rolled in manure, which is weird—I thought pigs were actually quite clean. Then again, this guy isn't a real pig; he's a Darkling. Resembling a pig is no guarantee he's piglike. For all I know, the dude eats steel and breathes fire . . . which may be why Reaper and his Renfields keep their distance from him, and why Calon gives the pig a wide berth as she leads me to the bar.

I finally notice the bartender. It's the Goblin from the Goblin Market, a little purple guy with big pointed ears. Like if Yoda fell into a wine vat. He has "cuddle me" written all over; when I was a kid, I would have loved a dozen of him arranged on my bed. Now that he gives away free liquor, he's pretty much my perfect man.

"Hello," he says shyly. He's standing on a stool to let him see above the bar. "What would you like?"

"Your best Scotch," says Calon Arang. "The *best* best."

"Goblin brand?" he asks in a hopeful tone.

Calon hesitates, then shrugs. "Why not?"

I ask, "Is this going to turn me into a frog?"

Calon doesn't laugh. She turns to the Goblin. "Is it?"

"I don't think so," he says. He looks me up and down. It occurs to me that the Goblin cast that self-repair enchantment on my costume, and that now, said costume resides in my slimewear bra. If the Goblin can sense his own magic, he might realize this normal-looking girl in a red dress is actually the awesome heroine Ninety-Nine.

But if he knows, he doesn't let on. He just says, "I haven't tried this batch of whisky on humans. But I doubt it will do anything *grievous*. And it tastes very good."

If I were smart, I'd tell him *No thanks*. But since I'm the stupidest smart person on the planet, I say, "Hit me."

* * *

THE GOBLIN HOPS DOWN from his stool and disappears into a back room. Calon's grip on my arm has loosened enough that I can turn to check out K and Lee again.

Definite signs of engrossed conversation. I don't even know if K has noticed me. I wish I had Spark-o-Vision so I could tell if Lee is enthralling K with magic. But as far as I can see, any enthrallment is purely hormonal.

K, K, K, you have got *to get over your infatuation with Darklings.*

Meanwhile, Pig Dude has finally worn out his welcome. Reaper moves in on the boar and says something I can't hear. I can't even read Reaper's lips; skulls don't have any. I assume he's doing the "That's enough, sir, move along." Gotta be polite—the were-boar may be dangerous and/or somebody important—but Reaper's clearly laying down the law. Pig Guy gives Reaper an angry look but grudgingly shuffles off and out through the blinder wall.

Reaper turns back to the gun case, but all is well. The glass isn't even smudged.

Uhhh . . .

Uh.

Why isn't the glass smudged? Pig Dude's snout was definitely wet and pressed directly against the case. I cast back my mind; yep, I can clearly recall moisture glistening on porcine nostrils.

Fuck. It was just an illusion. Magic? Or maybe Cape Tech. Whatever Pig Dude actually looks like, his nose wasn't damp at all.

«*Dudes,*» I transmit mentally, «*we've got a ringer. Guy who looks like a were-boar. He just left the third floor and is heading down the stairs.*»

«*You think it's Diamond?*» Miranda asks. «*Or Robin Hood?*»

«*Whoever he is,*» I say, «*he spent a long time scoping out the bazooka.*»

«*I'll stay with the gun,*» K says meeting my gaze from across the room. «*I'll watch it while you investigate.*»

I'm tempted to grumble. What K means is that ze'll cozy up with Lee while I chase a pig in a poke. At the moment, K and Lee are sharing a sofa and having a heart-to-heart. If it were anyone else but K, I'd think ze wouldn't notice a full production of *Cats* in the room, let alone someone trying to steal the bazooka. But I trust that Spark-o-Vision will show K what's happening, no matter how focused K's normal eyes might be on Lee.

I turn to Calon Arang. "Gotta go walkies." Calon is holding me loosely enough that I slip from her grip. If I headed for K and Lee, Calon might grab me again, but since I aim myself toward the stairs, she lets me go.

She knows I'll be back. The Goblin is fetching a glass of Scotch with my name on it.

ALL HELL WOULD BREAK loose if I sprinted to the stairs—drunk Darklings don't like to be jostled. Besides, I'm wearing high heels. Ginger Rogers notwithstanding, I might break my neck if I run too fast. There's also the problem of Gator Glaive standing just outside the blinder wall. If I burst into sight at high speed, she might summon her weapon and bisect me. At the very least, she'd grab the scruff of my neck and demand, "What's the hurry?"

So I move at an outta-my-way-I'm-gonna-puke velocity. I know this speed to perfection, even without my superpowers. I puff my cheeks and press my fist against my mouth. Gator Glaive jumps a bit as I bustle through the blinder, but she's not a stranger to people in my apparent condition. She gives me a wary reptilian eyeball, maybe wondering why I'm running downstairs instead of using the washroom on the third floor. But she's not so suspicious that she's going to venture into my spewing line of fire. I hurry unimpeded down the stairs, until I reach the second floor.

«*Anyone on floor two?*» I ask through my comm ring. I don't see the were-boar, but he could have disappeared into the crowd. The club is massive; the second floor alone can host two simultaneous weddings.

«*I'm on the east side of the floor,*» Grandfather answers. «*No were-boar here.*»

«*I have the west side,*» Invie reports. «*I do not see a were-boar either.*»

«*Hold position,*» I say. «*I'll keep going down.*»

«*I'm on the ground floor,*» says Miranda. «*But I can't reach the stairs very easily. The crowd is getting agitated—there's a whole load of ghosts that are freaking people out. I think the spells on the invitation cards are weakening.*»

«*Awesome,*» I say. And she's right. As I peel down the stairs, I see ghosts flickering in and out of existence. Ghosts with burns and ghosts with grotesque injuries. A couple of were-beast ghosts seem actually on fire, with their fur engulfed in flames. A great big Newfoundland dog wanders past me, and I swear I can feel the brush of its body.

The sensation makes me cringe. Feeling a ghost is exactly as creepy as you'd think.

So it's no surprise that human guests are scurrying away. Even Darklings are disconcerted. The closer I get, the more my skin starts to crawl. «*Keep an eye on the spooks,*» I tell Miranda. «*If the spell on the invites fails completely, this'll get ugly.*»

«*I see the were-boar,*» Shar announces. «*He's just arrived in the basement.*»

«*On my way,*» I say. «*Don't do anything rash till I get there.*»

Silently, I add, *Then I'll do something rash enough for both of us.*

SHAR SAYS, «THE WERE-BOAR is heading toward the back. He's in a hurry.»

«*Maybe he's just heading for the washroom,*» Miranda says.

«*There are washrooms on every floor,*» I reply. «*No point running from the top floor to the basement.*»

«*I can't read his mind,*» Shar reports. «*It's like nobody's home.*»

«*Could it be a robot?*» Miranda asks.

«*I don't know,*» Shar says. «*I've never encountered a robot.*»

Miranda says, «*Any robot convincing enough to pass for a Darkling must be made by a Spark. That means trouble.*»

«*Not necessarily,*» I say. «*If I had a robot that looked like me, I would* totally *send it to memorial services. And to any other event I wanted to skip.*»

Note to self: make a robot, so I don't have to go to class.

Miranda says, «*K, can you use Spark-o-Vision to see if it's a robot? Look inside and see if it has gears.*» Pause. «*K? K?*»

«*I'm here,*» K says after a pause. «*But the third floor is surrounded by a blinder wall. I can't see out at all.*»

I consider suggesting that K step outside of the blinder so ze can look at the boar. But no. One of us should keep an eye on the bazooka, in case this is all a diversion to draw us away.

«*The boar isn't heading for the washrooms,*» Shar says. «*He just went through a door marked "private, no admittance."*»

That's not good. On the one hand, the Transylvania Club is only a fest hall, so a private-no-admittance room is probably just a janitor's closet. On the other hand, no Darkling would make a beeline cuz he wanted to grab a mop.

By now, I'm rushing through the crowd in the basement. I can see Shar ahead of me—her spangled outfit sparkles in the candlelight. I can see where she's heading, and because I'm stronger and faster than she is, I catch up just as she reaches the door.

She whispers, "Should we get into costume?"

I look around. My hurried push through the crowd attracted attention, so lots of people are staring. "Let's stay in civvies," I whisper back. "But be prepared to throw up a force field the moment we're through the door."

Shar nods. I tap the door latch once with my fingertip, just in case it's electrified or cursed. Nothing happens, so I grab the latch and push the door open.

It's an ordinary utility room, with a furnace, two water heaters, and numerous doorless cupboards full of cleaning supplies. No sign of the were-boar; however, the room has a fire exit he might have gone out through. The exit has a sign saying an alarm will go off if the door is opened, but so what? Half the time, those signs are lying—either there isn't an alarm at all, or else it is always turned off so the janitor can go outside for a smoke without raising a ruckus. Even if the alarm is turned on, those things are child's play to disable . . . especially for Sparks or Darklings with inhuman powers at their disposal.

«*What's happening?*» Miranda asks.

«*Nothing,*» I reply, «*everything looks calm.*» Then I grimace, realizing I've jinxed the whole ball of wax.

And yep, here it comes. A voice out of nowhere announces, "Good evening! I'm called Diamond. Welcome to my evening's entertainment."

I'VE HEARD THE VOICE before—most recently inside my head when Diamond gloated about hacking our comm rings. But back before Christmas, I listened to similar words. The last time we fought Diamond, he left a prerecorded soliloquy that explained his master plan and defied us to stop it.

Déjà vu all over again.

"This is just a minor gig," Diamond says, "so don't expect anything elaborate."

Over my comm ring, I ask, «*Are you hearing this?*»

«*Unfortunately, yes,*» K answers. «*It's coming over the club's sound system.*»

«*A few people are running for the exits,*» Miranda says. «*Others look as if they think it's joke.*»

Invie says, «*Sensorium is tracking the source. He'll have a location soon.*»

"Since I'm recording this in advance," Diamond continues, "I don't know if this gun they've found is really one of mine. But I doubt it's genuine. More likely, some social climber in the Canadian law-enforcement community is trying to draw me out with trumped-up goods. That's extremely foolish—just ask the All-Stars. Attracting my attention is never wise."

«*The broadcast is coming from the basement,*» Invie says. I already know that. I've been searching the utility room and I've found a weird attachment stuck to the furnace. The furnace itself is just a sheet-metal box with ductwork feeding to the upper floors. One side of the furnace has a conventional control box for setting the temperature on each floor, but beside the box is a papery mass that looks like a giant wasp nest. Thin black tendrils run from the nest into the control box.

I rack my brain for explanations. I can see that the furnace burns natural gas. Diamond could easily set off a gas explosion, but that's far too pedestrian for a Mad Genius. Even if the recording said not to expect anything elaborate, a guy like Diamond wouldn't stoop to a mundane *kaboom*.

But the thing that looks like a wasp nest? Eek.

Shar joins me in front of the papery blob. "Should we try to rip it free before something happens?"

I say, "The moment we touch it, I bet we'll set it off."

"We won't have to touch it," Shar says. "I can use telekinesis."

"Whether you touch it with your hands or your powers, disturbing it will send the shit into the fan."

All this time, Diamond's voice has prattled on. It's his usual schtick: Darklings are parasites who must be obliterated, and if ordinary humans die, too, well, fuck 'em for being squishy. Gotta give Diamond credit for not using the eggs-omelet metaphor, but maybe he used it a long time ago and doesn't like repeating himself. Anyway, he's frank about his indifference for shedding human blood. I think his primary goal truly is to eradicate the Dark, but given a choice between a scheme that only kills Darklings and one that massacres a lot of humans, too, Diamond tends to pick Plan B.

Which is why I'm leery of touching the wasp nest. But I know bad things will happen whether I tamper with it or not. This is a clusterfuck waiting to happen, and I'm sure it won't wait long.

As Shar and I hesitate, an All-Star streaks through the door. It's one of the Blackmire twins. They're a fortyish brother and sister who share a single androgynous body. The body is strong and fast and capable of flying. Supposedly, when Missy is in control she revels in brute strength, while Maxim is more about finesse; but WikiJools tells me it's just PR, invented by a company that makes Blackmire action figures. Which one controls the body doesn't actually matter, because both are thoughtless hotheads who revel in smashing things.

Like wasp nests. Apparently.

Team Blackmire whooshes in, and faster than a speeding bull in a china shop, they rip the nest off the furnace. I don't even have time to say, "Wait." Just zoom, grab, yank, and the deed is done.

After which, no surprise, the air is full of wasps.

Big wasps. Little wasps. Babies. Goliaths. There are hundreds of the buggers, and I have no doubt they sting. Super-poisonous stings, and maybe with extras, like they set you on fire or drive you mad. These wasps were created by Diamond; I'm sure he made them killers.

But the swarm clearly hates Blackmire more than Shar or me. Blackmire stands there with tattered wasp-nest remains in zir hands. The wasps seem smart enough to put two and two together—they engulf Team Blackmire in a stinging frenzy that buzzes as loud as a scream. I have no idea how tough Blackmire's skin might be, but even if ze can shrug off the stingers, it's hard to ignore a horde of insects stabbing your eyes and crawling up your nose. Howling with fury and pain, Team Blackmire zips out the door.

Crashes. Shouts. The sort of sounds you'd expect when a super-strong Spark blunders blindly through a crowd while surrounded by raging insects.

This'll work out so well.

«*We've got bees!*» Miranda yells over her comm ring. «*They're coming out of the heat vents!*»

«*Actually, they're wasps,*» I correct her. «*They belong to the same taxonomic order as bees, but you can tell difference by—*»

«*Shut up!*» K snaps. «*They're on the top floor, too, attacking everyone.*»

«*Including you?*» I ask. «*Or did you go stony?*»

«*I can't Zirc out here, too many people are watching,*» K says. «*But

I'm fine. Lee sprouted gigantic wings; she's flapping up a wind to blow the wasps away.»

«*I've raised my force field,*» Miranda says. «*I had to switch to Aria, but I hope everyone else was too busy hiding from wasps to see me change.*»

Shar says, «*Maybe Ninety-Nine and I should change, too.*»

«*Don't do it,*» Miranda says. Or should I call her Aria? «*The moment I changed, the wasps zeroed in on me. They can't get through my force field, but they're trying super hard to sting me.*»

Shar says aloud to me, "Could Diamond program the wasps to attack people wearing costumes?"

"Not costumes," I say. "But Diamond might have engineered the wasps so they target Darklings and Sparks."

"Then why aren't they going for us?" Shar asks. "We aren't in costume, but we're still Sparks."

I say, "Maybe it's connected with Shadows and Halos. Diamond has somehow keyed these wasps so they only attack people who emit an aura."

"So if we don't change, the wasps will leave us alone?"

"Knowing Diamond," I say, "the wasps *prefer* to attack people who have auras . . . but they'll sting the fuck out of anyone."

Almost all the wasps that emerged from the nest have left the room, chasing after Blackmire. A few, however, must have lost the scent, because they're coming for Shar and me.

I whack one out of the air with my purse. It's like hitting a very small baseball; I knock the insect into the side of the furnace, but that only makes the wasp angry. I hit it a few more times until it finally falls to the ground. Even then, I have to grind it hard with the sole of my shoe. I push down with my full weight to make sure it's good and dead.

Another wasp goes for Shar. Violet light extrudes from Shar's forehead and captures the wasp in a thread-sized lasso. After a moment, the thread lets go and the wasp flies straight into the flame of the furnace's pilot light. It hovers in the flame for at least five seconds before it succumbs to the heat.

Meanwhile, three more wasps buzz in. They plunge toward Shar's head, aiming at the precise spot on her forehead where the violet strand came from. I guess wasps take it personally when someone mind-controls their sister to make her self-immolate.

None of the wasps comes for me. I move to Shar's side and help her stave them off, beating up another wasp with my purse as Shar deals with the other two. Instead of burning them, Shar uses telekinesis to grab the pair. She stabs the stinger of one into the other, then vice versa. The poisoned jabs cause instantaneous death, but five seconds later, more wasps show up.

"Where are they coming from?" Shar yells.

"Teleportation?" I suggest. They certainly aren't coming from the wasp nest. The ruins of the nest seem empty. I think the nest on the furnace was merely intended to attract attention when Diamond started speaking. The actual source of the wasps is elsewhere.

The point on Shar's forehead starts to glow again. I snap, "Stop using your powers! It attracts them."

Shar snaps back, "But then I'll get stung!"

She's right. And even though Shar is a Spark, I don't know if she'll survive a sting. As best I can recall, she hasn't taken a hit since she got superpowers. She's always protected herself with telekinetic barriers. Since it's never been tested, her skin could be tougher than rhino hide. But probably not; and if the wasps are as bad as I think, a single sting could be lethal.

"Fuck," I say, as I fend off the wasps that are trying to sting her. I drop my purse and grab the nearest two, one in either hand. I squeeze as hard as I can, and feel their exoskeletons crunch in my fists.

But I also feel their stingers stab my palms. Pain explodes through my hands.

I open my fists. The crushed wasps drop. The skin of my palms is turning black.

Then I'm falling and—

Selective Pressures

OOF, I'M AWAKE AGAIN. So, yay?

I'm still in the furnace room, lying on the rough concrete floor. My hands hurt like hell; they feel as if someone pounded nails through them. But when I stare through watery eyes at my palms, they're undamaged. My power of miraculous recovery saved me from a death worse than Fate.

As I try to stand, I twist an ankle. Stilettos are damned unforgiving when you're wobbly on your feet. I take off my shoes and try again. Now my ankle hurts like hell, but if I can heal from a lethal wasp sting, a sprain is de nada. Just give me a minute.

Meanwhile, I look around. I don't know how much time has passed since I got stung, but when I examine the room, I see a buzzing mass of wasps where Shar should be. There must be thousands of insects, clumped so thickly I can't see what lies beneath.

«Shar!» I yell mentally. «Are you all right?»

«I am furious,» she replies, «but not hurt. I changed to Dakini and enclosed myself in a telekinetic envelope without getting stung. And you're well?»

«Well enough,» I say.

I stare at the buzzing swarm. The general shape tells me Shar is standing upright, but I can't see her for all the wasps crawling over her body. Every now and then, I catch a glint of violet beneath the insects' yellow bodies. That must be the shield that keeps my friend from getting stung. I don't know how she can breathe in there, but I'd better not ask. Never question the mechanics of superpowers, or else you might bugger things up. If I ask, "How can you breathe?" Shar may start suffocating.

There's also no point asking, "How can I help?" Even if I had a flamethrower, I couldn't kill wasps fast enough to get them all—not before they stung me to shit. I'd pass out again for sure . . . and considering that two small stings put me down for an unknown length of time, who knows what a hundred stings would do? I don't want to test the limits of my recuperation.

But at least, no wasps are attacking me now. Shar (or rather Dakini) is a human-sized sugar cube drawing the wasps' attention. Let's not disturb them. The wasps focused on Dakini aren't killing anyone else. In a way, she's doing her part to keep people safe.

But I don't have a comparable option. I can't produce force fields, so if *I* get costumed up, I'll get stung and stung and stung. I have to stay Jools until I figure out some clever way to kill a million insects.

«*I'll get help,*» I tell Dakini. I hurry away before I'm noticed by the wasps.

I SPRINT FOR THE utility room's door. With my shoes off, my feet are only covered by stockings; the concrete floor shreds the nylon to ribbons in 2.73 seconds. This leaves me in bare feet—my cute uncallused feet, as soft as a baby's soft spot. I stop and mutter, "Let's get something straight. My feet may look demure, but they're as tough as the toughest human's toesies. As tough as an African long-distance runner who marathons daily without shoes."

My feet don't visibly change—from the ankles down, I could still model sandals. But my pampered-looking skin pulls taut around my bones. It hurts for a moment like a foot cramp; then abracadabra! My *Vogue*-model feet fast-forward through a lifetime of shoelessness, leaving them ready to race over cobbles without getting cut.

I crack open the furnace-room door. The basement outside is a shambles—an appropriate word, since "shambles" originally meant "slaughterhouse." I don't bother counting the bodies sprawled motionless across the floor, nor do I check whether they're all dead. Even if some are alive, I don't know how to keep them that way. What would be able to counteract the poison injected by a Mad Genius's wasps? Maybe there's something that'll work as an antivenom, but I don't know what it is and I sure as hell don't have any with me.

No wasps within sight. I throw open the door and hurry past the corpses. I breathe through my mouth to avoid inhaling. The club's aged-in scent of wood polish and beer has been replaced by the stench of body fluids: everything that spills out when dead muscles go slack. The reek is appalling. But if there's such a thing as a bright side, the smell seems to have driven away the wasps. Whatever species they belong to, the wasps have no interest in carrion.

Tables and chairs lie scattered in all directions. From the pattern of dispersal, I can tell that people stampeded toward the stairway. They cleared the route by tossing furniture out of their way. Vampires and were-beasts can throw really hard—the club's wooden chairs were sturdy, but some were reduced to flinders when they smashed against the wall. Let's try not to imagine what might have happened if ordinary humans got hit in the process.

Here and there, I see human-shaped lumps covered by wasps. They look a lot like Dakini did, except they're lying on the ground.

Darklings? Sparks? Innocent bystanders? I can't tell. But the insects targeted people with powers, whether Dark or Light. I wonder what happened to Grandfather and Invie, or the Australian All-Stars. I wonder if I'm all on my own.

No. My friends will be all right. They have to be.

I tiptoe past the wasp-covered forms, then race up the stairs two at a time. I stop when I reach the ground floor. The doors to the outside world have been torn off their hinges. Furniture has been scattered like I saw in the basement, and dozens of dead bodies lie sprawled. But I also see human-sized cocoons of black chitin scattered haphazardly around.

I've heard of such cocoons. Since vampires are vulnerable to sunlight, some clever vamp wizard developed a spell to surround himself with a lightproof black chrysalis. The wizard then taught the spell to other Darklings (for a suitable price, of course). I don't know how much the dude charged, but clearly, a lot of Darklings paid up.

The cocoon spell locks in its occupant till sunset—in this case, sunset tomorrow. The chitin of the cocoon is so hard it repels bullets. Maybe it also repels superpowered wasps. Guess we'll see at tomorrow's sunset whether the wasps could get inside.

In the meantime, I hear buzzing in the barroom. I tiptoe to the door and take a peek. A gigantic sphere stretches from floor to ceiling, covered with angry insects trying to plunge their stingers through the outer shell. Underneath the wasps shines a familiar golden light: the beaming goodness of a force globe produced by Aria.

«*Aria!*» I say with my comm ring. «*Is that you in there?*»

«*Me and a lot of people,*» she replies. «*As many as I could manage.*» She pauses. «*How are you doing? Dakini told us you got stung.*»

«*You know me,*» I tell her. «*There's dead and then there's mostly dead.*» I look at the huge buzzing sphere. «*How long can you keep that up?*»

«*I've achieved equilibrium,*» says Aria, ever the physics student. «*I've adjusted the size and thickness of the sphere to levels I can maintain indefinitely—like walking at an easy pace. But if I try to do anything else, I'll burn out fast.*»

«*Dakini is in the same boat,*» I say. «*But don't worry, I'll figure out something before you get tired.*»

I feel a sudden chill, as if someone dropped an ice cube down my dress. I whirl and see a ghost; it was running its hands down my spine. The ghost is so dried up and shriveled, I can't tell if it's male or female—just a mass of burned skin and bones. Its lips move, but I can't hear anything over the buzz of Aria's wasps. The ghost reaches out again and I shy away, feeling a brush of the phantom's icy cold.

I back away farther, thinking, *Damn, I've lost my invitation card.* The card was in my purse, which I dropped in the furnace room.

Will I have to face dozens of spirits like the one in front of me? It reaches for me, but I don't think it means any harm; it just senses my body heat and longs to make itself warm.

I retreat, keeping an eye out for other phantoms who might want to paw me. None in sight. That worries me. Before we got the "good" invitations, this part of the fest hall was full of lost spirits. Where did they go?

I doubt they ran from the wasps. A wasp can't sting a ghost. And even if Diamond's wasps are so damned special they affect the spirit world, the poor bozo spooks we saw probably didn't have enough intelligence to run away. If they got stung, they'd just huddle in misery, wondering why they hurt.

So where did the ghosts go? Did something lure them elsewhere?

I run for the stairs and head upward.

A COLD WIND SLAPS me as I approach the second floor. It's blowing through broken windows. Looks like some people made their own exits when they saw how bad the wasps were.

Hey, the chill has affected the wasps. Hah! Diamond may be a Mad Genius, but he's Australian. When he engineered his killer wasps, he didn't make them tough enough to withstand Canadian winter. And it doesn't help that his wasp nest *messed up the frickin' furnace*.

So wherever the wind can reach, the temperature has fallen below freezing. None of the wasps are moving. Waterloo's local wasps go dormant and hibernate through the winter. Diamond's wasps are doing the same . . . or else they just die and good riddance. Candy-assed poikilotherms.

Even better, the cold guarantees the wasps won't spread beyond the Transylvania Club. If this were summer, the broken windows would let wasps swarm the city. But tonight, the windchill is a slow but certain solution to our problems.

«Aria! Dakini!» I call through my comm ring. «*The wasps can't stand cold. Break some windows, or get outside.*»

«*Damn,*» says Aria. «*I should have thought of that. But I'm trapped in this big fucking bubble. No way I can squeeze through a door.*»

I say, «*Want me to smash the windows near you?*»

«*No, my cou . . . uhh . . . there's a guy named Todd here with me in the bubble. He's called 911. He can tell the fire and police to break the windows.*»

«*That works,*» I say. «*Just make sure the window-breakers back off fast. It'll take a few minutes for the wasps to freeze. In the meantime, a single sting is lethal.*»

As I continue up the stairs, the temperature keeps dropping. Ice has caked on the metal pipe that serves as the stairway's banister. There's even a sheen of ice on the wooden steps. My bare feet hate it to pieces. But I pick my way through the ice till I reach the blinder wall at the top of the stairs.

Deep breath. Then I crouch, so I won't be too noticeable as I come out the other side of the jet-black curtain.

Good decision, Jools! Just as I'm ready to sneak through the blinder, Wrecking Ball flies out over my head like she's been shot from a cannon.

Flight isn't one of Wrecking Ball's powers. Something must have hit her hard enough to send her sailing. She clatters through the guardrail at the side of the stairs and disappears toward the floor below. I can hear her crashing through furniture, plowing into tables and chairs. When she finally comes to a stop, silence reigns for a moment before she yells in outrage.

More sounds of breakage ensue. Wrecking Ball is not a happy camper.

Something drops onto the step beside me. It's a device the size of my pinkie and it's obviously Cape Tech—mostly black, but covered with strands of dark green. The strands glow, and move in a random-seeming pattern all over the surface. Specks of light circulate through the strands like little creatures racing through a maze. The device reeks of pine, like the D-grade air freshener that gets sprayed inside used cars.

This thingie must have fallen off Wrecking Ball when she

crashed through the guardrail. I gingerly touch it with my fingertip. My hand changes: it becomes semi-see-through and puckered like a raisin. I don't feel different, but now my hand looks like it belongs to a withered ghost. My other hand does, too, and when I press my fingers against a stair step, they sink a short distance into the wood. It feels like pushing a taut tarpaulin as it gradually yields to the pressure.

"Fuck," I say. My voice sounds hollow. Sepulchral.

"Fuck," I say again. Robin Hood and his posse snuck in disguised as ghosts.

I THINK ABOUT THE invitation cards. Did their enchantment literally blind us to the presence of Robin's gang? Or maybe the ghosts Miranda saw were Robin and his homies: visible to invitation-holders, but dismissed as surplus specters. They arrived on the ground floor and made their way toward the bazooka. Then Diamond unleashed his wasps, and in the confusion, Robin's gang made their move.

Wrecking Ball roars. Her thunderous footsteps pound the floor as she starts to run. The building shakes in response.

The density of cast iron depends on how it's made, but Wiki-Jools says it averages seventy-two hundred kilograms per cubic meter. I take a guess at Wrecking Ball's volume, mentally scribble numbers on the back of a fictional envelope, and end up with an estimate that the woman weighs close to a metric ton. That's a lot of stress on the wooden floor . . . especially since Wrecking Ball's weight gets concentrated on a small area each time one of her feet smacks down. The Transylvania Club was constructed to hold a crowd of beer-belly drunks dancing the polka, but Wrecking Ball may exceed the building's tolerance.

And she's only one of Robin's Merry "Men." The gang has several other Sparks. No one else matches Wrecking Ball's weight, but they all wield serious firepower. A shooting match could blow the club to bits.

Staying low, I finally shove myself through the blinder to see what's happening. Much gratuitous sound and fury: it's more than a brawl with a dozen combatants, it's a fucque du cluster à la mode.

Let's deal with the least important people first: Stevens & Stephens. They're crouched behind a flipped-up table and shooting at God knows what. They seem to be popping off their Glocks at random. Maybe this is the gunfire version of typing madly when you hear your boss coming down the hall. You don't want to look like a slacker by having leftover ammunition at the end of a firefight.

Next there's Reaper himself. He's battling blade to blade with Ninja Jane from Robin Hood's gang. Reaper's scythe versus Jane with a pair of daggers. They're off in their own little world, far from the bar and the bazooka. They're on the opposite side of the building, going full *Princess Bride* as they leap over tables, throw chairs at each other, and swing from the building's rafters.

It's hard to tell who's winning. It's hard to see much at all. Reaper is in his dirty gray robe, while Jane wears head-to-toe black: loose-fitting silk that covers her completely, except for a narrow eye slit. Since the candles have all blown out, the fight looks like shadow puppets flitting through the darkness. I catch flashes from Jane's knives, and the black glow of Reaper's scythe, but apart from that, my eyes don't see much.

On the other hand, their fight gives my ears a lot to hear. First, the weird crinkling of the air as it recoils from the scythe. Next, a series of thuds as Reaper hops over and onto furniture. Jane herself makes no sound, despite numerous superhuman jumps. WikiJools tells me she's never been heard to speak, but she's surrounded by apophenic whispers, a chorus of white-noise voices, mostly unintelligible but occasionally saying things you think you understand. *"I saw you do it." "No escape." "Blood on your hands."* Whatever language you speak, you can hear sinister phrases. Different people hear different things, and all at the same time.

I've heard about this before, and said to myself, "What a cheap gimmick." But hearing the voices for real is a whole other thing. They get under my skin like maggots; if not for the noise from the rest of the fight, I'd be totally creeped out.

But the rest of the fight is *loud*. You might expect the fighters would be mostly Darklings; after all, the building was full of them. But the great Dark majority are locked in cocoons or have bailed out of the building completely. The only Darklings left are Vandermeers: Nicholas, Elaine, and Momma Lee.

Elaine and Nicholas flank the bazooka case. They're fighting off Robin Hoodlums who want the gun. To me, this proves what K suspected: both Vandermeer kids belong to the Dark Guard. Otherwise, they'd have buggered off like all the other Darklings— the ones who didn't give a flying fuck about the gun. I sympathize with the Darklings who fled; why risk your life over a stupid MacGuffin? But if Nicholas and Elaine are Dark Guardians, they have to oppose rogue Sparks like Robin Hood.

I have no idea where Lee fits in. Maybe she's Dark Guard, too. Maybe she's protecting her children. Or maybe she's a pissed-off Elder of the Dark who has totally run out of fucks.

The why can wait. At the moment, let's concentrate on the how. And the what-can-Jools-do-to-stay-alive.

Crouched beside the bazooka, Nicholas plays the ghost card on both offense and defense. The offense part is against a pair of robots I assume were built by Maid Marian. They're big metal golems abristle with weapons: cannons in their bellies, fire and lightning in their hands. As I watch, Nicholas surrounds them with mist. Their fire goes out, their lightning gets grounded, and corrosion laces through the robots' metal.

The robots try to fire their cannons; the barrels rupture, spewing fragments in all directions. Several shrapnel-like pieces fly straight at Nicholas . . . but he's a ghost, and the shards pass harmlessly through him. They don't stop until they hit the glass case that holds the bazooka. Flares of magic erupt where the shards hit the case. The metal fragments melt in the blink of an eye, becoming molten blobs that dribble down the glass.

So as expected, the case is awash with defensive spells. It's not gonna be breached by mere ricochets.

On the other side of the case, Elaine is going full Dungeons &

Dragons, casting spells like a tenth-level wizard who's prepped for combat. Unlike her ghostly brother, she seems quite solid. For defense, she's surrounded herself with enchanted barriers. They glow like bloodred ramparts that Elaine crouches behind as she tosses sorcerous nastiness over the top. But the barrage of attacks from Robin's gang are whittling down her defenses. Elaine's cheeks have been gashed and her horn-rimmed glasses have literally melted onto her face. Her glittery black dress is in tatters; if she were human, she'd be bleeding to death.

But vampires don't bleed like humans. Some experts think vampires have conscious control over every drop of blood in their bodies. Like cars that use gasoline judiciously, vampires use blood to fuel their many abilities.

Case in point: Elaine now faces a Spark named Multiplier, one of Robin Hood's merry outlaws. WikiJools tells me he's a low-grade speedster with the added trick of making multiple copies of himself. He can't move so fast that he turns to a blur, but when you're facing three guys zipping around ten times quicker than normal human beings, you've got trouble.

The only upside for Elaine is that the copies share a single consciousness. Basically, Multiplier has a single brain running the whole show. The more duplicates he produces, the less he can manage them well. If he made, like, a hundred copies of himself, most would just stand around like dummies because he can't split his concentration between them all.

So the three Multipliers don't triple-team Elaine as effectively as three separate people might. They aren't as inventive or tricky. On the other hand, Multiplier's single brain is superfast, so his three-man attacks are quick and well coordinated. One guy swoops in from the left, another comes from the right, and the third guy goes up the middle. If any of the three gets close enough, a punch at super-speed is very $\frac{1}{2}mv^2$.[*]

But Elaine is a wiz at wizardry. Three bolts of crimson magic

---

[*]The formula for kinetic energy.

shoot from her fingertips, targeting each of the attackers. Two Multipliers dodge, but the third doesn't react fast enough. *Hiss-boom*. The Multiplier clone collapses in a smoking heap. The other two Multipliers say, "Fuck!" in unison. They race off to a far corner for a breather; they need time to recover before they can make a new duplicate and try the same tactics again.

So it seems like Elaine won the bout. However.

Each magical smackdown she delivers consumes a portion of the blood in her veins. Sooner or later, she'll run out; then she's pooched. Vampire sorcerers are wicked-ass threats, but they don't have unlimited ammo. This is the trade-off that keeps them on an equal footing with were-beasts: were-beasts aren't nearly so adept at casting magic, but they never run out of juice when they do.

Elaine is living on borrowed time. But she has an ace in the hole: her mom.

Lee stands atop the gun case, looking like Old Lady Winter personified. Hell, she might actually *be* Old Lady Winter: some Arctic goddess, unspeakably old and mad as hell.

Lee is the source of the ice on the stairs. Her braids have come undone, and her long silver hair whips up a fierce freezing breeze. Her kaftan billows around her body; the turquoise beads that speckle her skin burn like stars in a frigid northern sky. Snowy gusts stream off her with a vengeance. Even Wrecking Ball, with all her super-strength, can't prevail against the wind. Wrecking Ball looks like a cartoon character trying to push forward into a blizzard. Her eyes have iced up and she's white with frost, like a window on the coldest day of winter.

As if holding off Wrecking Ball isn't enough, Mama Vandermeer has plenty of strength left over. She's surrounded herself with a shell of ice that repels every attack aimed toward her. But the ice shell only works one way: it stops incoming assaults, but not the outgoing blasts that Lee shoots at anyone who threatens her children. Even as I watch, Lee hurls a barrage of hail at the two Multipliers. They go down under the volley, battered by hundreds of hailstones flying almost as fast as bullets.

But Multiplier is a side dish. The entree is the greatest threat of all: Robin Hood.

He's a dark-skinned dude in Lincoln green, exactly like the selfies he posts several times a day on Facebook. He wears a green eye mask, which doesn't cover up his cheekbones or his perfectly kissable jawline. He has a trim beard and mustache I'd love to nuzzle into. The next time the Royal Shakespeare Company needs a smoking-hot Othello, they should speed-dial this guy's agent. Because yes, Robin Hood is a hunk, built like a tennis pro, lean and lithe and lovely.

He moves like a tennis pro, too. Robin romps around the room like he's playing at Wimbledon. Every time Lee shoots an icicle at his head, Robin ducks it. He laughs as ice spikes past him. Amidst the chaos of wasps, black magic, scythes, and winter gales, Robin Hood is having fun.

He's a swashbuckling rogue who never breaks a sweat: that's why the public loves him. Or at least that's one reason. WikiJools informs me that Robin's lovability is also a superpower. It's not as extreme as with Spark mind-masters who turn people into adoring slaves, but Robin Hood has a shine that makes you like him. I find myself cheering him on as he skips around the barroom, shooting multicolored arrows.

According to WikiJools, Robin Hood's bow is nothing special. I can see that it doesn't have any of the attachments used in modern archery: no sights, no stabilizers, no pulleys. It's a simple recurve bow that unscrews into three separate pieces so it's easier to sneak into venues like this. And it's probably homemade to make it more untraceable.

But it's just a prop. If an enemy breaks the bow, it doesn't slow Robin at all. He uses the bow for the sake of appearance but can fire his arrows barehanded.

The arrows emerge directly from Robin's hands. Fire arrows. Explosive arrows. Arrows with lassos. Even a ridiculous arrow with a boxing glove on the end, for punching enemies in the nose. The public *loves* that one. When Robin is pulling a caper against the Dark, he always tries to end the fight with a Muhammad Ali knockout.

Unless Robin goes with a pie-fight arrow; he has those, too. Nothing dampens a Darkling's dignity like a coconut cream in the face.

There's every chance this fight will end with the Vandermeers wiping off pie. That's another of Robin Hood's powers: controlling the media narrative. Somewhere in the room, there'll be a flying camera drone that's filming this whole encounter. Footage will go up on YouTube within minutes . . . and it won't show Ninja Jane going apeshit with her blades or Wrecking Ball screaming obscenities. You won't see Darklings dying of wasp stings, or Lee bludgeoning Multiplier with hail. The reality of the fight is NC-17, but Robin will edit it to PG, with himself as the only star.

«Jools!» says a voice in my head. *«Is that you on the stairway?»*

It's K. No doubt, ze's Zircon now, shrunken too small to see.

«Yep, I'm on the stairs,» I reply. *«Where are you?»*

«Stuck on Lee's head,» Zircon says. *«When the wasps showed up, I shrank and hid in her hair. It seemed safe—she turned so cold, the wasps couldn't touch her. But then Robin Hood showed up and she encased herself in ice. Now I can't get out. I can't even see much outside.»*

«You mean the ice blocks your Spark-o-Vision?»

«Don't know if it's the ice,» Zirc replies, *«but I'm getting interference from something. I can only see with my actual eyes, and it sucks. My comm ring is having trouble, too—I've been trying to call you and the others, but the signal doesn't carry.»*

Zirc is right. I try quick calls to Dakini and Aria, but no response. I say, *«Maybe Robin Hood can jam transmissions. Impose silence so no one can call for help.»*

«And it affects Spark-o-Vision, too?» Zircon asks.

«Maybe.»

But I can't help thinking there might be a different reason why Zirc's Spark-o-Vision is messed up: Elaine Vandermeer and her blood bond. I don't know shit about blood bonds, but Elaine's very presence might cause distortion—like a strong magnetic field messing with the picture on an old TV screen.

I don't mention this over the comm ring. If Zircon is compromised, best not to let on I suspect. Instead, I grab a chunk of debris lying near me on the floor: the leg of a wooden chair, likely broken by Wrecking Ball. I wait for an opening, then hurl the heavy leg directly at the side of Elaine's head.

I'VE PICKED MY MOMENT well. Elaine's mother is looking in the opposite direction, so she doesn't notice what I'm doing. Elaine doesn't notice, either—she's fighting another outlaw, a guy named Sinquisitor, whose schtick is pretending to be a priest in the Spanish Inquisition. He's waving a crucifix and yelling stuff in Latin, the sort of nonsense that captures a vampire's complete attention. So Elaine doesn't see the chair leg coming.

It helps that the leg is wooden; vampire magic has trouble with wood. WikiJools tells me ash and rowan are best. The chair leg is only oak, but it's good enough. When it reaches Elaine's magic ramparts, it slows down a little but still gets through.

The chair leg hits Elaine like Colonel Mustard with the candlestick. She staggers—she's low on blood and not as resilient as when the fight began. It provides an opening for Sinquisitor; he runs up to Elaine's ramparts and heaves a handful of small silver crosses at her face.

The crosses are like shuriken: those sharp-edged throwing stars you see in kung-fu movies. They gouge Elaine and burn her undead skin. She screams for a fraction of a second, then falls to the floor.

The crosses keep smoldering where they're embedded. They aren't enough to kill her—once they've destroyed the surrounding flesh, the crosses slip out of the holes they've made and drop like sated leeches—but Elaine is definitely down for the count. She'll be a mess of cross-shaped scorch marks till someone pours a bucket of blood down her unconscious throat.

Lee howls. Sinquisitor runs like hell for the stairway. He takes several ice spikes in the back before he vanishes through the blinder wall. He has Kevlar hidden under his surplice and I think it's thick enough to prevent him getting skewered, but he'd better stay out of Lee's way from now on, or he'll end up with icicles stabbed through his eyeballs.

Lucky for me, Lee didn't notice that I was the one who threw the chair leg. She likely blames her daughter's defeat entirely on Sinquisitor. In fact, if Lee ever notices me at all, she might be inclined to protect me. I'm K's roommate, and if sparks are flying between K and Lee . . .

No. Let's not go there. I don't want to think about it.

I don't want to think about this whole damned thing. Why the hell are we fighting over Diamond's bazooka? I don't care if Robin Hood steals it. Diamond himself doesn't care! He took a look then walked away, leaving the wasps as a parting gift.

The wasps are what we should care about. Lee could freeze every wasp in the building. She could rescue Dakini and Aria, no sweat. *That's* what ought to be happening. Not this squabble over a dumb hunk of metal.

I'm tempted to turn into Ninety-Nine and bust heads, whack everyone in the face and yell, "Smarten up!" That's the superhero way. It's also the way of the hockey enforcer. I could bust loose and keep stomping ass till everyone listened.

But that's crazy. Apart from Stevens & Stephens, no one here will be easy for me to beat. All of them combined will be impossible. I'd get pounded into a pulp, and for what?

So I stay plain old Jools . . . if I can call myself that when I'm wearing a fortune in diamonds. And when I'm super-augmented with every skill known to Wikipedia. And enough Mad Genius intelligence to create underwear from slime.

Basically, I'm nothing like the Jools I was. Except for the rash stupidity of what I'm about to do.

I put my fingers in my mouth and whistle. I don't have Aria's supersonic volume, but I can whistle as loud as any human ever.

It's louder than a referee's whistle. It pierces the air like a knife.

In its wake it leaves silence: everyone in the room stops and ducks, for fear of some new attack.

I stand so everyone can see me. "Ladies, gentlemen, and bold independents! Might I have a moment of your time?"

I can yell almost as loud as I can whistle. And I set my charisma on max, whatever that means. Earlier in the day, K pointed out I can be as good as the best persuader ever. It's a terrifying thought, but what the hell, let's take my winning ways out for a spin.

In the pin-drop silence, I say, "This fight: can we all agree it's a crock of shit? Yes. I think we can. While people in the rest of the club are dying of wasp stings, we're fighting over a popgun." I start walking toward the bazooka. "Is this a sensible use of our time? Is it respectful toward the dead folks we're here to remember? Will it accomplish anything except wrecking this building? And in the end, what will decide who gets the gun? Random luck. You know I'm right. Someone will fumble or get a critical hit, and whoosh, the fight is over."

I pause. Nobody speaks. They don't try to kill me, either.

"So let's stop playing with our peepees and cut to the chase. Anybody got a coin?"

Wrecking Ball gapes. "You want a coin toss?"

"Capital idea!" Robin Hood cries. "Brilliant!"

"No way in hell," Reaper snaps.

"Oh, why not?" Lee says. "Makes more sense than fighting."

She lets her ice shell melt into rain. Well then, I've done at least one good thing. Zircon isn't trapped in the shell anymore. But before I can call Zirc on the comm ring, Calon Arang says, "A coin toss. Interesting."

Finally, she puts in an appearance. I'd wondered where Calon got to. She emerges from a pool of unnatural shadows in the back of the club. I don't know why she stayed out of the fight; maybe because she also realized it was pointless.

Calon produces a coin from her purse. She tosses it to me across the barroom's whole length. The throw is bang on; I catch the coin without having to reach.

Naturally, the coin is gold. WikiJools tells me it's a Krugerrand: a currency of choice for drug barons and others who need untraceable bullion. What does it say that Calon carries Krugerrands on her person? Probably just that she's a Darkling.

I say, "And the coin is fair? No magic that makes it come up heads every time?"

"Please, Jools," Calon says. "Don't be insulting."

"That's not an answer."

Calon glares at me. "It's fair. One hundred percent."

I don't know if I believe her, but I also don't know how I'd tell one way or the other. I look around the room with a glare almost as steely as Calon's. "No magic from anyone, right? And no superpowers. No telekinesis, no tinkering with Fate, no nudging the gravitational constant to make the coin spin the way you want. Everybody clear?"

Surly mumbles all around.

"Okay," I say. "Winner gets the gun." I point at Robin Hood. "Call it in the air."

I balance the coin on my thumbnail, and flip.

I WATCH THE COIN carefully as it spins. I'm so focused, I barely hear Robin yell, "Heads! I pick heads!" (As if he'd pick anything else.) I'm watching for the slightest wobble suggesting unnatural interference.

I see nothing suspicious. I catch the coin on the back of my wrist and slap my other hand to cover it.

Everyone in the room leans in toward me.

I look. I say, "Tails. Sorry, Robin."

I REALLY DON'T KNOW if the coin toss was clean. I didn't see any hanky-panky, but that don't prove squat. Still, it looks like Robin and his gang just lost fair and square.

Whispers explode behind me, the mind-fucking apophenia of Ninja Jane when she fights. I don't have eyes in the back of my head, but who needs them? I can guess crazy Jane is displeased by the coin-toss results.

So I throw myself to the floor. My reflexes are as fast as an Olympic fencer's, but I still feel the wind from a dagger as it whips a millimeter above my head. If my hair were as long as Miranda's, the knife would have cut off my updo.

An instant later, the knife takes on a mind of its own. I don't know who's responsible, but the blade does a U-turn just after it misses me and flies off toward Wrecking Ball. Wrecking Ball is too slow to get out of the way. She only just manages to twist her head away, so that the dagger slams into her cheek instead of her eye.

Wrecking Ball's cheek is iron. A normal blade would surely bounce off. But Ninja Jane's knife stabs deep into Wrecking Ball's face, spilling rusty orange blood from the wound.

Wrecking Ball goes ballistic. She roars as she rips the dagger from her flesh, then charges straight for the bazooka.

Oh, well. I tried. For one glorious moment, it looked like this would all end peacefully. I thought I could be the hero: as Grandfather put it, one of Waterloo's official babysitters who'd tuck everyone safely in for the night.

Stupid Jools. You can be best in the world, and still be a fuckup. Not even superpowers can make a silk purse from a drunken sow's asshole.

Abruptly, things turn just as bad as before. Maybe worse. Lee hurls ice at Wrecking Ball. Robin shoots arrows at Lee. Wraith casts hexes at Robin. Reaper and Jane go at it again, cuz lame don't change its game.

Fucktastic.

Once again, I'm tempted to bury my foot in some crotches. That would be the easy way. Turn into Ninety-Nine and burn off frustration. I could grab Reaper with one hand, Robin Hood with the other, and hold them face-to-face as I said, "You two work this out, or I will work it out *for* you."

Yeah. That'll work. I'm an Olympic-class diplomat, Olympic-class fighter, and Olympic-class peacekeeper. No problem at all knowing when to be which.

«*Screw this,*» I say mentally to Zircon, «*I'm leaving. Call me at home when it's over.*»

Zirc doesn't reply. Maybe there's too much interference on the comms. Or maybe ze doesn't have anything to say.

I take a disgusted step toward the stairs. Calon Arang snaps her fingers and says a word.

IT'S NOT A HUMAN word—WikiJools knows every human language, but draws a blank. Besides, no human vocal apparatus could produce the sounds Calon makes. Some syllables are like blades scraping on bone. Others are hisses or just jumbles of noise. Even the parts of the word that a human could pronounce are guttural agglomerations. But somehow I know that it's still a single word, although it takes several seconds to say.

I also know it's an *awful* word. The sort that opens doors that ought to stay closed.

When the word is finished, I turn back from the stairs. At least my body does. There's still a me inside who sees and thinks clearly, but Jools isn't the driver anymore. I'm strapped in the passenger seat, or maybe locked in the trunk.

My body begins to walk. I try to stop it, but no dice. My muscles have disconnected from my brain. I try to use my comm ring: «*Zirc, can you hear me?*» No answer. Radio silence.

This is going to be bad.

I suckered myself into thinking Calon Arang wasn't evil. Oh, sure, she's an Elder of the Dark, but that just means she's smart and shrewd. As if smart and shrewd guarantees benevolence.

At least, whatever happens, Calon will break K's blood bond. Right? Except who's gonna force Calon to keep her promise? Nobody even knows about our deal. And even if someone did, who's got the strength to hold an Elder's feet to the fire?

I walk through the middle of the fight. No one attacks me.

Why bother? I'm just a mortal in shredded stockings and a dress that used to be nice but now is tattered and dirty as hell from the crap I've gone through. Nobody even looks in my direction. Maybe Calon has used an ignorance spell to make me dismissible.

So I cross the room like some Jedi crossing a battlefield where blasts sizzle through the air but always miss. It takes me by surprise when I abruptly crouch behind an upturned table. I'm still Calon's puppet, but I've reached a turning point: in position for Phase 2.

Robin Hood is to my right, and Lee to my left. Lee sends a wall of sleet in Robin's direction. He produces an arrow of flame and nocks it on his bow. The arrow is bigger than anything I've ever seen him use. Perhaps he's been holding back, but now he's decided to escalate. Lee has proved she's tough, so Robin is free to use his heaviest attacks.

He draws back his bow. My muscles tense, ready to leap into his line of fire. Damn, piss, and fuck, I understand now. If Robin kills an innocent human, even in the chaos of a firefight, his reputation will be tarnished. This isn't even a noble cause—he's trying to steal a terrible weapon. The Dark can spin this into a PR nightmare. Robin is about to prove he's willing to kill a harmless girl, just to get his hands on a horrible gun.

Everything leading up to this makes it worse. I tried to arrange a truce. I showed the world I'm a mensch. Considering how I pumped up my charisma, I'll come across great on TV.

Cuz Robin isn't the only one who's filming this fight. Calon will be, too. Maybe she's even broadcasting it live. She wants the world to witness my terrible fate.

My body moves without my control. I rise and place myself between Robin and Lee, my arms outspread, as if I'm protecting Lee from what Robin will shoot at her.

Robin draws back his bow. Yes, I definitely must be hidden by an ignorance spell; it prevents him from noticing me, even though I'm standing right here. But I'll bet the spell won't affect the TV cameras. Someone watching this scene will see clear as day that Robin Hood intends to shoot me with a giant flaming arrow.

At the last instant, he smiles.

The fireball comes straight at me. Halfway along its path, a figure pops out of nowhere to intercept. Zircon zooms from microscopic to a size big enough to block the arrow. Since Zirc is literally made of stone, the arrow does far less damage to zir than it would to me. Still, the impact explodes into a fireball that knocks Zirc out of the air. Ze plummets like a meteor, smacking hard on the floor.

I want to dash forward to see if Zirc's all right. But I still can't control my body. Besides, I don't have the time. There's only a fraction of a second between when Zirc blocks the flame arrow from hitting me and when . . .

. . . I explode in a fireball anyway.

THAT STUPID DRESS FROM Calon Arang. I thought it was just a gown, but it's a suicide vest. If all else failed, Calon wanted to make 100 percent sure I died at Robin Hood's hands.

Zircon's sacrifice meant nothing. I saw it because I was right up close and because my perceptions are fast. From other perspectives—especially from the cameras Calon must have set up at just the perfect angle to capture this the way Calon wants—I'm sure all you'll see is a bloom of fire, then a girl engulfed in flames.

Me. Burning. Jesus.

I can smell my flesh as it bakes. I hear the hiss of me frying.

My perceptions are fast.

First extreme heat. Then extreme cold, as my cremated nerves go dead.

Fade far too slowly to black.

10

Pupation

I WAKE.

Well, that's a surprise.

And it's not a groggy completely-out-of-it awakening. One moment, I'm in nothing-nothing-land. The next, I'm fully conscious, though I can't see or hear. I'm floating on my back in goopy fluid, but I barely feel it: it's the same temperature I am and soft on my skin.

I'm not moving—not even breathing. The fluid covers my face. I can feel my heart pumping, but no movement anywhere else. When I try to wiggle a finger, nothing happens. I'm not frozen, I'm just limp.

But I'm alive. So there's that.

This isn't my first resurrection. Since becoming a Spark, I've gone down hard several times. Injuries on the edge of being lethal, maybe even *over* the edge. And each of those times, I came back with a lurch into the light, like leaping out of the penalty box the instant the clock runs down.

This time . . . no light. I don't want to think what that means.

My sister Jamie is a good Catholic girl. She believes in the classic heaven and hell. Sistine Chapel stuff—clouds and rainbows in one direction, fire and brimstone in the other.

My sister Jen is Catholic, too, but more progressive. Heaven is connection with God; hell is separation. It's a self-chosen thing: if you want to be stubborn and proud, you'll suffer, but it's still your choice. It hurts when you choose to wall yourself off. God will wait till you change your mind.

My sister Jill refuses to label herself, but says she believes in rebirth. No heaven, no hell, just a trip to the memory-eraser. Then out again for another kick at the can.

And finally, sister Jo is a militant atheist. She was a dick this past Christmas, going out of her way to pick fights. She demanded I tell her what exactly I believe, and was quick to put words in my mouth.

Before I became a Spark, I didn't know what to believe. My four older sisters said four different things, and I was just, "Why do I have to decide?" But now that I'm the world's best authority on everything, I've got a thousand religions in my head. They're all going at it with each other: the Vatican's best theologians, Hindu swamis, Taoist sages, and shamans galore.

You want to argue points of the Talmud? I'm your girl. You want to navigate the niceties of Santería, candomblé, Obeah, and all their cousins? Just say the word. I've got the Mormon president on speed dial, plus a couple of ayatollahs.

I'm up to the gills in conflicting narratives. But do any of them apply, now that I'm a Spark? For superheroes, death is a colander. Sparks always leak back eventually.

Hope it happens soon. I may not be able to see or hear, but I hurt like a son of a bitch. That exploding dress literally blew off my tits.

Fucking Calon Arang. She set me up.

She hooked me with a spell that co-opted my body and positioned me so Robin Hood would shoot me. Then the dress blew me to shreds, making Robin look like a killer.

Shit. I died for that?

No. I died to save K from the blood bond. If Calon frees K, then burning my snoobies will be worth it.

But I'mma kick Calon's ass when I'm back in the land of the living.

TIME PASSES. I ACHE. Then the goop that surrounds me begins to seep away. I still can't make myself move, but my lungs start breathing on their own. As the fluid level subsides, I settle downward, ending up with my back on a cushioned surface.

A crack of light appears above me. A soft female voice says, "You'll want to close your eyes. You'll find it bright until your vision adjusts."

The woman has an English accent: Received Pronunciation, like Calon Arang's. The softness in her tone is like somebody speaking to a child—gentle and warm, but also a bit fake. It makes me want to keep my eyes open, just to be contrary. But as the crack of light widens, my retinas feel like they're being smashed with hammers.

Grudgingly, I shut my eyelids. Even with my eyes closed tight, the reddish brightness hurts.

"What's going on?" I croak. My throat feels raw. Cold air settles down on me. Oh, crap, I'm naked.

"You were seriously injured," says the woman. She's standing close above me. "To be honest, I'm surprised you survived. I was certain you were dead. But Robin persuaded Friar Tuck to transport you here anyway."

"Where is here?" I ask through my raspy throat.

"The sick bay of Sherwood Forest. For the last fifty minutes, you've been in a medi-tank. I thought you'd be in there for hours or days, but apparently, you weren't as badly wounded as I thought."

The woman slips her arm under my shoulders and helps me sit up. Her arm is much cooler than I am . . . or perhaps I'm much hotter than normal. That makes sense: a medi-tank must be a machine that accelerates healing, and one way to do that would be by increasing my metabolic rate.

"I'll get you clothes in a jiffy," the woman tells me. "But first I want to check that you're fully recovered."

I force my eyes open a crack. The light still hurts, but hell, if I can survive getting blown up, I can tolerate a little eyestrain. Besides, my eyes adjust within seconds. They focus and let me see a fiftyish woman examining my stomach with a magnifying glass.

She's big. Close to three hundred pounds, even though she's considerably shorter than me. Her face has a million freckles, and her plain brown hair . . . it's like she invented a hair-cutting machine, then couldn't decide how to program it. Eventually, she went with default settings: medium length, straight, and shapeless. She wears safety goggles, the kind we all had to buy for Chemistry 120. But somehow I know they aren't really for safety; they're actually this woman's version of a mask.

Cuz she's a Spark. I can feel her Halo working on me. It soothes me, making me want to talk in the same soft voice the woman uses herself. A nursery-room voice, reassuring and slightly removed from reality. *You're safe now, Nanny will protect you.*

The woman wears an unbuttoned white lab coat. Underneath is an orange muumuu, embroidered with a multicolor pattern around the bodice. It's the dress a woman might wear around the house when she wants to be comfortable and isn't expecting anyone to drop by. Also when she doesn't give a fuck who sees her. Just to complete the effect, she's wearing orange rubber flip-flops. But of course, the lab coat, muumuu, and flip-flops are really a costume: the woman's Spark identity. In civilian ID, she probably wears jeans or yoga pants just like anyone else.

I'm guessing she's Maid Marian. I have no mental picture of Marian—Robin Hood and his gang often mention her in their videos, but she never makes appearances on-screen. Clearly, she likes to be cautious . . . as evidenced by the fact that she's hiding her true identity from me, even here in Robin Hood's stronghold.

"Maid Marian?" I ask.

"Just call me Marian," she says. "I'm nobody's maid."

I ask, "Did your crew get the bazooka?"

She finally looks up from examining me. She shakes her head. "When you got hurt, Robin called for an immediate retreat. He's quite upset about what happened. I had Wrecking Ball drag him away a few minutes ago, so I could open your medi-tank in peace. Otherwise, he'd be falling all over you to say he's sorry."

That would be awkward. I can fantasize scenarios where I wouldn't mind Robin seeing me naked, but not when I'm covered with goo and lying in a hospital bed.

Of course, it's not a bed at all. It's an immersion tank raised off the floor to Marian's waist height. It's like a bathtub with a lid and exotic built-in gadgets. Nozzles and arms and needle-tipped cables sprout from the bathtub's walls. No doubt while I lay unconscious, I was injected, debrided, and heaven knows what else. My skin feels sticky; the goo that I lay in must have been designed to heal my crispy singed flesh.

I wonder how much healing was necessary. Would my powers have healed me without the tank's help? Or did the tank keep me alive through something I wouldn't have survived?

One thing for sure: the tank has preserved my secret identity. Marian will think my recovery is due to her wondrous invention, not to my miraculous regenerative abilities. Marian has no reason to suspect I'm a Spark.

Then again, Marian says, "I must be smarter than I thought." She straightens up and sets aside her magnifying glass. "You don't even have scars. My most recent improvements to the tank turned out better than expected."

"Well, thanks then," I say.

I look down and see I'm completely intact. Undamaged Jools wherever I look.

Uh, wait. My tattoos are gone. Shit, I paid good money for those: two sleeves from my shoulders to my elbows! Dozens of beautiful plants and animals . . . wiped out completely, like a mass extinction.

I'm missing my hair extensions, too. And my nail polish: the pretty little birds Miranda painted.

I must have lost *all* my makeup. It saves me the trouble of washing off the gunk I slathered on for the party, but wearing no makeup at all . . . well, fine, since becoming a Spark I don't look too bad without makeup, but it's still not how I'd choose to meet new people.

Especially somebody hot like Robin Hood. He's hanging around here somewhere, right?

Oh, fuck, something else is missing: my slimewear. No cnidarian undies. The explosion must have vaporized both halves of the bikini. Either that or the medi-tank purged them, just like it blotted away my ink. Whatever the cause, my jellyfish are gone. So is my Ninety-Nine costume. On top of that . . .

I blurt out, "Where's my ring?" I wave my bare hand. Belatedly I add, "And my earrings and all. They were, uhh, keepsakes from my mother."

"Uh, well, Ninja Jane took them," Marian says.

"She *took* them?" I think about how tightly the ring clung to my finger. Then I think about Ninja Jane's knives.

Marian looks uncomfortable. "Look, you can't be wearing anything in the tank. Otherwise, it throws off the calibration." Marian turns away quickly, as if embarrassed. "I'll see what I can do about your jewelry. Jane likes to take pretty things and stash them in secret hideaways. But Robin can usually persuade her to give them back. He just has to catch her in a good mood."

Awesome. Insane-o Jane stole my comm ring. I can imagine her putting it on and admiring it. Next thing you know, it reshapes itself and screams, "Hey, I'm Cape Tech!" Or one of my friends says, «*Ninety-Nine, is that you?*»

I groan at the thought. Marian says, "What?" She lays a hand on my shoulder and stares keenly into my eyes. "Does something hurt?" She steps back and worriedly looks me up and down. "The healing process is as safe as I can make it, but Cape Tech is always an adventure. Nine times out of ten, it's brilliant—works better than you could hope. But the tenth time . . . have you seen that movie *The Fly*?"

"I'm fine," I say, pulling away from her. "And I'm not turning into a fly. I just . . . the truth of what happened is starting to sink in."

"Yes, of course," Marian says in her soft soothing voice. "I'm sure it's a lot to handle."

"Yeah," I say. I take a deep breath, then hold out my hand. "Hi. I'm Jools."

This isn't the first time I've been completely naked before I got around to introducing myself. But it's the first time I've only shaken hands.

MARIAN HELPS ME OUT of the medi-tank. My legs are wobbly, my throat still hurts, and my skin feels scoured too hard by a loofah. But I'm a fuck of a lot better than most people who slow-dance with a fireball.

As I try to stand upright, I peer at my surroundings. Marian called this the sick bay of Sherwood Forest. It's actually a curtained-off area four paces long and the same distance wide, like the space around a bed in a hospital ward. The bed, of course, is the medi-tank. There's nothing else nearby except a metal chair with a green padded back and seat, much like the chairs at our town house's kitchen table. It's the sort of chair where anxious friends or family might sit while waiting for a loved one to come out of the tank.

Marian sweeps aside the curtain to reveal the rest of the room. It's a lab the size of a basketball court, with twenty-some lab desks and tables, mostly covered by half-assembled machinery. By reputation, Maid Marian specializes in robotics, and that certainly seems to be true—I see numerous prototypes scattered around. Robotic arms with weapons instead of hands. Mobility devices: legs and wheels and tank treads. Artificial eyes. Power supplies of all kinds; I recognize batteries, fuel cells, photovoltaics, and Mr. Fusions, but there are unfamiliar others I immediately want to dissect.

Or maybe I should start by dissecting the guns. Weapons of all kinds, actually: energy blades and things that go *boom*, in addition to all the handheld firearms that shoot deadly things. The weapons sit shiny and new on workbenches or are clamped in vices as they await completion. Ammunition lies strewn about—not just conventional rockets and bullets, but loading-packs filled with toxic chemicals or alien microbes. (I know what the packs contain because some of them are labeled. Others aren't. Russian roulette must be even more fun when you don't know what the pistol will shoot. Ice? Gamma rays? Acid? Or a stream of plasma as hot as the heart of the sun?)

Maid Marian clearly spends a lot of her time devising new means of murder. Utterly typical of Mad Geniuses: not only do they build medi-tanks, they come up with a thousand new ways to make you need one.

Yet Marian looks nothing like a homicidal maniac. More like someone who works at a health clinic: the woman who asks, "Do you smoke?" and takes your weight before the actual doctor comes in. Or maybe I just get that impression because she's inspecting me again. Circling around to check me out, front and back. "You've really recovered brilliantly," she says. "Just look at your abs! When we first brought you in . . . no, shan't go into details, you'd get upset. But it was bad, very bad." She stares for a moment longer, then looks away. "Sorry, don't want to embarrass you. But I have to ask: Did you have those muscles before, or did the medi-tank give them to you?"

I say, "You invented the tank, but you don't know what it can do?"

"Exactly so," Marian says with a sheepish laugh. "A fact of life for Spark inventors. The whole is so often greater than the sum of its parts." She smiles and focuses back on my body again. "So. About your muscles?"

"One hundred percent earned," I reply. "Crunches and clean living."

This is not the time to discuss how becoming a Spark tightened and toned me. This *is* the time to feel awkward for standing around like the Venus de Milo while Marian admires my sculpting. Her Halo has that soothing *Don't worry* effect, but this is still a bit weird.

My feelings must show because Marian steps back and turns

her eyes away. "I said I would get you clothes, didn't I? And you probably want to shower—the fluids in the medi-tank have likely made you feel gummy."

"Kind of," I agree.

She *tsks* her tongue. "No matter how I improve the tank, I can't make that go away." Marian makes a face. "You'd think it would be easy. Compared to repairing damaged organs, doing a final rinse-off should be a piece of piss. But the Light refuses to play along." Her face takes on a thoughtful expression. "Perhaps it's symbolic. The Light will deliver miracles, but always with some niggling imperfection. An Achilles heel. Or a recognizable motif that's always present no matter how hard you try to avoid it."

She stops and looks embarrassed. "Or like the tendency for Sparks to soliloquize. Sorry." Marian points to a corner of the lab. "The shower is over yonder. I'll go find you something to wear."

She takes two steps toward a door marked EX T. (The I has been obliterated. In a lab where you make superweapons, I guess that happens.) Then Marian stops and turns back. "Please just shower, all right? Don't touch anything while I'm gone." She waves her hand vaguely around the room. "Dozens of things here could kill you so badly the tank would never bring you back. Neither of us wants that."

Marian smiles apologetically, then leaves.

I HEAD FOR THE shower. It's not the sort you see in normal bathrooms; it's the type you install in a lab where you may need to drench yourself in a hurry because you're covered with hydrochloric acid. There's only one tap to turn on and I'm certain the water is icy cold. That's what you want when your lab coat is smoking, since low temperatures slow down chemical reactions.

But oh, this is gonna hurt.

I consider not showering at all; freezing my delicate lady parts may be worse than feeling gooey. But when I think of the gloop the tank left on my skin, I can't help but worry. I was soaking in Mad Genius fluids that never went through medical trials or even casual safety tests. Like all Cape Tech gizmos, the medi-tank is a work in progress, probably whipped up impromptu to deal with some emergency, then sporadically toyed with thereafter.

Showering in frigid water is the lesser of two evils. Besides, I'm a tough-ass superhero. I should be able to stand . . .

Fuck, fuck, fuck, that's cold! Splash, wipe, one sweep of my hands to spread water everywhere, then I turn off the tap so hard I might have damaged it.

Good thing I don't possess actual super-strength. Otherwise, I might have ripped the plumbing out of the wall.

And oh, look, there's no towel. Just a roll of rough brown paper that's less absorbent than my butt. This is exactly what you want if you're dealing with a chemical spill, since a real towel would get damaged. But paper is damned useless for drying off quickly when you're dying from a case of the shivers. My hair is also a mess, and there's no shampoo. But who cares? Even if there *was* shampoo, there's no fucking way I'd go under that water again.

I truly feel as if I'll expire of hypothermia. What I need is—

Now I'm warm. Things went blank there for a second.

Maybe longer than a second. Cuz now I'm halfway across the lab, and standing in front of a workbench where I've cobbled together a heater from random parts.

My hair is clean and dry. It smells like peaches.

No, *all* of me smells like peaches. I must have mixed a shampoo and body wash from random chemicals lying around. Which is worrisome, since pretty much all the chemicals I've seen here are either toxic or incendiary.

But I feel fine. I smell *great*.

Sniff

Everywhere.

Note to self: start a bath-and-beauty store.

Additional note to self: you're an idiot. You should never have a Mad Genius blackout in enemy territory, especially when you're trying to pretend you're human.

I sprint back to the shower before Marian returns. I debate

forcing myself under the water again—being peachy clean and dry is hella suspicious. But getting wet again could do the same as before: another hypothermal blackout, whereupon I might get caught making something even weirder.

Better to cross my fingers and hope Marian doesn't notice. Just because she's a genius doesn't mean she's *observant*, right? Plenty of bright people go through life completely oblivious.

I point no fingers.

I'm barely back in position before Marian returns. She takes no special notice of how I look or smell. She just hands me a bright-red outfit that's very Men in Tights: red jacket, red shirt, red leggings, red leather buskins.

There's a codpiece. A very noticeable codpiece.

I say, "There's a codpiece. A very noticeable codpiece."

"Yeeessss," Marian says in a tone that's only making a token effort to be apologetic. "I made this for Multiplier when he first joined our band. Robin wanted him to be Will Scarlet, but it never really clicked. By tradition, Will Scarlet was the best swordsman in Sherwood; Multiplier was just *dreadful* with a sword. Terrible archer, too. So we set the costume aside. That's why it's available now."

Marian pushes the outfit toward me. "It's more or less your size, and it adjusts. Its fabric can stretch or tighten more than an inch in any direction."

I say, "It has a codpiece."

"Yes, I know," Marian replies. "But the outfit is tougher than Kevlar, resistant to caustic chemicals, and insulated enough to keep you alive at forty degrees below zero. If you'd been wearing this when Robin's flame arrow hit you . . . well, the shirt doesn't cover everything, but you wouldn't have ended up with burned intestines spilling on the floor.

"And," Marian adds, "if you don't like this costume, the alternative is wearing some of *my* clothes. Unless you'd prefer borrowing something from Wrecking Ball? Or Ninja Jane?"

"You make a compelling argument," I say. Besides, I'd like to

examine a costume that's so resilient to damage. It resembles ordinary cloth and leather—not bulky like the bulletproof suits you
see on TV. If I put on these duds, I can look them over real carefully as soon as Marian gives me a minute . . . the only price being that the red fabric makes me look like the next person to die
on *Star Trek*.

No underwear, but whatever—ending up without undies after
a party is the story of my life. I worry about chafing, but slipping
into the clothes, I find them amazingly comfortable. As Marian
said, they reshape to fit: a little more in the hips, a little less across
the shoulders.

There's a deep V down the front, which I guess must have been
intended to show Multiplier's manly chest hair. On me the V
shows my cleavage, such as it is . . . but as the outfit continues to
reshape, it provides some moderate push-up action.

Really? *Really?*

Did Marian design the shirt to work like this on Multiplier?
Why? But if Marian has blackouts like I do, she made this outfit
while lost in the throes of creation. Instead of thinking about
Multiplier or anyone else, Marian just invented a generic super-
athleisure wardrobe, adaptable for male, female, or off the axis.

Except for the codpiece. The rest of the clothes adapt to my
body, but the codpiece doesn't go away. I rap on it with my knuckles. It's hard. Armored. Well, okay, I won't object to extra armor
down there. But it feels weird.

I try a few kicks; the bulge doesn't get in the way. And hey, if
my skill set includes the absolute peaks of human accomplishment, I must be a wiz at working around certain lovely but
ridiculous bits of anatomy.

So I opt for denial. *La-la-la*, the bulge isn't really there.

La-la-la.

La.

There, I'm good. Tucked up, tucked in, and tucked down.

Marian looks me over and says, "You're a picture. Now come
with me; Robin wants to meet you."

She heads for the door. I don't. I say, "Wait."

Marian turns back. "Yes?"

"Where's this going?" I ask. "I mean, don't get me wrong, I'm grateful you saved me from joining the choir invisible. But you folks are outlaws, right? And the Darklings have a hard-on to throw you in jail. The more I see, the deeper I'm in, aren't I? As in *I can never go home again*."

Marian waves away my words. "Don't worry, I have a widget to erase your memory. Whatever happens while you're here, you won't remember after you go."

"Will the Darklings believe that?" I ask. "Or will they work me over with enchantments that rip up my brain?"

"I'm sure they realize it's pointless," Marian says. "Robin entertains many overnight guests. I always wipe their memories before they leave. No doubt, the Dark tried to interrogate our first few visitors. Maybe the first several dozen. But by now, they must have come to accept they'll never obtain useful information."

She says it like it's no big deal. As if the Dark have truly given up, and don't browbeat every "overnight guest" in the hope that this time the brain-wipe missed a scrap of useful data. Even if Marian is right and the Dark don't bother anymore, what about the ones who got tortured before the Darklings decided it was a waste of effort?

But I don't say any of that. Instead, I demand, "Does Robin consider *me* an overnight guest?"

Marian shrugs. "You're our guest. And I imagine you'll stay several hours. Or days."

"With Robin?" I ask.

She shrugs again. "Probably."

"What if I don't want to?"

"Then don't," Marian says. "But you will."

She turns away and goes to the laboratory's door. She holds it open for me.

I'm tempted to tell her and Robin to jointly fuck off. Sure, he's cute, but I refuse to be taken for granted: number 3,057 in an endless parade of bimbos. Brought in for a bounce, then brain-washed and sent on my way. I mean, shit, I'm all for meaningless one-night stands, but they ought to be win-win, not win-and-don't-remember-losing.

On the other hand, what happens if I say, "Go to hell"? The best-case scenario is that Friar Tuck whistles up his teleporting horse and tells it to take me home. But only after I get sent through the memory laundromat.

No way. This is my first time inside a Spark's secret base; whether or not I remember, I want to see what it's like. Otherwise, this will be like getting up to the door of some awesome location like NASA Mission Control, then saying, "Nah, I'm not in the mood."

So I plod along behind Maid Marian as she leads me out into Sherwood Forest.

11

Courtship Display

WE EMERGE FROM THE lab building. When seen from the outside, it resembles a medieval hunting lodge: flagstone walls and a thickly thatched roof. It's much larger than such lodges actually were. It's even much larger than the lab room I saw—the building extends far enough to contain a dozen labs of equal size.

But forget the building. What grabs my attention is Sherwood Forest.

It really is a forest. Giant oaks cast their shadows over the front of the laboratory. Unseen birds chirp and chitter in the canopy. Four dirt paths lead away beneath the trees, weaving through the kind of underbrush you might see in parts of the *real* Sherwood Forest.

But this *can't* be the real one. It's too bright and sunny, and it smells of warm summer green. England's winters may be milder than Ontario's, but still—in January, the real Sherwood Forest should at least be frosted over. And even if the actual forest experienced a fluky heat surge, oak trees wouldn't have all their leaves and the brush wouldn't grow in such abundance.

Besides, Marian said I was only in the medi-tank for fifty minutes. I don't know how long I blacked out for in the lab, but adding everything up, it can't be later than midnight, Waterloo time. Five in the morning in England. But the sun here shines brightly almost directly overhead. That puts us on a line of longitude somewhere around Beijing . . . but farther south, since Beijing is shivering its toes in deep winter, too.

So we're in the tropics or the southern hemisphere. The

Philippines, Indonesia, Australia, or one of those famous uncharted islands that don't really exist.

"I give up," I say to Marian. "Where are we?"

"Sherwood Forest," she replies with a smile.

"Can't be the one in England," I say. "Not where it's January, and five A.M., Greenwich time."

"Very good, Jools," Marian says. "But it's still Sherwood Forest."

"Time travel?" I ask. "Or some alternate universe?" If Marian is a Mad Genius, she could totally build a gate to, let's say, Sherwood Forest a million years ago, during some toasty time between ice ages. That would explain why no one has ever found Robin's base.

Marian says, "No, we're still in the present, and still in our own home dimension. I've tinkered with going elsewhere, but it just causes headaches. Time paradoxes, for example—that whole kill-a-butterfly-bring-on-a-nuclear-war scenario is no joke. Took us *ages* to set that right. And alternate realities are worse: alien invasions, worlds overrun by zombies, places where Satan won the war with heaven . . . no thanks!"

"So if we're still on our Earth," I say, "where are we?"

Marian smiles again. "It's a secret."

"So what? You're going to erase my memory."

"Better safe than sorry," Marian says. Before I can protest, she takes my arm. "Come now, Jools. Robin's waiting."

WE WALK THROUGH SHERWOOD Forest. Botany has never been my bud—I rank the kingdoms starting with Animalia, then Protista, Archaea, Bacteria, Fungi, and finally Plantae hanging off the bottom like toilet paper on Linnaeus's shoe. But now I recognize every damned species that flutters its fronds in my face. That's why I realize this forest's carpet doesn't match the drapes.

Oak trees are rank bastards; they don't play well with others. Their leaves contain a whopping amount of tannic acid, so when the leaves fall in autumn, they rot and poison the dirt. The oaks themselves don't mind acidic soil, but most other plants can't handle it. Result: either an absence of undergrowth or a preponderance of plant species with high acid tolerance.

But *this* Sherwood Forest is different. The ground cover varies too much. I see mosses and holly, mushrooms and lilies, ivy and jack-in-the-pulpits. It's all very pretty and woodsy, but wrong. Ninety percent of the species I pass couldn't survive in a full-grown oak forest.

So Sherwood has to be fake. At the very least, someone has worked their ass off, planting things that normally wouldn't thrive and mitigating the acid in the soil. More likely, Marian used Cape Tech to make these plants grow despite their innate characteristics. Cape Tech can do that—there's a loony German dude who calls himself Baumfuhrer, and every now and then he gets mad at some city and turns it into a jungle. Last year, he Guatemala'ed Gdansk in less than a day, with giant trees sprouting in the middle of streets, inside buildings, and half a mile out to sea. He made the city look like a Mayan ruin, completely enveloped by rainforest.

Maybe Baumfuhrer produced Sherwood as a favor to Robin Hood. Baummie Boy is an outlaw himself; he'd love providing a gang with suitable surroundings. Or Marian might have concocted the forest on her own. Anything that a Spark can do, a Mad Genius can usually replicate with enough time and money.

I say none of this aloud. Marian may not be the kind of Mad Genius who screams, "Bow down, peasant!" and talks about herself in the third person. But we call them *Mad* Geniuses for a reason. Marian might get miffed if I say, "Nice fake forest, dude."

Besides, I've noticed a glitch in the gestalt: a total lack of animals. No squirrels. No ants. And despite the abundant tweeting, no actual birds. The trees must have hidden speakers that broadcast birdsong.

I approve of the notion. Without any twitters and chitters, these woods would be eerie. Not Merrie Olde England, but Creepy McCreepPlace.

Still, I wonder why there *aren't* any animals. If we're really in the present day on normal old Earth, how could there *not* be animals? There should at least be insects.

Unless something killed them all.

Don't want to think about that. Instead, let's strike up conversation with Marian. She's ahead of me, leading the way. We're following a trail too narrow for us to walk side by side. I say, "So how did you get your powers?"

Without turning, she says, "Why do you think I have powers?"

"Because you invented that medi-tank," I reply. "Definitely Cape Tech. If people could make it with ordinary technology, you'd mass-produce it and become the richest gazillionaire in the world."

"True." She sighs. "I've tried to make more than just one, but I just can't get motivated. I dawdle around the lab till I think of something different I could build. Then *boom*, I'm off and running on that, instead of a second medi-tank. Mind you, when I think of a way to improve the tank I've got, it's full speed ahead."

She stops and turns. "Can you imagine what that's like? Having the know-how to make a machine that can save people's lives, but only being able to do it once? It makes me lose sleep. I lie awake at night, imagining all the dead people who might have been saved if I could force myself to concentrate."

"That's not how it works," I say, even though she must know already. "Remember when Myoblast tried to generate electricity with that super treadmill? He passed out after a few minutes, and when he woke, he'd lost all his powers. The Light refuses to be used that way."

Marian looks at me curiously. "You remember Myoblast? Not many people do. History swept him under the rug. Are you one of those people with a thing for Sparks?"

"No," I say, "I just . . . I have a head for trivia. Pub quizzes, stuff like that. Gives me an excuse to hang around in bars."

Marian's gaze gets more piercing. Then she turns her back and starts walking again. "You asked about my powers," she says. "In a way, I resent them. Some people think the only reason I can invent things is because I became super. But I've always been an excellent engineer. I earned my Ph.D. from . . . I'd better not say, but one of the best universities in the world. I earned a research position in a leading robotics firm."

"So what happened?" I ask.

"Have you ever heard of Byte Bitch?" Marian asks.

"Sure," I say. "A supervillain. A punk Mad Genius who loved to make creepy-looking robots. She had a mohawk haircut, piercings everywhere. Blathered about 'music of mass destruction.' She was only around for a month or two, then disappeared. No one knows why."

"Actually, *I* know why she disappeared," Marian says, "but you're correct about everything else. Byte Bitch was quite the throwback to Sid and Nancy. I assume she grew up in the punk-rock era, even though she looked as young as you are, Jools." Marian sighs. "Some people get younger when they're taken by the Light. Others . . ."

Marian picks a piece of leaf litter off her lab coat. She looks at the leaf in disgust, then flicks it away.

"I was talking about Byte Bitch," Marian says. "One night she broke into the lab where I worked. She wanted to use our equipment and steal some components. So she zapped my lab mate and me with a taser, then tied us up and dumped us in a corner. She went to work building God knows what—some kind of weapon, I think. Several hours later, Tuxedo Rex came bursting in. I have no idea how he knew she was there, but he immediately started thrashing her. They had an *enormous* fight that ruined our lab . . . but eventually the dinosaur threw Byte Bitch into the weapon she'd been building. She literally exploded. Burst into multicolored sparks. I got showered with the sparks, and *ta-da*, that was my origin."

"Sparks, eh?" I don't say it, but I know all about sparks and getting superpowers. "Let me guess. Your lab mate got Sparked up, too. He's now Robin Hood."

Marian glances back over her shoulder at me. "When it's time to erase your memory, I'll have to send you through the wash twice." She gives a rueful smile. "But that gives me the luxury of being honest. Yes, my lab mate transformed into Robin."

"Transformed?" I say. "What was he originally like?"

"Ordinary," Marian says, "like me. A man you could sit beside on the tube and never give him a second glance. He lived alone with his cat, did seven crossword puzzles a day, and never hurt a fly. But then he got superpowers, and . . ." She sighs. "You know how some people become Sparks and turn into berserkers? Eight feet tall, astronomically strong, and a totally different personality? My lab mate's change was equally extreme. Other people believe it was a vast improvement, but—"

Robin Hood swings out of the trees, holding onto a vine.

This isn't the kind of forest where trees have vines; however, for Robin they'll make an exception. He lets go with perfect timing and lands at our feet in a low courtly bow. He sweeps off his hat, bends his knee, and gestures his hand in a move that seems simultaneously deferential, tongue-in-cheek, and sexy.

Oh so sexy.

Under his hat, his hair is a mass of natural ringlets. My fingers *ache* to run through those curls. Preferably while he's on his knees in front of me, with neither of us wearing a stitch.

I tell myself these fantasies aren't my own. They're imposed by his Halo as it plays me like a self-juicing violin. But who am I kidding? I don't need a whack from a Halo to be horny for a guy. I'm the Queen of Hormones, the Empress of Hasty Horizontals.

Robin says, "Milady Marian," and kisses her hand. She gives it a little flick and taps him reprovingly under his chin. She wears a smile, but there's sadness in it. Maybe she's remembering the guy you wouldn't give a second glance to on the train. But she only has a moment to reminisce. Robin straightens up quickly and turns his brown eyes on me. "And you, my unfortunate misstep! I'm delighted to see you recovered. I beg your forgiveness for my unpardonable mistake."

He takes my hand and kisses it. I try not to swoon. Until this second, I had no idea what swooning felt like. Now, Marian could wipe my memory a hundred times over, and I'd still lie in bed every night trying to bring back this great swoony gush.

"Her name is Jools," Marian tells Robin. "In case you don't think to ask."

He gives Marian a wounded look. "Why must you think the worst of me? I'm not always well behaved . . ." He gives me a meaningful look. ". . . but I am always well mannered."

Marian rolls her eyes. She takes Robin's wrist in one hand and mine in the other, then delicately detaches us. (All this time he's been holding my fingers as if he hasn't finished kissing them.) Marian drags Robin off his knees and up to his feet. "So you see, Robin, Jools is fine, despite your best efforts."

"I truly am sorry," Robin tells me. "It's a mystery why I didn't see that you were there."

"No mystery at all," Marian says. "Someone must have cast a spell. *Several* spells, I suppose: one to make the girl move into the way; another to prevent you from seeing she was there; and maybe a third to make sure she was hurt as badly as possible."

Clever Marian, I think. And since I'm mad at Calon Arang, I'm on the verge of confirming what happened. But when I open my mouth, I nearly pass out . . . and not in a nice swoony way. It's more like an ice pick plunging through my head. I want to scream, "Ow, fuck!" but I can't say that either.

So this is what a nondisclosure agreement feels like.

Robin and Marian notice as the magic stabs me to silence. Robin seizes my hand. "Are you ill, milady?" Marian reaches for my throat and feels my pulse. Her eyes inspect me quickly from head to toe, perhaps to see if I'm bleeding. As if blood would show up on this bright-red costume.

Calon Arang's NDA continues to screw its way into my skull like a drill bit. It doesn't ease up for at least five seconds. When it finally lets me go, I slump. "I'm fine, really," I say. "Just a bit . . ."

I don't know how to finish that sentence. My go-to fallback kicks in. "Is there anything here to drink?"

Robin laughs, as merrily as only a dude named Robin Hood can laugh. "You wonder if we have aught to drink in Sherwood? Milady, I am crushed that you doubt our hospitality."

He takes my hand and begins to lead me down the forest path. Marian gives a snort and stays where she is. "You two have fun," she says. "I'm going back to my lab."

I turn to look at her. Her face is . . . what? Resigned? Bored? *I told you so?*

What does she feel for the man who Robin was before he changed? I wonder what he and she were to each other.

But whatever. I'm not the first whom Robin has led down this path. Probably not the last, either. It's nothing to make a thing about; it is what it is.

Maid Marian turns and walks away. Soon she's hidden by underbrush.

WALKING WITH ROBIN IS different than walking with Marian. The pace is faster—he's bursting with energy and barely contains it. Any second now, he might sweep me up in his arms and carry me off, swinging through the trees.

He has the muscles to do that; Robin is known to be as strong as five normal men. He could pick me up and have plenty of strength left over for acrobatics through the forest. But I don't know how he'd hold me and a vine simultaneously. Maybe that's what stops him from doing it.

The narrowness of the trail also slows him down. I can see he'd love to be walking side by side with me—perhaps even arm in arm. But whenever he tries to drop back and join me, he's blocked by a thornbush or a mass of thistles.

It makes me laugh: he's such a *guy*. So damned panting eager, but baffled by logistics. It amuses me so much, I don't try to help him. Eventually, he just speeds up so we'll get out of the forest faster.

I keep pace. Cuz after all.

Soon enough we come to a clearing with a house in the middle.

I recognize the house immediately: it's a reproduction of Shakespeare's birthplace, a Tudor-style building with lots of gables and bay windows.

It's a good-sized house, especially compared to the Elizabethan average. It's three stories high, with a tile roof, multiple chimneys, and a wattle-and-daub exterior. I don't know why Robin lives à la Shakespeare—Willy S. was born several centuries after the legends of Robin Hood supposedly took place. But maybe for our modern-day Robin, old-timey England is one big pre-Enlightenment mush. Little John and Shakespeare and William the Conqueror all played darts together at the local pub (the one run by Lancelot and Boudica with King Lear's daughters as serving wenches).

So why quibble about specifics? Besides, a place like Shakespeare's house is ten times more livable than anything true to Robin Hood's era. That was what, the twelfth century? So the floors were cold stone, with dried reeds strewn around to soak up piss. The lice fought the fleas to see who'd become king of the castle. By contrast, Shakespeare's day was no pristine picnic, but at least they'd figured out chimneys. And I doubt if our current Robin enjoys suffering for the sake of authenticity.

"Welcome to my home," Robin says, as he leads me into the house. "It's a little cramped, but Lady Marian has updated it to have all mod cons. So, food? Drink? A hot bath, milady?"

I don't answer right away; I just look. Robin's right that the place is cramped. The ceilings are low and the rooms are small, as per normal with Tudor architecture. But the raw dimensions are only part of the problem. Robin has filled the room with fripperies; it looks like a junk shop that was heaped to the rafters when it opened in 1905 and has kept adding stock ever since.

I can tell at once that the contents are all loot that Robin stole. Since he steals from rich Darklings, the booty divides into three categories: generic bling, heavy on gold, silver, and jewels; antiques, including a Rembrandt, a Chippendale chair, and a Ming jade lion;

and occult Things of Power that strike me as disasters waiting to happen.

I mean, it's one thing to stack gold bars in the corner. It's quite another to toss a dozen bottles bearing the Seal of Solomon into a rune-engraved crucible. Letting magical things lie on top of each other is like clacking together rods of plutonium . . . except with plutonium, you can use nice precise math to calculate how sorry you'll be, whereas with sorcerous knickknacks, nobody knows what the hell will happen. Maybe nothing. Maybe Revelations 6, verse 8.

"So what do you think?" Robin asks.

I say, "I think I need a drink."

He smiles. "As the lady wishes."

ROBIN LEADS ME THROUGH the house. Every room has a similar decor: clogged with trinkets, many of which are traditionally found in dragon hoards or handed out by women who live in lakes.

When we get to the kitchen, it has the same degree of congestion. This time, however, the problem isn't dangerous occultrements; the kitchen is cramped because of a large Cape Tech gadget in the center of the room.

The device doubles as the kitchen's table. Its surface is an appropriate height for dining, and its electronics are recessed enough that there's space for your knees to go when you pull up a chair. The machine is exactly what you'd think Maid Marian would build for a man like Robin: a gizmo for serving hot meals or cold drinks upon command. I'm tempted to say, "Tea, Earl Grey, hot." But let's not be totally stupid. I say, "Scotch, single malt, neat" . . . which is what Captain Picard *really* ordered when the cameras weren't rolling.

A glass rises out of a hatch in the center of the table. I take it, but don't belt it down. Partly that's because I don't want Robin to think I'm a desperate alcoholic. But it's also because I don't feel a sense of urgency.

Or interest.

Or any of the scarier words that usually fill up my mind when I think about my drinking.

Did the medi-tank do something to me? Put me through a cleanse?

Or is this a side effect of nearly dying? Maybe *actually* dying. I could have been forced to reboot, coming back without, uhh, an inclination toward sometimes mismanaging alcohol.

Maybe this newfound lack of compulsion was caused by my bout of Mad Genius, when I built that heater to warm me up and the shampoo to make me smell peachy. That really took the edge off. I'm still feeling pretty relaxed.

Yeah, no, I *was* relaxed. Now I'm freaking out. Something has changed, and I don't know whether it's good or bad. Nervous tingles flutter up and down my arms. But surprisingly, my impulse is to go and run hard for an hour, till I'm too hot and tired to think about anything. What I don't feel is any urge to chug the Scotch that's in my hand.

What is *wrong* with me?

Robin tells the kitchen machine, "My usual mead, if you please." A moment later, the machine's hatch opens and out comes a tacky Toby jug presumably filled with spiced fermented honey.

Robin and I clink: his pottery, my glass. He takes a hearty swig, then waits for me to do likewise.

I can't bring myself to go through with it. Instead, I flip to whisky-judge mode. I swirl my glass; I nose the aromas. The Olympic-level taster inside me reports that I'm holding an excellent specimen of its kind. I don't know if Marian's machine teleported it here from its home distillery, or if the whisky was assembled atom by atom to duplicate a prestigious original . . . but it's good. Very good. Very very.

I don't want to drink it.

I don't know why not, and that scares me. I could *force* myself to drink, but the prospect makes my mouth rebel. It would be like drinking some horrid concoction of urine, Liquid-Plumr, and blood.

All I can do is cradle the glass in my hands and look at Robin. "So what happens now?"

He grins. "To what are you referring, milady?"

I debate which way I want this to go. And how soon. "Naturally, I'm asking about your bazooka. The one you were trying to steal. Marian told me you pulled out prematurely—as soon as I got injured. Think you'll try to steal it again?"

Ha! I've taken him by surprise. I hate to be predictable. But Robin recovers quickly. "We'll try again if the opportunity arises. I dislike the Dark having a powerful weapon in their arsenal. And this weapon in particular—according to rumor, it only works when held by someone imbued with the Light. That's disturbing. It would mean the gun could be used to determine who is or isn't a Spark."

I say, "Diamond claimed the gun isn't his."

"Diamond is hardly a paragon of truth," Robin says. "Besides, are you referring to the message Diamond broadcast through the fest hall? That message was recorded before Diamond saw the weapon. At that time, I'm sure Diamond believed his self-destruction measures were foolproof. But he may have been mistaken."

"So you'll definitely go after the gun again?" I ask.

"If we locate it," Robin replies. "Of course, as soon as we left, its keepers moved it. We attempted to track where it went, but between the Darklings, the All-Stars, and Waterloo's local Sparks, they managed to confound Lady Marian's surveillance."

I'm stabbed with guilt. "Tell me about those local Sparks," I say. "Are they all right?"

"As far as we can determine, yes. The winter witch, or whatever she was . . . she had no trouble freezing and killing the rest of the wasps. Overall, deaths were few: one of Diamond's least successful exploits. Then again, his previous project ended in failure a mere two weeks ago. He's had precious little time to devise something new. This wasn't a full-blown scheme, just an improvised sally."

I nod, forcing myself to hold my tongue. It's not public knowledge, but when we fought Diamond before Christmas, he got seriously hurt. A normal person would still be in the hospital, possibly in a coma or under sedation. The fact that Diamond did *anything* is amazing. On the other hand, he likely has a medi-tank of his own. That has to be one of the first things a Mad Genius builds.

"You seem most interested in these matters," Robin says. "And knowledgeable." He gives a dimpled smile. "Are you what is known as a fangirl?"

"You wish," I say.

"Not at all," he replies. "I am weary of fangirls. Individually, they each have admirable qualities, but their approaches toward me are repetitive."

"Poor baby," I say. "You get all the groupies you want, but they're all the same."

He gives me a rueful smile. "Money for nothing and the chicks are free."

"Okay, let me break the mold." I slap my hand on the table. "Hey, machine, make me a quarterstaff."

Robin's eyebrows lift. "What are you . . ."

The table's hatch opens and a pole begins to emerge. I grab the end. I pull out seven feet of polished wood, thick enough that my fingers just barely go around it. When I've extracted the whole thing, I tell the table, "Now make another."

Robin laughs. "You can't possibly think . . ."

"I can and I do." A second staff begins to emerge. I toss Robin the staff I'm holding. He catches it one-handed. I pull out the second staff and give it a twirl.

Robin quirks an eyebrow. "Wearing a codpiece has affected you, milady." His face goes serious. "You do realize, don't you, I'm a Spark?" He takes a breath. "I'm Robin fucking Hood."

"Yeah," I say. "That's why I'm not challenging you to an archery contest. But you legendarily suck with a quarterstaff. While me, I've been playing hockey since I was four. Stick handling is my thing."

He puts his hand to his heart. "Oh, milady!"

"I'm no lady, and I'll prove it."

I head out the door, leaving my untouched whisky on the table.

THE DOOR FROM THE kitchen exits into a classic English garden: lupins and columbines, hollyhocks and roses. On a warm day like this, the flowers should be busy with bees and butterflies. Nope. No buzzing, no flits. No sound except our footsteps as Robin and I cross to a swath of grass between the garden and the forest.

I say, "What, no river with a log across it?"

"No streams of any kind in Sherwood," Robin replies. "At least not *this* Sherwood. Besides, I've never found a suitable Little John. The closest substitute I have is Wrecking Ball, and if she walked onto a log, it would snap." He gives me a rueful smile. "If I fought her with a quarterstaff, she'd snap *me*."

"Have you ever fought with a staff at all?"

"Not that I recall." He raises his staff in one hand and gives it a spin, ending with it tucked under his armpit and his empty hand extended in a press-palm, the sort of show-off maneuver you'd see in a martial-arts movie when a warrior wants to say, *I'm totally hot shit.* "But I'm Robin Hood," he says. "Fighting with a staff is bred in the bone."

I know the feeling. When my friends and I got our powers, there was no learning curve: our bodies knew exactly what to do. The first time I tried fancy gymnastics, I leapt and rolled and bounced like I'd practiced each trick a million times. No questioning what to do next. Instinct just took over.

So it's no surprise that Robin has quarterstaff skilz. They're part of his legend.

Howsomever, legend says he's not as good as he thinks.

He's not the best in the world. *I* am.

At least I'm as good as the best true human. There are six living Sparks who rank way beyond humans when it comes to fighting with staffs, but Robin ain't on the list. He's supremely agile and super-strong, but darling, he doesn't have the range.

I don't indulge in wuxia moves to show I'm ready to fight. I'm not Robin Hood, I'm Ninety-Nine. Before we fight in hockey, we sure as hell don't bow.

I just hold my staff two-handed, spacing my hands apart so they divide the length of the staff into thirds. Then I move in hard and fast.

Maybe it's what Robin expected. If I truly were a newbie, I might go into maximum frenzy right off the bat, trying to score a hit by the power of surprise. I swing one end of the staff in a downward blow toward Robin's head. He easily blocks, and he's quick to block again when I snap up the other end of the staff, going for a cheap shot to the groin. What he doesn't expect is my follow-through: as his staff blocks my upswing, I let my staff slide downward, riding along his until the butt of my staff jabs his foot like a spear.

He makes an "uhh" sound of pain. Then he shoves me back hard enough to lift me off my feet. I go flying into the lupins. Instead of landing on my ass, I plant one end of my staff on the ground as I hurtle backward. I use the staff like the pole in a pole-vault jump: my legs go up to the sky then arc over and come down. I land on my feet and casually swing around to face Robin again.

The whole move unfolds as a reflex—a demonstration that Spark powers don't need practice or forethought. But it looks acrobatic as hell.

"Well, well, well," Robin says. "You have hidden depths, milady."

"And they'll *stay* hidden," I say. Using the staff to pole-vault again, I jump over the flower bed and the fight *really* begins.

It's fun in the same way that a hockey game is fun—exhausting, sweaty, and bruising. I hit him two more times before he truly gets up to speed, a smack on his thigh and a jab that scuds along his rib cage when he doesn't turn fast enough. At that point, he drops his smirk and his chivalrous restraint. Perhaps he thinks, *If I hit her too hard, we can always put her back in the medi-tank.* Perhaps he's also thinking, *She moves like a Spark.*

I'd love to disguise that possibility, to stay within the limits of an average girl on the street. And Robin should be able to see I'm not super-strong or -fast. I don't even have superhuman skills. But I'm a Wudang mountain beyond your typical Jane Jock. I'm Donnie Yen good—Donnie Yen at his prime, with Tsui Hark as choreographer.

So fuck it. Let's make this a fight. One that's worthy of Robin Hood.

We take it into the forest, and up into the trees. It's easy to bounce off three trunks in a row to attack from surprise directions. Or pole-vault from branch to branch, then somersault down to the ground where I can slash at a patch of poison ivy and flick leaves at Robin with the end of my staff. Meanwhile, he does the Tarzan thing, always finding a vine exactly where he wants it so he can swing past and try to fracture my skull.

Whackety-whack. Snicker-snack. Back to the house and onto the roof, balancing on the ridges of two adjacent gables as we exchange flurries.

My hands soon hurt like hell. Each collision of staff on staff sends vibrations through the wood, making my fingers sting. Other parts of my body ache, too—I block every strike Robin slams at me, but he's so damned strong, the impact still shakes me to the bone.

It's a wonder the staffs haven't broken. They're thick, and I do my best to turn each direct smash into a glancing blow. Even so, some part of my brain that thinks like an engineer is adding up all the damage my staff takes, then subtracting the result from a decreasing endurance limit. If the score reaches zero at an inconvenient moment, Robin's staff will break mine and splatter my face.

Unless, of course, I use the moment to my advantage.

I wait for the right opportunity, when Robin's incoming strike has just the proper angle so I won't get flattened by the follow-through. Then, instead of discreet deflection, I spread my grip wider and slam the center of my staff into his swing. The quarterstaff shatters in the middle, giving me two half-length sticks to his one.

Now I switch to fighting Eskrima-style: *clunk*, feint, *clunk*. It's faster and two sticks to one. Robin blocks the stick that snaps toward his head, but misses the one jabbing his solar plexus. He gasps and stops breathing. A moment later, he collapses. The staff falls from his fingers.

Even before he hits the ground, my brain shifts from fighter to paramedic. I drop to my knees beside him and check his vitals. His pulse is strong, beating like mad from all the exertion. After a moment, he wheezes and starts breathing again . . . but his eyes stay shut and his body stays down for the count.

Awesome, Jools: was this what you wanted? To knock out the hottest guy you've ever met?

At this moment, the two of you could have been drunk and naked, but oh, no. You got weird about the whisky, then suddenly you were all, "Let's fight."

With quarterstaffs, no less. You couldn't just have a little squabble over who got to be on top?

First?

Oh my God, it's so *stupid* being a Spark!

I think I may have ruptured Robin's spleen. Now he's just lying there with internal bleeding.

Fuck.

It's a damned good thing I have an eidetic memory. I might have to find my way back to Marian's lab so I can carry Robin to the medi-tank.

I'm about to sling him over my shoulder when his body begins to shrink. His arm muscles go soft. His beautiful ringlets revert to short curls, his beard turns to patchy ungroomed stubble, and his cheekbones vanish under a layer of pudge.

In five seconds, Robin is gone, replaced by a much more average-looking dude who opens his eyes and asks, "What just happened?"

12

Alternative Ecosystems

I HELP THE GUY sit up. He's dazed but healthy. Breathing well. No signs of injury.

I touch my fingers to his throat to take his pulse. He goes tense, like he's afraid I might try to strangle him. But he doesn't bat me away; he's fatalistic.

The dude's heartbeat is fine. The same speed as Robin's, but not as strong.

Seems to me, "not as strong" is the phrase to mark with highlighter. Even if I hadn't watched Robin turn into this guy, I'd see a resemblance. He could pass as Robin's couch-potato older brother: a dude in his forties who's not Nigeria's answer to Errol Flynn, but the hardworking chartered accountant who pays bail when baby-bro Robin gets busted on a DUI.

"How are you feeling?" I ask.

"Disorientated." His accent is British, but not posh. With a few more sentences, I could pin down his accent precisely, regional, class, and ethnic influences all factored in. But that would be showing off.

"I'm Jools," I tell the dude.

"I know," he answers. "I'm . . ."

He hesitates, obviously debating whether it's wise to give his real name. Then he shrugs. "I'm Vernon."

Awkwardly, he reaches to shake my hand. I take it. I stand and use the handhold to lift him to his feet. He seems steady enough; when I let him go, he doesn't teeter. He just looks at his surroundings, taking in the trees, the garden, the house. He breathes in deeply, leaning toward the flowers nearby. He inhales their perfume, then smiles.

"It's strange," Vernon says. "I know everything Robin gets up to, but I don't actually experience it. I'm *aware* of what Robin is seeing, but I don't see it myself. Same with feeling, hearing, and smelling."

"That sounds awful," I say.

"Not really. It's like reading a book: no direct sensory input, but I still get vicarious enjoyment." He gives me a rueful smile. "And at the moment, it means I don't feel black and blue with a terrible ache in my gut. I've just set down the book and I'm fine."

He takes another deep breath, clearly inhaling the pleasant scents around us. "I feel rather good, actually." He gives himself a shake, shifts his balance, flexes his fingers. "Nice to have a body again."

"Have you been stuck a long time as Robin?" I ask.

"Almost eight months," Vernon replies. "The last time I got out was when Robin slept with Tigresse. You know, the super-goddess. The one who looks so damned amazing. Sex with her wasn't much different from being smashed around with a quarterstaff. Draining, even for Robin. The third time through, he folded like a lawn chair."

"Leaving you alone with Tigresse?"

"Yeah." Vernon has a distant look on his face. "I thought she'd bloody well murder me. But actually, she was very, very kind. She tried to make tea. She kept apologizing for having no idea how to be '*ordinaire.*' We spent the rest of the night just talking."

"Shut up, you're making me cry." And it's true, I'm getting teary. Poor guy. But good for Tigresse. I say, "Maybe I should pound the crap out of Robin on a regular basis."

Vernon laughs. "It's really not so bad. I get to be Robin Hood! I even sort of know what it's like to have sex with Tigresse. Lots of other women, too. Also a few men, and a couple of . . ." He stops and shrugs. "With so many Sparks and Darklings around, sexuality has more dimensions than M-theory."

"M-theory," I repeat; the great-grandma framework that unifies all versions of string theory. "Yeah, I heard you were a science dude before you got Robin-ized. I got the four-one-one from Marian. Hey, would you like to see her?"

"Marian?" Vernon looks baffled a moment, then laughs. "Oh, right: Marian. She absolutely hates that name. But Robin just *had* to have a Maid Marian."

"She seems okay with Marian," I say. "She just doesn't like the 'Maid.'" I take Vernon's hand. "Let's go see her."

He resists my pull. When I look, I see him surveying himself with disgust. He does look kind of saggy, considering he's still wearing Robin's costume. Not many guys can rock tights.

On the other hand . . .

I say, "Dude, do you think Marian cares what you're wearing? I mean . . ." I stop myself from making an asshole-ish remark about Marian's muumuu. I say, "She doesn't come across as a fashion snob. She's also not . . ." I stop myself again. "When she and I talked, I could tell she misses the real you. I'm sure she'd love to spend time together. Speaking of which, how long do you have?"

Vernon shrugs. "I don't know. This has only happened four times since I turned into Robin. I guess it depends on how long he takes to recover."

"I didn't hurt him too badly," I say, hoping it's true. Ruptured spleen . . . internal bleeding . . . minor things for a Spark. He'll snap right back. "You may not have long," I say. "Let's hurry."

Vernon looks down at himself once more. He grimaces.

"Stop comparing yourself to Robin," I tell him. "I guarantee Marian won't care."

Vernon hesitates a moment longer, then nods. "Okay. Let's go."

I TRY TO SET a quick pace back to Marian's lab, but Vernon doesn't keep up. I think he's still ashamed of himself and afraid of meeting Marian. In other words, he's just as much of a *guy* as Robin was: he completely misunderstands Marian's feelings.

Or maybe Vernon just sucks at stomping through the woods. He strikes me as a city boy, not to mention the geeky sort of dude who always fled when jocks like me entered the room.

I slow down and let him catch up. When he does, he says, "You're a Spark, right? You're pretending you aren't, but you are."

The question takes me by surprise. And I feel so sorry for the dude, the way he's trapped in nowhere for months at a time, I don't want to lie to him. So I say nothing.

"Don't worry," he says, "I won't tell. I just . . ." He gives an exasperated sigh. "Robin meets Sparks all the time, but he never *talks* to them. He's forever bumping into people by chance, fighting at their sides, and usually shagging them after. But he never has an actual conversation. That time with Tigresse . . . it's the only chance I've had to hear someone else's thoughts on being a Spark. Robin is a doer, not a thinker. Whereas me, thinking is all I do for months at a time."

I meet his eyes for a moment. He has nice eyes. Big and brown. "Yes, of course, I'm a Spark," I say. "But I'm pretty new at it, so I don't have a lot of insights."

"What do you do?" Vernon asks. "What powers?"

"I'm human max in everything. Strength, speed, skill . . . probably intelligence, too, though that doesn't seem to stop me from acting like an idiot. And I heal crazy fast. One of my teammates says it looks like time-lapse photography."

"How did it happen?" Vernon asks. "Getting powers, I mean."

"I got zonked by a supervillain's machine." I turn away and start walking again, partly so I don't have to look Vernon in the eye. "Not so different from what happened to you. Marian told me about you, her, and Byte Bitch."

Vernon is quiet for a moment. Then he says, "How much did she tell you?"

"Not a lot. Not enough for me to figure out your true identity, if that's what you're worried about."

"Jools," Vernon says, "if you ever figure out my true identity, I wish you'd let me in on it. But that's not why I asked."

Vernon puts on a burst of speed so he's walking beside me rather than behind. The trail isn't really wide enough for that, but me being the best backwoods girl in the history of the planet, I can slip and slide through the undergrowth without Vernon noticing that I'm letting him monopolize the path. Besides, he's focused so hard on choosing his words, he's not paying attention to much else.

He says, "I've never had a chance to talk about this with . . . Marian." He's not comfortable using the name, but he presses on. "And when I talked with Tigresse she did her best, but she's not very introspective. She has hundreds of funny stories, but they're all about clawing people and shoving them off cliffs. Not about coping with . . . stuff."

"Just FYI," I say, "I haven't won medals for coping with stuff either. I specialize in avoidance."

"But you're human," Vernon says. "Tigresse is a tiger goddess, supposedly thousands of years old. For all I know, she's actually like Robin Hood, a human who recently changed into a Spark, and only *thinks* she's a goddess. But even if that's true, she's completely invested in the goddess identity. It's endearing when she tries to come down to a mortal level, but she's really *bad* at it. You, on the other hand—do you remember the moment you changed?"

I shudder. "Of course I do."

"What was it like?"

I want to say, "You're the one who wants to talk; you go first." But I don't want to be a shit. This guy spends his life locked in Robin Hood's head. Am I going to stonewall him during his few minutes of freedom?

I'd do almost anything to avoid discussing stuff that's close to the bone. I have an outstanding track record in that department. As in, *Dude (whatever your name is), do you really want to talk? Wouldn't you rather just have a beejer?* That's ma girl Jools.

But fuck it. Marian is going to wipe my memory, so I'll never have to remember how squirmy the next few minutes will make me feel.

I take Vernon's hand. Don't ask me why.

I say, "There was this portal . . ."

THERE WAS THIS PORTAL, created by the Mad Genius Diamond. Call it a door to another reality, a rip in the fabric of our world. Multicolored candle flames swarmed from the portal, like the sparks when you're close to passing out. My head went woozy and the sparks shot into my brain—parasites shouting, "Free food, free food!"

Once the flames got inside my head, they made me remember horrible things. I don't bother giving Vernon specifics, but I know what people mean by, "My life passed before my eyes." A Jools montage zoomed past at a million frames a second . . . and the memories that stood out were the ones I'd rather forget.

Missing crucial shots in hockey. Being jerked around by my sisters. Literally getting caught with my pants down. Stuff like that. I realized what the worst was going to be . . . and *boom*, as soon as the thought crossed my mind, we were there.

The awfullest day of my life.

But that day didn't zip through at high speed. The million frames a second came to a screeching stop, and suddenly I was *there* again.

In the park. With my mom.

It was the summer between grades seven and eight, the summer I got serious about training. I'd always been a jock, but mostly to distinguish myself from my sisters. Between the four of them, they were good at so many things, they hadn't left much I could make my own. None of them cared about sports, though, so I latched onto that.

I played hockey and soccer and softball like a lot of kids do: nothing special, but having fun. When I started going through puberty, my sisters teased me that I'd soon give up on dirt and sweat. The four of them were boy crazy (it runs in the family) and as women of the world, they predicted that any day now, I'd trade my team uniforms for tight tops and Daisy Dukes.

Mom assured me it didn't have to be either/or. She wasn't a jock herself—she was fifty pounds overweight, and couldn't give up cigarettes—but she supported me, even when I decided to spend the summer in a rabid exercise program. I did everything I could to prove to my sisters they were wrong. I woke up at 6:00 A.M. to go swimming at the pool, then an hour lifting weights, and biking, jogging, all that. Plus every little league sport they'd let me sign up for.

In other words, I went overboard. Typical Jools, right? No such thing as too much.

But Mom supported me. Which was how we ended up in a park beside the North Saskatchewan River on a sunny afternoon: me running a half-K jogging loop while Mom sat on a bench, reading *Chatelaine* and timing my circuits with a stopwatch. By the end of the summer, I wanted to run the eight-K in under half an hour.

I ran hard and fast, less than two minutes a lap, which is pretty darn good for a twelve-year-old. The first time I passed my mom and saw that she'd slumped on the bench instead of sitting straight up, I was mad that she'd fallen asleep. She was supposed to be timing me!

I felt the same anger when I relived it years later. As those alien sparks ignited memories in my brain, I was two separate people: twenty-one-year-old Jools in a Waterloo lab, and twelve-year-old Jools in that Edmonton park. I felt my young irritation and my present-day horror. I shouted to myself, *Stop! Don't keep going! Go check on her!*

I didn't. Twelve-year-old me didn't stop till I finished my laps. Then I ran to my mother and started to grump that she'd fallen asleep on the job.

She wouldn't wake up.

I still did nothing useful. First, I wasted time nudging her shoulder, harder and harder. Then I panicked, feeling helpless and dumb cuz I didn't know CPR. Couldn't remember how they did it on TV. Finally, finally, I ran to look for help . . . but somehow I got the desperate idea that I couldn't just scream my head off, I had to pick exactly the right person. If only I chose correctly and found a doctor, everything would still turn out okay. That wasted even more time, until a guy walking his dog asked, "Are you all right?" and I fell apart.

For a long time afterward, people kept telling me nothing would have made a difference. "She died instantly, Jools. You couldn't have helped her."

But what else would they say? It's what they had to tell me.

To this day, I don't know if it's true. No one in our family does. Whatever the truth, would any doctor say, "Of course, the girl could have saved her mother. She was just too stupid and self-centered."

Anyway, that's what happened when I was twelve. And that's what I relived when the sparks got inside of me. I lived through the moment I ran past my mom and saw that she'd slipped sideways. That she'd dropped her magazine. That her position was far too awkward for anyone to be able to sleep. I felt annoyed that she wasn't paying attention to me; as I started my next loop around the trail, I ran even faster because I was pissed off.

But inside Younger Me, Older Me screamed, "Stop, stop!"

Suddenly, the two of us split. My older self broke out of my younger body, separating and drifting upward to a bird's-eye view. I saw myself running. I saw my mom lying so limply it brought me to tears—how clueless I was to think she had fallen asleep. I floated above the world, screaming and crying . . .

Then my mother was floating with me.

Not like a ghost from the movies. Neither of us was visible. I was disembodied, a viewpoint looking down on the scene; Mom was even less, just a *presence*. But she radiated disapproval, all the blame and loathing I've aimed at myself ever since.

A good daughter would have seen the truth immediately. A *smart* daughter would have called for help and started CPR. It was the middle of the afternoon; plenty of people were within earshot. Maybe one was a doctor or a nurse. Maybe somebody had a cell phone; they weren't so common back then, but somebody probably had one. An ambulance could have arrived within minutes, instead of the forever it took.

My mother was so *disappointed* with me. I was twelve years old, not five. You could forgive a little kid, but I was old enough to use my pitiful excuse for a brain.

I floated above my mother's corpse and felt her soul accuse me.

It nearly killed me. I truly think I might have died with those sparks inside my head. When people get superpowers, often a crowd of folks are exposed to the same conditions—the same radiation, or chemicals, or cosmic forces. Some people survive and become super; the others die.

But as I floated . . . as I felt the blame squeeze crushingly around me . . . something within me said, *No, you aren't my mom*.

My mother was good and she loved me. The last thing she'd do would be to shame me. The entity judging me couldn't be my mom. It was some goddamned horror pretending to be her, and I silently screamed in outrage, *Fuck off, fuck off, you leave her alone!*

Something snapped. I woke up. My eyes, nose, and throat were burning. I was still surrounded by those little colored sparks trying to get inside me . . . but now they couldn't.

As if I was armored against them. Immunized. Saved.

Eventually, my friends and I closed the portal and got the hell out of that lab. But that stuff was only aftermath. I became a Spark the moment I said no to whatever it was. To *all* the whatevers that wanted me to curl up and die.

And that's the story I tell Vernon. I fuck up a lot; there's stuff I can't put into words. I don't even know how much I say out loud. A ton of it sticks in my mouth.

But Vernon gets it. By the time I finish, he's holding my hands and nodding, over and over. I don't know what he went through himself, but he's on the same wavelength.

"Thanks, Jools," he says, very softly. He takes a deep breath. "So now, I guess it's my turn." He inhales again. "Okay, I can do this. I can tell you."

But he doesn't. Because Ninja Jane leaps down from a tree and claps her hands three times loudly.

THE CLAPS ARE SURPRISINGLY sharp, given that Jane wears gloves. I start to ask, "What do—" but she makes a chopping gesture. I'll interpret that as *Shut up!*

Jane stares hard at Vernon. She thrusts her finger at a trail leading who knows where.

Vernon gives me an apologetic look. He says, "I guess—"

Jane makes her chopping gesture, and jabs her finger at the trail again.

I say, "Jane apparently wants you for something."

"No," Vernon replies, "it's Marian. Jane is just the messenger."

Jane claps her hands even more loudly and points to the trail.

"I'd better go," Vernon says. "Jane doesn't take no for an answer."

"All right," I say, "let's go."

I step toward the trail, but Jane blocks my way. She's shorter than me and maybe thirty pounds lighter, but she's intimidating, like a black-pajamaed time bomb. With most Sparks, that would only be her Halo getting under my skin, but with Jane, there's nothing artificial about it. Her eyes drill into mine without blinking, dark brown eyes surrounded by greasepaint and the black of her ninja mask.

I stare back and don't blink, either. Hockey instincts: don't let other girls scare you. If I had any booze in my bloodstream, I might even escalate. I wouldn't outright head butt her but I'd send the message, *Don't mess with me, sis.*

But really, what would fighting Jane get me? Bruises and bupkes. I'm just annoyed she interrupted before Vernon could tell his story.

I want to know what he went through when he got superpowers. Did he have to face some mental ordeal? Reliving a horrible thing from deep in his past?

I want to know.

Even more, I want to know what K, Miranda, and Shar went through the night we got powered up. But then I'd have to tell them my own story, and I don't know if I could stand it. Telling a stranger is one thing, especially when my mind will soon get erased so I won't have to live with the memory. But confessing to my friends? When I know it'll make them think badly of me? Nuh-uh.

I don't do emotional spillage. It clashes with my brand.

Maybe I *should* start a fight with Jane. That'd get my mind off my mother. A fight would get me out of my head, maybe better than sex or alcohol. And hey, I outfought Robin Hood. Why couldn't I beat Ninja Jane, too?

Yeah, no. I'm just being stupid.

Robin's powers are charisma and shooting strange arrows. He's never been known as a hand-to-hand guy. Jane, however, is one of the top ten scrappers in the world. I don't know where I rank in the list of Spark brawlers, but it probably has three digits. Or more.

And Jane's too crazy to hold herself back. She might not kill me outright, but she'd happily gash me bloody with her scary whispery knives. I doubt if Jane understands the concept of sparring for fun or practice. It's always a fight to the finish for her, preferably damaging opponents so badly she'll never have to fight them again.

Fuck that. I step back.

Consider it a sign of budding maturity.

Or sobriety. Frightening, inexplicable sobriety.

I turn to Vernon. "Are you sure you'll be okay?"

"Jane won't hurt me," Vernon says. "She just wants to take me to Marian."

"Got any ideas for what I should do to amuse myself?" I ask.

Vernon laughs. "Stay out of trouble."

I think, *Yeah, that's going to happen*, as Ninja Jane hustles him off.

13

Migration

LEFT ALONE IN SHERWOOD Forest, I have three choices.

Choice one: Go back to Robin Hood's house. Where that gadget in the kitchen will cheerfully make me food and drink. Especially drink. Except I don't want to find out that I still can't face the prospect of alcohol. Also, I'm not hungry at all, even though it's been hours since I ate anything. Wouldn't be surprising if Marian's medi-tank topped up my blood sugar; I won't need to eat for a while.

Choice two: Wander through the forest till I find something of interest. The paths in these woods aren't game trails; I still haven't seen any animals. So let's assume human beings made these pathways to connect between places like the lab and Robin Hood's house. The members of Robin's gang must have living space somewhere in the forest. And who knows what else I might find? A mead hall. I'll bet there's a mead hall. Cuz duh. But a mead hall could be just as traumatic for me as the dispenser in Robin's kitchen. What if I can't drink anymore?

Which leaves choice three: Marian's lab. I can find where it is, no problem—I remember the way. And it's full of interesting gadgets, including the medi-tank.

I really should learn how the tank works. Partly so I can build one for my friends if they get injured, partly to figure out what the hell the fucking tank did to me.

Why can't I stand the thought of booze? And what else has changed inside me? Like for instance, why did I decide to whack Robin with a quarterstaff instead of straddling his mighty manhood?

Wasn't that weird? It was weird. What was I thinking?

So I head for the lab. It only takes a minute to get there. And when I poke my head inside, nobody's home . . . at least not in the room closest to the door. The building itself is large enough to hold multiple labs, and now that my brain isn't mucked up from time in the medi-tank or freezing to death after a cold shower, I can see that the lab in front of me has doors leading left, right, and center. It makes me wonder what else the building holds . . . but as soon as the question crosses my mind, ideas flood in. The rooms that *I* would build if I were Marian.

Research lab. (I'm looking at it.)

Manufacturing facility. (She seems to have an unending supply of battle-bots. Means she needs a place to build them.)

Storage area. (Because once you have robots, you need to put them someplace.)

Power plant. (It must take gigawatts of energy to run this place, and an outlaw can't plug into a public power grid. Marian must have built her own generating station. Nuclear maybe, or fusion. Or something beyond all conventional science, and likely dangerous as hell. A super-Fukushima waiting to rumble.)

A Mad Genius needs all that stuff. And that's only for starters. After that, it's time to get *creative*.

The possibilities start my juices flowing. Notions and plans leap spontaneously out of nowhere.

I can tell when WikiJools feeds me data. I feel downloads arrive from some exterior source, maybe literally from Wikipedia and similar sites on the triple dub. But other info just seems like it's always been inside of me. I don't have to access how to fight or do parkour; it's as natural as walking. It doesn't feel like something external putting thoughts into my head. It's completely me.

Except I never had Mad Genius ideas until I got powers. My brilliant insights leaned more toward "It's time to go to the pub" and "I'm horny as hell, let's fix that." Not a dozen new ways to break the laws of physics.

But now my brain is filled with Cape Tech designs. And I'm staring at a lab that can make the designs a reality.

I wander, taking inventory as I pass tables covered with cruft. In a mundane lab like the one where I tried to analyze Diamond's bazooka, most gizmos look like sealed boxes with computers attached. Cape Tech is more photogenic. At the very least, there are flashing lights, and gauges with big red zones labeled DANGER. But you also see shit that is just plain weird: a helmet with deely bobbers controlling a 3-D printer, or a four-keyboard pipe organ with mummified hamster heads for stops. I'm tempted to pick a gadget at random and take it apart to see how it works . . . but after mature consideration (ha ha), I head for the medi-tank.

THE TANK IS THE same place I last saw it, in that curtained-off alcove. From a nearby workbench, I grab some tools—a funky little oscilloscope with attachment clips shaped like actual alligator heads, and a solid copper rod that seems to read my mind as it sprouts anything from screwdriver tips to perfectly sized wrench sockets. I set to work examining what makes the medi-tank tick.

Time passes while I have fun. Unlike with Diamond's bazooka, I have no trouble understanding the tank. Maybe I just have better equipment. The lab on campus was perfectly adequate for analyzing mundane devices but bush league for the needs of Cape Tech. And maybe when Diamond designed his gun, he deliberately made it confusing to figure out. Or maybe, since Diamond is nuts, his inventions are too deranged for me to grasp, whereas Marian is more on my mental wavelength.

One way or another, I catch on quickly. The tank works by infusing human cells with extra chromosomes that contain genes from various reptiles—the kind of reptiles that can grow back parts of their body if something gets bitten off. The new chromosomes also have genes to inhibit scarring, which is the main impediment to regrowth of tissues. A scar is an impenetrable barrier: it permanently seals off blood vessels, nerves, and so on.

Scars provide an evolutionary advantage because they quickly cap off a wound, thereby preventing infection and further damage. But they also prevent regeneration. They're immovable blockages to growth.

So Marian's medi-tank suppresses the scarification process, while expediting restoration through gene therapy, hormones, and other bio tricks. It makes me smile—Marian had to get the requisite genes from quick-healing animal species. But me, I've got something better. I could use my own Spark tissues. Since I regenerate much faster than any natural creature, a Jools-based medi-tank could patch people up in record time.

Even better, a Joolsian tank would minimize the need for post-repair cleanup. Marian's tank has to remove the reptile chromosomes after the healing is finished. That takes a lot of effort, and it's *fiddly* work because you have to be careful not to reopen wounds.

But my tank will use my own DNA. That's human already (except for the Sparkness). There'll still be some cleanup to make the regrown cells compatible with the host—wouldn't want my lovely new tissues to be rejected by their owner's immune system—but that's easier than dealing with completely foreign stuff like reptile genes.

Oh, wait, that raises another problem. Spark immune systems tend to be more ornery than vanilla human ones. Some Sparks fight off germs so thoroughly, they'd reject the reptile chromosomes too fast for the process to work. Sparks have other abilities, too: mutations that might clash with the added DNA, or armor that's simply too tough to get through. Take Wrecking Ball, for instance—the tank could immerse her in a million weird-shit chemicals, but none of it would soak through her cast-iron skin. So how . . .

. . .

Whoa.

Sneaky. And scary as hell.

Before the tank does anything else, it turns off superpowers.

Shuts 'em down completely. So Wrecking Ball would revert to flesh and blood. And someone like me . . .

Crap. This fucking machine could have killed me. The very first thing it did was turn off my power of regeneration. If it had just left me on my own . . . well, okay, I might have died, but otherwise I would have healed from my wounds in minutes.

This stupid medi-tank made me *human*. That's why I needed a full hour to recover. And why I might have died if the tank hadn't come through and put me back together.

So note to self: when I make my own version of a medi-tank, leave out the stuff that turns powers off.

Except what about Zircon? Zirc is made of rock. I'm not sure, but Zirc might not have internal organs, just rock all the way through. If Zirc gets hurt, my medi-tank will *have* to turn zir back to flesh and blood before the machine can inject its restorative DNA.

Translation: canceling the patient's powers may be necessary. But how would that actually work? How did Marian make a tank that de-supers the person inside?

I poke at the tank some more. And oh, look, there's the trick: the machine drains off energies of the Light and stores them in a weird metal canister. It leaves the patient totally human. Once the healing is finished, the energy gets shoved back inside the person it belongs to. You basically have another superhero origin, with the Light invading your soul and giving you powers.

The thought of that makes me shiver. While I was unconscious in the tank, did I have to go through the ordeal with my mother again? Or did I manage to avoid reliving those terrible few minutes? Since the Light had already tested me and found me suitable as a host, maybe it went back inside without a fuss—as if we'd both been metamorphosed to fit together.

Except.

My sudden new aversion to alcohol. It's like the way vampires avoid garlic, or werewolves run from wolfsbane. Could that be because of the medi-tank?

Lots of Sparks have strange quirks and vulnerabilities. When my powers left and came back, maybe something changed in the process. My stats got slightly rewritten to include a new disadvantage: a prohibition against booze.

Crap. Is anything else different?

I think hard about everything I've been through since I got out of the medi-tank. When nothing comes to mind, I consult Wiki-Jools.

Hello, Wiki? It's me, Jools.

Shit. No answer. At least, nothing obvious. But just for the sake of experiment, I try listing the atomic weights of every element, starting at Lawrencium and going backward.

Easy peasy. Automatic.

No sense of downloading data. I just *know*.

Fuuuuuckk. Now I can't tell where my own brain ends and WikiJools starts. The connection seems completely transparent.

How could that happen? Or why?

An idea pops into my head: maybe from me, maybe from elsewhere.

What if resurrection has a price?

We Sparks are creatures of myth: larger-than-life people subject to Fate and other intrusive tropes. We can come back from the dead; we can beat unbeatable odds. But in stories, you can only do the impossible by paying a price. You have to give up some piece of your life . . . and you'll never get it back.

Is that it? The cost of my survival is becoming incestuously linked with WikiJools? And never drinking again?

Harsh.

Oh, shit, what about fucking? I hope I still like it. I can live with giving up booze, but giving up sex would *break* me.

Or maybe I've got everything wrong. Something else is affecting me, and I just haven't figured it out yet. Like maybe the medi-tank does such a wonderful mental cleanse that I just *feel* more tightly linked to WikiJools. And the tank might also implant an urge to live healthily until you've fully recovered. For a few days,

I'll want to get eight hours of sleep, eat whole grains, abstain from intoxicants, yada yada yada. But once I'm 100 percent, the urge for clean living will wear off and my linkage with WikiJools will go back to having some friction.

That makes sense. And I like it a whole lot better than the alternative. I start examining the tank again, to see if it has features that do that . . .

Someone clears their throat behind me. I don't know how long I've been lost in thought, prodding the medi-tank's tech. I'm learning so much, I don't want distractions, but something grabs my elbow and a voice says, "Really, you ought to stop."

THE GRIP ON MY elbow comes from a big black shaggy Newfoundland dog. It's really quite gigantic. Not unnaturally so—it's not, like, eight feet tall. But Newfoundlands are humongous beasts, nearly the size of Saint Bernards.

This one has my arm in its mouth. It pulls me inexorably away from the tank. It's not biting hard at the moment, but I get the impression it could chomp through my bones if I caused any trouble.

Wait a minute. I've seen a dog like this just recently. In the Transylvania Club—I brushed past a Newfoundland that I thought was a ghost. It was probably this very dog, wearing one of Marian's doohickeys: the Cape Tech gadgets that let Robin Hood's gang look like ghosts.

"Her name is Nana," somebody tells me. It's a scrawny kid in blue jeans and a ratty black hoodie. He's fourteenish. Korean face but Midwestern American accent.

He's trying not to stare at my codpiece. Or my boobs. Or my ass. Basically, he's got the whole approach-avoidance thing going on: he's shy and I scare him, but he's also fourteen and chemically heterosexual. He has no idea where to aim his eyes. Eventually, he decides to look at the medi-tank, since it's not going to judge.

"You shouldn't play with Marian's equipment," he tells me. "You might hurt yourself, or break something."

"It's okay, I'm a science major," I say. "I'm Jools. Who are you?"

"Friar Tuck."

Well, that's a surprise. My mental image of Friar Tuck is like the pictures by Howard Pyle . . . and I know frigging well that half a second ago, I had no idea who Howard Pyle was, let alone what his drawings were like, but never mind. Our modern Robin and Marian have done an excellent job making everyone believe that Friar Tuck is a roly-poly middle-aged man with a tonsured haircut. Either the photos I've seen are fakes, or else this kid is like Robin: completely different as a Spark than as a civilian.

I tell him, "You don't look much like a friar."

"I didn't pick the name." He does a turn-away/zoom-back thing with his eyes. This whole shy-boy routine will be endearing for another ten seconds, and then I'll want to smack him.

"Robin just decided I had to be Friar Tuck," the kid tells me. "He wanted us all to have names from the stories. But when Wrecking Ball signed on, she refused to be called Little John. I thought about doing the same, but by then I'd already been seen a few times looking . . . you know." He mimes a paunchy belly, then pats his head on the spot where Friar Tuck is traditionally bald. "Marian decided I needed a disguise, cuz people would freak if they found out how young I was."

Marian's right. Friar Tuck has appeared alongside Robin for over four years. So this kid must have been ten years old when he first started going on Robin's heists. Can you say, "Reckless endangerment and corruption of a minor?"

I can't help asking, "How do you change your appearance? Did Marian invent a gadget that makes you look older?"

"No," Tuck says, "I found a rat named Harold. He's good at illusions."

My brain has nothing about a rat named Harold. But nobody knows how many superpowered animals Friar Tuck can call on. In fact, people argue if his pets are even real. Does Tuck have a way of breeding animals with Spark powers? Does he sense where super-animals hang out, and then he tracks them down to befriend them? Or are Tuck's pets mere projections from his own mind?

His teleporting horse, for example: is it a real horse that lives in a Sherwood Forest barn? Or is it just a manifestation of something in Tuck himself?

I could easily believe this boy has a ton of superpowers that he externalizes as imaginary animals. It's the kind of thing a kid might do if he got powers when he was really young. Like, say, if a bully went after him, Tuck might imagine a bear with super-strength showing up to save him. Tuck may be older now, but the way his powers work got cast in stone long ago.

On the other hand, Tuck's power may be that he's a magnet for super-animals. Somehow they find him. I was like that myself when I was little—always finding snakes and bugs that my sisters didn't notice. Jools, the born biologist.

Do I really need to know how Tuck's abilities work? They're basically magic, like all other superpowers. The veneer of a scientific explanation is just for plausible deniability.

"So tell me, your holiness," I say, "what brings you to the lab? Looking for Marian?"

"No, looking for you." He drops his gaze apologetically. "Polly said I should watch you, cuz you're going to cause trouble."

"Who's Polly?" I ask.

He gestures at a lab desk outside the curtained area that surrounds the medi-tank. A bright red parrot perches on a robot arm that's propped up on the desk.

Where the hell did the parrot come from? Shouldn't I be, like, the most observant person in the world? How could I not notice a flashy-colored bird only a few steps away?

Polly glares at me. Bird faces don't have the proper muscles for emotional expressions, but Polly does a damned good job of hostility.

I glare back. "Polly's wrong. I won't cause trouble at all."

"Polly's never wrong," Tuck says. "She knows things."

"So do I," I snap back. But I have to ask, "What kind of things does Polly know?"

"Future things. What's going to happen."

"Oh," I say. "One of those."

Prognostication is a rare superpower, but some Sparks definitely have it. Usually, it's just short-term prediction of events that are pretty much certain: stuff like *Person X is about to come through the door*. It may be a handy heads-up, but it's not much of a stretch—you may not be able to see it, but Person X is just outside the door and heading in your direction.

Long-term predictions are rarer and not cast in stone. What will happen in a month is subject to unpredictable randomness. Strong influences may push toward a particular outcome, but there's just too much chance for other factors to get in the way.

As for me causing trouble, I don't know if that counts as short term or long term. I don't *intend* to shit the bed in the near future, but when did my intentions ever matter? I have a knack for doing dumb things without even knowing.

Maybe I've already screwed the pooch, what with turning Robin into Vernon. I'll also bet that my roommates are raising hell trying to find me. For all I know, Aria might come blasting into Sherwood Forest three seconds from now.

One. Two. Three. Nope.

But picturing Aria makes me think of something important. "Your holiness," I say to Tuck, "can you help me with something? I got brought here and put in the medi-tank. You know about that?"

"Sure," Tuck says. "It was Lightning who brought you. My teleporting horse."

"Right. Your teleporting horse. And before I got put in the tank, Ninja Jane took all my stuff. I don't care about most of it, but I had a ring, a ring that belonged to my mother before she died."

Telling this lie makes me wince, considering that memories of my mom are pretty damned raw right now. But I want my comm ring back. I'm ready to fib if I have to. I say, "Do you know where Jane hid my ring? Maybe Polly knows. Polly knows things, right?"

I can see that Tuck is torn. Thanks to the parrot's warning, he's afraid I'll mess up his world. But he's also afraid of *me*, in that awkward intimidated-by-girls manner you see in a lot of boys his age.

Tuck must have led a sheltered life. He's stuck in Sherwood Forest, where the only females are middle-aged ones like Marian and Wrecking Ball, or crazies like Ninja Jane. He might also catch glimpses of the women Robin Hood brings home as fuck buddies, but they're probably too busy in bed to spend time socializing with a fourteen-year-old. I may be the first girl anywhere near his age Tuck has talked to.

I shouldn't take advantage of his shyness. But too bad; I want my comm ring. So I let the kid sweat till he cracks. "Nana could find the ring," he mumbles. "She's got a good nose. And tracking is her specialty; she led me to you."

He pats the huge dog at his side. She gives him a slobbery lick. Fantastic. I'm positive Nana has powers—her ability to track things is probably super—but otherwise she seems like a normal dog. It would weird me out if she could talk, or anything similar. I don't know why that is. After all, I'm fine with the Inventor being a telepathic basset hound. But I just couldn't handle words coming from a dog's mouth.

I'm a biologist. I don't like anomalous animal behavior.

Tuck says, "Let Nana sniff your hand. The finger where you wore the ring."

I raise an eyebrow and give him a look. Why would one of my fingers smell different than the others? But superpowers follow idiosyncratic rules. I stick my ring finger under Nana's nose.

She snuffles. She presses her wet cold nose against my finger. She gives me a lick with her huge sloppy tongue. Then she turns and sticks her nose in the air.

After a few seconds, she huffs without actually barking, then plods across the lab. Newfoundlands aren't excitable hunting dogs who race after fleeing targets; they're working dogs who patiently drag drowning people out of the sea.

Tuck and I follow as Nana walks past half a dozen desks covered with mechatronic miscellanies, then to an exit door hidden behind a giant Gundam head. Nana waits for one of us to open the door. Tuck hesitates, clearly worried about taking me places I shouldn't go, so I do the honors myself.

I pull the door open and move quickly into a corridor that ramps at a downward angle. The walls are white plastic, very antiseptic-looking, like walls you'd see in a research center where they study diseases. It occurs to me that Marian might well do the same. However much she resembles an orange muumuu'ed hausfrau, she's actually a Mad Genius. Considering her use of reptile DNA inside the medi-tank, it's a slam dunk that Marian tinkers with genomes whenever she's bored.

She may well have a lab where she plays with deadly diseases. Naturally, she'd separate it from all her other labs, to minimize the risk if accidents happened. And if Ninja Jane wanted to hide my ring where no one would ever look for it, where better than a lab full of viruses?

I just hope Jane didn't stash it in a vial of bubonic plague. But I guess we'll find out, won't we?

NANA LEADS US DOWN the sterile corridor. Polly arrives in a great flap of wings and lands on Tuck's shoulder. She stares at me with hostility as we descend.

At the bottom of the ramp, we go through a door into another sterile-looking room. Three walls are made from the same white plastic as the corridor. The fourth wall is a clear glass window. Finally, I see what lies outside Sherwood Forest.

Nothing.

Empty sky. But not our familiar blue one. The sky is a cloud-less purple, even though the sun shines brightly a short distance above the horizon.

The purple extends downward as well as up. Far below us, I see the tops of clouds.

"Huh," I say. "Where are we exactly?"

Tuck turns to the parrot on his shoulder. "Polly?"

The parrot answers in a parroty voice. "Latitude forty-three degrees twenty-eight minutes north. Longitude eighty degrees thirty-one minutes west." I recognize the numbers as the coordinates of Waterloo. Then the bird adds, "Altitude twenty-five kilometers."

All righty then: we're in the stratosphere. Well above commercial air routes. Also above the jet streams and most other factors related to the weather. That's why the sky isn't blue. The usual blue color is caused by Rayleigh scattering off particles in the atmosphere. Up here, the air is much thinner, so particles are fewer and farther between.

I can now fill in a lot more details about Sherwood Forest. It's a pressurized airborne environment, big enough to hold a fair-sized forest, not to mention Robin's house, Marian's gigantic lab, and who knows what else.

You'd think people would notice something so huge floating high above Waterloo. Apparently, nobody has; otherwise, the location of Robin's headquarters wouldn't be such a deep dark mystery. Sherwood must be invisible. Also cloaked against radar, IR-sensing satellites, and whatever else might look in our direction.

How did Marian build such a thing? I don't mean the cloaking devices; I take it for granted that Marian could invent invisibility machines. But my mind is blown by the resources required. You need a fuck of a strong shell to contain a breathable atmosphere when there's virtually no air pressure outside. And then to keep it in flight! Where does the energy come from? Solar power is guess number one, but nuh-uh. Intercepting sunlight casts a shadow. The more solar energy you absorb, the less reaches the ground, and soon you're a big dark blob in the sky.

How can it all work? How much did the building materials cost? And how can you construct a great honking aircraft the size of a supertanker without anyone noticing? A gazillion spy satellites watch every inch of Earth's surface, precisely because they're trying to catch Mad Geniuses making shit like this. Yet apparently, Marian built this place and launched it with nobody being the wiser.

I don't understand how that's possible. But even as I contemplate the difficulties, my mind toys with possible solutions. And heck, it must be doable because here we are.

Besides, Marian isn't the only Spark outlaw to build something colossal without being caught. Mad Geniuses regularly pump out robot armies, Godzilla-sized monsters, and super dreadnought-destroyers without being spotted till it's too late.

One thing for sure: Sherwood Forest represents a shitload of money. No matter how much Robin steals, there can't be a lot left over for healing the sick and feeding the hungry. Robin robs from the rich and gives to construction cartels.

It makes me sad. I'd hoped Robin Hood would be noble. But honestly, the Robin I met didn't show a laser-like focus on charitable deeds. Marian has more potential in the focus department, but given the choice between inventing awesome new gadgets or sneaking cash donations to UNICEF, I can guess which she'd find more attractive.

I shouldn't judge her. I can feel my own brain tugging on its leash, wanting to race back to the lab and play Frankenstein. But when I compare Robin and Marian to someone truly altruistic like Miranda . . .

I miss Miranda.

I miss K and Shar, too. I miss my own bed, Shar's new kitten, and watching Netflix with my friends.

I pat Nana's rump. "Let's find that ring."

But at that very moment (dammit!), Polly says, "Incoming report from spy code name Gisbourne. Darkling agents intend to transport the Diamond gun from Waterloo to an Ottawa research center. It will be loaded onto a train within the hour."

"Oh, for fuck's sake!" I say. "A train? They're putting it on a *train*?"

"That seems weird," Tuck agrees. "Plenty of Darklings can cast teleportation spells. Wouldn't that be safer than transporting the gun on a train?"

"It's a trap," I say. "They're dangling this big fucking bait in front of Robin's nose. *Dude, how can you resist a fucking train robbery?*"

Tuck grimaces. "Yeah. Robin would never refuse a chance like that."

"Good thing he's not Robin right now," I say. "Let's hope Marian keeps him Vernon for a while."

But how long is a while? Without any sense of a WikiJools download, I know the schedule for every train in Ontario. "It's seven and a quarter hours from Waterloo to Ottawa. But that's the passenger train, with a ninety minute stopover in Toronto. High-speed special express would take four or five hours. If Marian can keep Robin as Vernon that long . . ."

"What ho, Merry Men!" cries a cheerful voice from a speaker in the ceiling. "The game's afoot! The prey is on the wing! Assemble, my hearties, for we have villains to thwart!"

I bury my face in my hands. Robin Fucking Hood is back.

Feeding Strategies

STILL ON THE OVERHEAD speaker, Robin calls for the shortest possible meeting to discuss strategy, then off for the great train robbery.

I say to Tuck, "Before the meeting starts, can we take just a minute to get my ring?"

The room we're in has a door leading onward, presumably to the place where Ninja Jane stashed my stuff. But Tuck refuses; when Robin says, "Hurry!" everyone else has to hustle their butts.

"It'll only take a second," I say, heading onward anyway.

Next thing I know, Nana bites the seat of my pants and yanks me back. Lucky for me, the Will Scarlet costume is as tough as Marian claimed—Nana's teeth don't break the fabric. Still, it's a major-league grab-ass and it hurts like hell, even if it doesn't draw blood. Just to drive home the message, Nana growls. She may not be able to talk, but she can communicate with excellent clarity.

Sigh.

I let myself get herded back the way we came. Tuck hurries up the slanting corridor, while Polly glares from his shoulder and Nana trails behind us like a sheepdog. We make our way through the lab and into the forest. Tuck leads us along yet another game trail until we arrive at a mead hall.

The exterior is similar to Robin's house: Tudor-style, with walls made of wood laths and wattle and daub. The interior is a single big room with a table in the middle. No doubt the table has supported zillions of suckling pigs with apples in their mouths, plus tankards of Viking hooch sweet enough to make your teeth ache. The rafters have rung with many a rowdy song and the echoes of farts. Tales have been told, bets have been betted, toasts have been quaffed and queefed.

By the time we arrive, the hall is full. Full of people: familiar faces like Robin, Marian, and Wrecking Ball, plus Multiplier, the Artful Dodger, Middlemarge, Posit, Sinquisitor, Shtum, and Mistah Kurtz. Also full of animals: a sturdy gray quarter horse, an orangutan, a kangaroo, a komodo dragon, a family of otters, two eagles, and an untold number of insects, spiders, etc. lurking in the shadows. Everyone seems to be squawking without paying attention to anyone else . . . but as soon as they notice Tuck and me, everything goes silent.

"Excellent!" Robin exclaims. He stands at the head of the table, with Marian on his right and Wrecking Ball on his left. He shows no injuries from our quarterstaff frivolities. He shows no ill will either, because he gives me a beaming smile. "Fellow outlaws!" he says. "Allow me to introduce the beauteous Jools. A jewel of a woman indeed, and a fine addition to our band."

"Hey, wait a minute," I say. "I'm not an addition, I'm just passing through. In fact, it's time you sent me home."

"That won't be possible," Marian says. "I can't let you leave with your memory intact, and I don't have time to erase it now. You'll have to wait till we've robbed the train."

"But waiting is tedious, don't you think?" asks Robin. "Surely you'll join us for the robbery? You'll see what jolly times we have together."

I glare at him. "My dad always warned me against falling in with a bad crowd and committing felonies. Especially since any moron can see this is a trap. Why are you so obsessed with getting this gun?"

"Better for us to have it than the Darklings," Robin replies. "They'll use the weapon for villainous ends. And of course, dear Jools, we all realize this is a trap. But that's what we live for: to confound those who think they're smarter than us rabble."

"Pass," I say. "Have fun storming the castle."

Robin stares at me with his dark glittering eyes. "Milady, might we have a word in private?" Without waiting for me to answer, he takes my arm and escorts me to a corner of the room. It never crosses my mind to resist—he suddenly got so charming, I literally stopped thinking. For ten seconds there, my mind was just putty in his hands.

Fucking superpowers. And if I weren't a Spark myself, I'd *still* be under his spell, a blank slate for Robin to write on. Even now I feel tempted to give in and swoon.

I wonder if he realizes what he's doing. He might just believe he's a suave handsome guy whom women instinctively adore. He may not know he literally compels their minds.

"Milady," Robin says (and his voice makes me want to cream), "you and I both know you're a Spark. If you join our sport, you'll enjoy it, I guarantee. But if you insist on staying in Sherwood, we'd be forced to ensure you don't escape during our absence. We couldn't afford to weaken our numbers by leaving someone to watch you—as you have observed, this is a trap. That means we'll require our entire company for the operation. I will therefore have no choice but to hobble you before we set out on our mission."

Hobble? I don't like the sound of that. I say, "What do you mean, 'hobble'?"

"Marian has a device that neutralizes powers of the Light. It will put your Spark to sleep, so to speak. Render you unpowered. I'm told the experience can be upsetting. If one has grown accustomed to being more than human, reverting back is stressful."

My breath catches in my throat. Reverting back? Is that possible?

But of course it is. That's how the medi-tank works. The first thing it does is shut off your powers. So why is it any wonder that Marian built a device that did the same thing?

Something that could make me plain old Jools. The stupid Jools who flunks her courses. Not an Olympic-level anything, but a slutty alcoholic whose biggest claim to fame is klutzing around with an intramural hockey team that only went four-for-eight last season.

They're threatening to reduce me to *that*?

I couldn't bear it. Stupid Jools is worse than ordinary; she's pathetic. Before she became a Spark, she was circling the bowl into nothingness.

I can't go back.

I can't go back.

"Bastard," I say to Robin. "Fucking bastard."

"You're not the first to call me that," he answers. He takes my hand and kisses it. (Why do I let him?) "But when the wind of adventure blows through your hair and you stare danger straight in the eye, you'll change your mind, milady."

I want to yank my hand free and backslap him hard. But something in my head refuses to do it. The most I can manage is a gentle pulling away, like a shy little maiden blushing prettily as she says, "Good sir, you mustn't."

What I actually say is, "Fine. I'll rob your fucking train. But after that, this is over. You erase my memory and send me on my way, with my powers one hundred percent intact."

Robin gives me a smile that flutters my heart, despite how much I hate both him and myself for the reaction. "Whatever milady wishes."

He kisses my hand again.

ROBIN LEADS ME BACK to the table, where the others are working out tactics. Not that we can do much planning in advance—we know virtually nothing about what we're facing. Apparently, Robin gets info from a Darkling spy, a rebellious rich girl they've code-named Gisbourne. (She gets off on betraying the Dark in exchange for "forbidden pleasures" with a super outlaw. Yeah, sure, whatever.)

Robin knows she'll eventually double-cross him; she's just bored and doing this for kicks. And the info she supplies is pretty sketchy. Still, it's all we have to go on, so we'll have to make do.

According to Gisbourne, the bazooka will be transported as part of a regular passenger train. That's a pain in the ass, since it means we'll have to be careful of innocent bystanders. On the other hand, it's trivial to learn the train's schedule and the route it'll take. This lets us figure out the optimal place to attack: a long stretch that parallels the shore of Lake Ontario, where the rail line runs through relatively empty farmland. A Dark-Spark battle there shouldn't cause much collateral damage. Since it's winter, there won't even be cows in the fields, so no livestock will be killed in the fighting.

And yes, there *will* be fighting. We don't know who or what will be on the train, but presumably Reaper and his bosses will want overwhelming force. That gives them lots of options; they could, for example, hire mercenary Sparks to act as guards. Plenty of superpowered people sell their services by the hour. But Robin and Marian have good connections in the merc community, and they haven't heard a peep.

This suggests the bazooka will be protected by other types of guard. Most governments have secret Spark military units, but that's a double-edged sword—Spark super soldiers have a habit of going rogue. They rebel against their Darkling masters, and either become renegade heroes fighting governmental corruption, or else crazy villains who name themselves after war crimes.

When it comes to capturing a popular Spark like Robin Hood, the Darklings in our government will probably opt for non-Spark minions: Renfields like Stevens & Stephens, and full-fledged Darklings like Reaper. But it's hard to find Darklings willing to fight; how do you persuade multimillionaires to risk their lives in brawls? Robin is a high-prestige target, so he'll attract more interest than a random Spark off the street. But Gisbourne reports no calls for volunteers. Apparently the feds have something different in mind.

Nobody knows what it might be, and nobody cares. Robin's plan will be the same, no matter what: attack in full force, grab the bazooka, then vamoose.

My own plan should be to run the fuck away while the others fight. Just one problem: running is literally my only means of escape. Let's say I jump off the train and race away across the surrounding fields. I'll either get caught by one of the outlaws, or else the Merry Men will just abandon me and teleport back to Sherwood. I'll be left alone and on foot, forced to deal with whatever army the Darklings have mustered to guard the gun. They'll be able to track me down with magic, or even just a werewolf's keen nose. The only question is whether they'll kill me on the spot, or just rough me up and throw me in jail forever.

My best chance for avoiding an ugly orange jumpsuit is to stick with Robin and his gang. Cling to their coattails when they run home, and hope that Robin eventually lets me go. Yes, it means Marian will erase my memory, but that's better than getting killed or locked up.

I'm still thinking through these thoughts when Robin asks, "Anything else?" We have nothing that resembles a plan, but the outlaws shout, "No!" and jog off to gather their gear. Within seconds, the only ones left in the hall are me, Robin Hood, and Nana, who's circling the table and lapping up any mead left in the tankards. (The tankards are big enough for her to get her muzzle inside. I can't see what happens next, but I can hear her tongue going *flap*, *flap*, *flap* inside each tankard's echoing interior.)

"Milady," Robin says, "you make a most bewitching Will Scarlet."

"*Willow* Scarlet," I correct him. I feel clever for coming up with the name. Then I realize I'm not the first—I know of twenty other Willow Scarlets in the world. This must be the work of WikiJools, though I didn't sense any download; how else would I have heard of, say, a writer in New Zealand? But if I'm going out in public as a Spark, I need to construct an identity, even if it's not unique. I've got the fancy red costume, and now I have a code name. But . . .

I say, "I need a mask."

"That's easily arranged." Robin goes to the mead-hall table. For the first time, I notice that it has a delivery hatch like the one in Robin's kitchen. He taps on the hatch. "Might I please have a suitable mask for Willow Scarlet?"

The table whirs softly, then the hatch slides open. Up rises a simple eye mask, the same shade of red as my costume. The mask is totally basic, like the kind you buy for a buck at Halloween, except it doesn't have an elastic band to hold it in place. Robin dangles the mask in front of me. "Would milady pay a kiss for this bauble?"

I roll my eyes. "Cut the crap. I'm not in the mood."

"Not in the mood for a kiss? A kiss, nothing more?" He gives me a look of mock disapproval. "You wound me, milady."

I can feel his Halo flare. I don't know if he's doing it intentionally, but it's suddenly all I can do not to grab him and nuzzle his beard. I snatch the mask from his hand and mash it against my face.

Better. With a costume, a mask, and a code name, I'm now a full-fledged Spark. My own Halo flares, insulating me from much of Robin's aura. He's still the sort of dude I keep pictures of in the drawer of my nightstand, but he's not a roofie on legs.

Robin clutches his heart. "Milady!" Which I guess must mean he got hit by my Halo's clout.

I wonder if Willow Scarlet's Halo feels different from Ninety-Nine's. My roommates assure me that Ninety-Nine's Halo is "inspirational," not sexy. That's mucho disappointing, but what else would I expect when I put on a bulky hockey uniform? Not the stuff that wet dreams are made on. By contrast, the Willow Scarlet costume isn't a tight-fitting catsuit, but it's red and it's lithe and it's leather. That has to help.

I'd love to investigate if my Halo gives off different vibes when I change my costume and code name. Is my Halo part of *me*, or is it created by whatever identity I assume?

That question has to wait. Robin is still pretending to be smitten by me. He taps the table's delivery hatch, and without him saying a word, a shot glass of whisky rises into his hand.

He drains it in one gulp, as if I'm so dazzling I drive him to drink. He taps the hatch again like he still needs bolstering.

"Oh, stop it," I say. "You've slept with Tigresse. Don't pretend to go wild over *me*."

"You underestimate yourself, milady," Robin says. "And you

slander me as a man. Do you think a single night with Tigresse leaves me jaded and blind? I am still most able to appreciate beauty in its multiplicitous forms."

"If you want multiplicitous forms," I say, "fuck a shape-shifter. I have one form only, a form that pounded you unconscious once, so don't make me do it again."

"The lady doth protest too much." Another glass of whisky has appeared in response to Robin's tap on the hatch. He picks up the glass and offers it to me. "Mayhap you are simply on edge before battle. Will this settle your nerves?"

"Fuck off," I say wearily. I don't want a drink; I just wish I did. I know who I am when I'm hard up for booze.

But no. And no on sex offers, too.

I picture ripping open the V of my shirt and smothering Robin's face in my cleavage. That would be natural. Simple. That would be *me*. I could check my brain at the door and float away.

But my brain doesn't want to float. It's thinking about . . . what? The mask I put on a minute ago. How does the mask stay in place without strings? It doesn't even have glue. I think that it's bonded to my skin, as if some kind of tissue on the mask's interior has merged its cells with my face.

I realize exactly how I could do that with hagfish slime.

Robin asks, "What's wrong, milady?"

I don't answer. I just start to cry.

A GUY ONCE ACCUSED me of being without shame. What a douche. He just wanted me ashamed of sleeping with people who weren't him.

The truth is that I *do* feel shame. I'm ashamed of being a crier.

Big tough Jools. Hockey enforcer. Superhero. Takes no shit from anyone. But prone to outbursts of tears. Sometimes, I don't even know why.

I hate it. Then I get mad at myself for crying, and that makes me cry harder.

Robin Hood moves toward me . . . and I swear to God, if he

tries to take me in his arms for a reassuring hug, I have no idea what I'll do. I might try to rip him apart. Or I might fuck him. Won't be the first time for either—I've cried in front of other men, haven't I?

Stupid emotional bitch.

But before Robin reaches me, Nana moves between us. She has a worried look on her face. She nudges my chest with her nose, as if to ask why I'm crying.

I fall on the big dog's neck and hug her hard. Nana licks me with her huge wet tongue. Robin comes in close, but then wisely steps back. After watching me cry into Nana for a bit, he goes back to the sideboard and has a quiet conversation with the delivery hatch.

I keep hugging Nana. I kiss her, too, pressing my lips hard against her fur. She leans her weight against me . . . although maybe that's just a counterbalance so I don't push her over.

Time passes. I truly don't know why I'm crying. I could make a list of reasons, but they're all dumb.

It's a good thing Newfoundlands are water dogs. I'd fucking drown a Chihuahua.

Eventually, Nana gives a soft *wuff* and pulls away from me. I let her go. Robin is gone, so Nana and I have the hall to ourselves.

The tears in my eyes have cleared up enough that I can see my snot on Nana's fur. I pull myself together and go to the table; I need to order some wipes to clean up me and the dog. But I stop when I see what Robin has left for me.

Two swords. Specifically sabers.

Appropriate, I guess—according to the Robin Hood stories, Will Scarlet was Sherwood's greatest swordsman. And I'll need weaponry for the robbery; I can't fight stuff like Reaper's scythe with my bare hands.

But swords?

I slide one from its sheath. The blade looks sharp as fuck. And the people I'll be fighting aren't bad guys as such—technically, they're on the right side of the law. I don't *like* Stevens & Stephens, but I won't hack off their arms just to steal a stupid gun.

I'm not Ninja Jane.

I heft up the swords. They're beautiful examples of their kind—duplicates of the military sabers carried by German cavalry officers in the First World War. I'm a superior sword *maker* as well as wielder, and from both points of view, these weapons are awesome: the last generation of swords made for actual battle. The idiots actually believed they'd be riding in cavalry charges, waving their blades as they rode down on the enemy. That turned out well, didn't it? And now Robin wants me to do the same, facing guns and superpowers?

The door to the mead hall opens and Marian enters. She's still in her lab coat and muumuu, and still wearing safety goggles. It doesn't look like a battle costume, but if my Willow Scarlet outfit is bulletproof, Marian's must be, too.

"Shake a leg," Marian says. "We'll be leaving in just a few minutes."

I point to the table. "Robin wants me carrying these swords. How useless is that!"

"What would you prefer?" Marian asks. "A gun? The table can provide you with a nice M16. Or an M4? An M82? I can get you an Uzi or AK-47, but only if you'll use them ironically."

I say, "What about a weapon that knocks people out instead of killing them?"

"Ah, yes," Marian says, "head trauma and permanent brain injury are *much* more humane, aren't they?" She sighs. "Willow, darling, if you're fighting Darklings or Sparks, you can hack them or shoot them and they'll be fine, relatively speaking—unless you deliberately go out of your way to kill them. Whereas, if you're fighting normal humans, they're so damned *breakable*! People have been killed by a single punch. An ordinary punch, not even superstrength. What you did to Robin with that quarterstaff . . . for him it was just a time-out and a lesson against arrogance. If you did the same to a normal human being, they'd be ready for a toe tag. It's the zeroth law of Dark and Light: we play by different rules than mortals."

She picks up one of the swords and tests its weight. "The real question is," Marian says, "can you use this effectively? And do you have an alternative? If you can shoot lightning out of your nostrils, then by all means, leave the swords behind. Or if you're a mediocre sword fighter, take something you're more adept with. A quarterstaff, for example. But from a practical point of view, any weapon is lethal against normal humans, but only good clean fun against people with powers. Given that, you might as well take the swords to keep Robin happy."

She offers me the sword she's holding. I don't take it. "Keeping Robin happy isn't one of my high priorities."

"It should be," Marian says. She says it lightly, but I hear the threat behind her words. "As long as Robin likes you, the rest of us will, too. If you give us reason to reconsider . . ."

She lets that hang in the air. I can fill in the blanks. It would be easy to hang me out to dry during the train robbery. When the fighting starts, the outlaws could simply not guard my back. Hell, someone like Ninja Jane could stab me in the back during the chaos. That would solve a lot of problems for Marian: she wouldn't have to erase my memory and run the risk that I'd still remember something; she wouldn't have to worry about some wild card running around Sherwood Forest, messing with her lab and building stuff of my own; and if I get killed during the robbery, the feds will take off my mask and discover that the poor girl supposedly shot by Robin Hood was actually a member of his gang. Robin stops being a thug who hurt an innocent bystander. Marian would surely concoct a story saying that my apparent death at Robin's hands was just a clever ruse . . . and hey, he's back to being a roguish dude who'd never harm a fly.

But no one will stab me in the back if Robin likes having me around. Essentially, I'm safe as long as Robin wants to fuck me.

Awesome.

I take the sword from Marian and strap it onto my back.

I take the other sword, too. No sense having one hand empty.

15

Mechanisms of Fight or Flight

MARIAN LEADS ME THROUGH the forest to a clearing that's being used as a staging area. She points me toward a handful of jet packs lying on the ground. "Suit up," Marian tells me, then hurries away.

I go to the jet packs and examine them. Each has a pair of meter-long wings attached to a central cylinder with a jet cone at the bottom—the type of personal flight unit that humans have dreamed of since Icarus, or at least since reading *Popular Science* in the 1920s.

Engineers have coughed up hair balls trying to make such devices, but never with much success. They've produced half-assed flight units that lumber through the air for embarrassingly short periods of time, but nothing that lets you swoop across the sky like a bird.

Then along came Cape Tech, which pumped out swoop machines by the dozen. Every Mad Genius feels obliged to make their own personal flight-pack design, in the same way that classical musicians wrote fugues just to prove they knew how.

I pick up one of the units. It's heavy, like a backpack equipped for a ten-day hike. I have no idea how to strap it on or work it, but Wrecking Ball comes over to lend a hand.

"You're the new girl," she says. "You clobbered Robin. Good job."

This is the first time I've heard Wrecking Ball say anything beyond hollered curses. Her accent is Filipino, and her manner is hearty. She strikes me as one of those people who never represses emotions: if she's angry, she's furious; if she's sad, she cries without feeling guilty; if she's happy, she'll slap you on the back and buy the first round of beer.

Up close, she's huge, a head taller than me and twice as wide. She's human at the moment—her skin is just brown, not rusty black iron. I wonder if she has to be human in order to use the jet pack. Maybe turning to metal would make her too heavy. Or maybe she's just more comfortable as flesh and blood . . . like wearing casual clothing instead of a work uniform.

Wrecking Ball smacks the side of the jet pack's central cylinder. The top of it detaches; it's actually a steel skullcap. She makes me take off my red Robin Hood–style hat, then she presses the skullcap tightly onto my head. I can't see what happens next, but I think the cap resizes itself for a snug but not too tight fit. Wrecking Ball nods to herself, then tells me to put on my hat again. I do. She adjusts the hat slightly and says, "There. Can't see the cap at all."

"What does the cap do?" I ask.

"Reads your mind," Wrecking Ball replies. "It has a Wi-Fi connection with the jet pack's control unit. Just think where you want to go, and the pack does the rest."

Seems simple. Also potentially disastrous. What if somebody blasts the area with radio static to scramble the Wi-Fi? I'll just have to trust that Marian thought of such dangers, and took appropriate precautions.

Wrecking Ball must see the worried look on my face. She laughs. "Come on, girl, if someone like me can use one of these packs, you'll get the hang of it, too. Tuck's horse, Lightning—he's over there—will teleport us to the scene, one by one. We'll be hundreds of meters in the air, so you'll have plenty of room to experiment while you wait for others to arrive."

"That's assuming I don't crash and burn," I say.

"Can't happen," Wrecking Ball assures me. "Marian built in fail-safes. If the wings detect you're in a nosedive, they automatically pull up before you hit the ground."

I'm still not thrilled, but I have to assume Marian knows what she's doing. She's off on the other side of the clearing, giving orders to several dozen robots. They look like run-of-the-mill cannon fodder—bulky metal contraptions painted Lincoln green. They're roughly human shaped, with guns instead of hands. I doubt that the robots have much speed or intelligence, but they'll add to our numbers and provide covering fire for our attacks. They'll also provide cover for our retreat . . . which brings up an important topic.

I ask Wrecking Ball, "What happens when one of us gets the bazooka?"

She says, "Just think that thought clearly. Your skullcap will signal the jet pack to fire a flare. Very bright, very loud—we'll all see it. If you trigger the flare yourself or see it from somebody else, just fly straight up. Keep going till the air gets thin enough that it's hard to breathe. That'll be high enough to be safe from anything the Darklings shoot at us. Then just wait; Lightning will teleport us out, one by one."

"What if something happens to my jet pack?" I ask. "What if I *can't* fly away?"

"Someone will help you," Wrecking Ball tells me. "Probably Robin. He likes rescuing pretty girls."

Wrecking Ball gives me a wink. She probably believes Robin and I have already got consummatory together. I don't correct her misimpression. She might take better care of me if she thinks I'm balling the boss.

I say, "Speaking of being rescued, how do I call for help? Do we get radios? Maybe cell phones?"

Wrecking Ball taps the side of her neck. "We have radio implants," she says.

"I don't," I reply. "At least I sure as hell hope Marian didn't put anything inside me while I was unconscious."

"Then if you need help, you'll have to yell," Wrecking Ball says. "But don't worry. Watch the rest of us and follow along."

I could ask a million more questions, but the answers would likely be hand waving. Robin and his outlaws are all off-the-cuffers. Not a single one has asked what my powers are. No one has even asked if I *have* powers. They've apparently heard I beat Robin in combat, so they assume I must be a Spark.

They must leave all the thinking to Marian. Without her and her inventions (including Sherwood Forest itself), Robin and his posse would be easy pickings.

Speaking of Marian, where is she? She's not talking to the robots anymore. I look around, but she's nowhere in sight. Instead, I spot Robin striding to the center of our assembly.

"Good my friends," he shouts, "the time has come! Pray to your gods, then gather round. Lightning awaits."

Robin leaps onto the back of the gray quarter horse I saw in the mead hall. The horse has been quietly grazing on the clearing's grass . . . but when Robin mounts its back, the horse doesn't bolt in surprise. It simply stops eating, gives a long-suffering look in Friar Tuck's direction, then disappears.

Five seconds later, the horse is back. Ninja Jane appears from the shadow of the trees and places her hand on the animal's neck. The horse disappears again, taking Jane with it. The process repeats—Lightning in, Lightning out—for each of the outlaws. No one except Robin makes the effort of mounting the horse; touching is obviously enough for the teleportation to work.

Wrecking Ball nudges me forward when most of the others have left. Most of the *human* others, I mean; Marian's robots wait stoically, last in line behind the Sparks. I pat Lightning's shoulder and feel his strong muscles under his skin. He's sweating now, as if hopping back and forth requires exertion. But quarter horses are tough animals bred for working on ranches, and Lightning is nowhere near his limits. He leans into my hand, and abruptly I'm slapped hard by a winter wind.

MY ALTITUDE: HIGH AS fuck. The temperature: inversely proportional. Southern Ontario is approaching an Edmonton level of cold, and here I am, wearing red tights.

Suddenly, I'm thankful for the codpiece. It blocks more wind than the leggings. But the V down my front is bronchitis waiting to happen.

At least I have a wonderful view. It's midafternoon, and sunny. Farmland spreads out below me, fields white with snow framed by forests of bare dark trees. Gray lines of roads form a haphazard grid, with occasional zigzags to scoot around oddities of terrain. Barns and houses clump here and there, but they're scattered sparsely enough that they probably won't get hit in the coming firefight.

I can barely see the train tracks. They're under a dusting of snow that must have fallen since the previous train passed. No flakes are falling at present; cirrus clouds wisp like my dad's hair when it needs cutting, but they don't block the sunshine at all. The train we're going to attack is visible many miles in the distance as it chugs along through the pastures.

Lightning the Flying-slash-Teleporting Horse disappears. I'm whipped even harder by the wind, now that I'm not in the lee of the horse's body. I start to plummet. Apparently, touching the horse prevented me from dropping, but now I'm on my own.

My gut clenches, but only for a millisecond. Then I muster all the skill and coolheaded nerve of the world's best paratrooper. I project calm thoughts toward my jet pack, and in a heartbeat, I'm flying for real. Jools the F-18. I'm still freezing my ass off, but who the hell cares? This is awesome.

It isn't my first time flying without an airplane. I've been carried by Miranda, and I've ridden a flying carpet powered by Shar's telekinesis. But this is the first time I do my own driving; it's glorious. I practice zooming around till I almost crash into Robin.

I don't see the dude till the very last second. Lightning must have spaced us out widely when he brought us in. That way, we'd be spread across a big swath of sky to avoid accidental collisions. I haven't even seen any other outlaws yet—they're smart enough to keep their distance. But Robin has gallantly swooshed up to join me, in case the dumbass newbie needs help. I have to make a barrel roll to dodge him midair, combining the skills of a combat pilot with everything else that's in my head. I yell nasty things as I spin, but there's no way that Robin can hear me. The jet packs aren't super noisy, but they're as loud as a gas-powered lawn-mower. Between that and the rush of the wind, nothing I say will be audible unless I get up close and personal.

Robin grins, as if he didn't just nearly get me killed. I almost grin back—his Halo hits me hard with its charming brashness—but my Willow Scarlet Halo immunizes me enough against Robin's charisma. His smile still affects me all the way to my toes, but it doesn't shut down my brain.

So I turn and jet away to a safe distance. Keeping my back toward Robin, I hover to look at the train. It's still too far away to see much detail, but I can make out the basics: it has a single engine in front, then two bog-standard freight cars, three passenger cars, two more freights, and a caboose.

The passenger cars are double-deckers, painted green and white like the normal GO trains that make commuter runs between Waterloo and Toronto. Some of the passengers may be ringers—Darklings or Sparks who'll jump out of their seats when the shit hits the fan. It's possible the bazooka has been stashed with the passenger luggage to make it harder to find. The gun is too big for a standard suitcase, but it would fit in a duffel bag like I use to carry hockey equipment. Odds are, however, that the bazooka is stored in one of the freight cars: locked in a heavy vault and surrounded by enough combat power to ruin our day.

Assuming the gun's on the train at all. This whole setup might be fake. The bazooka may be sitting in the back seat of a minivan, cruising along the highway in a completely different direction. Reaper may be a bonehead (ha-ha), but someone in the Darkling community might be smart enough to arrange such a bluff.

Only one way to find out. I drag my gaze away from the train and scan the sky around me. As far as I can tell, almost everyone has arrived. The other outlaws drift on the breeze—some hugging themselves in the cold, some sizing up the train, some apparently zoned out. No sign of Tuck, but several of his animals are present. (There's nothing I've ever seen as cute as a fennec fox with its own tiny jet pack.) No sign of Marian, either, but a dozen of her robots hover nearby, so maybe she's controlling them from Sherwood.

Lightning arrives with a final robot clutching the horse's mane. Robin shouts something I can't hear. It's probably "Tallyho!" or something equally Robinesque. He tilts forward into a power dive straight at the train. Others plunge close after him. For a moment, I imagine them crashing into each other fifty feet above the target. I tell myself they've done this often enough to be good at group operations. Still I give them a good head start, so I can steer clear of collisions.

It's only after I'm heading down that I see Ninja Jane behind me. Somehow, on a clear afternoon in a wide open sky, I didn't notice her.

But obviously, she's decided to keep an eye on what I'm doing. If I try to escape, she'll stop me with extreme prejudice.

I'll bear that in mind.

THE OTHERS DON'T SMASH together above the train. On the way down, they do a reasonable job of dividing into equal-sized parties for each of the four freight cars. Someone must be issuing orders over the radio implants; it might be Robin, but my money is on Marian, wherever she is. She can probably see through the eyes of her robots, so she's getting twelve different views of the robbery scene. By checking out the feeds, Marian has a great bird's-eye view of what's going on.

In orderly fashion, the Merry Men align themselves with the freight cars. They match the train's speed and hover a few hundred feet above their targets. It's possible no one on the train knows we're here, but I doubt it—even Reaper should be smart enough to cast some spell that would let him watch for attacks coming from overhead. In fact, he'd just need a few GoPros mounted on the train and aimed in different directions to get an overall view of the situation.

But no one attacks us. After a moment, Wrecking Ball makes the first move. Like a diver doing a cannonball off the ten-meter platform, she drops and hits the roof of the freight car connected to the caboose. Blue sparks of lightning shoot upward from the point of contact—the train roof must be wired like an electrified fence. I don't know if Wrecking Ball can be hurt by electricity, but in the short run, it doesn't matter. Her impact bashes clean through the roof and into the freight car below.

I'm at an angle that should let me see through the hole, but I can't: it's just a sheet of blackness. Someone cast a blinder wall to hide the car's interior. I should have expected that. All four freight cars must be shielded with blinders to block any remote senses the outlaws have.

At the opposite end of the train, a Friar Tuck warthog hits the frontmost freight car with its tusks. Gouts of lightning spark on contact, but the animal doesn't flinch. Flying along with the same speed as the train, the warthog digs its tusks deep into the car's roof. The hog yanks its head hard, ripping enough of a hole for the Artful Dodger to get through.

The Dodger and his jet pack immediately go invisible, so I can't see what happens next. Presumably, though, the Dodger dives through the hole, after which he ducks and dodges any enemies he meets. (I don't know what powers the Dodger has apart from invisibility—whatever he does, nobody's ever seen him do it. But let's assume he's like his namesake, with the skills of a master thief. If there's a vault inside that freight car, the Dodger will artfully open it.)

Speaking of people with unknown powers, Middlemarge taps her foot on one of the untouched freight cars. The car's entire roof lifts like the lid of a box. I see hinges on the side where the roof connects with the car, hinges that weren't there two seconds ago.

According to expert consensus, Middlemarge is a higher-dimensional being. She doesn't look like one; she looks like your middle-aged aunt. I mean *literally*, she looks like your aunt.

Whether you're white, black, Western, Eastern, if you have a middle-aged aunt, that's who Marge looks like. If you don't have a middle-aged aunt, you have an uncanny feeling that Middlemarge would be a dead ringer for your aunt if you had one.

Everyone sees her differently. In photographs, she looks like the photographer's Aunt Marge, whoever that might be. And her powers are unpredictable, except (perhaps) to Marge. Basically, the universe does her favors. Maybe she's the *universe's* Aunt Marge, and it wants to help her out.

Nobody knows. Because Marge doesn't speak any known language. She natters away when she feels like it, but she's incomprehensible. Sometimes she seems to say, "Thank you," after the world transforms itself in response to her desires, but even *that* sounds different every time. It's a mystery why she hangs around with Robin Hood, but she showed up one day out of nowhere and she's been with him ever since.

Maybe she thinks he's hot. Or maybe it amuses her to help him; she's not the only otherworldly creature to throw in her lot with the Light for no apparent reason. Whenever aliens come to Earth, they seem compelled to join the conflict of Darklings versus Sparks on one side or the other. No one ever stays neutral and just hangs out.

Anyway, Middlemarge flips the lid of the freight car, exposing the blinder wall below. After a moment, she dabs her finger toward the blinder. She doesn't actually touch it, she just mimes a tap from a distance. The blank black surface vanishes to reveal what's below.

Ick. Zombie vultures.

It's like one of those train cars that transport livestock, crammed full of animals going to slaughter. Except in this case, it's not pigs or chickens, but vultures who look like they've been slaughtered once already. Half of their feathers have fallen off, leaving naked blotches beginning to rot. The birds' heads are scabby, but their beaks are sharp. They take to the air as soon as the blinder wall vanishes, like a flock of killer geese rising from a pond. In a roar of flapping wings and bone-chilling squawks, they surround Middlemarge and the two closest outlaws, Mistah Kurtz and Tremens.

Which is fine. Mistah Kurtz is a big crazy dude with super-strength and a penchant for going berserk. The only serious threat from the vultures is if he bites off one of their necks and catches a disease. Tremens is a scruffy little guy who's a one-trick pony, but it's a heck of a trick. If you come within three meters, you're hit with DTs: hallucinations, high fever, the shakes, and confusion. Even better, the power is selective—it only affects enemies, not friends, and when you're confused, you lash out at targets that Tremens wants you to hit.

So when zombie vultures get too close to Tremens, they suddenly start pecking at each other. It's pretty damned sickening. Like zombies in movies, the vultures keep attacking long past the point where any living animal would be too torn up to move . . . so we get treated to the spectacle of vultures with guts dangling out of their bellies still flapping around in search of victims. Some birds are missing one or both of their wings; they shouldn't be able to fly, but hey, *it's magic.* Once something comes back from the dead, defying Bernoulli's principle ain't no thing.

The biggest weirdness is that when the vultures' blinder wall disappears, the blinders on *all* the freight cars go pop. But maybe that shouldn't surprise me. This is, after all, a trap; when any one part gets sprung, you'd want to set loose the full barrage.

So what to our wondering eyes should appear? The roofs of the freight cars dissolve and we've got trouble with a capital "truh."

One: Winged golems. Like naked Frankenstein monsters that can fly.

Two: Reaper, Stevens & Stephens, and a dozen other dudes in black. They're packing pistols with a variety of weird shapes and protrusions. Undoubtedly, the guns shoot something more spicy than lead slugs.

Three: And saving the best for last, we have several supervillains. They all have pasty white skin and costumes of pale washed-out colors.

Oh, shit, they're *bleached*. I've never heard of bleaching before this second, but suddenly I know all about it. Well, not *all* about it; no one knows much about bleaching except privileged bigwigs in the Darkling community. But I know plenty enough to turn my stomach.

The whitening effect suggests that bleaching is done by powerful vampires: an ultrapotent blood drain that wreaks havoc on vital parts of the cerebellum. Another theory centers around parasites of the type used on Chekov in *Wrath of Khan*—hideous insects that snack on your brain till you're pliable. Other possibilities include magical lobotomies, demonic possession, or gaggerific horrors from exotic folklore.

But whatever bleaching is, its results are simple. It rips out a Spark's mind and makes them a puppet for a Darkling master. In the process, either as a side effect or for added intimidation, it makes the Spark's skin almost white. Just for shits and giggles, Darklings dress up bleached Sparks in faded versions of their original costumes . . . so a dude who used to wear a bright red outfit ends up wearing a lifeless pink, all sad and wan.

It's enough to give you chills. And that's the point. Darklings want everyone to know, "This dude is *broken*. We can break you, too."

Legally, bleaching is equivalent to execution. It can only be done after a public trial, and only on Sparks who commit mass murder or worse. But does anyone believe that? What would happen if, say, the Vandermeer family caught the Artful Dodger trying to steal their stuff? Would they turn him over to the cops for an open trial, during which who knows how many family secrets might come out? Or would they consider how useful it would be to have a Spark as a mind-slave?

Lucky for Dodger, he has friends. If the Artful went missing, Robin and the outlaws would look for him. If they found him bleached, they'd raise so much hell, the bleachers would end up regretting it. But plenty of Sparks work alone, especially folks who rob banks and commit similar crimes. What happens to *them* when they get caught?

Apparently, they end up on a high-speed train, with their skin the color of ashes and their skulls scooped clean by a magical melon baller.

So we got a pale pudgy dude who breathes fire, a starved-looking teenage girl who stretches, a thirtyish woman whose arms and legs are silver, and an old Chinese guy with no apparent powers except being able to fly. All four are obviously bleached: their faces and clothes look like they've gone through the laundry a hundred times too many. Their expressions are slack, their eyes are dull, and their hair is ditchwater gray.

Unlike ordinary Sparks, these four won't bluster or banter during the fight. But they won't be dimwits, either. Bleached Sparks are super focused on whatever they're ordered to do. They don't hold back, and they're never ever distracted by doubts or second thoughts. Bleached Sparks aren't stupid, they're *streamlined*. Like living torpedoes.

The four that were hiding in the freight cars attack those of us who aren't engaged with other opponents. Flame-breath dude huffs a blast that I evade by ducking behind one of Marian's robots. The bot gets hot, but takes no damage—fire attacks are so common in super battles, it'd be professional malpractice if Marian didn't make her robots fireproof. I could stay where I am and let the bot soak up fireballs, but fuck that shit. I'm a superhero. I don't hide from fights, not even when the fight is ridiculous and neither side are good guys.

On the other hand, it's ridiculous just to mill around with no strategy. And I'm Ms. Super Strategy—as good as Napoleon or a dude in his underwear playing *StarCraft II*. So let me end this as quickly as possible: by finding the bazooka. Grabbing the gun will lead to a nice little cutscene where we all teleport away safely. Then it's back to the mead hall for backslapping self-congratulation.

Also booze. Surely by then I'll be ready for booze. It's impossible to win and not want a drink in celebration.

STRATEGY MEANS GETTING THE big picture. I leave the lee of the robot and fly higher for a better view.

With the blinder walls gone and the freight cars open, I can see what was previously hidden. It doesn't take long to start cursing, because whoever set up this trap had an actual brain.

Each of the four freight cars contains several dozen crates big enough to contain the bazooka. Each crate is identical: they're made of wooden slats, which makes it easy to see that each has an inner blinder wall. We'll have to smash into every crate and grope around. No, wait, you can't *feel* inside a blinder wall any more than you can see. Blinders block neural impulses. So we'll have to tip over each crate and see what falls out, hoping that we find the bazooka instead of a booby trap. Meanwhile, the bad guys will keep pounding our—

Something grabs me: the scrawny bleached super-stretcher. She's standing in the freight car right next to the caboose. She's at least twenty meters below me, but elastic enough to reach the distance and grab me by the ankle.

She yanks down hard: super-strength as well as super-malleability. I'm caught in a tug-of-war between her pull and the power of the jet pack. I can tell I'm the weakest link—with the girl dragging me down and the jet pack holding me up, I'm close to breaking. First my spine will separate; then it's a question of whether my leg rips off before my guts split in half, or vice versa.

But I have other options. Without even thinking, I find that I've drawn my two sabers. I could easily slice at the girl's outstretched arm. *Snicker-snack*, off with her hand. Problem solved.

Yeah, no, I don't want to do that.

It's irrational, I know. She's bleached; she's as good as dead. No, she's *worse* than dead. Sparks come back from the dead all the time, but no one has ever come back from bleaching.

So severing the girl's wrist is no worse than slashing up a zombie. Grisly but safe moral territory.

I still refuse. That girl could be me, except for a bad roll of the dice. Hell, I could be like her tomorrow if the Darklings bring me down. And maybe bleaching isn't as permanent as everyone thinks. If this poor little Stretchkin ever returns to her right mind, what will she think about the person who lopped off her hand?

But the girl is still pulling me down. And she's standing right beside Stevens & Stephens, who blast away with their fancy pistols. Their guns shoot incendiary nuggets—not nearly as fast as bullets, but they burst like miniature grenades wherever they make impact. Lucky for me, the Renfields shoot as accurately as Stormtroopers. Shots singe the air around me, but only a few hit home. They feel like stones thrown hard at point-blank range, but they fizzle against my Willow Scarlet costume. It really is bulletproof and flame resistant.

So, yay.

But the costume doesn't cover my face or that open strip of cleavage. Who thought that the V was a good idea? Sooner or later, as the scrawny bleached Stretchkin pulls me closer to the Renfields, someone will get lucky and it won't be me.

Okay, fine. Let's get proactive.

STRETCHKIN STILL CLUTCHES MY ankle. I bend and grab her wrist in both my hands. I give it a sharp snap, the way my sisters used to do with skipping ropes. In accordance with Physics 112 (which I hated), a sine wave travels fast and furious down Stretchkin's arm. When it reaches her shoulder, the energy in the wave lifts the girl off her feet like a rat being shaken by a dog.

She's such a puny kid: maybe fourteen, and underfed. I'd bet good money she was a mutant who manifested powers soon after puberty. The girl left home or got kicked out for being a freak, and eventually ended up living in alleyways. She probably resorted to petty crimes so she wouldn't starve, until she got harvested by the Dark and bleached to oblivion.

She's as light as a feather. She'd anchored herself in the freight car by grabbing a support strut with her free hand, but my snap caught her by surprise. It shook her loose and now she's untethered. I snap her again, this time sideways, and when the wave propagates down her arm, she jerks into Stevens & Stephens hard enough to knock them off balance. Add in the motion of the train, and both Renfields stagger.

It earns me a few free seconds of not being shot at. During those seconds, I tell my jet pack to boogie, and up we go, me with my darlin' wee Stretchkin hanging from my leg. Between the two of us, we still weigh less than Wrecking Ball, so the jet pack holds us just fine.

Speaking of wrecking balls, I now have one of my own. She dangles below me on an arm twenty meters long. But Stretchkin isn't as docile as a normal wrecking ball. She flails like a fish on the end of a line, frantic but without any good options.

I feel bad for her. Especially considering what I aim to do next.

I look at all the crates in all the freight cars. Any one of them may contain Diamond's bazooka. For a moment, I envision swinging Stretchkin like a chestnut on a string, clonking one crate after another to see what's inside.

But that's such an obvious thing to do. It feels expected. So I swoop with my jet pack and swing poor Stretchkin at the caboose.

It's a crack-the-whip maneuver. Surely, it won't hurt much—as Marian said, Sparks are seldom injured too badly in combat. If they aren't naturally durable, then they have some other defense: a force field perhaps, or rapid healing like me.

Stretchkin is so rubbery, she ought to be really resilient. When a rubber ball hits the ground, it doesn't break, it just bounces off. (Physics 112 reminds me that bouncing off isn't what I want. To smash things, I need an inelastic collision. No, wait, that was Physics 111. No, wait, I'm distracting myself with trivia so I don't have to admit that I'm using an emaciated street kid to bash through a solid wall. Shit.)

Like an Olympic hammer thrower, I do a swing and kersmash.

The caboose is made of metal. Stretchkin crashes into it harder than I intended, rupturing the caboose like she's a battering ram. I say, "Oh, fuck," and fly in fast to see if Stretchkin is still breathing . . . but when I get close to the hole, I say, "Not important," and fly away.

I'm halfway across the nearest snowy field before I think, *What just happened?* I might have just killed a defenseless kid. And I blew it off?

I wheel around and fly back toward the train. But again, as I near the caboose, I think, *What's done is done. If I look to see the results, it will only come back to haunt me later.*

I turn away. Maybe I should go beat on someone at the front of the train. That'll make me feel better. I can smack that old Chinese guy—he's bound to be interfering somehow, even if I can't tell what he's doing.

Maybe he's affecting my mind. I should punch him in the face.

No, wait. What the living fuck. I head back toward the caboose.

But come on, Jools, why this obsession? You're being irrational. There's nothing there.

Nothing but an ignorance spell. That has to be what's happening.

K told me about the damned things. They mess with your mind to make you ignore stuff. *Hey, there's no point in looking in that direction. Nothing to see. You're wasting time.*

Fucking Darkling fuckery.

I point myself toward the caboose once more. I barrel forward. Immediately, I ask myself what's wrong with me. I'm making terrible choices, like all those times I got drunk instead of studying or doing lab projects.

You know what would be fun? Heading straight for a lab and building something with slime.

FUCK, FUCK, NO, NO, I HAVE TO CHECK ON STRETCHKIN!!!

Something snaps: the mental block holding me at bay. I

head for the caboose, zeroing in on the hole I made by slinging Stretchkin.

The hole is just big enough for me and my jet pack. Inside, the girl lies in a heap, like a bleached sheet of melted rubber. She's shapeless, no bones, just slack flaps of skin. Her sloppy head is enough to make me puke. No sign of a skull inside. Her face is like a mask made from nylon tights, but baggy, not taut.

I can't tell if the girl is unconscious or dead. She's like a collapsed parachute. The only thing that gives her any shape is what's beneath her.

She's lying like a tarp over Diamond's bazooka.

I GATHER UP THE girl and the gun. It nauseates me to use Stretchkin like a canvas wrapping, but I focus on the thought of getting her into the medi-tank. I don't know if the tank will help her—maybe she's too far gone—but it's still worth a shot.

So I make a girl-gun bundle. That's partly from paranoia—I don't want to touch the gun, for fear it's guarded by curses and other magical surprises. Instead, I drape Stretchkin over the weapon, like a blanket around a baby. It's a big baby and a bigger blanket, but I'm as good as one of those people who wrap Christmas presents as a profession.

I get the job done. By the time I'm ready to go, Ninja Jane is peering through the hole in the caboose.

I yell, "I've got the bazooka!" I don't know if Jane can hear me over the pandemonium outside: pistol shots, the howl of the wind, and the myriad sound effects of Spark powers. (*Crash! Whoosh! Sizzle!*) But Jane should be able to read my lips. That's a necessary skill for anyone who regularly takes part in super fights.

Jane slithers through the hole and lifts a corner of Stretchkin enough to see the gun. Jane stares a moment, then nods. Holds a finger in a *wait* gesture. She slides to the hole in the wall and looks out, scanning with slow deliberation to check in every direction. When she's satisfied that the coast is clear, she gestures for me to follow, then dives out the hole.

I'm right behind her, hugging the girl and the gun. Their combined weight is something like 175 pounds. I may be as strong as that weightlifter named Boris, but this isn't a featherlight load. It's also bulky and awkward, despite my packing skilz. So maneuvering through the hole takes time—like getting a heavy sofa through a doorway. Before I get all the way outside, I'm already under attack.

IT'S THE OLD CHINESE guy, the bleached dude who could fly but had no other obvious powers. He swoops past the caboose as I'm halfway out the hole. Immediately, my clothes try to kill me.

It's so damned simple. Everything I'm wearing just shrinks. It feels like when the doctor puts a blood-pressure cuff on your arm: *pump-pump*, and your blood stops circulating. My shirt squeezes my arms, and my tights squeeze my legs. I can't bend my elbows or knees. My hat clamps my skull, and my mask pinches my face as if it's trying to drag the flesh off my cheekbones.

And the codpiece . . . fuck! I *knew* that bulge was bad news. Like a weaponized thong. I ought to have my feet up in stirrups.

Everything squashes tighter. Normal cloth would rip to tatters, but my outfit is bulletproof. It ain't gonna shred anytime soon.

I'm just lucky for that V down the front. My clothes don't encircle my throat, so there's no way to crush my windpipe. Even so, I can feel the shirt collar moving—as if it's reaching for a better grip. If it finds one, it'll squeeze off my carotid artery and cut the blood supply to my brain.

Shit! My shoes are contracting! The bones of my feet grind against each other. It hurts like fuck. Strangling my arms and legs may partly immobilize me, but at least there's a layer of muscle to absorb the compression. No big muscles in my feet—just a hell of a lot of nerves. They squeal like pigs as my bones and tendons and ligaments crunch together.

I'm still stuck half in, half out of the caboose as Clothes Crusher flies by again. My clothes ratchet in another notch. Fuck, that hurts! Especially my feet. It's like they're caught in conveyor-belt gears. I can't move at all now. But none of the clothing rips. The damned things have suddenly acquired super-durability.

Ninja Jane flies close to me. She jerks her thumb hard toward the sky, with a get-going gesture.

"I can't," I try to shout back. My lungs and diaphragm are so squished, I don't have air for yelling. But my mouth still moves, even if my voice is just a wheeze. "Old bleached dude is giving me a lethal wedgie."

I'm an idiot. Instead of making a joke, I should have just said, "Stomp that bastard!" Luckily, Jane has smarts in her black-hooded head. Whether or not she understands me precisely, she's caught the gist. She rockets toward Mr. Clothes Control with both of her daggers drawn.

Thank baby Jesus, the guy can't squeeze two victims at once. I feel the exact moment when he switches his attention from me to Jane. My clothes go slack; they feel like they're going to slough off like fig leaves, but it's only the sense of contrast. My outfit reverts to ordinary cloth, merely hanging instead of constricting.

Now Jane is the one under attack—I can see it. Her ninja pajamas go taut around her, like the clingiest of spandex. But I doubt her costume is spandex or any other common fabric. Jane's pajamas are likely bulletproof Cape Tech wonders like mine.

All the stronger to strangle you with, my dear. Her hood grips her skull like a vice . . . and unlike me, her costume completely surrounds her throat. It's close to garroting her.

My turn to move. I should probably go after Clothes Control Dude, but then he'd throttle me again. I don't want that to happen; my feet are in agony, even if they're no longer being crushed. They're like two bags of bone chips swimming in blood. I won't be able to walk till I regenerate. And if that's not bad enough, the only obvious way to stop Mr. Dressup is to gut him with my swords.

Nuh-uh. Sherwood Forest has only one medi-tank, and it's reserved for my poor Stretchkin. I hug the girl to my chest and fly toward Ninja Jane.

* * *

JANE FLIES UPWARD ON the trajectory she was traveling when her clothes started shrinking. It occurs to me that our jet packs are controlled by our skullcaps. Can clothes-crushing affect a cap made of metal? Or has the cap simply been squeezed too hard by Jane's ninja hood and is no longer working? One way or another, Jane doesn't seem able to change course. Otherwise, she'd be trying to ram Clothes Dude in the kidneys.

I rev my jets to catch up with her. When I get close enough, I match her velocity. She might be screaming, but I can't tell for sure. Her ninja mask covers her mouth with a strap of unbreakable fabric.

I can fix that.

With one arm holding the Stretchkin-bazooka bundle, I draw a sword with my other hand. Hack, hack at one of Jane's sleeves. A lesser sword wielder might have trouble slicing the cloth without cutting Jane, especially since the fabric clings so tightly to her skin. But hey, I'm the best, blah blah blah.

It's like that moment when you break the package of Poppin' Fresh dough: Jane's arm flesh bulges out of the gash. Then the tensions in the cloth go past critical and the whole sleeve rips itself to pieces. Before it's finished unraveling, I split the other sleeve, too, releasing both of Jane's arms.

She's not out of the woods yet. Jane's still being strangled, and cocky though I am about precision cuts, I'm reluctant to take a swing at the cloth on Jane's throat.

But I don't have to. Jane still has her daggers and now she can move her arms freely. Lightning fast, she makes a scalpel-like incision down the clothes garroting her neck. She makes another cut down the length of her hood, from the top of her head to her jaw. The cloth snaps like an elastic band and splits down the middle, revealing the true face of Ninja Jane.

It's Marian.

A thinner version, like the "after" weight-loss picture on one of those magazines that haunt grocery checkouts. Jane's a good 150 pounds lighter than Marian. Still she has the same freckled cheeks and the same ill-chosen haircut as the original.

Quelle surprise. But I'd never seen them together, had I? And if the explosive death of Byte Bitch turned Vernon into Robin, why couldn't it do the same to Marian?

Multiple forms and personalities. Different identities. Except that I'd guess Marian has more control over the switch than Vernon does. Marian can become Ninja Jane when she wants to, not just when she's knocked out. As Marian, she's a Mad Genius; as Jane, she's just plain mad.

Jane clearly realizes I've figured out the truth. She gives me a furious glare, but doesn't have time to do more in the midst of a battle. Instead, she gestures angrily, pointing up to the open sky: *Get the bazooka out of here!*

Without waiting to see if I obey, Jane goes back to slashing her clothes. Their squeezing must hurt like hell. I know from experience.

Within seconds, Jane is naked, wearing nothing except the skullcap controlling the jet pack. She rolls in the air and zooms off toward Clothes Crusher Dude. He has no way to hurt her now . . . and as soon as Jane catches up with him, he won't bother anybody again.

I turn away quickly. Some things, I don't want to see.

I FLY UP AND away from the train. After several seconds, I remember to signal that I've got the gun. As soon as that thought crosses my mind, a flare erupts from my jet pack, whistling like a banshee. It goes off like a multipack firework, spilling red and green bursts into popping cascades. At the very end, there's an earsplitting bang, all the louder because it's only a stone's throw away from me.

Note to self: next time, keep your distance until the flare finishes doing its thing.

But one nice part about being deafened is the quiet that follows immediately. My eardrums bleed and my inner ears hurt, but I'll heal.

In the meantime, I'm several thousand scenic feet above the countryside. The air is frigid, but I don't feel cold. After all the exertion of combat, I'm as warm as if I've just finished a five-kilometer run.

The fight is over. Far below, the outlaws battle their way to freedom. Anyone in trouble will get rescued. Scores will be settled, and Robin will showboat to get it out of his system. He'll smile at the people in the passenger cars and blow kisses to any woman who smiles back.

I'm not part of the fun. I'm all alone with the bazooka and a girl I've probably killed. A teenage kid I whipped through a wall, just to see if something was behind it.

Why did I do that? I have a perfect eidetic memory, but I still don't know what I was thinking.

*Epigenetic Inhibition**

THE OTHERS EVENTUALLY JOIN me. Robin slaps me jovially on the back and delivers a lengthy speech. I can't hear him over the wind. I could read his lips if I wanted, but I don't.

Marian-slash-Jane hovers nearby without speaking. She's borrowed a cape from another outlaw; it's a swath of coppery silk, which she's wrapped around herself like a bath towel. It covers her from breasts to thighs, but doesn't hide the blood spatter speckling her shoulders and face.

Clothes Control Dude was bleached. His blood wasn't.

I wonder about the mental conjunction between Marian and Jane. Is it the same as between Vernon and Robin? Vernon knows everything Robin does, even if Vernon doesn't experience it directly. Does Marian know what Jane gets up to? And how does Marian feel about that?

Then again, how sure am I that Marian and Jane are mentally different? The whole "Jane never speaks" routine could just be an act, a trick to make Jane seem more spooky. Marian and Jane could be no more different than "me as Jools" and "me as Ninety-Nine." Or "me as Willow Scarlet."

As I ponder the question, Jane flies up to me. She points at Stretchkin, whom I still cradle in my arms. Jane shakes her head violently, then jerks her thumb to indicate, *Get rid of her.*

I say, "I want to put her in the medi-tank."

Jane shakes her head again and jerks her thumb.

I look around at the other outlaws. They're widely dispersed

*Alteration of a gene to prevent it from being used.

across the sky, but none of them looks seriously injured. A few gashes, some burns, and Sinquisitor seems to have broken his arm, but nothing immediately life-threatening. I tell Jane, "No one else needs the tank. This girl does."

Jane glares at me furiously. Then she grabs the cape she's wearing and loosens the knot that holds it around her. Jane's body balloons, muscles being replaced by fat as she adds on 150 pounds.

The cape can't go all the way around her anymore. She does her best to hold it in place, at least to cover her front . . . but it's a losing battle. She scowls in exasperation, then rolls her eyes and gives up. She turns to me and says, "There's nothing my medi-tank can do for that girl. Just leave her."

No doubt she's speaking in Marian's soft nursery-school voice. I can't hear it over the wind and the sound of our jet packs. But I can read her lips.

"The girl might not be dead," I say. "After the mess in the Transylvania Club, you thought *I* was dead. But the tank saved me."

"You weren't bleached," Marian says. "The tank can't do anything about bleaching."

"But it might still heal her physically."

Marian says, "Think, Jools. This girl is a Darkling mind-slave. It's magic. Cape Tech can't fix magic. So if the medi-tank heals her body, what's the point? The moment the girl leaves the tank, she'll attack us. We'll have to bash her unconscious again. Keep her locked up forever. Sooner or later, she's bound to escape— Sparks always do. Then she'll rat us out to her masters, and the next thing we know, Sherwood Forest is under full-scale attack from Darklings thrilled that they've finally found us. Even if we drive them off, our secret base won't be secret anymore. We'll be attacked over and over until Sherwood is blasted to pieces."

I start to object, but Marian continues. "The Darklings might find us, even if we keep the girl completely under wraps. I'll lay you odds that the bleaching process creates a permanent magical link to her—similar to a vampire's blood bond. If we take her back to Sherwood, the Darklings may be able to use her as a sorcerous homing beacon."

I want to argue but can't. Enchantments do have a habit of establishing sympathetic connections. Bleaching likely produces a magical Find My Phone app.

"Leave her," Marian says. "She's as good as dead anyway. We're doing her a favor."

I don't respond. I simply do nothing as Marian gestures to Mistah Kurtz. She must be saying something to him using her comm implant, because the big hulking dude flies over to us.

Kurtz grabs the girl and bazooka out of my hands. He pulls little Stretchkin off the gun and tosses the girl aside.

Stretchkin falls like a sheet in the wind, carried away on the breeze. She'll flutter for miles before she reaches the ground. Maybe she'll get caught in the branches of a tree and hang there for who knows how long, gradually turning into unidentified tatters.

A street kid whom nobody cared about.

My eyes are so full of tears, I don't notice when Lightning the Wonder Horse takes me back to Sherwood.

THE OTHERS ARE BOISTEROUS. I'm not.

I got their fucking gun for them. I only had to kill a kid to do it.

I don't even care about the gun. I want to go home.

And I want my memory erased . . . if there really is such a machine. At this point, it wouldn't surprise me if Marian's memory wipe is actually performed with Ninja Jane's daggers and a cremation furnace.

But that's my anger talking. Marian, Robin, and the rest aren't utter monsters. They aren't even villains. They're adrenaline junkies.

Takes one to know one.

They're all in the mead hall now, getting rip-roaring drunk. Me, I still can't stand the thought of alcohol. And unlike before, I'm *happy* that I don't want a drink.

So there, I've discovered the cure for alcoholism. All you have to do is murder someone. Then you absolutely don't feel like carousing.

It's no challenge to slip away from the celebration. Robin tries to paw me up a little, but I slap his hands and he gets the message. I worry that maybe Marian will keep a watchful eye on me, but she's distracted. She can't stop looking at Diamond's bazooka.

The gun sits proudly on the mead-hall table. Everyone wants to take selfies posing beside it. The outlaws won't let Marian take it away to her lab, so she tries to examine it right where it is. She gets so caught up trying to figure out how it works, she forgets about me completely.

I know what you're going through, sister, I think, as I sneak unnoticed out the door.

It's night in Sherwood. Down in Waterloo, it must be late afternoon, but the forest operates on a different schedule. Or maybe there *is* no schedule. Maybe Robin and/or Marian arbitrarily decide when it should be day or night. Getting drunk goes best with darkness, so they've turned off the simulated sun and fired up the mead hall's hearth. Flames crackle under dark rafters: the perfect party ambience.

Outside the forest is full of the sound of crickets and nonexistent owls.

I race through shadow toward the lab. Pockets of mist are forming—likely through artificial means because I can't think of a natural explanation. Maybe Robin requested a fog-laden atmosphere, and Marian made it so.

What Robin wants, Robin gets.

I reach the lab and go inside. (No locks on the door—we're all friends here.) I retrace the route I took with Nana, the one that was supposed to lead me to my comm ring. I go down the ramp to the viewing gallery that looks out over the world . . . and here, the sun still hangs in the sky, with more than an hour till dusk. The ground is hidden by clouds a long way below us. We float in stratospheric sunlight, disconnected from the world.

If I find my comm ring, will it even work? We're twenty-five kilometers above the nearest cell-phone tower. But I have to believe Invie's rings don't use the conventional grid. For all I know, they can transmit through all of space and time like the phones on *Doctor Who*.

I leave the viewing gallery and go through the door I saw earlier in the day. It leads to a Cape Tech clean room, sealed off and isolated, which explains why it's so far from the main part of the lab. It's actually outside the shell of Sherwood Forest, like a barnacle clinging to the ship's hull. I'll bet it's completely detachable. If something goes wrong—if a virus gets spilled or a robot goes berserk—the room can be ejected before the problem spreads. When the jettisoned room has fallen a safe distance from Sherwood, incendiary bombs will likely go off to purge the place clean.

And this is where Jane put my comm ring? Well, as I thought before, it's not a bad place to cache treasures. Who would go snooping through a lab full of cholera?

Unsurprisingly, the door has a lock—you don't want anyone wandering in by accident. But the lock is controlled by a standard Singatec security pad. It's a Model 3L as opposed to the 3C I dealt with two nights ago; it locks and unlocks the door, as opposed to just setting off an alarm. But details, shmetails. I take off the faceplate, yank the right wire, and knuckle-punch the chip.

Hope I didn't just release a zombie plague or a rogue AI.

Oh well. Omelets. Eggs. Human civilization. These days, nothing is built to last.

EVEN WITH THE LOCK broken, the door takes serious muscle to open. It's steel, thick enough to withstand high pressures. The room on the other side is the size of an elevator cab, but with extremely solid metal walls. The room's exit is another steel door identical to the one I just opened . . . so basically, this place screams "Air lock!" on the off chance I haven't yet got the message that I'm breaking into Pandora's box. I should probably be wearing a biohazard suit; either that, or pristine white coveralls, with a puffy plastic hat to cover my hair and frost-colored makeup to finish the look. But my Willow Scarlet suit will have to do. I'll burn the fucking clothes when I finally get out of here.

Oh, wait, the costume is flameproof. Well, that just makes it a challenge. Mad Genius time!

I push a blue button that closes the outer air-lock door. Time passes as fans whir. *La-la-la.* I think of all the movies I've seen where someone's being chased by monsters or dying from loss of blood and has to wait while some mechanical door takes for-fucking-ever to open or close.

La-la-la.

But at last the inner air-lock door swings open. The room beyond is appropriately white, all the better to see any schmutz I might shed from my clothes or unsterile body.

The furnishings are sparse: just two heavy steel tables, one in the center of the room and another up against a wall. The surface of the central table has a network of grooves designed to channel fluids to a drainage hole at the foot. Not ominous at all. The side table has tools laid out on a pad of gauze—scalpels, clamps, etc.— plus an autoclave machine and a dozen glass containers that might be used for tissue samples.

Ooo-kay. Strong Dr. Mengele vibes. But maybe I'm judging too harshly. The labs I'm used to are for undergrad biology classes. They're cramped and chronically underequipped, with everything scuffed and a few years behind the times. I shouldn't label Marian as a Nazi just because her lab is squeaky clean and state of the art.

But where the hell is my comm ring? I survey the room and finally realize that one of the walls is slightly different than the others. It's the same white color, and at first glance has the same texture. But it's made of a different material—smooth metal as opposed to ceramic tile.

I walk over for a better look. For the sake of experiment, I give the wall a light little push. Something goes click, and one side of the wall swings outward a few centimeters. Aha: a door in disguise. I slip my fingers around the edge and swing the door open on its hinges.

Behind is a second door, as big as a walk-in refrigerator. Embedded in the door's surface are two numeric keypads (both hexadecimal), plus a trackball, four display screens, fifteen levers, six USB ports, and a docking slot for a cell phone.

Cape Tech. Nothing else could possibly need such a complex interface. But what are all the bells and whistles supposed to do? This can't just be a plain old storage vault. That would be too easy. And it wouldn't be "fun." When you use Cape Tech, your keywords are "weird," "overcomplicated," and "disastrously unsafe."

So what's the craziest shit I can imagine?

This door in the wall leads to other times and places.

I hate to say it, but that makes sense. If you enter the proper coordinates on the keypads, you can toss your toxic trash into the sun. Different coordinates, and you can store your valuables in some postapocalyptic desert so far into the future that you don't have to worry about people or even bacteria messing with your stuff. Or maybe you'd prefer to keep your goodies on the moon where there's nothing but hard vacuum. For sheer joy in life, you could deposit your stash in some alternate universe that has completely different laws of physics. True, that'd be a crapshoot, since there's no telling what happens to terrestrial substances when the fine-structure constant of the universe becomes something radically different. But that's the sort of dickery a Mad Genius loves.

Marian *could* have made an ordinary vault and a garden-variety incinerator for dangerous waste. But no. That's boring. Isn't it more entertaining to dump stuff in the distant past, and take the chance of completely changing the course of evolution? Besides, if you steal some magical doodad from the Darklings, do you really want to keep it close at hand? Or would you rather plop it onto an airless ice world five galaxies away, so that if it summons Cthulhu, nobody cares?

I'll bet that Marian is pissed off she can't bring the bazooka here to her sanctum. If Robin and the others didn't want to drape themselves all over it, Marian could keep the gun on ice just by typing some numbers into—

Zap.

I WAKE UP FEELING like crap.

I mean seriously. Exactly like that coiled-up-turd emoji.

Worse than a cold. Worse than a hangover. Worse than when I got mononucleosis, and could barely rub two brain cells together.

Wha' hoppen?

A head appears in front of my blurry eyes. I squeeze my eyelids shut, then open and try to focus.

It's the kid. Friar Tuck. Nana is here, too. She licks my face.

I go, "What the fuck just happened?"

"You triggered a defense system," Tuck says. "It shot you with a taser. You've been unconscious a long time. Hours."

Fuck. I've come back from fatal injuries in a matter of minutes. That taser must be one bad-ass weapon.

But it would have to be, wouldn't it? Gotta be designed to knock out a Spark or Darkling with a single shot.

Fierce.

Tuck goes, "Marian's super mad at you. You broke into her special lab. You might have released something *awful.* Like, extinction-of-life-on-Earth awful."

"Why is Marian working with stuff that could kill all life on Earth?"

Tuck shrugs. "Sometimes we fight villains and capture their equipment. Marian takes it apart to see how it works. She likes knowing things. And sometimes she does research, trying to make extra-good inventions. Not normal Cape Tech, but even crazier. She says that one tiny mistake, and instead of a cure for cancer, you get a sentient cancer life-form that wants to replace humanity."

I'm like, "Tell Marian I'm sorry. But you know why I was there. I wanted my ring."

The boy actually does the Awkward Turtle thing with his

hands. Wow. I thought that was an internet hoax. Tuck goes, "Marian looked at your ring. She says it's actually a Cape Tech communicator. That made her *really* mad. Ninja Jane–level mad. So she . . ."

Tuck doesn't finish his sentence. He looks down at his hands and keeps turtling. Nana licks me again, but this time slurps my ear instead of my face. I may be super, but wet willies are my kryptonite. I jerk away from the dog, and finally sit up to see where I am.

I'm on a cheap couch in a tiny living room. The place is just big enough to hold the couch and two big-screen TVs, one on the end wall and one on the side. The end screen has an Xbox One X attached and the side one a PlayStation 4.

There's something around my neck. A metal collar. It's lightweight enough that I didn't notice it with my muddy head. But now I grab hold of the collar and try to pull it off.

Immediate stabbing headache. Like, super vicious.

Tuck goes, "Don't do that. You'll hurt yourself."

I let go of the collar. The headache fades but the muddiness doesn't.

Tucks turtles some more. "The collar, umm, it's a neutralizer. To suppress your powers. So you don't cause any more trouble."

I stare at Tuck a moment, then start to cry.

IT'S AN UGLY CRY, I know that. And I hate it. I hate being a crier.

I hate all the bullshit about crying and not crying. I hate how when I cry I think, *Don't be a baby*, then I think, *Crying is okay, who told you otherwise?* Then I think, *People will call you a hysterical bitch*, but then there's, *Fuck those people*, and *Fuck everyone*, and *Fuck me most of all*.

I can't cry without thinking I'm bad. I can't cry without thinking I'm bad for thinking I'm bad. I can't cry without thoughts of *You're stronger than this* heaping up on top of why I'm crying in the first place.

I wish I could just cry. I wish I were really as stupid as I feel. Then I wouldn't have the spare brainpower for hating myself at the same time that I'm bawling my ass off.

So be proud of yourself, Jools! Even without superpowers, you're not dumb enough to cry unselfconsciously.

And yeah, my powers are truly gone. I try to rhyme off π, and I only get as far as 3.14159. WikiJools doesn't come to my rescue. I can't even remember who played Elsa in *Frozen*. If I tried to sing now, I'd break the Auto-Tuner.

I hug Nana as if I'm drowning. That's what Newfoundlands are for: they rescue people who've fallen into cold deep waters. But Nana's not going to rescue me from the collar. She's on Marian's team, not mine.

WHEN I'VE CRIED MYSELF out, I wipe my nose on my sleeve. With my other sleeve, I wipe my eyes.

No sign of Tuck anymore. The kid's only fourteen. He likely stayed in the room as long as he could stand listening to me, but eventually he convinced himself that leaving me to cry in private was doing me a favor.

Can't blame him. I've done the same. Once I walked in on my hockey teammate Zaynab while she was crying in the locker room. I stood in the doorway a long, long time, wondering what I should do. Then I backed off into the hall and went to sit in the bleachers until I was sure she'd be gone.

Never found out why Zaynab was crying. No way I could ever ask.

What a fine human being I am.

I tell myself I'd be different now. I'm a Spark, and Sparks don't hold back when people are suffering. A lot of Sparks literally can't—they're driven to get involved.

Besides, I'd be an Olympic-level therapist. The best hotline counselor ever. The best at emergency psych. I would have known exactly what to say to Zaynab and everyone else who's hurting.

But I'm not a Spark anymore. Not while I'm wearing this collar. I'm stupid hide-from-people Jools. Nothing but a waste of biomass.

If my tear ducts had juice left, I'd start crying again. But unlike dry heaving, there's no such thing as dry crying.

At least I don't think so. Without WikiJools, I don't know for sure.

Nana huffs and licks my nose. She likes the taste. She licks some more. Whoopee, my tears are good for something: providing Nana with salt.

But there's only so long I can stand a canine tongue bath. I pull back and hold Nana at bay when she tries to keep licking. She gives me a reproachful look. Then she pads out of the room.

I prop myself up on the couch and feel like shit for a minute or two. In a sudden burst of anger, I try to rip off the slave collar. The pain almost makes me puke. Even poking at the collar with the tip of one finger turns my stomach. When I actually grab the metal, my guts do a flip-flop. I do it again, promising myself I'll hold on no matter what . . .

I wake up, covered in vomit. My brain hurts so bad, it's like I've had the concussion my sisters warned me about ever since I started playing hockey.

The collar is as tight as ever. It's not going anywhere.

With nauseating dabs of my finger, I map out the collar, checking for weak points. There's a hinge in the back and a seam in front where the two halves lock together. Nothing that feels like a keyhole. If I were still super-smart, maybe I could figure out how to get the collar off. But dumb old Jools has no ideas except using brute strength.

I try that again.

I pass out again.

I wonder how often I can do this before I get permanent brain damage.

Smart Jools would know. I don't.

EVENTUALLY I GIVE UP.

I brush half-dried puke off my clothes. Good news! The Willow Scarlet outfit cleans up pretty well. Resists vomit as much as bullets.

But that V down the front where the costume exposes my skin . . . it's crusty and totally disgusting.

* * *

IT TAKES ME TWO tries to get off the couch. Is this what life was like when I was unsuper? Clumsy as a hog, and three-quarters drained of energy?

Shit, no, I refuse. I'm still a jock, aren't I? Even without powers, I'm healthier than, like, 95 percent of the population. This has to be left over from getting whazzed by Marian's taser. It stomped my nervous system with hobnailed boots.

But in a while, I'll be back to my hockey-goon self . . .

Shut up, Jools. You aren't fooling anyone.

17

Junk DNA

I HAVE TO PSYCH myself up just to leave the room. I'm useless compared to the superpowered outlaws. I feel like a mouse surrounded by tigers.

Fuck, Jools, get your act together!

But it's hard. I remember how cocky I was before I got superpowers. I always thought I was the strongest one in the room. Tougher than all the other girls. Even most guys. As for the few guys bigger than me . . . well, I had equalizers and knew how to use them.

But in Sherwood Forest, I'm roadkill. After only two weeks of being super, I know how much Sparks outpower normal human beings. Even a kid like Tuck could destroy me.

I feel timid as hell. But eventually, I scrape up the nerve to stick my nose out the door.

No one in sight. I sneak farther, always on tiptoe and listening hard.

I'm in a barracks for Robin's outlaws. Looks like each of them has a suite made up of little rooms. It makes me think of stories I've heard about tiny apartments in London or Manhattan, where you get a kitchen, bathroom, and bedsitter with the floor space of a postage stamp.

But in my current condition, any bathroom is better than none. As a Spark, I could go all day without a bladder break. Didn't even think how unusual that was. Being super has all kinds of perks nobody ever talks about it. But now that I'm mortal, biology is a bitch.

Fine. Whatever.

Afterward, I stare at myself in the mirror over the sink. I look like hell. Puke all over me. I'm still wearing the Willow Scarlet mask. I reach up to take it off, but then stop. I don't really want to look at myself.

Makes no difference. I'm not super, so the mask is just a mask, not a separate identity. I look like Jools with something big and red and stupid on my face. I can see my bloodshot eyes through the mask's eyeholes.

So I do take off the mask. I'm tempted to toss it in the garbage, but decide it might be useful later on. Maybe a time will come when I need to pretend I'm super. I won't have a Halo, but I can still try to fake it.

I've had practice trying to fake being better than I am.

I tuck the mask in a pocket of my jacket, then use the sink to wash myself. The process takes a while, but it makes me feel more human.

As if human is a thing I want to feel.

I WANDER THROUGH THE barracks another few minutes, but most of the doors are locked. Nobody's home, not even Tuck's animals. It's strange that I'm not locked up if Marian is so peeved with me. I guess the collar is considered enough of a jail.

Anyway, I'm sure none of the outlaws want to waste their time guarding me. They're either still drinking in the mead hall or else they've passed out.

I still can't believe they'd give me free run of their base. So I look around hard, and eventually spot a pebble-sized fleck hovering close to the ceiling. It's silent and neutral gray. When I reach toward it, the thing backs off. But when I move away it follows, as if it's programmed to stay at a specific distance.

Must be a spy drone the size of a peppercorn. Cape Tech, of course. You couldn't make something that small with *real* science. It'll have a camera and microphone to watch me . . . something to raise an alarm if I get out of line . . . an engine that lets it fly, and a battery to run the show. No way conventional technology could cram so much into something the size of a piece of snot.

I show the drone my middle finger. That's the limit of what I can do. How can nonsuper people defy Cape Tech? I've got nothing. Nothing at all.

I can't stand this. Time to find Marian. I'll get down on my knees if I have to: "For fuck's sake, just wipe my brain and send me home."

There's no reason to keep me anymore. They've brought the damned gun back to Sherwood. Now Marian has all the time in the world to erase my memory. Hell, if she makes me forget what I did to Stretchkin, I'll name my firstborn Marian. Or Robin. Or whatever these fuckers bloody well want, so long as they let me leave.

I BLUNDER THROUGH THE barracks till I find an exit. Out I go.

But when I get outside, I have no clue where I am. I'm still in Sherwood Forest—the trees are just a few steps away. But this is my first time at the barracks, and I don't know how to get from here to anywhere else.

Overhead, the Milky Way smears across the night like a photo from *National Geographic*. Maybe I'm being stupid, but the sky looks real, not like the fake sun or fake night that was simulated earlier. It's like Marian has turned Sherwood's roof transparent so we can see what the universe really looks like from the stratosphere.

No clouds at all. So little air, the stars don't twinkle. Just hard cold points of light with galactic dust around them.

Miranda would love the view.

I miss Miranda.

I look around for any sign of how to get out of here. The barracks building resembles Robin's house: Tudoresque. Lots of windows made from diamond-shaped panes of glass. It could be a copy of some famous historic building, but how would I know? Without WikiJools, I'm a bumpkin who knows fuck all about her own country, let alone England.

Screw it. I just want to leave.

The night is crazy dark—the kind of dark you never get in cities, where streetlights shoo the darkness away. Despite the stars, I can barely see anything. The moon is nowhere in sight, and the trees will block the starshine as soon as I enter the forest.

I stumble around for a while and finally find a trail leading into the woods. It starts a few paces from the barracks' front door, and thank God, it's not too hard to follow. With people like Wrecking Ball using the path on a regular basis, the dirt gets stomped down hard and undergrowth doesn't have a chance to grow.

I can't see a thing once I'm under the trees. I have to walk with short slow steps, grossly embarrassed at my awkwardness. I'm all hunched over with my hands out in front of me. I can picture people laughing their heads off if they're watching me through the spy drone's camera. (For sure, the drone must be able to see in the dark. It follows me perfectly through the night, a little wee nugget glowing faintly behind me like a firefly jail guard.)

For all my caution, I still bump into tree trunks and lurch into brambles. The only thing that saves me from serious injury is Willow Scarlet's costume. It shrugs off the collisions and scratches that would otherwise mean death by a thousand cuts. Padded bulletproof boots are awesome when you stub your toes in the dark.

But the clothes can't save me from my own stupid fear. My nerves jangle as I grope through the woods. Primal instincts, right? Back when we were monkeys, we knew that the forest was full of predators. Intellectually I know that Sherwood has no big bad wolves, but tell that to my hindbrain.

Besides, there are worse things than wolves. I imagine Ninja Jane watching from the shadows. Marian hates me for breaking into her clean room. Also for learning that she's actually Ninja Jane—that must be a secret she wants to keep hidden. And thanks to the spy drone, Marian surely knows where I am. Ninja Jane could slit my throat, and who would stop her? In this jet black night, who would even know?

I'm vulnerable. A minnow among sharks.

I'm soggy with fear sweat by the time I stagger out of the woods. I can smell myself; it's not pretty. And this isn't the time to relax just because I'm out from under the trees. In every movie ever, the moment you go "I'm safe" is the moment you die.

After a while, I choke down my nerves enough to look around.

Still no lights to speak of, but I think I'm facing Marian's lab. I smell warm thatch from the roof, and when I reach out, I touch a flagstone wall. I want to run inside immediately; there'll be light and and escape from the dark.

But as I move toward the door, a thought hits me. What if Marian stops me from entering the lab? What if the spy drone, or the collar, or some other automated defense zaps me?

Marian can't be eager to let me back into her lab. She may even kill me for trying. Robin is too chivalrous for cold-blooded murder, but I'm not so sure about Marian.

Still, I have to see her. I want this over. I fumble around till I find the door.

I go inside.

FOR A SECOND, THE lab is as dark as the forest. Then a sensor detects my arrival, and the lights come on.

They're so bright it's blinding. I have to cover my eyes.

But nothing shoots me. I don't even set off alarms.

As I wait for my eyes to adjust, I realize that Marian can't be here. Otherwise, the lights would have been on already. Maybe she's still in the mead hall, guzzling champagne and pawing at the bazooka. But I'm not ready for another dark trip through the forest. I'll wait till my heart stops pounding.

What if Marian catches me here? What if she hurts me?

Fuck, Marian has broken me. I'm walking on eggs, for fear that someone super gets angry.

I stay standing two steps inside the doorway, afraid to go farther. I stare at the gizmos on desks close to the door. I remember when I got my first glimpse of this lab—I recognized almost everything. Now, I don't.

What's the name of that thing where you can't recognize faces? *Pro*-something. (Without this damned collar, I'd know the word.) I have that same condition, except for gadgets. I look at the stuff around me; everything seems half-familiar. But there's a wall between me and my memories.

I flash back to writing exams last term. I would read a question and think, *I've seen that before*. But my mind would come up blank. Like some YouTube dog that can't get up the stairs.

For a while, I stopped being that dog. That girl. But now I'm back at the bottom of the stairs. Without WikiJools to cheat and pass me answers, I got nothing.

Shit.

Shit.

Shit.

TIME PASSES IN BLANKNESS. Not productive blankness, like when I enter Mad Genius mode. Instead, I shut down like some sedentary sea creature that attaches itself to a rock and spends its life eating plankton that just happens to drift into its mouth.

I know such species exist, but I can't name any. I should be able to cite phylum, class, all that Latin bullshit. But I can't. I stand like a miserable dummy . . . until Marian opens the door and comes in behind me.

She goes, "What are you doing here?"

I try to get my shit together. "I came looking for you, okay? I want to go home. So please, just wash my brain and get it over with."

Marian doesn't answer. She stares at me like a problem she hasn't solved yet. Finally, she goes, "What do you want, Jools? Apart from leaving Sherwood. What do you really want?"

I'm like, "I don't know what you mean."

Marian keeps staring at me, but I think she's putting together a speech. Finally, she goes, "Being a Spark is an infection. It's gets inside and changes you. With someone like Robin, the changes are obvious: impetuousness . . . an impulse to beat up bad guys . . . an utter certainty that he's personally a good guy. Every other Spark is the same, just more subtly. Even people we call supervillains, from monsters like Diamond to the petty little sods who rob banks . . . they're all true believers. Moral crusaders, even when they do horrible things.

"Ordinary humans are different. A human mob boss . . . he

knows he's shite. He'll rationalize what he does, but he'll admit he's a greedy violent smeg. He doesn't think he's *good*, he just thinks he's justified. 'Everybody does it'—that kind of excuse. But Spark mob bosses think they're heroes. Absolutely doing the right thing."

I go, "Like they pretend they rob from the rich to give to the poor?"

Marian laughs. "Exactly. Sparks offer many explanations for what they do, but seldom any doubts or self-reproach."

I'm like, "You want self-reproach, just ask."

"Well, Jools, that may be your *thing*," Marian says. "Some Sparks are oh-so-conflicted . . . as if they got super-angst as part of their power set. But in that case, they deeply *believe* in angst: that the world is an anguishing place, and people who don't feel tormented are monsters."

"Nope, that's not me, either. I don't *want* to be down, I just am."

"Oh, well, blame that on the collar," Marian says. "I don't mean the collar artificially makes you feel bad. It doesn't *impose* any particular feeling. But when you stop being a Spark, you stop being certain of your . . ."

She doesn't finish her sentence. Instead, she crosses to a lab desk and opens a cupboard. She pulls out a metal collar like the one that's clamped on my throat.

"I made this for myself," Marian says. She holds it up so that it catches glints from the overhead lights. "It doesn't have a lock, but apart from that, it's a twin of the collar you're wearing."

She lifts the collar and latches it around her neck. Marian's eyes unfocus a moment. She shuts them and takes deep breaths. "Bugger, I always forget what it's like."

"You do it to yourself? Voluntarily?"

"Yes." Marian opens her eyes. "It's useful to stop thinking like a Spark once in a while. To be my old self for a bit." She makes a face and mutters, "As if I can ever be my old self."

Marian hops up to sit on the desk. She waves her hand at the desk directly across from her. "Why don't we talk?"

"About what?"

"Whatever." She gestures again. I don't want to talk, but I go sit anyway.

Marian waits for me to say something. When I don't, she goes, "Jools, tell me what you want."

"I still don't know what you mean by that."

"That's because, at the moment, you aren't a Spark. Neither am I. At the moment, I'm just . . ." She hesitates. "Ah, what's the fuss, you won't remember this, will you? I'm Vanessa. My real name is Vanessa. *Was* Vanessa, anyway."

I snort. "You and Robin were Vernon and Vanessa?"

She shrugs. "I rather liked that. It sounded like we were a pair."

I go, "Have you ever put one of these collars on Robin?"

"I asked him once if he was interested," Marian says. "He took it as a sexual proposition. A Spark version of bondage." She sighs. "The man has a one-track mind."

"You never just sneaked up and collared him by surprise?"

Marian glares. "There's this word, Jools: 'consent.' You might have heard of it."

"I didn't fucking consent when you put the collar on *me*."

Marian—or should I say Vanessa?—looks guilty. "You gave me no choice. Besides, when I put the collar on you, I was Marian. Convinced of my own morality."

"But you aren't now? Then take the collar off me."

She shakes her head. "I recognize that at the moment, I'm not smart enough to make that decision."

"For fuck's sake," I say.

I hop off the desk and am half a second away from storming out the door when Vanessa puts her hand on my arm. "Jools, please. Another minute. Tell me what you want."

I shake off her hand. "What the fuck do you want me to say?"

"Anything," Vanessa goes. "I'm not doing this for me, but for you, the real you. When you're a Spark, you'll want . . . oh, let's call it truth, justice, and the Canadian way. (Is there such a thing as the Canadian way? No, let's not get sidetracked.) The point is that as a Spark, you'll have an agenda. You won't even have to think about it. You'll feel a calling, and see it as your destiny."

She grimaces. "When I'm Marian, I know that stealing from Darklings is the ideal way to spend my life. It feels so *obvious*: I have to keep the Darklings from winning. And taking their treasure is the best way to do that. *I feel. No. Doubt.* Don't you have a similar conviction, Jools? Not necessarily that you ought to steal Darkling treasures, but that you have to fight the Dark in some specific way. Haven't you ever felt that? A sacred calling?"

"No," I say. "Not unless you count kicking your ass once I get this collar off."

"Then you must be new," Marian says. "New at being a Spark. It takes a while for the Light to seep into your mind and make adjustments. But it will. After a month or two as Sparks, we end up as different people."

I don't like the sound of that. But hell, I'm a university student; I've seen the same thing in action. First-year students come to uni from high school, all fuzzy-headed and random. They get whipped into shape over the months of first term, so that by Christmas they think like scientists, engineers, or whatever they're supposed to be. Their whole perception of what's true and important gets transformed, like religious converts.

Is that going to happen to me and my friends? Is the Light going to change us that much?

Marian pats my arm, then gives me a little push back toward the desk where I was sitting. "This time-out is a gift, Jools. For a while, you're a normal human. So now, while you're not under the influence of the Light, what do you want to do with your powers?"

This whole conversation just pisses me off. I'm like, "Why do you even care? You keep talking as if you've done me a favor, fucking up my brain."

"I *have* done you a favor," Marian says. "And I don't consider it fucking you up. I consider it disinfecting."

"Oh, fuck off."

If I were Ninety-Nine or Willow Scarlet, I'd punch her in the face. But since I'm Jools, I'm not that crazy. I don't trust that the collar she's wearing actually does anything. She *says* it makes her normal, but why should I believe that? If I lay a finger on her, she might turn into Ninja Jane. And even if that doesn't happen, we're in a lab surrounded by robots and superweapons. How do I know some robot won't suddenly leap to Marian's defense?

I glare at her. She stares back, but doesn't look pissed off. Finally, she slides down from the desk where she's been sitting and takes off her collar. "You know what your trouble is, Jools?"

"Yeah. I'm locked in a fucking slave collar and I want to go home."

Marian acts like I didn't even speak. "Your trouble is you don't have goals. No matter how often I ask, you can't tell me what you want." She puts her collar away in the cupboard. "Maybe you need someone to hate, Jools. If you don't have something to fight *for*, you should at least have someone to fight against."

"Are you trying to make me hate *you*? Cuz, lady, it's working."

Marian rolls her eyes. "No, Jools, you're just angry. And anger isn't hate—anger's hot, hate is cold. Besides, I truly am not your enemy. I'm just pragmatic. And I'm trying to tell you something important."

"What?"

"That you should do some serious thinking while you have that collar on. Decide what's genuinely important to you, a goal truly worthy of your powers. Figure it out, then commit to it. Otherwise . . ." She stops to think. "You may not realize it, but you've been all over the news. *The innocent girl who was murdered by Robin Hood.* They say you're a biology student. Is that right?"

"Yeah."

"I'm no biology expert," Marian says, "so you may know more about this than I do. But you've heard about those viruses and parasites that make certain animals foolhardy? The bugs that get inside animal brains and change their behaviors?"

"Sure. Like *Toxoplasma gondii*. Mice usually run away from places that smell of cat urine; but when mice get infected with

T. gondii, they stop being afraid. *La-la-la. Cats. LOL.* So the mice get eaten, and *T. gondii* ends up where it wants to be: inside a cat's gut, which is the parasite's favorite place to reproduce." (And thank you, baby Jesus, that I still remember this stuff. I may be a dumbed-down loser, but I'm still a third-year biologist.)

"Okay, then," Marian goes. "The Light works exactly the same. It has an agenda. The Light changes your behavior to further its goals, even if that means putting you in harm's way against your better interests. I don't know if Sparks can completely shrug off the Light's manipulation, but at the very least we ought to be aware of what's happening. Then we can try to achieve something that's meaningful to our own lives, rather than whatever the Light wants."

In spite of myself, I have to ask, "What do you think the Light is making us do?"

"Fight. Primarily against Darklings. But also against fellow Sparks whose agendas clash with our own."

"Don't we *have* to fight? I mean, when dudes like Diamond try to murder hundreds of people . . ."

"Yes, of course," Marian says. "Sparks have to deal with emergencies if they arise. We can do things others can't, and we often end up in positions where we have no choice. You may not realize it, Jools, but our band of outlaws deals with supervillains on a regular basis. It's an occupational hazard—we stumble onto some horrid conspiracy and are forced to save the world. It happens with ridiculous frequency. But heroic derring-do is not the Merry Men's core competency. It's not how we define ourselves."

"How *do* you define yourselves?"

"Jools, please," Marian says. "We rob from the rich, and give to the poor."

"You really give to the poor?"

"Yes. But not the actual treasures that we steal. When we break into a Darkling office tower, our primary goal is never the golden statue or the fifty-million-dollar Van Gogh. While Robin makes a show of swinging from chandeliers, the Artful Dodger quietly hacks into computers. He steals whistle-blower information, or tech developments that the Darklings are suppressing to preserve their monopolies. Then we leak everything to the public. *That's* why the Darklings hate us: stealing a Van Gogh hurts their pride, but revealing illegal practices hurts them for real."

"But," I say, "you still get to keep the Van Gogh."

"True. So every week, I publish schematic diagrams for easy-to-make items that will improve the lives of as many people as possible. This week was a water purifier that removes pollutants and bacteria. Last week was a solar-powered battery charger. The week before that, a neural soother for alleviating arthritis. I put every invention into the public domain. And these designs aren't Cape Tech—you don't have to be a Spark to construct them. I try to keep the build price below ten pounds, with off-the-shelf DIY components."

Well, shit. I'm impressed. I still hate Marian's guts, but I'm impressed. And I believe she's telling the truth. I don't have WikiJools to check for sure, but I've heard of wonderful gadget designs showing up anonymously on open websites.

Still, I'm like, "Couldn't you do all that stuff *without* stealing the Van Goghs?"

"I need funding for resources," Marian says. "You think all this lab equipment was free? And robberies keep the Light inside me appeased. As I told you, I feel as if I *have* to steal from the Dark. So I do. It placates the urge. Then I can concentrate on making the world a better place."

Marian turns away and starts walking toward the door. "I'll leave you to think about that, Jools," she says. "Oh, and here."

She turns back and tosses something to me. I catch it. It's a shapeless nugget of metal. "That's what's left of your ring," Marian says. "It melted itself into slag when I tried to analyze it. But I assume it was a communication device?"

I nod.

"If it's any consolation," Marian says, "the ring wouldn't have worked, even if you'd retrieved it from my vault. Sherwood is thoroughly shielded against transmissions out. That's why we can't be detected—I've blocked every form of emission known to science. Conventional science *and* Cape Tech."

I bet if I were still smart, I could find a way around that. But I'm not. I just tuck what's left of the ring into my pocket, and simmer with resentment. I go, "When are you sending me home?"

"Not quite yet," Marian says. "Robin wants to see you before you go."

"Why? Because he still hasn't fucked me?"

Marian shrugs. "Yes, that's basically it."

"Well, fuck *him*."

Marian sighs. "Jools, I'm surprised you aren't more sex positive."

"I *am* sex positive. I'm triple sex positive with sprinkles. But there's this word, Marian: 'consent.' You might have heard of it."

"Oh, you'll consent, Jools. You'll be gagging for it. That's Robin's gift."

"It's not a gift, it's mind rape, and you know it."

Marian doesn't answer. She doesn't look at me.

"For fuck's sake," I yell. "Why are you doing this to me?"

Marian goes, "I'm not doing anything."

"Then why are you letting Robin do this to me? You could send me home right now, before anything happens."

Soft and quiet, Marian says, "Robin gets what he wants. He's our leader."

"Bullshit," I say. "You're the one who's in charge."

"No," Marian says. "I may be the power behind the throne, but I don't have the charisma to lead Robin's followers. They only listen to me when Robin tells them to. So I need Robin to need *me*." She gives me a hard look. "I'm a Spark, Jools. I have goals. Keeping Robin happy is a means to that end."

"So you'll use me as a means to an end, too?"

"I'll tell you a secret, Jools: Robin needs sex or else he starts to lose his powers. It's no different than Popeye needing spinach or Ocean Girl dying without seawater. But what is your problem,

Jools? Millions of women would kill to make love with Robin. And women like Tigresse . . . she could have any man on the planet, but she practically threw herself at Robin. He's an extremely handsome man; I can tell that you find him attractive. I also doubt that you're a stranger to one-night stands. You strike me as an actively heterosexual young woman. You'd bed Robin in a heartbeat if you'd just get over your huff."

"My *huff*? That's what you think this is? When you've put me in a fucking slave collar?"

Marian rolls her eyes. "It's not a slave collar. You still have control of your mind. Complete free will."

"Which is fine right up to the moment when Robin's Halo hits me. Then I'm Cosby'd."

Marian shrugs. "You'll want the sex while it's happening. Immediately thereafter, I'll erase your memory. So where's the harm?"

I grab a metal gadget off a lab bench and throw it at Marian's head. But I'm Jools, not Ninety-Nine. Marian bobs to one side and my throw misses.

Marian gives me a pitying look, then turns her back on me. She stops in the doorway a moment, looking out at the darkness. Without turning around, she says, "If you fuck him, Jools, then I don't have to. And at least there's a chance *you'll* enjoy it."

She steps outside, and the door closes behind her.

AFTER SHE'S GONE, I look around wildly, searching for something I can use to break the collar. I still don't recognize any of the crap on the tables. God, what a loser I am! I'll bet my roommates would recognize *some* of this shit, even if a lot of it is Cape Tech.

I suddenly realize I have to run. Marian will tell Robin where I am. He may show up any minute.

I flee into the dark woods. I stumble at random through the brush until I find a trail. I follow it blindly. I'm lost, but I'd rather be a moving target than cowering in the shadows.

I look behind me. I don't see Robin. But the spy drone glimmers along after me in the darkness. I imagine Marian watching. I imagine her talking to Robin on his comm implant, informing him about my every movement.

I flounder through the trees and undergrowth. Maybe Robin will take the hint that I don't want him. Or maybe if this takes too long, he'll just get bored and give up. He must be used to instant gratification.

But as I stagger through the dark, I can't help thinking of Marian's question: what do I want? It's stupid to think about that now when I should focus on getting away. But I'm not going to get away, am I? And I can't face what's going to happen, so my brain flies off elsewhere.

Me. Jools. What do I want?

Whatever happens in the next few minutes, I'll soon be back home. Starting a new school term. A new life as a superhero.

What do I want?

I fucking well don't want to be Maid Marian. Or Robin Hood. Or Diamond. If I thought I'd become like them, I'd build my own version of this collar and quit the super game completely.

But can't I just be sane? Not a Mad Genius, and not an egomaniac crusader who plows over anyone who gets in the way.

I want to be smart, but kind. I want to be happy with my friends. I want to get laid when I feel like it, on my own terms, maybe with a guy who knows and likes me.

And I want to be rich, famous, and beloved, and to win umpteen Nobel Prizes as well as the Stanley Cup, because shit, only a moron thinks small.

THE TRAIL THROUGH THE woods ends up at the barracks. Well, at least it's not Robin Hood's house.

Behind me, I hear whistling coming through the trees. Not a wolf whistle, but an actual tune: *Robin Hood, Robin Hood, riding through the glen . . .*

Shit! I run into the barracks. I try to lock the door behind me, but the door doesn't have a lock. Without turning on a light, I race down the corridor. I know where the bathroom is, and I know it has a lock. I also know that a lock won't keep Robin out—he's as strong as five ordinary men, and he can shoot energy arrows that will blast the door off its hinges. But maybe a locked door will shield me from his Halo and I can tell him to fuck off.

I find the bathroom. I shut myself in. The room is so small, it's like hiding in a cupboard.

The spy drone flits around me, glowing in the dark. I imagine Marian watching with interest, to see the moment I get hit with Robin's aura. I'll probably unlock the door and melt into his arms.

Fuck you, Marian. I refuse to put on a show.

The bathroom is so small, the spy drone can't keep away if I really try to get it. It takes me a couple tries, but I finally grab the drone and clutch it in my fist.

The drone struggles like a fly trying to escape between my fingers. I don't let it. Instead, I try to squeeze it to pieces.

No good. The drone is only the size of a small green pea, and I can't clench my hand hard enough to damage it. I raise my fist and glare at the little monster as its light seeps out between my fingers.

The drone gets a bit bigger. From a pea to a brown bean.

Weird.

Some kind of defense mechanism? Am I going to get tased again?

Nothing happens.

I think about the drone, all the things it must have in it. Camera, control circuits, flight mechanism, battery. You couldn't build anything powerful yet so small, except by using the flaky quasi-magic of Cape Tech.

What if . . .

I lift the drone in my fist. I press it against the slave collar. The bean-sized drone expands to a chickpea.

Without this damned collar, I'd probably comprehend exactly what's going on. Since I'm only stupid Jools, I have to guess.

The drone contains too much stuff for its size. When it's close to the collar's suppression field, it can't stay as small as it is. Maybe

Marian actually built the drone on a larger scale so its parts were easier to work with. Then she shrank it somehow, the way Zircon shrinks from full sized to microscopic.

So.

Am I really going to do this?

Robin's whistle is coming down the hall. Any moment, he's going to knock on the door. I don't know if I'll be able to resist throwing the door open.

Hope this doesn't kill me.

I shove the drone under the metal collar.

THE COLLAR DOESN'T FIT super tight. Anyway, my neck is soft enough to yield under pressure. Still, I have a hard time shoving the drone between my throat and the collar's metal band.

The good news: the drone stops struggling to get away. Close to the collar, it goes dead. It obviously doesn't work in a No Cape Tech zone.

The bad news: I get a splitting headache whenever I touch the collar with my hands. But I grit my teeth against the pain, and use my thumb to poke the drone deeper under the collar.

The drone starts out the size of a chickpea. It doesn't stay that size for long.

The little drone expands like a balloon: a balloon as solid as a steel ball bearing. It pushes into my neck as hard as it pushes out on the collar. Equal and opposite forces—damn you, Newton! And my neck isn't nearly as unyielding as the collar's metal.

Basically, I'm using the drone as a type of crowbar to pry off the collar. Too bad the only fulcrum is my neck.

By the time the drone reaches the size of a golf ball, it's pressing against me like a hammer. I'm not completely stupid—I didn't insert the drone where it would crush my windpipe. But it's compressing my whole fucking neck, squashing my airway and blood vessels so hard . . .

. . .

. . .

* * *

I COME TO, SPRAWLED on the floor. I'm still alive.

The drone lies on the floor in front of my nose. It's a blackened mess—its circuits have gone electrically kablooey.

Little bugger couldn't take the strain. Good. Now Marian can't watch.

Even better, the collar feels loose. Either the strain of the drone's growth damaged the lock, or else being next to the drone's electrical meltdown fried the collar's circuits.

One way or another, the collar is dead. I feel half-dead myself, but I muster the strength to open the collar far enough that it falls off my neck.

I'm not okay. I can barely breathe. But now that I'm *her* again, I can regenerate.

If there's time.

The door of the bathroom bursts open, slamming its wooden edge into my gut. Now I can't breathe at all.

But it's okay. It's Robin Hood. Beautiful, kind Robin. He leans over me, a look of concern on his face. In a moment, he'll sweep me up in his arms and take me someplace warm and safe . . .

Something white blooms out of nowhere. It starts on the floor and shoots upward, catching Robin full in the face as he leans over me. It's a fast-rising uppercut delivered by a fist made of rock.

The sucker punch knocks Robin backward out the door, slamming him into the opposite wall of the corridor. He slumps unconscious.

I scream in dismay that my Robin is gone.

Then I moan in relief that I'm free of his spell.

I wrap my arms around Zircon and cry into zir cummerbund.

18

*Ecdysis**

ZIRC STROKES MY HAIR for a few seconds, then says, "We should leave. Can you walk?"

I'm still weepy. "How did you find me?"

"Let's walk and talk." Zirc tries to help me off the floor, but the bathroom is too constricted and besides, strength is not Zirc's forte. That super-uppercut trick is only powerful enough to knock out Sparks because Zirc's growth spurt adds a huge extra force to an otherwise nominal punch. I love Zircon madly, especially at this moment, but ze's still a four-foot-ten flyweight.

"I can help," says a voice from the hall. Vernon. When unconsciousness closes Robin Hood's door, it opens Vernon's window.

Zircon steps toward him with stony fists raised. "It's okay," I tell zir, "Vernon's cool."

Vernon snorts. "First time anyone ever said *that*." But he hurries and helps me stand. My legs feel as weak as putty. Cutting off blood flow to the brain completely sucks.

I realize I might have died. Maybe I *did* die. But once the collar got broken, I healed.

I put my arm around Vernon's shoulder and totter as he walks me down the hall. I say to Zirc, "Where to?"

"That's one of our problems," Zirc says. "I haven't found any way out. I don't even know where we are."

I say, "We're twenty-five klicks straight above Waterloo."

"Huh," says Zircon. "I didn't even know we were airborne. Something prevents me seeing past the walls of this place."

*Shedding of skin, e.g. in snakes.

"Maid Marian told me Sherwood Forest can block all transmissions, both conventional and Cape Tech. I guess that includes your Spark-o-Vision."

"Yeah," Zirc says. "And my comm ring. Can't send or receive squat. Otherwise, I'd have called Aria and Dakini."

My spirits sag a little. "They aren't here?"

"Nope, sorry," Zircon says. "But even if we're twenty-five kilometers up, Aria could fly here in . . . uhh . . ."

"In 72.85 seconds," I say. "Assuming she flies at the average speed of sound."

Yeah, baby, I'm back.

As Vernon and I maneuver awkwardly to get through the front door of the barracks, I can feel my wobbly legs getting stronger. Oh, regeneration, if it were possible, I'd totally go down on you.

When we're outside, Zircon uses Spark-o-Vision to look for trouble. The night might be as black as a Goth's corset, but Zircon's weird eyesight doesn't care. Zirc says, "The coast is clear. But Maid Marian won't be happy that you destroyed her drone. How many people do you think she'll send to see what you're up to?"

"If it were just the spy drone," I say, "she might not get too upset. Robin was hot on my heels; she'd assume he could handle me. But she might also realize I broke the slave collar. It likely had a tracker in it, and now it's gone off the grid. Oh, and all the outlaws have comm implants, so maybe she knows that Vernon is here and Robin isn't." I stop and look at Vernon. "Do *you* have an implant? Like, do you and Robin share the same body, and it just reshapes itself? Or are you completely separate?"

"Separate," Vernon says. "As if Robin and I are truly different people. And Marian has never given me an implant."

"Good on you," I tell him.

Zircon says, "We're in trouble if too many Merry Men run to the rescue. I've seen ten Spark outlaws so far, and that's not counting the robots or Friar Tuck's animals. No way we can face them all."

"And next thing you know, we're *both* in collars," I say. "If it comes to that," I tell Zirc, "shrink out of sight and run like hell."

"And leave you here with them?" Zirc says. "I heard how Marian wants to use you. It's sick."

I say, "Robin's not around. My man Vernon is here." I still have my arm propped around his shoulders. I give him a squeeze. "Now, Vernon, I'd be happy to give a tumble. He's a nice guy."

I mostly said that to make him blush. I can't see him in the dark, but I'm sure it worked. Even so, it wasn't a lie—Vernon's okay. I've slept with worse bros for less reason.

Vernon squinches away. (He's such a chicken!) "I'll head for the mead hall," he says. "I'll tell them everything is fine."

"They won't believe you," I say. "And they won't like me roaming around unchaperoned, now that I have my powers back."

"I'll tell them you're hurt and weak," Vernon says. "And I won't mention anything about . . ." He gestures toward Zircon. "You destroyed the drone before your friend showed up. If Marian thinks you're on your own and seriously injured, she won't send *everyone*. Maybe just one or two."

"Okay, go ahead," Zircon tells him. "We'll run in the opposite direction."

Vernon looks at me for confirmation. Our eyes meet. I smile. "Be safe. And don't trust Marian. She may look like Vanessa, but she's not. She thinks she's trying to save the world, but she's cutting too many corners."

"I know," Vernon says. "I see what Robin sees, remember? But unlike him, I know what it means."

Vernon gives me a sad little look. For a moment, I think about what his life must be like, watching day after day. How can he bear it?

But the answer is obvious. He bears it because he has no other choice. Besides, it can't last forever—neither the good nor the bad.

I grab him and give him a kiss. He doesn't kiss me back. When I let him go, he just turns and vanishes into the woods.

* * *

IN A LOW VOICE, Zirc asks, "Any thoughts on where to go?"

"Back to the lab," I answer. "I might be able to whip together something to teleport us out of here."

"Can you do it fast?" Zirc asks. "Because from what I've seen of Marian, she won't leave her lab unprotected. She knows that's where you're most likely to go, so she'll send over serious muscle."

"How much have you actually seen?" I ask. "How long have you been here?"

"A few hours," Zircon says. "But when I found you, I couldn't get close because of that collar. As soon as I flew anywhere near you, I lost my Spark-o-Vision and felt myself growing. That spy thing was watching you, too. I figured that if it caught sight of me, Robin's whole gang would come running and we'd both be screwed. I had to hold back till you dealt with the drone and collar. Nice work, by the way—you killed two birds with one stone."

I say, "But how did you get to Sherwood in the first place?"

"Less talking, more walking," Zircon replies. Ze grabs my hand. It's like getting chummy with a statue—Zirc's hand is rock hard, and while it's not particularly cold, it's not nearly as warm as flesh. "Come on," Zirc says. "Gotta keep moving."

We do. Zirc pulls me along the path, much faster than I could go myself. I'm glad *someone* can see in this darkness. And with 360-degree Spark-o-Vision, Zirc should pick up on incoming outlaws long before they reach us.

Except, I think, *for the Artful Dodger, and anyone else who can turn invisible.* In an arm-wrestle between Spark-o-Vision and super invisibility, there's no predicting which would win. But one problem at a time.

Meanwhile, Zirc explains how ze got here. "Grandfather called and told us the feds wanted to transport the bazooka on that train. We all knew it was a trap, just like the memorial service. The Darklings made sure that word leaked out so Robin would take the bait. We talked it over—Aria, Dakini, and I—and we decided to play it low key. I got to the train before it left the station. With the blinder walls, and crates, and everything else, I couldn't find the gun, not even with Spark-o-Vision. So I just shrank to the size of a virus and hid. Aria and Dakini tracked the train from a few miles away, staying in touch with me through the comm rings. We didn't care what happened to the bazooka, but if Robin and his outlaws showed up, we wanted to follow them back to their lair so we could rescue you."

"Why didn't you do anything when you saw me?" I ask. "If Aria was there, she could have swooped in and pulled me out so fast no one could stop her."

"But we didn't know it was *you*," Zirc tells me. "I thought you were a member of Robin's gang. You wore that red costume, mask and everything, right? Nice codpiece, by the way; are you finally joining me on Team Nonbinary?"

"Sorry, no," I answer. "I've still got a double X in the cis-het-female check box. But you really didn't recognize me?"

Zirc shakes zir head. "It never crossed my mind the chick in red might be you. Spark anonymization, right? I literally couldn't recognize my best friend when she was wearing a dumb little mask."

Best friend? I give Zircon's hand a squeeze. It's like squeezing a hunk of granite, but I hope ze can feel it anyway. "So," I say, trying not to choke up, "are you and I okay again?"

"I'm gonna make you do my laundry as penance," Zirc replies. "But shit, Jools, we had no idea where you were or even if you were alive. The Darklings ran hour after hour of TV footage showing Robin Hood blowing out your guts. How could I stay mad when I was so worried?"

"My guts really blew out?"

Zirc nods. "It was horrible. We knew you could regenerate, but healing from something that awful? It didn't seem possible. And cops and politicians, even the prime minister, were saying, *See? Robin Hood is a monster. We'll pursue him and his terrorists with everything we have.*"

"They still have to find him," I say. "And this base is way off the map."

"*Pffft*," Zircon says. "I found him easily enough. As soon as you found the bazooka during the robbery, I just flew over and hid on it, real small. Then I rode it back here to Sherwood."

"Yeah, but . . ."

I stop.

I think.

"Fuck," I say. "The gun is a Trojan horse."

DIAMOND SAID THE BAZOOKA wasn't his. I finally get that he wasn't lying.

And I realize why I couldn't figure out how the gun worked: because it didn't.

I understood the medi-tank. It made sense—it was real Cape Tech. But the bazooka was only a mock-up, like a prop for a superhero movie. I'll bet it was actually made by some A-list props master. Who else would the Dark Guard hire to make something convincing?

The gun looked so good, even Marian couldn't tell it was fake. It drove both of us crazy. We kept thinking we ought to comprehend it, but always came up short.

The Dark kept showing the gun out in the open, hoping someone would steal it. Hell, all that rigmarole at the airport, with the ice-cold strap on my wrist . . . I don't know if Reaper realized the gun was fake, but his boss must have. The whole magic ritual was just an excuse to keep the airport vault unlocked long enough for one of Robin's outlaws to arrive.

I thought the Darklings were only using the bazooka as bait. I didn't grasp how the trap actually worked.

When Zircon first saw the bazooka, ze said it had a little glowing speck of power. We assumed the speck was Cape Tech. But what if it was magic?

A magical homing beacon. As soon as the outlaws brought it back to Sherwood, the Dark got a fix on Robin's HQ.

Marian told me that Sherwood blocked all transmissions, specifically, "every form of emission known to science. Conventional science and Cape Tech."

But I'll bet it doesn't block magic. The Light and the Dark are nonoverlapping magisteria. Weird science has trouble counteracting spells and vice versa. A strong but subtle sorcerous signal might shine as clear as day.

As part of the same plan, Calon Arang arranged for an innocent victim—i.e. me—to be killed dramatically on camera, supposedly by Robin Hood. For years, superpowered good guys have given Robin a pass: he's just a rascal, not a villain. But now everyone thinks he's crossed the line. If the Dark Guard announces, "We know where Robin is," they'll have no trouble assembling a team to smack the Merry Men down. Heroes of the Light will think it's their duty. The Aussie All-Stars were already in Waterloo, and plenty of other Sparks would volunteer, too. As for Darklings, they've always hated Robin. You could muster an *army* to invade Robin's den.

Mounting an assault won't be simple—Sherwood Forest is up in the stratosphere. But I can picture the Dark Guard assembling Sparks and Darklings with powers that can cope with the tactical difficulties.

They'll need people who can fly. Enchantments to keep attackers alive in thin freezing air. Advance scouts to check Sherwood's defenses. Containment spells to prevent the outlaws from teleporting away.

How long before the onslaught is ready to go?

Soon. It's gotta be soon. The clock is ticking.

Suddenly, getting caught by Marian is the least of our problems.

I SPELL IT OUT to Zircon, or at least I start to. Zirc catches on fast, and sees the implications without me explaining. "Shit," Zirc says, "it may be too late already. They'll have people watching outside. Like Sensorium—that suit of his won't have trouble operating in the stratosphere."

I say, "And his sensors are the best of any Spark in the world." (I didn't feel WikiJools feeding me that factoid, but I doubt if I knew it two seconds ago. Welcome back, my wiki pal.) I say, "If we break out of Sherwood, Sensorium can track us all the way to the ground. He'll send his buddies to arrest us once we're within grabbing distance."

"But that's great!" Zircon says. "They won't arrest *you*. You're the victim, Jools, the innocent bystander. Everyone saw Robin Hood shoot you, then run off with your body. If you bail out of Sherwood, everyone will think you've managed a miraculous escape."

"I'll tell everyone you rescued me," I say. "Noble Zircon, infiltrating the outlaw hideout." I stop. "Just one problem. This miraculous escape involves falling twenty-five kilometers."

"Falling yes, crash-landing no," Zircon tells me. "As soon as we're outside Sherwood, my comm ring should work again. I'll call Aria and have her catch us. She'll have plenty of time to do it; we'll take a long time to reach the ground. And Aria can be careful so there's no sudden snap."

"We still have to survive the first few minutes," I say. "There's virtually no air outside, and the temperature is in negative triple digits."

"Jools," Zircon says, "I got ninety-three in Atmospheric Science. I'm not an Olympic-level aerologist like you, but I'm not a total ignoramus. And by the way, I'm also a rock. I don't need to breathe, and in negative triple digits, I'm just a *cold* rock. NBD. As for you, I've seen you regenerate from all kinds of lethal crap."

"Yes, but it *hurts*!" I say. "Before we jump, let me build some survival equipment."

It occurs to me I've already made a heater that can deal with the cold: the gadget I built to warm myself after the freezing shower. The only other thing I'd need would be an oxygen tank. Oh no, wait. "Problem," I say. "Here in Sherwood, air pressure is normal. Outside, it's basically zero. Explosive decompression isn't a real thing, but terrible shit will still happen. To me, if not to you. Embolisms, the bends, a *serious* case of the farts . . ."

"Okay, yes, your farts are truly dangerous," Zircon says. "If it'll stop you whining, take a few minutes to build a space suit. But then we have to go. Has it occurred to you that instead of attacking Sherwood with an assault team, they may just shoot it with a big-ass bomb?"

Crap, that never crossed my mind. And it would certainly be simpler than gathering a strike force for a not-CG act-three fight. On the other hand, blowing up Sherwood would send its burning remains plummeting onto whatever lies below. Not a forward-facing public relations move. Besides, Sparks have a habit of surviving big explosions and showing up later for revenge. Attacking with an actual army reduces the chance that anyone slips through the cracks.

"I don't think they'll use a bomb," I tell Zircon. But I hurry my pace. This'll get messy.

WE MAKE IT SAFELY to Marian's lab—no attacks from outlaws or Dark/Spark assault squads. Inside the lab, I no longer have gadget prosopagnosia. (*That's* the word.) I recognize every weird-science widget on the lab desks: the molecule ticklers, the energy spoons, the Maxwell demon drunk tanks, and all the other impossible gizmos you can assemble with Cape Tech.

I say to Zircon, "Did you see the jet packs we used during the robbery?"

"Jools," Zirc says, "seeing is what I do best."

"Then look around the lab for something like that. A backup plan, in case something has happened to Aria and she's not available to catch us."

I expect Zircon to walk through the lab, opening cupboards in search of jet packs. But Zirc simply leans against a desk and relaxes. Apparently, Spark-o-Vision can see through cupboard doors.

Zirc's powers are scary. Then again, so are mine.

Ideally, I'd make my pressure suit out of whale blubber. Whales can dive from the ocean's surface to crushing depths of two kilometers, so *obviously*, they're your pressure-control market leaders. But Marian doesn't have whale parts stocked in her lab. *Tsk*. Exactly the kind of shortsightedness you expect from someone in robotics.

Apart from the medi-tank (which obviously *had* to deal with living tissue), Marian's inventions use metal instead of organics.

But I can cope. I'm a master of every known science, not just the fun ones. And Marian has plenty of human-shaped robot shells lying around in various stages of assembly. I find one that's the right size to hold me once I pull out the wires inside. I hope I'm not killing an intelligent being, or destroying some brilliant new breakthrough in cybernetics. But screw it: I rip out everything in the robot's metal shell and set about outfitting it with enough of an oxygen system to keep me alive the four minutes it'll take to fall twenty-five kilometers.

As I work, Zircon lugs over a jet pack ze found. It's not quite the same as the one I wore earlier today—it looks like a more advanced prototype. I hope it actually works . . . but even if it doesn't, Aria will be waiting to catch us. Right? In fact, Aria's feelings will be hurt if we try to save ourselves without her.

But I still want a Plan B. Cuz I'm a grown-up who's all cautious and shit.

"CRAP!" ZIRCON SAYS. "WE have company."

I say, "Who?"

But Zirc has already shrunken too small for me to see. A moment later, Marian barges through the door. She has Vernon in tow, and she holds a nasty weapon I've never seen before. It's only a pistol, not nearly as imposing as the fake Diamond bazooka. Even so, it has "blow your brains out" written all over it.

"Leaving us, Jools?" she asks.

"I thought it was time," I say. "Considering that I finally figured out what the Dark Guard is up to."

"Enlighten me," Marian says, training her gun on my face.

I tick off on my fingers. "One: Gisbourne. That's what you call your Darkling informant, right? And Gisbourne was the one who told you the bazooka was at the airport?"

Marian nods.

"Wrecking Ball tried to steal it, but that went to hell when the airplane exploded. So two." I tick off another finger. "Gisbourne gave you another crack at stealing the gun—this time from the memorial service. But why would they have the bazooka there in the first place? Forget that nonsense about auctioning the gun off; the truth is they *wanted* you to steal it. They put up a token resistance so it wouldn't look too easy, but they wanted you to end up with the gun. They must have been furious when Robin ordered a retreat so he could save my life.

"Then three." Another finger. "The Darklings decided to move the bazooka by train. *By train!* They could have transported it a million other ways, but they chose a method Robin Hood couldn't pass up: a great train robbery. Which Gisbourne told you about, too. At last, you finally succeeded in stealing the gun. You brought it home . . . and ever since, it's been sending out a sorcerous homing signal telling the Dark Guard where Sherwood is."

"We scanned the gun for magic," Marian says. "It's clean."

"Cape Tech has trouble detecting magic," I say. "So how did you scan it? Did you perhaps get Gisbourne to do it?"

"Oh," Marian says. "Bugger."

I say, "Dude, you named your spy Gisbourne. In the Robin Hood stories, Guy of Gisbourne was a shithead. So what did you expect?"

Marian mutters something. At first I think she's swearing under her breath, but then I realize she's using her comm implant to speak to the other outlaws.

While she's distracted, I dive for cover behind the robot shell I've been working on. But Zircon also takes advantage of the moment: Zirc uses zir trick of growing real fast to uppercut Marian the same way ze did to Robin.

It almost works. Zirc hits Marian with good solid contact, strong enough to knock out a rhino.

But two things go wrong.

First, Marian's finger was on the trigger of the gun. Twitch, and the gun goes off.

Second, saying bye-bye to Marian means hello to Ninja Jane.

19

Territorial Aggression

ZIRCON ISN'T STUPID. WHEN Zirc sucker punched Marian, ze stood out of the pistol's line of fire. But Marian's gun is Cape Tech. Straight lines mean nothing.

The shot explodes out of the gun's muzzle, then circles like a heat-seeking missile. It might be designed to target Sparks. The projectile spikes forward several meters before it loops and hits Zircon from behind.

I can see it as if in slow motion. Zirc has zir back to me, between me and Marian's gun. I see everything, but can't react fast enough to yell a warning.

Zircon's rocky skin shrugs off normal bullets, but Marian's ammo isn't normal. The slug pierces Zircon's stone and vanishes inside. I don't know if Zircon has any internal organs, but on a normal person, the bullet would have just embedded itself in the lower lobe of zir right lung.

The professional surgeon inside me knows it's not the worst place for a gunshot. It's still pretty bad.

Zircon collapses. Ze falls like a curtain dropping to reveal what's behind: that lean mean version of Marian I saw when Ninja Jane slashed off her costume.

Jane immediately drops the gun, and draws two daggers from beneath Marian's lab coat. Vernon cringes away, but Jane ignores him. Marian may be fond of Vernon, but Jane doesn't give a damn.

"Jane!" I snap. "Don't be stupid. We have to get out of Sherwood before things go to hell."

Jane doesn't answer. Just twitches her knives. Her face is grim.

It's crazy how she can look exactly like Marian—same face, same clothes, same haircut—yet be nothing like Marian at all.

Still, she has a share of Marian's intelligence. Without taking her eyes off me, she places her foot on the gun she just dropped. With a quick backward jerk, she scuffs the pistol out through the door behind her.

She's much stronger than she looks; the pistol flies out of sight into the darkness. I'll never be able to find it in the shadows of the forest. Too bad—a gun with Spark-seeking bullets would come in handy right now.

"Vernon," I say, "do you know first aid?"

"Not really," he says.

Shit. And Jane won't let me doctor Zircon myself. Jane won't let me do anything except fight to the death.

"Get Zircon out of here," I tell Vernon. "Find the other outlaws. When they evacuate Sherwood, make sure they take Zirc to a hospital."

Vernon bends and picks Zircon up. Zirc is usually four-foot-ten, but is now less than half that, about the size of a ventriloquist's dummy. When Zirc was shot in the back, ze must have tried to shrink out of sight—an automatic defensive reflex. But lucky for Zirc, ze fainted before ze got too small. If Zirc had gone microscopic, we never would have found zir. One other lucky thing: at this size, Zirc is light enough for Vernon to lift, even though ze's solid rock.

Vernon cradles Zirc in his arms. He takes one step toward the laboratory exit, but Jane gets there ahead of him. She raises a knife and shakes her head. I don't know why Jane won't let Vernon leave, but it's clear she's made up her mind. Maybe she wants Zircon to die; Jane knows that Sherwood will soon be attacked, and she's decided Zirc and I are to blame.

Only one other way out of the lab. It's crazy, but we don't have a choice. "Vernon, head for the clean room," I say. "You know where that is?"

He nods.

"Then go."

The way should be clear. I doubt that Marian has had time to fix the lock that I broke.

Vernon keeps a wary eye on Jane as he heads for the ramp to the clean room. Jane doesn't try to stop him; her gaze stays fixed on me. Whatever Jane intends to do about Zircon, she must think she has plenty of time.

After all, I don't look like I'll put up much of a fight. I'm empty-handed against Jane's two daggers. And of course, they aren't ordinary daggers. They've already started whispering. And those blades can cut steel as if it's Brie. Or maybe it isn't the knives that are so lethal, it's Ninja Jane. She's super-strong and -fast, even compared to other Sparks. Compared to nonsuper me, she's a buzz saw facing a rubber knife.

All righty then. Let's even the odds.

I wait for Vernon and Zirc to get clear, then I scrunch up my forehead and concentrate. I may be dressed like Willow Scarlet, but I'm really Ninety-Nine. I hold out my hand and a glowing green hockey stick appears in it. The stick hums softly, like a light saber.

I say to Jane, "Okay, dude. It's hockey night in Canada."

JANE'S FACE GOES WARY. One nice thing about being new at the superhero game: nobody knows what tricks you have up your sleeve.

Of course, I don't really know, either. This is only the second time I've summoned the stick, so I have no idea what powers it has. Being a hockey stick, it probably can't shoot fire or read minds—the Light prefers form to match function. But I know that my stick can whack things really hard, and I hope it's tough enough to ward off Jane's fancy knives.

First things first. I vault onto the nearest lab desk and start taking slap shots with the components strewn across the desktop. They're the bits and pieces I pulled out of the robot shell while I was trying to make a survival suit: chunks of steel and silicon that can be flicked at high speed straight at Ninja Jane's head.

I'm the best in the world at making slap shots . . . and maybe it's my imagination, but I could swear each hunk of metal that I shoot *accelerates* after it leaves the blade of the stick.

Each shot is a bull's-eye, targeted at the middle of Jane's face. But Jane is faster than any goalie. Her knives cut the air so fast I see them as a blur. She deflects my shots with ease, sending shattered electronics in all directions.

Some pieces even ricochet back at me. I knock most aside with my stick. The rest smack harmlessly into my Willow Scarlet costume. Bulletproof is good.

I'm not discouraged that Jane shrugged off everything I aimed at her. I didn't expect to beat her in the first few seconds. Maybe I won't win at all, but the longer I keep Jane busy, the longer Vernon has to get Zircon to the clean room. Also, the more likely—

Everything lurches. I'm thrown off the lab desk, but I somersault in the air and land lightly on my feet.

Something goes bang in the distance. Someone returns fire with a rattle of bullets.

The assault on Sherwood has begun.

THE FLOOR TILTS.

It only tips a little, but glassware rattles and things slide across the lab tables. Behind me, something clatters to the floor. I'm not stupid enough to turn and see what it was, but the noise still grabs my attention for a moment. Jane takes the opportunity to hurtle toward me, leapfrogging on top of a workbench and using the height to plunge down toward me.

She must hope I'll hesitate in surprise. Not a chance. In fact, she only slows herself down.

Because gravity. It's a well-known fly in the ointment for superfast-moving Sparks. As long as they stay on the ground, they can travel at ridiculous speeds; as soon as they jump, however, they're ballistic projectiles. They can only fall with the usual acceleration of nine point eight meters per second squared. The result is a lot less velocity than Jane can produce with muscle power.

Translation: when you're super speedy, running is fast but falling is slow. Or at least slow*er*. Which is why I have no problem batting Jane out of the air with my hockey stick.

The glowing green stick leaves a scorch mark on Jane's white lab coat. It reminds me of the first time K tried to do zir own ironing.

But one whack isn't nearly enough to put Jane down. In fact, she might have planned on me doing exactly what I did. At the same time I hit her, she lashes out with a dagger, slashing at the hockey stick's shaft. I feel the impact in my hands, the way that you feel a sting when you hit a baseball with an aluminum bat. If my stick were a normal stick, Jane's knife might have cut clean through. My fancy green stick is stronger than that, but green sparks splash from the point of contact, like when a blacksmith hits molten metal with a hammer.

Jane lands on her feet several meters away. My eyes meet hers. I want to yell, "We're wasting time, let's just leave." But the moment I inhale in order to speak, Jane comes at me again, a Cuisinart of Cape Tech daggers moving at superhuman speed.

My only advantage is reach—the hockey stick is longer than her knives. As she drives toward me, I jab at her face. My move is high enough that she can duck her head to one side to avoid the thrust. She does exactly that . . . whereupon I snap the stick downward like an ax on her shoulder, then slap it sideways to cuff her on the ear.

The flat of the blade makes solid contact. It might well have ruptured her eardrum. The pain doesn't stop Jane's attack completely, but it throws off her balance and timing. I can tell she meant to plunge straight in and stab me. Instead, she wobbles enough that she steps on a sharp metal rheostat that fell when I was taking slap shots. For Jane, it must be like stepping on a piece of Lego, especially since she's only wearing Marian's flimsy flip-flops. She twists awkwardly as she tries to avoid putting down her full weight.

It gives me time to dodge behind the nearest lab desk. As I move, I flail at Jane with my hockey stick. I don't connect, but Jane dips back to avoid getting hit. In a moment, we're standing with the lab desk between us like a waist-high parapet.

I know she's going to come at me over the desk. I move my eyes right, then dodge left—the best I can do for a feint. She's not taken in, and she's faster than me. Jane nicks my arm with a dagger before I get clear.

Note to self: the bulletproof costume ain't proof against Jane's knives.

It's not a serious cut, but it burns like fire—far worse than it should, considering it's just a shallow gash on my forearm. Maybe her daggers are poisoned. After all, she's *Ninja* Jane. Poison is a ninja thing.

Even worse, she's smiling. Not pressing her attack. As if that one little prick was all she needed. Now she'll wait till I start to slow down.

Regeneration powers, now would be a good time to show your stuff.

But the cut just keeps burning. Getting worse. Shit, shit, shit.

I retreat. Jane follows. She doesn't try to close the gap between us, but she stays close enough that I'm forced to focus my attention on her. If she wanted, she could reach me in a fraction of a second. I keep the blade of my hockey stick ready to meet an attack. She doesn't try, but when I edge toward the door that leads to the clean room, she darts around to block me.

Okay, then. New plan. I plant the end of my hockey stick on the floor and use it as a vaulting pole to jump the lab desk behind me. Two more steps take me to the medi-tank. I drop my stick, throw myself inside the tank, and pull the lid shut on top of me.

It whirs. My brain's getting muddy. Familiar feeling: like the slave collar, starting to suppress my powers. This raises an interesting question of timing:

A: My regeneration is trying to fight off Jane's poison.

B: The tank is trying to shut off my regeneration.

C: The tank must also be trying to neutralize the poison from Ninja Jane's knife.

And D: The poison is trying to kill me.

So which competitor will win the race? And will I be alive at the finish line?

But there's a fifth contestant in the mix. I don't believe Jane will just leave me in here.

She's a crazy blood-spilling killer. She won't shrug and walk away. She'll run straight up to the tank and heave it open.

I can picture her doing it. A normal person might be wary, using one hand to lift the lid while keeping her other hand free, dagger at the ready in case I try something tricky. But Jane isn't normal. She's a hacky-slashy Spark, and she's furious that the tank might save me from her poison. I'm as good at psychological prediction as I am at everything else; my guess is that Jane will yank open the tank as fast as possible, using both hands.

Wait for it . . .

Yank.

For a moment, Jane has both hands on the lid, like a funeral director opening a coffin. She still holds her daggers—she's not an idiot—but she's grappling with the lid and the knives, so she's not in good position to attack. Also, I'm ready: the tank hasn't totally suppressed my skills yet. And opening the lid shoots me back to full strength.

I grab her wrists and pull her inside on top of me.

Jane thrashes against my grip, and she's way too strong for me to rein in completely. Luckily, her instinct is to pull away rather than drive the daggers through me. It gives me the time I need to twist her wrists sideways. The knives stab into the sides of the tank, embedding their blade tips deep.

Jane knees me in the groin—another standard fighting instinct. Too bad, booboo: I've got a codpiece. Jane's knee goes in like getting swallowed by a pillow, and it doesn't hurt at all. In fact, with her knee half buried in my crotch, it leaves one of my legs free. I kick out with my foot, hitting the medi-tank's lid. The lid bounces up, then down, slamming home and squeezing us both into darkness.

JANE STRUGGLES BUT DOESN'T have room for drastic maneuvers. I still have hold of her wrists, and the daggers are too deeply impaled in the medi-tank wall for her to pull them free. She doesn't have space or leverage; after a moment, she's short on strength, too. The tank is sapping her powers.

Once we get down to my normal muscles against hers, I'll win. I'm bigger than her, I'm stronger, and I haven't spent years relying on superpowers to pull me through fights.

Still, it's not an easy victory. Jane tries a head butt, but she's out of position—her forehead is level with my chin so it's her hard skull against my hard mandibular prominence. Call it a tie.

Jane tries to bite but can't reach any of my vulnerable bits. Her mouth is pressed against my shoulder, so all she can chew on is Willow Scarlet's jacket. I don't think the jacket is bulletproof anymore—the proofness comes from Cape Tech, which the tank detechifies. But the jacket is still good leather, tough enough to stand up to Jane's teeth.

After ten seconds of tussling, Jane gives up. I don't let her go—this might be a ruse. More seconds pass. The weight on me suddenly increases, from Jane's weight to Marian's.

"All right, Jools," she says. "You win."

I say, "Marian?"

"Yes, Jools. Can we get out of here, please? I find this unpleasant."

"Let go of the daggers," I say.

She does. I ease my grip on her wrists; when she doesn't attack, I let go completely and push upward to open the tank.

Marian gingerly peels herself off my chest, trying to minimize the amount of contact she makes with me. She clambers out; I follow. My brain still feels muddy and the gash on my arm is still burning. Even so, getting out of the tank is literally a breath of fresh air.

Gunfire erupts in the distance. "We have to get out of here," Marian says.

"How about the clean room?" I ask. "It has that Cape Tech disposal chute. The chute can go anywhere, right?"

"Not *anywhere*," Marian says. "But a great many places safer than here."

"Can you send us to Waterloo?"

"Certainly."

"Then go," I say. "Punch in the proper coordinates."

"Aren't you coming with me?" she asks.

"In a minute," I say. "But . . ." I jerk my thumb toward the medi-tank. "I need that for my friend."

20

Immune Responses

MARIAN WANTS TO STAY and help me with the tank. I order her
to git—she's the only one who knows how to work the disposal
chute. If she gets caught by the people attacking Sherwood, we're
all screwed. On the other hand, if *I* get caught . . . well, it's bad if
I can't put Zircon into the medi-tank, but if I don't show up in the
clean room, Marian can at least deliver Zirc to a hospital. I'm
pretty sure Marian will do that, if only because Vernon will insist.

Marian is indispensable. Me and the medi-tank aren't. Besides,
if I get caught on my way to the clean room, I can talk my way
out of trouble. I'm the innocent bystander, right? Supposedly
killed by Robin Hood. It looks bad that I'm wearing Willow Scarlet's costume, but thanks to WikiJools and being an Olympic-level
actor, I can totally fake Stockholm syndrome.

The medi-tank has casters, so getting it mobile is no big deal—I
just have to detach it from Sherwood's electrical grid. The tank is
directly connected to a funky Cape Tech power box, but after a few
seconds arguing with myself about red wire/blue wire, I open the
tank, use all my strength to pull one of Jane's daggers from the
medi-tank's wall, and slash the connection cable. The dagger cuts
the cord like a Ginsu knife, and bonus, I don't even get electrocuted.
(I consider claiming both Jane's weapons for my own, but Zircon
has a scary set of daggers, too, and I don't want to steal zir schtick.)

I take a moment to examine the severed cable. It's just a bundle of
normal wires. I probably can't just connect it to a household outlet,
but at least I don't have to find a source of upsilon particles and a
feed of helium-3. When the time comes, being an Olympic-level
electrician and a Mad Genius will have to be good enough.

I can hook up the tank and save Zircon. All I need is a power supply.

I drape the severed cable over the tank, lay the dagger beside it, and start rolling the whole shebang toward the clean room. The medi-tank rolls slowly, and the casters are for shit. Marian obviously didn't foresee she might need to move this puppy at emergency speed. I'm only halfway across the lab when I hear a shout behind me: "Stop or I'll shoot!"

I recognize the voice—my long-lost ghoul-friend, Staff Sergeant Barbara L. Stevens.

Shit.

I stop pushing the tank. I remember that the Willow Scarlet mask is still in my jacket pocket. I pull it out and slap it onto my face.

The mask sticks. Hallelujah! So when things get kung-fuey, as I'm sure they will, Staff Sergeant Barbara L. Stevens won't recognize me as the once and future Julietta Walsh.

"Last warning!" Stevens snaps. "Freeze!"

I have to give her credit. Since I couldn't hear her over the rolling medi-tank, Stevens could have shot me in the back without any warning. That would have been her safest play. After all, I look like a Merry Man, i.e. an outlaw Spark. Even if Stevens is a more-than-human Renfield, she'd be better off hosing me down with bullets than giving me a chance to surrender.

But she didn't. She's playing it straight. Which is why I don't reach for the dagger that lies on the tank. Instead I raise my hands without turning around. I step away from the tank so it doesn't get damaged when shots inevitably get fired.

Only then do I turn. Stevens has her gun propped against the frame of the lab's outer doorway. Her head is visible, but the rest of her body is out of sight around the edge of the door. Unsurprisingly, her partner Stephens has propped himself and his gun on the doorway's other side. And look, there's Reaper emerging from the forest behind them, his ugly-ass scythe moaning like a porn star.

"Well, this sucks," I say.

I keep my hands in the air as Reaper moves to the doorway. He stares with his empty eye sockets. "Who are you?" he says. "You aren't in our files."

"Willow Scarlet," I say. "I'm new."

Reaper tells Stevens & Stephens, "Then no reward for bringing her in alive. Kill her."

BY THE TIME HE finishes his speech, I've taken cover behind a lab desk. During the time when I was moving, Stevens & Stephens could have peppered me with lead, but neither one fired. Being Renfields, they have trouble making decisions on their own. They literally couldn't pull their triggers until Reaper said, "Kill."

As soon as Reaper gives the order, both Renfields shoot. But by then I'm out of sight behind the desk.

Not that I'm safe. Two thunderous shots blow cannonball-sized holes through the cupboards below the desk. But Stevens & Stephens aren't shooting actual cannonballs. All I can see hurtling past me are blobs of black energy without anything solid inside them.

The blobs are still fucking lethal. To hammer that message home, the two blasts punch through the desk behind me, and partly through a third.

Magical weapons, whipped up by Darkling sorcerers. And these aren't the pissy little blasters Stevens & Stephens brought to the great train robbery. The Renfields and the others were never supposed to win the fight at the train—they just had to mount a credible opposition until Robin escaped with the bazooka. So Stevens & Stephens were packing second-rate heat; they didn't want to be too effective.

Now, though, they've brought their A game. It's the grand finale, the final boss fight. Stevens & Stephens are going all in with their nastiest weapons, and John Woo is about to yell, "Action!"

My bulletproof costume no longer matters. We've gone light-years beyond bullets. If any shot hits me, I'll be splattered.

In a moment, Stevens & Stephens will fire again. So I dive, cartwheel, somersault, slide. I stay low behind desks so I won't be an easy target, but I never slow down. If I can reach the pressure suit I was making, it can give me some badly needed protection. It's the shell of a battle robot, designed to withstand damage better than unarmed laboratory furniture.

Shots keep banging, but the Renfields can't see me behind the desks. They're firing blind. It also seems the pistols can't shoot very quickly: they need a second or two to build up power between each discharge. Maybe they're literally summoning vaporizing energies from hell.

No, wait: the pistols aren't firing as quickly as I expect because only one Renfield is shooting. Shit! While one cop provides cover, the other must be tiptoeing in to get closer.

Stephens appears around the edge of the desk where I'm hiding. He has an unimpeded shot, and I can't get out of the way before his finger squeezes the trigger.

I close my eyes just before I hear the bang.

I DON'T GET SHOT.

I open one eye.

There's a wall of energy between me and the bad guy. Violet energy. Dakini's color.

Stephens fires again. The gout of blackness that emerges from his pistol smacks the violet barrier. The barrier shudders but holds.

A golden voice I know and love shouts, "Everybody chill!"

Aria's here. I've been rescued.

I YELL, "I SURRENDER!"

It doesn't work. Stephens fires at me again. The violet barrier goes wobbada-wobbada but stays intact.

Near the doorway, a second gun goes off. The other Stevens is firing at someone I can't see.

Chilling ain't gonna happen. I say, "Okay, fuck this noise."

With the violet shield still protecting me, I take a moment to concentrate. My lovely green hockey stick must have ceased to exist when the medi-tank neutralized my powers. But now I squinch my brain till the stick reappears in my hands. Then I hop the violet wall like jumping out of the penalty box, and I smack Mr. Stephens a good one upside the face.

Renfields are tougher than humans, but they can't compare to Sparks. A single slap dazes Stephens enough that he's not going to shoot me immediately. This lets me whack him a few more times, and he folds like a paper lantern.

Farther off, the other Stevens shoots up a storm. I can't see what she's trying to hit, but I assume it flies and sings opera. Reaper's scythe moans with excitement; it wants to spill blood, and soon. I can't help wondering how my hockey stick would fare against the scythe, but I doubt I'll have the chance to find out. Aria and Dakini will beat me to the punch.

I step over Stephens's body and stealth my way to the doorway of the lab. The female Stevens is just outside; she's popping her pistol at a sphere of golden light that flits through the nearby treetops. Inside the sphere is my dear friend Aria, who's quick enough to dodge most of the gunfire and whose force field deflects the few shots that manage to be on target.

Meanwhile, Aria sings sonic blasts at Reaper's skull. They don't have any discernible effect—Reaper spins his scythe like an airplane propeller in front of him, somehow forming a wall that Aria's attacks can't penetrate. In fact, the barrage of sound only increases the scythe's own moaning, as if the weapon absorbs the energy and keeps getting stronger.

I don't like where that might end up, but first things first: Staff Sergeant Barbara L. Stevens. I lean around the doorway and extend my hockey stick to tap Stevens on the shoulder. She whips toward me, trying to bring her pistol to bear. But that just makes it easier to poke her in the face, then slash the stick down on the gun. She doesn't drop the weapon, but the muzzle gets knocked downward. An instant later, the pistol goes off—Stevens must have pulled the trigger by reflex.

A hole opens up in the ground near Stevens's feet. Clouds of dirt spit upward like brown talcum powder.

I flick my stick and catch Stevens under the jaw. Her head snaps backward, and from there, it's just bashy unsportslike conduct until I batter her into neverland.

A voice speaks out of nowhere. "Who are you and how did you get Ninety-Nine's stick?"

Dakini. She sounds close by, but I can't see where. She must be making me blind to her presence: telepathic invisibility.

And I don't understand her question. Doesn't she realize . . . oh, wait, I'm dressed as Willow Scarlet. Even though Dakini can literally read my mind, she doesn't recognize me.

I step back into the lab and around the edge of the door. When I'm sure that Reaper can't see me, I pull off my mask. "Surprise!"

A moment later, Dakini's arms are around me. She gives me a giant bear hug. "We've been looking all over for you! Are you okay?"

"I am, but Zircon's not," I say. "And any second, this place is gonna—"

The floor beneath us lurches. Shit, I jinxed it.

SHERWOOD FOREST TILTS AGAIN. The angle is only five degrees or so, but off in the woods, I hear the collapse of an oak that's overbalanced. It's the sound you hear when a lumberjack chops down a tree: the unchopped portion of the trunk slowly crackles as it breaks, then branches snap as the tree slumps against its neighbors, and finally, *THUMP* as the trunk hits the ground.

Reaper says, "Fuck," then starts to chant in some language I don't recognize. Since I know every human language, he must be casting a spell in the special Darkling language called Enochian. I'm sure I'll hate the results if we let him finish.

I go back to the doorway, cock back my arm, and throw my hockey stick at Reaper's head. Butt end first, with the blade of the stick straight up like an airplane's tail rudder.

I'm as good as the best human spear thrower, and that includes people from back in the day when good throws meant survival, not medals. I'm confident my toss will hit Reaper bang on, even if a hockey stick isn't as well balanced as an actual spear.

But Dakini is bad at taking things on faith. As my stick flies through the air, violet tendrils wrap around to guide its aim and multiply its force. The stick veers midair and circles so it hits Reaper hard in the back of the skull.

It's not enough to knock him out, but it staggers him a moment. He can't continue his incantation. More importantly, he can't maintain the propeller-like spin of his scythe as it blocks Aria's song. A sonic blast gets through his guard and knocks him off his feet.

As Reaper scuds across the grass, Aria follows up with a coloratura volley pounding down on top of him. He's driven into a Reaper-shaped divot, and held there by the force of a recitative.

Reaper struggles to move his scythe between him and the sound. Before he succeeds, I grab my hockey stick from where it fell. I jam the stick's blade under the handle of the scythe. The moment of contact jolts my stomach with a sudden explosion of nausea, but I manage not to puke as I flick the weapon out of Reaper's hands.

The scythe sails away, screaming its head off in frustration. It bounces against a tree and releases the power it absorbed from Aria's attacks. The tree's trunk blows out like a truck tire bursting, leaving a gigantic hole.

The tree begins to topple, and for a moment, it looks like it might fall on Reaper himself. But Dakini intervenes to prevent the sort of poetic justice that likes to happen around Sparks and Darklings. She throws up a violet barrier similar to the one she used to protect me from Stephens. She tilts the barrier like a ramp, letting the tree slide down on an angle and hit the ground several paces from where Reaper lies.

Reaper tries to get up. Before he gets far, Sherwood Forest gives another lurch. It tilts farther, then shudders.

Aria gives Reaper another blast. This time he falls . . .

No, he doesn't. He just kind of floats.

And *I'm* floating, too. Totally weightless.

Aw, shit.

21

Potential Extinction Vectors

GRAVITY HASN'T STOPPED WORKING. Gravity works just fine. What doesn't work anymore is whatever keeps Sherwood airborne.

So crap. We're in free fall.

Sherwood plummets, and those of us inside drop with the same velocity and acceleration. In the stratosphere's thin air, it feels like zero g: *whee*, fun! But every second that we plunge, the density of air outside will increase. Soon we'll have enough air resistance for gravity to return . . . which sounds like good news, except it will also mean that the hull of Sherwood Forest will heat up madly, like a space capsule on reentry.

Was Marian farsighted enough to equip Sherwood Forest with heat shielding? More to the point, could she afford the cash and resources to do so? Even Mad Geniuses must sometimes get pinched by budget constraints.

To confirm my worries, a computer-generated voice starts booming from speakers in the trees: "Critical systems failure. All persons abandon ship. Sherwood Forest will crash in approximately four minutes."

"Aria!" I shout. "We have to move!"

She looks down at me. I realize this is the first time she's seen me without the Willow Scarlet mask. *CRACK!* She breaks the sound barrier zooming down to hug me, burying her face in my shoulder. "You're alive!" she whispers. "You're alive!"

"Um, yeah," I say, forcing myself not to joke that her hug might kill me. But seriously, Aria is nearly squeezing out my guts—splat, like a tube of lube. She's super-strong and not holding back. After a moment's more squishing, I have to say, "Dude. Four minutes from now, we hit the ground and splatter. Unless we burn to cinders first. Can we put a pin in this for later?"

"Sure," Aria says into my collarbone. She straightens up. "Sure. But we need to find Zircon. Ze's not answering our messages."

"I know where Zirc is. We have to go back into the lab."

Aria is still holding me, though not in as much of a death grip. She easily carries me with her as she flies through the laboratory's door.

Inside, lab equipment drifts in zero g: robot components . . . weapons . . . bottles filled with chemicals . . . oh, look, there's one of Jane's daggers. Let's not bump into that, shall we?

As I look around the room, I catch sight of Dakini. She's bobbing weightless beside the male Stephens. Violet tendrils reach from her forehead into the man's skull. "Erasing memories?" I ask.

"I thought it best," she replies. "I'm wiping away the last ten minutes, so they won't remember we fought them. That way our team won't get in trouble with the law."

"Good." As I speak, I spot what I've been looking for: the medi-tank. Since it wasn't anchored to the ground, it's floating like everything else—a priceless weightless bathtub of medical salvation. "That thing there," I say. "We need it."

"On it," Dakini says. She gives Stephens's brain a final rinse, then wraps the medi-tank in a mesh of violet strands. When it's suitably enveloped, Dakini throws another strand of violet around Aria's waist. We've become a little train: Aria is the engine and she's carrying me in her arms; when Aria moves, Dakini gets pulled along too, with the medi-tank tagging behind like a caboose.

"Critical systems failure. All persons abandon ship . . ."

I look down at Stephens, still lying unconscious. I sigh. "Dakini . . ."

She says, "Of course."

More strands of violet energy, one reaching out the door to snag onto Reaper. Within seconds, all of our recent opponents have been added to our little train.

We do *not* bring Reaper's scythe. With any luck, it'll be destroyed along with Sherwood. I suspect that destroying the scythe won't be nearly that easy, but a girl can fantasize, right?

"Awesome," I say when we're ready. I point toward the corridor that leads to the clean room. "That way," I say. "Fast."

Aria is good at fast. She zooms forward, still hugging me tightly. The rest of our train is in tow. We have to slow down through doorways, so Dakini can maneuver the medi-tank, but the tank is weightless and Dakini is getting quite dexterous at telekinesis. As for Reaper and Stevens & Stephens . . . screw 'em. If they bounce against doorframes, boo-hoo.

Within half a minute, we've reached the clean room's air lock. There's just enough space for us all to fit inside along with the medi-tank. Even so, we have to stand the tank upright, like an extra person in our midst.

And let me say, there's no good position for an unconscious skeleton and two Darkling minions when you're all crowded in together. You don't want them right in your face, but you don't want them behind your back either. We prop them behind the medi-tank, and push the tank tight back against them—partly to keep them from slumping to the floor, and partly so we don't have to look at them.

Since we've got a bit of time while the air lock cycles, Dakini goes to work erasing the memories of Reaper and the other Stevens. Meanwhile, I try to slip out of Aria's grasp, but she doesn't let me go.

"What *happened* to you?" she demands. This is the first chance we've had for a talk—while we were flying, conversation consisted of, "Go right . . . turn left . . . now slow down a second." Aria says, "We looked all over the forest for you, but . . ."

"How did you get up here in the first place?" I ask.

"The Darklings brought us. They put out a call for Sparks to help invade Robin Hood's base. Dakini and I volunteered. But as soon as we got here, we snuck away from the main attack force and started looking for you and Zircon." She looks around. "Where *is* Zircon, by the way?"

"Seriously hurt," I reply. "But if all goes well, ze'll be fine. There's a teleport thingie that will beam us to Waterloo. As soon as we arrive, we need to get Zirc and this tank to a power source." I hold up the tank's electrical cable, the one that I cut with Jane's dagger. "Standard power lines should do, but wherever we go, it has to be someplace Zirc'll be safe for three or four hours."

"What about the roof of a university building?" Dakini suggests. "We should be able to find a useful power feed. And no one will notice us up there—not until morning, anyway."

"Sounds good," I say.

"I'll keep you safe," Aria promises. "Both of you. All of you."

"Safe from what?" I ask.

"From this honking big forest that's falling straight down on Waterloo."

OOPS. FORGOT ABOUT THAT. But Polly the Parrot did say that Sherwood was parked above our city.

Basically, several million tons of foresty goodness is about to crash down on top of our home. Sherwood measures at least two kilometers in diameter. When it falls out of the stratosphere, hot from reentry, it'll flatten and incinerate everything below.

Then the force of Sherwood's impact will scatter debris in all directions. *Burning* debris. Burning debris that includes a shitload of Cape Tech, so assume extra explosions and spills of uncanny radiation.

Then there's the sheer earthquake shock that'll shake the ground. Waterloo houses aren't built for such tremors. For miles around the impact site, everybody asleep in their beds will have their homes collapse on top of them.

Three hundred thousand people currently live in Waterloo. I wonder how many will be alive three minutes from now.

"Critical systems failure. All persons abandon ship . . ."

The Darklings and Sparks who assaulted Sherwood must be hightailing it by now. Presumably they had an escape plan. They can leave the same way they got to Sherwood, however they managed the deed.

But did they think about the risk that Sherwood might crash? And even if they did, do the attackers have the strength to do anything about it? It's one thing to transport attackers up to a target in the stratosphere. It's a whole other thing to grab something that weighs millions of tons and shove it back into the sky.

In the past few seconds, a few percentage points of gravity have returned. The closer Sherwood gets to the ground, the thicker the air. It's now thick enough to push back.

The floor beneath us is heating up. Aria lifts me off the ground before my shoe soles start to melt.

THE DOOR OF THE air lock chimes and we all pile out. More precisely, Reaper and the Renfields *topple* out like corpses when you open the wrong closet . . . but to-may-to, to-mah-to. We let them lie because we're busy keeping the medi-tank from falling.

In front of us, Marian has laid Zircon out on the examination table. Zirc's costume has been removed to expose the wound on zir back. It's bad: like if someone used a sledgehammer to smash a hole in a rock face.

Nearby lie bandages and disinfectant, which Marian must have intended to put on Zircon's wounds. But the first-aid stuff hasn't been used. What would be the point? Zirc isn't bleeding, and rock can't get infected.

But rock can crumble. Zircon's face has changed from its normal gold tan to a bleached marble white. And the surface of the rock has started to flake off—what geologists call "spalling" or "exfoliation." Rocks exposed to harsh weather develop microfractures and eventually fall to pieces. With real rocks, the process takes centuries; with Zircon, I'm afraid ze may crack apart at any moment.

"You bloody well took your time," Marian growls. She's standing in front of an access panel in one wall of the room. Inside the panel are what look like conventional circuit boards. Marian is smearing the boards with toothpaste. I tell no lie. It is literally Colgate toothpaste with Total Advanced Whitening, and she's slathering the stuff across the capacitors, resistors, and logic chips. Oh, Cape Tech, I love you . . . especially in the hands of a master Mad Genius like Marian.

"I met some opposition," I tell her, "but I also found some friends."

"How lovely for you," Marian says. "Are you aware we're crashing?"

"No shit, really?" I asked. "I thought the weightlessness was because you didn't pay your gravity bill." I look around the room. "Where's Vernon?"

"None of your business," Marian says. "I sent him someplace safe."

She points to the door that leads to other places and times. It's open now. In the middle of the opening is a space-time vortex—an actual swirling eddy that resembles a cut-rate *Doctor Who* special effect. Multicolored bands spiral into a central vanishing point, and the whole thing turns slowly like the North Atlantic Gyre.

Very cheesy. Very weird science. But I repeat myself.

I say, "So Robin Hood will live to fight again?"

"Of course," Marian replies. "Now chop-chop, into the vortex. The sooner you go, the sooner I can finish rewiring."

I turn to my friends. "Aria, take Zirc. Dakini, take the tank. Get out of here now; I'll be right behind."

Aria looks like she wants to protest, but Zircon needs help more than I do. Aria cradles Zirc in her arms and flies into the swirling mass of color. The two of them vanish.

As Dakini begins to use her energy strands to move the medi-tank, I lower my voice and ask Marian, "Why the rewiring?"

"Because if I'm fast and clever, I can rig the vortex to suck in all of Sherwood." She jabs a soldering gun into the toothpaste. The toothpaste sputters, then sizzles. "It'll be like a snake swallowing itself. Everything will get pulled from this plane of existence . . . as opposed to falling on the heads of people below us."

It sounds insane. But that makes it perfect for weird science: a ridiculous gambit to save hundreds of thousands of people. The Light loves that shit.

I say to Marian, "What happens to you?"

"What do you think?" she snaps. "I get sucked in, too."

"And you end up where?"

"Nowhere," Marian says. "Just gone. Negated."

I jerk my thumb toward the vortex. "You can't escape through that?"

"No," Marian says with strained patience, "because I'm changing the vortex from *transport* to *annihilate*. And if you don't stop asking these questions, I won't have time to make the change and Sherwood will smash the shite out of your precious city."

I glance at the vortex. Dakini and the medi-tank have gone through now. I pick up Reaper and toss him inside. He disappears. As I pick up Stephens, I say to Marian, "Converting the vortex will go faster if I help. We'll be sure to finish in time."

I lean in to look at the toothpaste-covered circuits. Marian spreads her hands over them protectively. "I don't need your help, Jools. But your friend Zircon does. You're the only one who can hook up the medi-tank."

She's right, dammit. Aria and Dakini—Miranda and Shar— may be science students, but they do *real* science, not Cape Tech. I'm the only one who can jury-rig the medi-tank and save Zircon. I'll have to trust Marian to do what needs doing.

I toss one Renfield, then the other, into the energy swirl. Sayonara, S&S.

I pat Marian on the shoulder. "So long, dude. Good luck."

"Good-bye, Jools," she says. "I'm not sorry for being a bitch. But I'm sorry for being a bitch to *you*."

I hesitate in front of the vortex. A foot as strong as Ninja Jane's hits me from behind and kicks me through.

* * *

ABRUPTLY, I'M BACK IN Waterloo. I recognize where I am: the roof of the university library. The rest of campus spreads out ten stories below me.

The wind up here is fucking freezing. But it's blowing hard enough to sweep the place clear of snow. Nothing underfoot but a bare graveled surface.

Several huge antennas and receiver dishes rise above the roof. This is the highest point on campus, so it's the base of a major cell-phone tower and also perfect for satellite uplinks and other comm facilities. I even see a contraption that looks like a sea urchin made of copper and gold. A Cape Tech gizmo . . . unless it's a student art installation, which is not beyond the realm of possibility.

The antennas have the usual signal lights to warn off airplanes, but apart from that, I'm surrounded by darkness. The only lights level with the rooftop are dim glows from Dakini and Aria.

The two of them stand at the foot of the cell tower. They've parked the medi-tank beside an electrical transformer that feeds a satellite dish. The tank's lid is open and I assume they've put Zircon inside. Everything's ready for me to wire the tank to the transformer.

But Aria and Dakini aren't looking at me. They're staring up into the sky.

I follow their gaze. A ball of light shines directly over our heads. It's marginally bigger than the background stars, but it beams more fiercely than all the stars combined.

Sherwood has started its final descent.

But I won't let myself worry about that now. I have to plug in the tank and save Zircon. It's up to Marian to keep us from being crushed.

I race to join my friends. It's only when I stop in front of the medi-tank that I realize I don't have tools. Not so much as a screwdriver.

Shit.

I say, "Dakini, I'm going to need you."

"Of course," she replies. "What should I do?"

"Your telekinesis," I say. "Can you use it like a wrench? And maybe wire cutters?"

"I expect so," she says.

"Then open that up," I say, pointing to a service panel on the transformer. "Please."

While Dakini gets to work, I look into the tank. Zircon lies inside, still less than half human size. Also ze's fully dressed. "Aria," I say, "you'll have to take off Zirc's clothes. Comm ring, too. Otherwise the tank might not work."

Aria looks aghast for a moment—not mentally prepared for undressing a friend. Then she takes a sharp breath and says, "Of course." Gingerly, fingertips only, she reaches into the tank.

I watch for a moment to make sure she can force herself to do it. Then I grab the tank's power cable and start prying back the outer insulation to get at the wires inside.

A golden glow springs up around us. Aria is still working on Zircon, but she's also erected a force field around us all. I can't believe the field will protect us if something as heavy as Sherwood hits us at terminal velocity . . . and even if the force field holds, the library will be demolished under our feet. But Aria clearly wants to make the gesture. If nothing else, it's blocking the icy wind.

How long do we have left? It seems like more than four minutes since Sherwood started falling, but we're running on Spark time now. A hell of a lot gets compressed into just a few seconds, as if our time perception stretches out like a rubber band.

Dakini has unscrewed the bolts on the transformer's access panel. Inside is normal electrical wiring—nothing like the Mad Genius stuff Marian was coating with toothpaste. For a moment I think about what I saw, before Marian spread her hands to prevent me from getting a good look.

Stop it, Jools! This is no time to get distracted. "Dakini," I say, "can you detach that wire there?"

A telekinetic strand extends into the circuit box. Its violet glow changes the colors of all the wires. "You mean this one?" Dakini asks.

"No, that," I say pointing. But my finger blocks the view. "Look," I say, "just read my mind."

"People hate when I do that," she says.

"I'm not people. I'm a Spark. Do it."

I don't feel any change. Zircon says Spark-o-Vision can see when Dakini hooks into another person's brain, but to me the effect is invisible. I just watch the violet telekinetic strand finally move in the direction I want. Another strand joins it . . . and another, and another . . .

I zone out a little, getting my Mad Genius on. But this zoning out is featherlight, like the buzz I used to get from a single glass of beer. The wiring job is mostly vanilla—the medi-tank's cable is only a wee bit Cape Techy. So my brain stays clear. I feel a titch cheated that I don't have to use any toothpaste . . .

Why toothpaste? I try to understand, but can't.

Fucking hell. This is as annoying as analyzing Diamond's stupid gun.

Except it wasn't Diamond's gun, was it? The bazooka was only a mock-up designed to give the *impression* of being Cape Tech.

It didn't really work. It only looked like it should.

Behind me the medi-tank starts to hum. Red LEDs light up around the lid. Each LED is the size of a shirt button and separated from its neighbors by a space of three fingers. The pattern reminds me of the eye spots that circle the rims of bivalve shells. The fact that the lights are red makes me worry—red usually means something is wrong—but perhaps they'll go green one by one as Zirc is slowly put back together.

Yes. I tell myself that's how the tank works.

My brain defizzes from its Mad Genius buzz. I realize the roof is much more brilliantly lit than when we arrived. Fiery light blazes down from the sky. Sherwood Forest has grown to the size of the moon, but shines so incandescently, I can't look at it directly.

We watch the forest fall, Aria, Dakini, and I.

I can see Aria and Dakini asking themselves if there's anything they can do. Maybe Aria wonders if she should fly up to meet the plummeting forest . . . plant her hands on its underbelly and push up as hard as she can to slow its descent. Maybe Dakini is wondering the same. But as soon as they got close, they'd be cremated by the forest's enveloping flames. Besides, neither of them is strong enough to pull a tree out of the ground, let alone bear the weight of thousands of trees and the soil they grow in.

The oncoming fireball burns brighter, as bright as the noonday sun. I imagine the light waking people in their beds. They go to the window and look out, not understanding what they see.

Aria takes my hand. Her golden force field surrounds us. She says, "Jools . . ."

"Shush," I tell her. "Marian will get this done. Nick of time, right? The Light always likes a show."

And it's true: both the Light and the Dark love rescues with only milliseconds to spare. I just hope the Light gets the timing right.

The superheated Sherwood has grown so bright, the shine hurts even with my eyes closed. The roar of the forest plunging through the atmosphere is louder than standing next to a jet engine. I don't just hear it; I feel it shake my entire body.

I cover one of my ears with my free hand. Aria won't let the other go.

Then a colossal sucking sound. The light blinks out. Total darkness. And relative silence . . . except for car alarms going off all over the city.

I open my eyes. Sherwood Forest has vanished.

"See?" I say. "Marian had it under control."

Dakini says, "When I was in contact with your mind, I saw what she had planned. Dying heroically to save us all."

I wave my hand dismissively. "Nah. That's only what she

wanted us to believe. I mean, toothpaste. Really? Really? And when I tried to see what she was actually doing, she hid it."

"Why?" Aria asks.

"She was faking," I say. "Think about it: back when she built Sherwood Forest, she must have realized she couldn't keep it secret forever. Sooner or later, someone would track down where it was . . . at which point the Darklings would mount a full-scale attack. What could Marian do when that happened?"

Aria says, "Fake a crash?"

"Exactly. Why did Sherwood even start falling in the first place? You two were part of the assault; during the preparations, didn't somebody say, *Whatever you fucking do, don't make the forest crash?*"

Dakini nods. "Essentially in those exact words."

"But we all felt Sherwood lurch," I say. "And if somebody was tampering with Sherwood's machinery, that should have been a warning to stop. Then more lurches. Big old danger signals saying, *Leave things alone!* Would anyone be crazy enough to keep on messing with the equipment? Of course not. But the problems got worse, then we started to plummet. Meanwhile, in the clean room, Marian made sure she had witnesses to her heroic attempts to salvage the situation. Ending in her tragic just-in-time sacrifice."

"Are you saying it was all a trick?" Aria asks.

"Pretty much. Marian built Sherwood Forest so she could make it die spectacularly if and when an attack finally happened. That included what looked like obliteration at the last second: so bright and loud that no one could see or hear anything. Not even someone with amazing sensors, like Sensorium."

"But what really happened?" Aria asks.

"Sherwood was never as damaged as it seemed. No one on the attack squad was stupid enough to break whatever kept Sherwood airborne. The lurch-and-fall routine was a big dramatic production designed by Marian herself. And when Sherwood got close enough to the ground, it didn't self-destruct. The whole place just teleported elsewhere."

"So it's still intact," Dakini says. "Probably in the stratosphere again."

I nod. "Eventually, Robin and his gang will reappear, pretending they all evacuated before their HQ got sucked into oblivion. Neither Marian nor Ninja Jane will ever be seen again . . . but someone similar with a new mask and costume will appear at Robin Hood's side. No one will recognize her as Marian, any more than people recognized me as Ninety-Nine when I was Willow Scarlet."

"Damn," Aria says with admiration in her voice. "Hats off to Marian. I want to strangle her, but credit where credit is due."

"And she did let us have the medi-tank," I say, patting the lid. "I want to strangle her, too, but I won't give away her secret." I pat the tank again. "We owe her."

22

Population Renewal

DAKINI MAKES VIOLET LAWN chairs, so we can sit and wait. Aria surrounds us with a golden force dome; it shuts out the wind and holds in our body heat like a tent. After a while, I put on the Willow Scarlet mask to become a full Spark again. It's probably just psychological, but my Halo helps keep me warm.

After a few minutes, one of the red LEDs on the medi-tank's lid changes to green. We breathe a sigh of relief. There are dozens of red lights left, but now it's only a matter of time.

The ghost of dawn has begun to creep above the horizon when the last LED goes green. We leap from our chairs. Aria naturally reaches the tank first . . . but she holds back from opening it, stepping aside to let me do the honors.

I suppose she worries it's not as simple as it looks. But nothing fancy is involved—the lid doesn't even have a fastener. There's just a little resistance as I lift the top, and we gaze down on K.

Ze looks back at the three of us, hesitates a moment, then says, "Oh, Auntie Em, I had the strangest dream."

I CAN'T HELP MYSELF. I haul K out of the tank for the strongest hug I can give. Doesn't matter that ze's naked and gooey with medi-tank fluids.

Well, it doesn't matter to *me*. K seems a titch uncomfortable. Ze shrinks by an inch and turns into rocky Zircon. Still naked, of course, but looking like a classical stone statue.

It's a good look for zir. Next time I go over to Fine Arts and make money modeling in the nude, I should take Zirc with me.

I should take Zirc everywhere I go. I should take *all* my friends, and never let them out of my sight again.

Hugs, hugs, hugs, and attempted high fives.

My roommates all *suck* at high fives.

I love them anyway.

WE SMUGGLE THE MEDI-TANK into our town house's basement. I'll need to adapt it to run on household current, but that's a boring piece of cake. I'll have a lot more fun figuring out how to replace the reptile DNA with my own cells. Once I do that, the healing process will run much faster and will handle the direst of injuries. If any of my teammates gets hurt, they'll survive provided we get them back home quickly enough.

I'll have to make myself a new costume and a new costume-changer. I'll study the Willow Scarlet outfit closely—it would be great to have bulletproof clothes. I think I can make something just as light but a lot tougher. Maybe starting with hagfish slime.

For the costume-changer, I'll need more of Zircon's cells. But I'll get Shar to bake some cookies as a bribe.

Now that I think of it, I'll have to make Zircon a costume-changer, too. Zir old one will have been "cleansed" by the medi-tank. But at least Zirc still has the costume itself—Miranda saved the clothes after stripping Zirc down for the medi-tank.

Speaking of which, I'd better warn K about the "paying a price" possibility. I'm not certain the medi-tank really tweaked my powers and destroyed my ability to drink . . . but in case that's a side effect of using the tank, I'd better give Zirc a heads-up.

Yeah, that won't be an awkward conversation. Maybe I should practice doing the Awkward Turtle like Friar Tuck.

Other things: I'll need a new comm ring from Invie. Unless I make one myself.

Or maybe a comm IUD, so it's harder for someone to take away. Besides, how many villains would even think to check?

(Note to self: consider making communication IUDs for all my teammates.)

(Further note to self: make sure I'm channeling the most tact-ful person ever when I broach the subject with Miranda.)

But before I get back to being Ninety-Nine, I have to tie up Jools's loose ends. So I change into my cleanest leggings and a bright green T-shirt with Darwin's picture on it. I also put on appropriate makeup, which Aria criticizes for being excessive until I point out that you need more makeup than normal if you're going to be on television.

Yes. We intend to do some super PR. Which is why Aria hur-ries off to enhance her makeup, too. When we're finished, we agree we'll both look *fabulous* under bright lights.

We fly off to meet our teammates at the studios of CKCO TV. By the time we arrive, it's almost 7:00 A.M. Zirc and Dakini have wielded their Halos (and possibly Dakini's mind-control powers) to arrange an interview on the station's breakfast-time show. We're telegenic AF as my teammates lie about how they rescued me from the clutches of Robin Hood, and I (in my civvies) mostly tell the truth about my supposed death at the hands of the outlaws.

"Actually, the Merry Men saved my life," I say. "Maid Marian put me into a healing machine that made me as good as new. They treated me well while I was there. What? Oh. As far as I can tell, the only reason Sherwood nearly crashed was because of a care-lessly destructive raid organized by government forces. Maid Mar-ian sacrificed her life to protect thousands of lives from the irresponsible actions of Darkling agencies."

I lay it on thick. Have I mentioned I'm the most charming TV personality in the world? By the time I'm finished, the Dark Guard's name is shit. I imagine the Elders of the Dark giving Calon Arang a serious rap on her devious knuckles. It's one thing to fail at capturing Robin Hood, but it's quite another to get blamed for a near disaster that incidentally turns Marian into a heroic martyr.

Throughout it all, the interviewer seems dazzled by my team-mates' Halos. He practically drools over Aria—her Halo has that effect. But the man retains enough presence of mind to ask a pertinent question: doesn't Waterloo have *four* new Spark protectors? Where is good ol' Ninety-Nine?

Dakini answers with a straight face, "Ninety-Nine was injured at the Transylvania Club during a fight with the supervillain Diamond. We expect a full recovery, but she recuperates quite slowly compared to the rest of us."

"Yes, she's delicate," Zircon says. "Poor Ninety-Nine."

"Very delicate," Aria agrees.

"But in her honor," I say, "the team has decided to name itself the Ninety-Nine Percent." I smile at the others. "Isn't that what you were telling me before we went on air?"

"Well, you heard it here first!" says the interviewer. "Waterloo Region has a new super team named the Ninety-Nine Percent . . ."

My teammates and I all smile.

My smile isn't forced.

AFTER THE INTERVIEW, THEY all yell at me. "The Ninety-Nine Percent?!?!"

Aria says, "That's . . . that's . . . that's actually not bad."

"Could be worse," Zircon says.

Dakini narrows her eyes. "We'll talk."

WHEN WE GET HOME, I want to climb into bed and sleep the day away. I'm sure my friends do, too.

But it's Monday: the first day of classes for UW's winter term. Sigh.

K and Miranda would never skip class, even if they were literally on fire. Shar skips on occasion, but she still has to go to campus. Her boyfriend, Richard, will fuss if she doesn't meet him for coffee.

As for me . . . hell, I don't need to go to class. I know everything already. But my grades sucked so badly last semester, I've been put under academic review. Translation: I have to improve or I'll get expelled.

The actual challenge will be how to raise my marks convincingly, without pumping them so high the profs think I'm cheating. Step one will be going to class. Step two will be staying awake. Step three will be not drawing Cape Tech schematics while I'm sitting bored to death in the back row.

Anyway, all four of us grudgingly conclude that sleep is not going to happen in the near future. Instead, we decide to start the term self-indulgently with a full-calorie breakfast. Aria, Dakini, and Zircon become Miranda, Shar, and K, and we all hustle off to Mel's Diner.

Mel's is just a block from the university campus, the sort of place with pictures of James Dean and Marilyn Monroe on the wall, and ABBA's greatest hits on the sound system. Most people who eat at Mel's weren't alive when ABBA was around, let alone during Dean's or Monroe's lifetimes. But the food is good, so nobody minds the crypto-meta-nostalgic iconography. It's like having breakfast at Grandma's.

When we get to the diner, it's almost empty—no one except two guys dressed for a day in construction. (There's *always* construction around the university.) The guys check out the four of us, and of course they home in on Miranda; but she doesn't give them a glance, so eventually one smiles at me.

He's not creepy about it. He's kind of cute. I smile back.

I'm not horny, but I feel like I *could* be horny if it wasn't 8 fucking A.M. Thank baby Jesus, Robin Hood didn't break me. I'll be swiping right again in no time.

We pick a table in the far back corner where we can talk without being overheard. We order food. We guzzle coffee. We converse. My roommates want to hear what I did in Sherwood Forest. I want to hear what's happened in the outside world. Much catching up ensues . . . until suddenly everything stops.

My friends freeze midsentence. ABBA freezes mid-*mamma*. On the opposite side of the diner, the coffee being poured by a waitress becomes a motionless stream.

I sigh and turn toward the door. I'm not surprised to see Calon Arang.

"Show-off," I say.

She ignores me. She's looking at the fake memorabilia on the walls. She wants me to know she's appalled by the decor.

"Come on, Calon," I say. "You haven't always been part of the zero-point-oh-one percent. If you're the real Calon Arang, you lived in a grass hut with chickens in the yard."

She gives me a look. "Chickens only came to Bali when Europeans did. I prefer ducks."

"Greasy spoon diners don't serve duck," I say. "Not even duck eggs. But they make an awesome Western omelet."

I reach out with my foot and hook the toe of my boot around a chair from a nearby table. I pull the chair across the floor, then set it nicely at the end of our table. "Want to join us?"

Calon doesn't answer, but she makes her way toward me. She doesn't sit. "You seem in good health," she says.

"You mean, considering that you put me in a fucking exploding dress so you could make Robin Hood look like a murderer?"

"Yes, that." Calon shrugs. "Would you believe me if I said I thought you might survive? I knew Maid Marian had a healing machine. There was a chance you might be saved if she moved quickly."

I politely refrain from spitting in her face. "Doesn't matter if I believe you or not. All I care is that you keep our deal." I point to K. "This is my friend—the one with the vampire blood bond. Can you break it?"

Calon stares at K intently. Calon tilts her head . . . moves to look at K from another angle . . . leans in close and puts three fingers on K's forehead. Finally, Calon chuckles softly. "The blood bond is already broken. A bond did exist, but now it's gone."

"How could that happen?" I ask.

"Either someone persuaded the vampire to sever the bond voluntarily, or else someone cast an extremely powerful spell to break the bond by force."

"Those are the only two possibilities?"

"Those are the only two *probabilities*," Calon says. "I would never pretend to know what's *possible*. We live in a world where the Dark and Light mangle reality like two toddlers fighting over a toy. For all I know, your friend may have passed through a field of quaternion energy while hopping on one foot and reciting the Gettysburg Address, which somehow made the blood bond snap like a cheap rubber band. No one knows all the rules, Jools. And whatever the rules are at this moment, they'll change when we aren't looking."

She's right. All bets are off when the Dark or Light get jiggy. Like, take a for-instance: K's blood bond might have been cured by the medi-tank. The tank literally rewrote the DNA in all of K's cells. It inserted lizard genes, then took them out again. Temporarily, K's blood became qualitatively different. Could that have broken the bond?

Maybe. The medi-tank changed me, too, right? It stole my lovely ink, and I'm no longer tempted by booze. That *had* to be the tank's fault, right?

Because the only other explanation is that I've replaced one addiction with another. My drinking problem has become a tinkering problem, Mad Genius–style. And now I'll start going on benders during which I black out and start building death rays.

Naahhhh. It was the medi-tank's doing. It cleaned me out and sobered me up. I'm fine.

And the tank also broke K's blood bond. Because another possibility is that K broke the bond by making a deal with Lee. K's too smart to do that. It would be too out-of-the-frying-pan-into-the-fires-of-hell.

Oh, K, you dumbass. What have you done?

"Are we finished here?" Calon asks.

I bring my thoughts back to the here and now. I could ask a lot more questions—such as how Calon found me here, and whether she'll keep tempting me with proposals that will likely get me killed. But any answers Calon gives me will be half truths at best. She'll try to use *me*, and I'll try to use *her*.

Looks like the start of a beautiful friendship.

(Really, Jools? Yes. I'm stone cold sober and *still* making bad choices. At least I'm consistent.)

I nudge the empty chair with my foot. "Sure you don't want breakfast? Everything comes with home fries."

Calon doesn't smile. But she doesn't *not* smile. After a heartbeat, action throughout the diner suddenly resumes.

Calon sits in the empty chair and says, "Introduce me."

Acknowledgments

Thanks as always to my excellent agent, Lucienne Diver, and my equally excellent editor, Greg Cox. Also thanks to copy editor MaryAnn Johanson and Tor staffer Christopher Morgan. And thanks once again to Robert J. Sawyer for hosting "Rob's Write-Off Retreat" where some of this book was written.

Thanks to everyone who has said nice things about this series, including Alyx Dellamonica, Cory Doctorow, Kelly Robson, and Charles Stross. Thanks to all those in the comic book industry who continue to develop superheroes and help them change with the times.

Gratitude as always to Wikipedia and the people behind it, as well as the many other web resources I consult on a daily basis for nuggets of knowledge and trivia.

Thanks to various people, places, and things around the city and region of Waterloo for being such good sports as I lay waste to prominent landmarks. Also a big shout-out to the Kitchener Public Library for providing so many services I need and love. Oh, and speaking of Kitchener, thanks to the entire city for mutely accepting that it doesn't exist in the Dark/Spark world. There's a tragic story there, and maybe some day I'll get around to telling it.

About the Author

James Alan Gardner (Jim) started reading comic books near the beginning of the Silver Age, and never really stopped. Eventually, he picked up a couple of math degrees from the University of Waterloo, after which he immediately started writing fiction instead. He has published numerous novels and shorter works, including pieces that made the finalist lists for the Hugo and Nebula Awards. He has won the Aurora Award, the Theodore Sturgeon Memorial Award, and the Asimov's Science Fiction Magazine Readers' Choice Award. In his spare time, he teaches kung fu to six-year-olds and indulges the vices of his pet rabbit.